Rocked by

LOVE

The Bradens & Montgomerys
(Pleasant Hill – Oak Falls)

Love in Bloom Series

Melissa Foster

Cover Design: Elizabeth Mackey Designs
Cover Photography: Wander Aguiar Photography

WORLD LITERARY PRESS
PRINTED IN THE UNITED STATES OF AMERICA

A Note to Readers

Jillian Braden has waited a long time to find her forever love, and I knew she would need a strong hero who would appreciate her creative mind and strong personality and who wouldn't try to change her. Johnny Bad did not let me down. He is as strong as he is big-hearted, with a secret penchant for romance that I don't think *he* even knew he had. I don't want to give away spoilers, so I'll just say that I'm not sure any of us were prepared for the challenges they face, and I'm thrilled to give them their happily ever after. I adore their story, and I hope you will fall as desperately in love with them as I have.

For my avid fans who have been asking for more stories featuring more Bads (Bad Boys After Dark), I will answer the burning question. Yes, each of Johnny's siblings will be getting their own story. At the end of this book you'll find a preorder for Johnny's brother, Kane, and Sable Montgomery's story, FALLING FOR MR. BAD. Aria's and Harlow's stories are forthcoming.

If this is your first Love in Bloom book, all my love stories are written to stand alone, so dive in and enjoy the fun, sexy ride. You will find a Braden family tree included in the front matter of this book.

The best way to keep up to date with new releases, sales, and exclusive content is to sign up for my newsletter and join my fan club on Facebook, where I chat with readers daily.
www.MelissaFoster.com/news
www.Facebook.com/groups/MelissaFosterFans

About the Love in Bloom Big-Family Romance Collection

The Bradens & Montgomerys is just one of the series in the Love in Bloom big-family romance collection. Each Love in Bloom book is written to be enjoyed as a stand-alone novel or as part of the larger series, and characters from each series make appearances in future books, so you never miss an engagement, wedding, or birth. A complete list of all series titles is included at the end of this book, along with previews of upcoming publications.

Download Free First-in-Series eBooks
www.MelissaFoster.com/free-ebooks

See the Entire Love in Bloom Collection
www.MelissaFoster.com/love-bloom-series

Download Series Checklists, Family Trees, and Publication Schedules
www.MelissaFoster.com/reader-goodies

Love Audiobooks? I've got you covered
www.MelissaFoster.com/audio-books

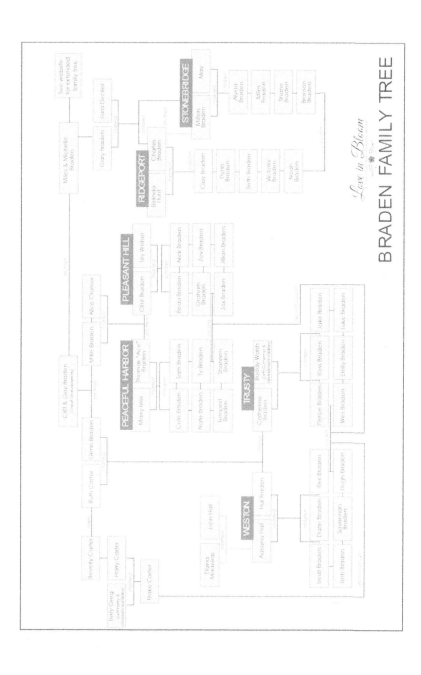

BRADEN FAMILY TREE

Love in Bloom

Chapter One

"ARE YOU FREAKING kidding me? He's canceling our meeting *again*? It's literally in twenty minutes. I've got a car waiting," Jillian Braden fumed into her cell phone to her cousin Victoria, aka Victory in the entertainment world. Victoria owned Blank Space Entertainment, and she was the agent who represented rock star Johnny Bad and his band, Bad Intentions. "Does Johnny have any idea how hard it was for me to clear my schedule for two weeks at the last minute and come to New York City? Dick called me *three* days ago and said this was the only time Johnny could set aside to work with me." Dick Waller was Johnny's manager. He'd hired Jillian, a sought-after fashion designer whose designs had graced the covers of the most prominent fashion magazines, been worn on red carpets, and commissioned by the wealthiest of women, to design the band's tour wardrobe to promote their latest album, *Brutally Bad*. "Why isn't Dick dropping this bomb? Why does he always have you do his dirty work? Isn't there some rule in your industry about not using family in this way? He doesn't even work for Blank Space."

"Don't get me started on Dick," Victoria said, exasperated. "I'm sorry this happened again, and Johnny is fully aware of how busy you are. Believe me, if there were any way around this, he wouldn't be canceling the tour or your meeting."

Jillian scoffed. "Sorry, Vic, but I don't believe that for a second. Johnny is an arrogant, self-centered ass, and I have no idea why I've put up with his bullshit for all this time." She needed to be jerked around by an arrogant rock star like she needed a hole in her head, but creating a wardrobe for a famed musician and his band would be a huge boon for her business, and working with rock stars had always been a dream of hers. A dream she was now regretting. "You *know* I put off the launch of my new Wanderlust line for the past year because of this opportunity. He's canceled the tour and put me off *three* times. I realize that makes me an idiot for accepting each of the contracts, but I really wanted to believe you every time when you said he had his shit together." It hadn't hurt that Dick had come groveling with a new, higher-paying contract and raving about Johnny *only* wanting *her* to handle his wardrobe, which made no sense since she was known as a women's designer, but she'd clung to that brass ring for all she was worth.

"He *did* have his shit together. It just keeps falling apart."

Jillian rolled her eyes. "What's his excuse this time? He's having too much fun with his *Baddies* and doesn't want the fun to end?" Johnny's female fans called themselves Baddies. She'd heard he'd dumped his long-term model girlfriend last year. He was probably making up for lost time with a handful of groupies.

"You know I can't divulge his reasons, but he wouldn't cancel for *that*."

"For a man with an entourage, he sure has a lot of issues. I should have walked away the first time he canceled." She'd heard that Johnny was hard to work with, but she'd grown up with five loud, opinionated brothers, and she'd never met a man she couldn't handle.

"I know how much this sucks, Jilly, and I'll make sure you're compensated."

"Oh, he's going to pay, all right. But I want to look him in the eye and tell him *exactly* what I think of him wasting my time like this, and *then* I'm going to tell him he can shove his tour wardrobe where the sun doesn't shine." She snagged her room key and clutch from the table and stalked toward the door.

"*Jillian*, I know you're mad and rightly so. But he's got a lot going on. At least give him time to fill in his team on the cancelation."

A grin slid into place as she realized her luck. "I'll give him the same courtesy he's given me. Thanks for calling, Vic. I appreciate the heads-up." She ended the call and stalked out the door. By the time she was done with Johnny Freaking *Butthead*, he'd think twice about disregarding anyone's time ever again. She headed out of the hotel and into the waiting car. The sooner she got this over with, the sooner she could get home to Maryland and back to her life.

JILLIAN CLIMBED OUT of the car and pushed past a mob of photographers in front of Johnny's building, hoping Mr. Butthead hadn't yet told the doorman he was no longer expecting her. "Jillian Braden. I have a meeting with Johnny Bad."

"Yes, ma'am." The doorman gave her directions to the elevator that serviced the penthouse.

"Thank you." She breathed a sigh of relief and made her way to the elevator, knowing there was a good chance the bodyguard Johnny's manager had mentioned would be manning it had probably been notified of the cancelation.

The mountainous man had cold black eyes and looked like he was chewing on glass, but his emotionless eyes trailed down her sleek, curve-hugging white sleeveless sheath. The dress was part of her Multifarious line and had a black abstract design and a splash of vibrant blue, yellow, and pink just below the hips. It was edgy, classy, and just sexy enough to show that she knew she had magnificent assets but didn't need to flaunt them. Based on the interest flickering in Mr. Serious's eyes, she'd chosen perfectly.

"Good morning. I'm Jillian Braden. Mr. Bad is expecting me."

"Yes, ma'am. I'm afraid I need to see some identification."

"Do I look like a groupie to you?" She fished out her wallet.

"Groupies come in all shapes and sizes."

She handed him her driver's license. "I bet they don't show up in five-hundred-dollar dresses that they designed."

"You'd be surprised." He glanced at the license and then at her as he handed it back and stepped aside, allowing her into the elevator.

"Black suits for bodyguards are overdone," she said with a cutting edge, her annoyance getting the best of her. "Tell your employer he can do better."

She rode up to the penthouse alone, her heart slamming against her ribs. The doors opened directly into the suite, and there in the massive living room was the famed rock star, with his dark hair messy, wearing low-slung jeans and a tight T-shirt, pacing as he barked into his cell phone.

Buckle up, bad boy. It's your turn to be barked at. Squaring her shoulders, Jillian stalked toward the man who had already stolen far too much of her time.

"KANE'S ON IT, and he'll be in touch." Johnny ended the conference call with his bandmates and turned around just as a hot burgundy-haired chick wearing sky-high heels and a deadly scowl nearly barreled into him.

"Who the hell do you think you are, demanding I show up in New York for two weeks to design your wardrobe and then putting me off for a *third* time?" she seethed. "I have news for you, *Mr. Bad Manners*: I am *done* with your arrogant, self-centered business practices. I don't care how much money your manager waves at me or if working with you would put my name at the top of the music-fashion industry. Nothing is worth the way you have continuously disregarded and devalued my time."

Johnny's mind was reeling. He'd fired his thieving, liar of a manager two hours ago, when the onslaught of Dick's misdoings had upended his life. "Who the fuck are you?"

Her eyes narrowed, shooting daggers. "Did you *not* hear a word I said about designing your wardrobe? Does *Jillian Braden* ring a bell?"

"*Jesus*. Victory was supposed to call you. I'm sorry, but I don't have time for this right now."

"You don't have time to explain yourself after you've wasted my time for an entire *year?*"

The bathroom door opened, and his eyes darted to Zoey, the disgruntled teen scowling at him from across the room, clutching her cell phone as she said, "This has been exhausting. Are you at *least* going to feed me now?"

Jillian's jaw dropped, and if he thought she was throwing visual daggers before, now she was breathing fire, too. "Are you kidding me? She can't be more than *fourteen*. You're not just an asshole—you're disgusting."

Zoey smirked and crossed her arms, amusement dancing in her eyes.

Christ. Could his life get any worse? He pointed at Zoey. "Don't say another word." He grabbed the dragon woman's arm and tugged her to the side of the room, lowering his voice. "You need to sign a new NDA."

"I will do no such thing," she snapped. "I'm not hiding your sick proclivity for young girls."

"I don't have a fucking proclivity for young girls," he snarled as the elevator doors opened and his brother, Kane, strode in. "She *might* be my *daughter*, and I can't afford for the media to get wind of this, so you're not leaving here until you sign a new NDA."

"Too late for that, little brother. Your hotel is already surrounded by paparazzi." Kane's jet-black hair was slicked back, his beard trimmed, and his neck tattoos peeked out above the collar of his dress shirt. A self-made billionaire, he was the first person Johnny had called after firing Dick. Kane owned businesses and properties up and down the East Coast, and he had agreed to step in to save Johnny's ass and take over as his manager. "TMZ's headline is JOHNNY BAD'S SECRET LOVE CHILD REVEALED. They've got copies of a DNA report that was done when Zoey Elizabeth Conrad was four days old. Mick is verifying that as we speak." Their cousin Mick Bad was Johnny's lawyer. They'd been through more than a handful of false paternity claims.

My daughter. Holy fuck. Johnny could barely keep his own life in check. How was he supposed to be a parent? How was he going to break this to *his* parents? They didn't need more stress in their lives, and what the hell was he going to do with a teenage girl? He knew nothing about teenage girls, other than they'd been all over him when he was a teenager.

Johnny, and an equally shocked Jillian, looked accusatorily at Zoey.

Zoey rolled her eyes. "Don't look at *me*. I didn't even know you were my father until a couple of hours ago. It was probably my *mother*, and I bet she got paid a lot of money to spill the beans about the daughter she never wanted. But good luck finding her. I'm sure she's long gone by now. She's not one to stick around. She spends all her time following bands around the country."

"I've got guys on it. They'll find her," Kane said.

"Just give me some cash, and I'll get out of your hair," Zoey said sharply.

"Where will you go?" Jillian asked as Johnny's phone rang.

Zoey shrugged. "Anywhere but *here*."

"You're *not* leaving." Johnny pulled out his phone and saw the name of his PR rep, Shea Steele, on the screen. He put the phone to his ear. "Yeah?"

"You've got to get out of town. Someone tipped off TMZ. Social media is blowing up."

"I heard, but what am I going to do with the kid? Where the fuck am I supposed to go?"

As Shea told him to take Zoey with him, Jillian seethed, "*Lan-*

guage. There's a teenage girl in the room."

"Yeah, watch your fucking language," Zoey said.

"*Hey,*" Jillian snapped, glowering at her, earning another eye roll from Zoey.

Shea was going on about making a statement asking the public to respect their privacy, but Johnny had missed whatever else she'd said. "The statement is fine."

"Johnny, not to add more pressure, but the music awards are only two months away. With *Brutally Bad* up for Best Album of the Year, this kind of media attention can go either way," Shea warned.

"Yeah, I'm on it. I'll be in touch when I figure out where we're going." He ended the call, more than a little worried about being in charge of a teenage girl. He needed help, but the likely candidates weren't options. His sister Harlow, an actress in LA, would only bring more attention to them, his youngest sister, Aria, had social anxiety and didn't fly, and his parents had enough on their plates with his mother's most recent battle with cancer. He was screwed.

He turned to Kane, wishing he could get him to go with them, but Kane had to manage the fallout from firing Dick. "I've got to get her out of here. Can we use your helicopter and possibly your plane?"

"You bet. The helicopter can land on the roof, and I'll distract the media while you take off." Kane pulled out his phone.

"Getting out of here sounds like a stellar idea." Jillian headed for the door.

"You can't leave me alone with *him,*" Zoey whined. She stalked over and linked her arm with Jillian's. "I'm not going unless *she* goes."

"What?" Jillian's eyes widened, pulling her arm free. "*Why?* You don't even know me."

"I don't know *them,* either, and at least you're a girl," Zoey insisted.

Jillian's expression softened. "Don't you have relatives you can stay with?"

Zoey didn't answer, but the sadness in her eyes cut Johnny to the core. *Fuck it. She's been hurt enough.* The last thing he wanted was to be stuck with two females who would rather be anywhere other than with him, but this wasn't about him.

He grabbed Jillian's arm. "You're coming with us." Problem solved. He needed a buffer, and she seemed to know how to handle Zoey, which was better than nothing.

"Like hell I am." Jillian yanked her arm away.

"You *have* to come," Zoey pleaded. "How would you like to be left alone with him?"

"I *wouldn't*." Jillian scowled at Johnny.

"Well, neither would *I*," Zoey insisted.

"He can bring his bodyguard to keep you safe," Jillian suggested.

"Another *guy*?" Zoey snapped. "No fucking way!"

"Watch your language—"

"Would you two *stop* arguing and give me a second to think?" Johnny's mind spun, and his phone was vibrating nonstop with texts. Another call rang through, and Harlow's name flashed on the screen. She had no doubt heard the news.

He answered, but before he could speak, Harlow said, "Is it true?"

"Looks like it. I can't talk right now. I'll call everyone later. Can you do some damage control with Mom and Dad?"

"I talked to Dad on the way over," Kane interjected. "I also have a team going over every move Dick has ever made on yours and your band's behalf."

"Thanks, man." To Harlow, Johnny said, "Kane already spoke to Mom and Dad, and I doubt Aria has heard yet, but can you talk to her so she has a heads-up?" Johnny added how this would affect Aria to his growing list of worries.

"Jesus, Johnny," Harlow said. "Are you okay?"

He eyed Zoey, who'd been abandoned by her mother and left with him, a damn stranger to her, and despite his anger, his chest constricted. "What do you think?"

"Stupid question. Sorry. I'll call Aria, but you'd better call us later. Love you," Harlow said.

"You too." He ended the call, even more stressed than he'd already been. Kane was on the phone, and Jillian was trying to talk Zoey out of needing her to go with them. As messed up as it was, Johnny needed her to go, too. "Neither of you knows what this life is like. The media will slaughter *all* of us. I've got to get Zoey someplace safe, and I have no idea where that is yet, so *please* stop arguing and let me think."

"Can't I just go with *her*?" Zoey pointed to Jillian.

"Um, *no*," Jillian said. "No offense or anything, but I'm not the mothering type."

"What*ever*. My own mother wasn't the mothering type, and you're already ten times better than her," Zoey insisted.

Jillian's brows knitted. "I'm sorry, but I have a business to get back to."

"Actually, you have a two-week contract with me," Johnny reminded her. "As I said, you're coming with us."

Jillian glowered at him. "In case you've forgotten, you aren't going on tour, and you canceled my contract."

"Not in writing. You're still legally bound to work with me for two weeks."

"*Work*, not sit around on my ass while you figure out your personal life," Jillian retorted.

"Then you'll design my fu"—he eyed Zoey—"freaking wardrobe."

Jillian folded her arms over her chest. "If you think I'm going to follow you like one of your groupies, you're wrong. I will make your life a living hell if you force me to go."

"And I'll make your life hell if she *doesn't* go." Zoey's eyes were locked on him.

Kane stifled a chuckle.

Johnny ground his back teeth, trying not to snap at the teenager who, according to her mother—who Johnny had apparently spent a few *forgettable* hours with—had no one but him to turn to...and the painfully beautiful dragon lady beside her. It wasn't their fault his life was suddenly beyond fucked up, so he forced himself to be calm. "I'm used to people making my life hell, so join the club."

Jillian's brow furrowed, as if she was coming up with a plan. Probably to slaughter him. She crossed her arms and lifted her chin. "I'll go under one condition."

"Are you shitting me? *What?*"

"If and when you do the *Brutally Bad* tour, you let Sable Montgomery's band, Surge, open for your show."

"Who?" *What the fuck?*

"Sable Montgomery. The band is great. But if you'd rather not." She headed for the door.

He didn't have the time or the energy to argue about this bullshit. He didn't give a damn if the band sucked. "*Fine.* She's got it."

Her eyes widened, like she couldn't believe it, but in the next second they narrowed with determination. "I want it in writing."

Fuming, he went to the armoire and pulled open a drawer, taking out a pad of paper and a pen and scrawled, *Surge can open for my next tour.* He signed it and tore the page off the pad, shoving it into her hand. Ignoring her smirk, he turned to his brother. "Any ideas where we can go?"

Kane shook his head. "The media knows where all my properties are."

"*Ohmygod.*" Jillian looked exasperatedly at Kane. "Aren't you *Big Daddy Kane?* Which kind of makes me gag. Some kind of billionaire business mogul with your own groupies at your beck and call?"

Kane cocked the grin that Johnny had seen melt panties across several continents. "Trust me, darlin'. I go down smooth. No gagging involved."

Are you fucking kidding me?

Jillian rolled her eyes. "Shouldn't you have hidden properties all over the world for exactly this reason?"

"Shouldn't you, *Ms.* Braden?" Kane asked with amusement. "I'd think that's precisely what the fashion industries' *It Girl* of sightly outlandish designs would be into."

Johnny shot him a dark stare. "*Kane,* cut the shit."

"For your information, I don't *need* a hidden property." Jillian's words dripped with defiance. "I don't have trouble with paparazzi like Johnny does, but when I want to keep a low profile, I go to my brother and his wife's inn in the Colorado Mountains. They've put up celebrities and know how to keep things on the down-low. They even have a private airstrip."

"Then that's where we're going," Johnny said. "Call your brother and make arrangements."

"*Excuse* me?" Jillian squared her shoulders. "I'm not your employee, and I won't be ordered around like one."

Shit. He was used to people asking *how high* when he said *jump*, not having his every word challenged. But if he thought *his* life was suddenly fucked up, that was nothing compared to what the fourteen-year-old girl who had lost her grandmother, been abandoned by her mother, and was now stuck with him was going through.

Forcing his irritation down deep, he kissed Jillian Braden's gorgeous ass, speaking as calmly as he was able. "Jillian, Zoey's been through enough for one day. We need a place to lie low while we figure this out. Unless you want the media attacking her and slaying your reputation for being here with us, will you *please* ask your brother if we can stay at his inn?"

She huffed hard enough to shake the room, but as those keen hazel eyes slid to Zoey, they warmed, and she pulled out her phone.

Chapter Two

JILLIAN STARED OUT the window of Kane's private plane, wondering how she'd gotten herself into this mess. She couldn't believe Johnny had agreed to let Sable's band open for his tour, assuming he was still going to have one at some point. She wasn't even sure if Sable would agree to do it. Surge played at music festivals and such, but Sable's brother, Axsel, was a rock star in his own right, and Sable had never tried to follow in his tracks. Jillian had been sure Johnny would refuse, and that would be her *out*. But would she have walked away if he'd given her the chance? She certainly would have wanted to, but whether he'd agreed to Sable opening or not, she knew in her heart she wouldn't have walked away. She couldn't have turned her back on the young girl who was trying so hard to hide her fear behind a surly attitude. Jillian had been trying to figure out what happened that had landed Zoey in Johnny's care and why neither of them had known he was her father until that morning, but she hadn't wanted to ask in front of Zoey, who seemed traumatized enough.

She studied the sleeping teen across the aisle.

Zoey hadn't said two words since they'd left the penthouse and had fallen asleep with her earbuds in an hour into the four-hour flight. She looked so young with her shiny brown hair draped over her shoulders. She hadn't even outgrown her baby face yet, but she wielded her attitude with the adeptness of an eighteen-year-old and dressed like one of Johnny's groupies, with too much makeup, a tight black skull-patterned belly-baring top that looked two sizes too small, skintight hip-huggers, a denim jacket, and black Converse. A thin leather choker circled her neck, several cheap plastic bracelets covered her wrists, and fake pearl earrings dangled from her ears. She was a pretty girl beneath all that armor. What had her guarded eyes seen in so few years?

Jillian glanced at Johnny lying on the couch with his jeans-clad legs crossed at the ankles, one hand behind his head, dark eyes staring up at the ceiling, just as they'd been since they'd gotten up in the air. There was no denying that he was infuriatingly gorgeous, with that chiseled jawline, pitch-black scruff, a mouth that she was sure was capable of all sorts of dirty pleasures when it wasn't spouting arrogance, and a body made for riding. But his attitude was no less abrasive than Zoey's. He'd barked orders at his assistant and his PR rep for twenty minutes before the helicopter had arrived, and his jaw had been tighter than a vault for the past two hours. How was a guy like him going to raise an ornery teen when they couldn't even talk to each other? The way he'd spoken at Zoey instead of to her had made Jillian want to slap him. That was one reason she hadn't put up more of a fight about going with them.

She pushed to her feet, and his dark eyes shifted, watching her approach like a rottweiler deciding if he should bite or bark. Why was that so hot? Annoyed with herself, she swatted his booted feet off the couch, forcing him to sit up.

She sat beside him, speaking quietly. "I went out on a limb for you with my family. You owe me an explanation."

"About?" he asked gruffly.

She gave him a deadpan look. "Give me the scoop, or I'm taking off the minute we touch down."

He glanced at Zoey and leaned his elbows on his legs. "You heard Kane. She's more than likely my kid."

"Yes, but it sounded like neither of you knew that until today. Were you just bullshitting? Where's her mother? Where has she been living?"

He shook his head, wringing his hands. "I'm still putting all the pieces together, but obviously I must have hooked up with her mother after a show when I was nineteen or twenty, probably blitzed out of my mind. I don't even know who her mother is. My manager showed up with Zoey this morning and said she was my kid and her mother wanted nothing to do with her." His jaw clenched, and his tone turned venomous. "*Then* he told me he'd been paying her mother off for all these years to keep her quiet, because he thought it would ruin my career if word got out." He turned his head, eyes full of ire. "I *never* got a chance to decide how to handle any of it, and I have no idea what I would've done, but I sure as hell *wouldn't* have taken that route."

Jesus. No wonder he'd been ready to kill someone. "That's awful. How does a mother just abandon her child after raising her for fourteen years?"

"She *didn't* raise her." He fisted one hand, rubbing it with the other. "She took the money Dick sent every month and left Zoey with her grandmother. Her grandmother died three weeks ago, and at that point her mother had no choice *but* to take care of her, which I assume is why she dumped her on me."

"And it sounds like she went for the payoff with TMZ," Jillian added. "No wonder Zoey is so angry. That poor girl has gone through so much, and you're obviously not happy about her being here, either. Talk about getting her legs knocked out from under her."

"You think *I* like any of this?" he fumed. "Having my world turned upside down? Letting down my band when we're supposed to be recording? Being betrayed by the guy I trusted with my entire life since I was fifteen years old?" He bit out a curse. "Do you think I like knowing *she's* hurting? I don't want to snap at her. She's a *kid.* But how would you react if someone put her in front of you and said, 'She's yours, twenty-four-seven, don't fuck her up'?"

"I couldn't do it. I stay up all night working, and I have enough trouble remembering to eat and take care of myself. I'd never cut it as a parent, and I like my life the way it is."

He splayed his hands, giving her a look that said *no shit.* "Then you get why I'm just as lost as she is."

"Yes, but you *created* her. This is the reason people use condoms."

"I've been using them since I was *fifteen*," he said through clenched teeth. "I'm not an idiot."

"It's hard to get pregnant through latex, but girls who are motivated to rope a rock star into paying them for the rest of their lives are sneaky. If you used their condoms, they can poke holes in them."

He cursed under his breath.

"Look, the how or why doesn't matter. The fact is, she's yours, and I guess she'll cramp your style. You can't really *entertain* groupies with a teenage girl around."

His eyes narrowed. "Is *that* what you think this is about? You think I'd put getting off above another person's life? Especially a kid's?"

"To be honest, I don't know what to think. I only know what I've experienced, which is your total disregard for my time, and frustration about having to take care of Zoey."

His jaw tightened, and he stared at her for a minute, as if he were trying to keep from blowing up. "What you've *experienced* isn't my disregard for your time. Canceling had nothing to do with you. I had more important things, more important *people*, to tend to than a damn tour for my fans. You just got caught in the crossfire, and I'm sorry for that. I really am. It sucks, and what you've seen today is me being too shocked to think straight." He lowered his voice even more. "I don't know a damn thing about that girl, much less how to take care of her. Where will she go to school? Does she need therapy? Does she use drugs?"

"She's fourteen—obviously you'll need to find a school for her." She wondered what things and which people were more important than his tour, but she let that go for now and tried to lighten the air. "And she's definitely going to need therapy. So are you, and if I stick around too long, I probably will, too." His expression remained serious and angry, reminding her of her older and most ornery brother, Nick. She knew how to diffuse Nick, and damn it to hell, she felt bad for Johnny and tried to help him the same way by softening her tone. "How about if you just try to get to know her and make her feel like she's not an imposition? It's understandable that you're mad about your life being turned upside down, but suck it up. None of this is her fault. She didn't ask to be born to a mother who didn't want her, and you said she lost the grandmother who raised her. Is she sad about it? Was her grandmother good to her?"

"I don't *know*. All I know is that her grandmother died of an aneurysm while she was at school, and she'd been the one to find her."

Oh my God. She looked at Zoey, struggling against a lump forming in her throat. She took a deep breath, and as she'd done her whole life, she looked past the heartbreak to find a way to mend it. "Well, now is the time to find out. Whether you like it or not, you hold the power to step up and try to salvage how she feels about you *and* herself, or you can fuck her up beyond repair by making her feel even more unwanted."

He sat back and raked a hand through his hair, blowing out a breath like he'd just run a marathon. "I thought you weren't the mothering type."

"I'm *not*. But I was fourteen once, and I know how much my relationship with my father shaped my life. You have two younger sisters, don't you?"

He nodded.

"If they were in this situation, how would you want the guy who just found out he was their father to treat them?"

He swallowed hard, his gaze moving to Zoey again before returning to Jillian with a hint of a plea. "You're going to help me with this, right?"

"Sorry, but I'll be busy working on your wardrobe." She rose to her feet, and he caught her hand, their eyes connecting with an unexpected jolt. It wasn't heat or hate but some kind of strange in-between, like two people hanging on to the same lifeboat.

"Thank you." He squeezed her hand, holding it for so long her pulse quickened.

She slipped her hand from his and made her way back to her seat, wondering what the hell had just happened.

Chapter Three

JILLIAN GATHERED HER things and glanced out the window, the tension in her neck and shoulders easing. There was something about the Colorado Mountains that had always calmed her. She spotted her oldest brother, Beau, with his short brown hair and serious dark eyes, and his wife, Charlotte, a warm, quirky brunette, and felt more of that tension ease. Before leaving New York, Jillian had given Beau and Char the rundown about Johnny and Zoey. If anyone could understand what Zoey was going through, it was them. Beau had lost a big piece of himself when his first love had died more than a decade ago, but he'd found an even better piece of himself with Charlotte, who had suffered the loss of both her parents and the grandfather who had raised her.

"Where are we?" Zoey asked, holding her cell phone like a security blanket. "I thought we were going to an inn."

"We are. This is just the landing strip. The inn has been in my sister-in-law's family forever. Wait until you see it. It's gorgeous, and it's surrounded by wildflowers, my favorites. There's a heart-shaped lake, and the inn and everything around it has a magical quality."

Zoey rolled her eyes.

Johnny shook his head.

"I'm not kidding," Jillian said. "Legend has it that once you're touched by the magic of the inn, nothing can break the spell. If you two are lucky, maybe you'll catch a little of that magic and get to a better place." That earned another eye roll, but it didn't dissuade Jillian. She believed in the magic of the inn and hoped it would help them. She pointed out the window. "See that guy? He's my brother Beau. He renovated the inn and all the other structures on the property for his wife, Char. That's her in the pink cowgirl boots, petting their dog, Bandit. You have to watch Bandit. He's a thief, and nothing is off-limits, so be careful where you put your things."

"I don't like dogs," Zoey said. "Is there anything to do here?"

"There's plenty to do, and there's a cute town not too far away."

"We're here to lie *low*," Johnny reminded them. "If the media gets wind of where we are, our lives will be a shit show."

Jillian glowered at him.

"I mean *chaotic*," he corrected himself. "Sorry."

"So? Isn't it better to get it over with than to hide like criminals?" Zoey asked.

"No." Johnny's jaw tightened again. "The media is probably already slandering the hell out of me."

"Then why do you care if they know where you are?" Zoey challenged. "Do you have other kids you're hiding?"

"*Look*," Johnny snapped. "I don't—"

"He doesn't want to fuel the fire," Jillian interrupted, taking Zoey's hand and dragging her toward the exit to diffuse the mounting tension. "He's right that something like this can make your life even harder if it's not handled properly."

"Why would I care?" Zoey grumbled. "My life is already a nightmare."

Jillian's heart ached for her. "I know it feels that way, and I'm sorry. Let's just get settled in so Johnny and his team can figure out the next step. I promise I'll do everything I can to make sure you won't be bored while you're here."

They descended the steps, and Jillian ran to Beau, slowing only long enough to pet Bandit. "Hey, Bandit. You're too cute with your yellow bandanna."

"That's so we can see where he's sneaking off to at night." Beau hauled her into a strong embrace, speaking quietly. "What have you gotten yourself mixed up in?"

"I don't know, Boo." He held her tighter at the childhood nickname. "But I couldn't just leave her alone with him."

"That's the big Braden heart that gets us all in trouble."

She smiled as she stepped out of his arms. "How were Jax and Jordan before they left? How is Sully?" Jillian's twin brother Jax's fiancée, Jordan, had recently reunited with her long-lost sister, Casey, who now went by the name Sully. Sully was staying at Redemption Ranch, not far from the inn, where she was getting therapeutic help while she put the pieces of her life back together, and Jax and Jordan had spent the last couple of weeks there with her.

"They're all doing okay, making progress," Beau said. "Jax and Jordan are planning another trip here soon."

"Good. Thanks for letting us come," she said.

"Are you kidding? We'll do everything we can to help." Charlotte, cute as ever in shorts and a sweater, pulled her into her arms and lowered her voice to a whisper. "What a mess, but Johnny is *hot*. I'm totally using him for hero inspiration. Are you two…?"

"*No*. He's a hot jerk whose life is a mess," Jillian whispered. "I'm here for Zoey."

She glanced at Zoey, doing something on her phone as the steward brought out their luggage and Johnny's guitar. Johnny, at six-plus feet, stood eye-to-eye with Beau as they shook hands, and her brother visually sized him up.

"Thank you for letting us hide out here." Johnny reached down to pet Bandit. "You'll be fairly compensated."

"No need for that," Beau assured him. "Given the circumstances, we thought it best to let you stay at our place. We've moved into the inn, so you'll have more privacy. You can use Char's SUV."

Johnny nodded, his expression serious. "I hate putting you out like that, but I appreciate the extra privacy."

"No problem." Beau said. "Should we expect an assistant, bodyguards, or anyone else to show up looking for you?"

"No. My assistant Jerry's wife just had a baby, and the fewer people with us, the better. I don't want to call attention to the inn."

"We appreciate that," Beau reassured him.

"Johnny, this is Char, Beau's wife," Jillian said. "She's a bestselling romance author, and I can't believe I'm only just realizing this, but your sister Harlow played the main character in the adaptation of Char's book *Anything for Love* on the Me Time channel."

A smile brightened Johnny's eyes, softening his sharp edges. Jillian didn't think he could get any hotter, but *Wow*. Tingles spread through her chest. *No, no, no. No tingles.* She didn't need to get caught up in a jerk.

"It's nice to meet you, Char." He shook her hand. "Harlow really enjoyed working on that project with Duncan Raz. Our family got together at my parents' place to watch it the night it was released. It was a great story."

"I'm so glad you enjoyed it. Harlow nailed the part. I'm glad Beau and I had a chance to meet her. She's super sweet," Charlotte said.

"Yeah, she's pretty great," he said. "I'm sorry for putting you and Beau out of your home, and I really appreciate you letting us camp out here for a while."

"You brought my favorite sister-in-law, so I should be thanking you." Charlotte lowered her voice as if she were sharing a secret. "Fair warning, though. Anything said or done around me might end up in one of my books. But don't worry. I won't use your real name."

"*Great*," he said a little sarcastically.

Jillian waited a few seconds for Johnny to introduce Zoey, and when he didn't, she said, "Okay, I guess I'm doing the introductions. Zoey, come meet Beau and Char."

Bandit trotted over to Zoey, walking beside her and pushing his nose into her hand. Zoey's expression remained sullen, her eyes trained on the ground. Johnny watched with a furrowed brow, tension rolling off him like the wind. Did it bother him that she was ignoring the dog and not looking at Beau and Char, or was he actually worried about Zoey?

Maybe Jillian had it all wrong, and he was trying to figure out an escape from the turn his life had taken only hours before. *There's no lifeboat, buddy. Please do the right thing by her.*

Pushing those thoughts away, she said, "Zoey, this is my brother Beau and his wife, Char. Guys, this is Zoey, who I'm looking forward to getting to know." Johnny's eyes flicked to her, as if he were shocked she'd said it. *Someone has to make her feel welcome.*

"Hi, honey," Charlotte said warmly. "It's so nice to meet you."

"Hi," Zoey said, quiet and clipped.

"We're glad you're here, and we look forward to getting to know you, too," Beau said.

Jillian could have hugged Char and Beau for their warmth. She elbowed Johnny, giving him a you-could-learn-from-that look that made his expression grow even tighter.

AS JOHNNY AND Beau loaded the luggage and his guitar into the back of Beau's truck, Johnny was struck again by Zoey's lone suitcase. He was pissed that his manager had duped him, but it made him sick to think his own kid had paid the price. How could a fourteen-year-old have only one suitcase to her name? Especially when he'd been unknowingly paying ten grand a month to her mother. He couldn't even think about Dick's betrayal without wanting to punch something.

"Hey, man, from what Jilly said, you've had a hell of a morning. Are you okay?" Beau asked.

"About as okay as can be expected, I guess." Johnny looked at Zoey kicking at the grass a few feet away from where Jillian and Charlotte were talking. Jillian glanced at her with concern in her eyes, and when Zoey looked over, Jillian smiled. Zoey looked as though she was thinking about smiling, but she averted her eyes. "I'm glad your sister agreed to stick around."

"Jilly said she's working on designing your tour wardrobe while you're here."

Shit. He'd forgotten about that. "That's right."

Beau looked at him skeptically. "She's a hell of a designer, but she also mentioned that you canceled your tour."

Fuck. "I did," he admitted.

"Then what's my sister really doing with you?"

Johnny met his gaze. As an older brother, he knew exactly what Beau was worried about. "It's not what you think. Do you have kids?"

"Not yet, but I hope to soon."

"Well, I *wasn't* hoping to, and now I'm supposed to be insta-dad, only I don't know the first thing about being a father. I needed help, and Jillian seemed to have a way with Zoey. Zoey begged her to come with us because she didn't want to be alone with me, so I used my contract with Jillian as leverage to get her to come with us. She will be designing the wardrobe, but with all that's going on, I have no idea when I'll be touring again."

"I get it, but you obviously don't know Jilly. She doesn't have a lot of experience with kids. She and my wife have a lot in common in the realm of focusing more on work than the world around them. So if you think Jilly's going to step in as some sort of mother figure to your daughter, you'd better think again. She's got a big heart, but she's also got a big mouth, a massive career, and a will of steel."

"I've witnessed that big mouth and her will of steel firsthand. I don't need her to be a mother, Beau. I just need a buffer so Zoey and I don't kill each other."

Beau chuckled. "In that case, you chose well. Jilly's been dealing with five bullheaded brothers her whole life. I think she can handle you and Zoey. It's too bad you didn't get here yesterday. You could've met Jilly's twin, Jax. He and his fiancée, Jordan, headed back to Maryland this morning."

"I don't think I could handle two of them."

Beau chuckled. "Jax and Jilly are nothing alike, except in their careers. Jax is very low-key. He's a wedding gown designer. Come on, let's get you and Zoey over to the cottage so you can get settled in."

A little while later Beau drove down a tree-lined road, and when they emerged from beneath the umbrella of branches, a gorgeous three-story glass, stone, and cedar inn came into view with grand terraces overlooking a lake, sprawling meadows, and a damn fine view of picturesque mountains in the distance.

"Wow," Zoey said with awe. "*That's* the inn?"

"Isn't it beautiful?" Jillian said as Beau drove past it and headed down a dirt road.

"Where are you going?" Zoey looked over her shoulder at the inn. "Aren't we staying there?"

"We're staying at Beau and Char's place, for privacy," Johnny said.

Zoey sank down in her seat, pouting.

"I think you'll like our cottage," Charlotte said.

Johnny didn't know what he was expecting, but as they pulled up to a rustic cottage with two brown A-line roofs that dipped in ways no roof ever should and sloped nearly to the ground, as if they'd melted from the sun, he was sure it was some kind of joke. Nothing was square or even. The edges of the cottage and roof were rounded and cockeyed, and the roof tiles were oddly shaped and misaligned. Between two tall roof peaks were a pair of dormers, also with drippy, uneven roofs, and just below, another sloping roof sheltered a bay window beside an arched barnwood front door. Johnny half expected the seven dwarfs to come out whistling.

Beau parked, and Bandit bolted out of the truck and around the side of the cottage. They climbed out of the truck, and Johnny looked down at the walkway made of oddly shaped maroon, green, and peach slabs of rock and cobblestones bound together with thick white concrete that led to the front door.

"What the hell is this place?" Zoey asked.

"*Hey,*" Johnny snapped. "Show some respect."

"This is our home," Charlotte said excitedly. "It's an exact replica of Snow White's cottage. My great-grandmother loved fairy tales, so my great-grandfather renovated the cabin that was on the property to create it for her, and then Beau fixed it up so we could live here. Do you like fairy tales?"

"They suck," Zoey said.

"*Zoey*," Jillian chided her. "That's not nice."

"Would you rather I lied to her?" Zoey asked.

Jesus. This kid has no manners. "Sorry, Charlotte. It's been a rough day." Johnny looked at Zoey and said, "If you don't have anything nice to say, please keep it to yourself."

She rolled her eyes. *"Whatever."*

"Including *that*." If he never saw another eye roll or heard the word *whatever* again, it would be too soon.

Zoey turned her back to him.

Johnny was in way over his head. He didn't believe in miracles, but he sure as hell hoped for one, or they were both in trouble.

"It's okay," Beau reassured him. "We know our home is different, but the good news is that nobody comes back here. You'll have all the privacy you need."

"Can't we just stay in the inn?" Zoey pleaded. "I promise I won't leave my room."

"We're staying here," Johnny said. "I'm not taking any chances with media hounds tracking you down."

"Why don't we go inside and check it out?" Jillian suggested. "It's actually really cool. One of a kind."

Charlotte pulled a blue and yellow polka-dot key from her pocket and handed it to Zoey. "Do you want to do the honors?"

Zoey couldn't look less enthusiastic as she trudged up the walk and unlocked the door.

"This place looks great," Johnny said. "I'm really sorry about Zoey's attitude."

"Don't be," Beau said.

"He's used to moody girls," Jillian said as she strutted past, following Zoey and Charlotte into the cottage.

Beau chuckled, and they headed inside.

The cottage smelled like warm cedar and happy family. The familiar scent nearly stopped Johnny in his tracks, reminding him of his childhood home on Cape Cod. He took in the dips and swells of the uneven frosting-like ceilings and crooked exposed beams, the stucco and stone walls, and what had to be a hand-carved wooden cap on the half wall separating the living room from a cozy eating area. They walked through an archway carved into a massive tree trunk to a good-size kitchen, which also had crooked, frosting-like walls. He admired the varying-sized pine cabinets with elaborately carved arched doors, three small arched openings between the countertop and the cabinets above, and the old-fashioned iron stove, with a flue that wound up behind it and disappeared into a stone wall that housed a rounded brick oven.

"This is incredible," Johnny said. "It's just like the pictures in the story."

"You know the story of Snow White?" Jillian asked with surprise.

"Yeah. Harlow and my other sister, Aria, are six and seven years younger than me. I read it to them a million times when they were young. They loved it." He looked at Zoey, staring at the floor, and was hit with a wave of sadness. Did she hate fairy tales because her life was hell or because it wasn't cool to like them? He hoped it was the latter, but his gut told him otherwise.

"Want to check out the upstairs?" Beau motioned to a set of steps tucked off to the side of the tree-trunk archway. Every step was a different size and shape. "The steps were made from trees on the property."

"The details in this place are unbelievable," Johnny said as they all made their way upstairs.

"Every piece of wood is hand carved," Beau said as he walked them through the unique bedrooms and bathrooms. The master suite had a stone fireplace that looked as though it had settled into place from a landslide. Two uneven hand-carved mantels made it appear even more off-balance. The walls were angled in like an A-frame, but they didn't meet at a peak. The ceiling was flat, and two large picture windows offered gorgeous views of the property.

When they headed back downstairs, Jillian said, "Isn't it wonderful?"

"It really is. A lot of hard work must've gone into it," Johnny said, heading for the door to get their luggage.

"A lot of *love*," Charlotte corrected him as everyone followed him out.

"Yeah, that, too." Johnny grabbed Jillian's and Zoey's luggage.

"You can leave mine in the truck," Jillian said. "I'm staying at the inn."

"What?" Zoey's head snapped up like her life was in danger. "Why do you get to stay at the inn?"

"Because I'm not as famous as your father, so I blend in," Jillian answered.

"Then why can't I stay with you?" Zoey asked. "People will think I'm your daughter."

"But you're *not*," Jillian said.

"You can't leave me alone with him. I don't *know* him. He could be a murderer," Zoey said angrily.

"That's a little dramatic," Jillian said flatly. "He's a lot of things, Zoey, but I don't think he's a murderer. And it's important for you two to spend time together so you can get to know each other."

"Why do we have to do that alone? *Please* stay with us," Zoey pleaded. *"Please?"*

The way she was begging made Johnny worry that some asshole might have hurt her in the past. He'd spoken to his cousins, Mick's brothers, Brett and Carson earlier. They owned Elite Security and were digging up everything they could on Zoey's life. But he also knew that Jillian was right. He had the power to royally fuck up Zoey, and that was the last thing he wanted to do. He needed to figure out how to talk to her, how to find common ground and build trust between them. It seemed impossible, but he'd find a way or die trying. But for now he kept his mouth shut and hoped for the best, because he wasn't keen on the idea of being alone with her, either, and he had a feeling Zoey's pleas would have a hell of a lot more pull with Jillian than his demands.

Jillian's shoulders dropped just a little, and he knew Zoey had won before Jillian even said, "Fine, but I get the master bedroom."

Chapter Four

JOHNNY HATED GOSSIP, and he'd long ago stopped reading online gossip about himself. But this wasn't about him. It was about the young girl who had locked herself in her room hours ago and hadn't come out. It was about his *daughter*, a fact that Mick had confirmed. That was why Johnny had forced himself to read the lies the media hounds were publishing, which ran the gamut from Zoey being his love child to his dirty little secret. They made her out to be a girl looking for trouble in all the wrong places, and for all he knew, they might not be far off. He read about her mother's fast lifestyle, the grandmother who had raised her, and dozens of theories about why he'd fired Dick. By the time he put his phone away, he was furious, and so fucking sad for Zoey, he'd had to go for a run to calm down before finally calling his family to discuss all that had transpired.

He looked at his parents' faces on his laptop screen as they waited for his siblings to join them on the video call. His father had worn his silver hair even shorter since his mother had lost hers from chemotherapy. Her hair had started growing back, and she had a soft sheen of blondish-gray waves, not much longer than his father's hair. They looked good, all things considered. Then again, even in the worst of times, they clung to any sliver of light in the darkness, and that light shined through them with vigor. Johnny wondered how they managed to exude positivity no matter what the situation. His mother had suffered from two types of cancers in the last year. She'd gotten through the first and was currently undergoing chemotherapy treatments for the second. Things looked good, but Johnny lived every day in fear of the disease rearing its ugly head again and stealing her from them.

A surprise disgruntled teenage granddaughter would only add to his parents' stress, and yet here they were, sitting nearly cheek to cheek, without a hint of judgment or unhappiness in their expressions. Their worry, however, was evident in the shadows in their eyes.

"How are you feeling, Mom?"

"I'm *fine*, honey. Don't worry about me. My tumor is shrinking, and I'm resting. All is well over here. We're just worried about you."

"I'm really sorry about all this."

"There's no reason to be sorry," his mother said. "We love you, and we'll love your daughter."

His throat felt like it was closing. He'd give anything for Zoey to have had that type of love from her damn mother so she'd never have to feel like she was now.

"How are you holding up, son?" his father asked. He was their family's rock, steady and stable in the worst of times, much like Kane.

"Ask me that in about a week," Johnny said. "I'm still in shock."

"That's understandable, honey," his mother said as his siblings' faces appeared on-screen. "How's Zoey doing? She must be so frightened. If she has a phone, I hope you took it away. The news reports have not been kind to her or her mother."

Damn it. He hadn't considered Zoey's phone. She'd probably seen all there was to see by now. "She's not doing great, but hopefully things will settle down now that we're someplace safe."

"Does that mean she's going to be staying with you?" his father asked.

"She's my kid. Of course she is."

Kane gave Johnny a supportive nod. As biological siblings, they shared their father's dark hair of his younger years and dark eyes, while Harlow and Aria were adopted and fairer haired.

"I knew you'd do the right thing," Harlow said with her typical enthusiasm. Her black knit turtleneck set off her side-parted blond hair, which hung just past her shoulders. "You two are all over the news, and there's a lot of speculation about why you fired Dick."

"I *know*. I read it." Dick had discovered Johnny when he was a fifteen-year-old YouTube sensation and had represented him for the past nineteen years. The betrayal cut so deep, if he let himself think too much about it, it would obliterate his ability to deal with Zoey.

"Johnny, are you okay? A teenage girl can be a lot to handle." Aria pushed her long dirty-blond hair over her shoulder, her short sleeves revealing the colorful tattoos on her arms. "Do you need help? Do you want me to come to wherever you are?"

He knew how big an offer that was coming from Aria, who was not a fan of traveling or being around people she didn't know, but before he could respond, Harlow said, "I can help, too, but only for a couple of days until I have to be back on set."

"Girls, that's sweet, but you know you can't do that without the media catching on," their mother said.

"She's right," Johnny said. "You have to stay put and act like you have no idea where we are. I'm really sorry this came out the way it did. I wish I could have brought Zoey home to Mom and Dad's so she could be around family, but that's not an option yet. For now, since everyone's looking for us, they'll probably have eyes on all of you." That was the reason his mother's illnesses had been kept under wraps. To keep the vultures from swarming and publishing horrific shit that no one needed to read. "I've spoken to Brett and Carson. They're arranging a security detail for each of you until this blows over."

"Mine's already shown up, and he's hot," Harlow said.

"*Ugh.* Do you have to send someone here? You know I hate having people watching me," Aria complained. "I'm safe. Zeke is parked outside my cottage right now. He and Tank won't let photographers get anywhere near me."

Aria was a tattooist at Wicked Ink on Cape Cod, which was owned by Tank Wicked. His cousin Zeke had tutored her when she was younger and had been watching out for her ever since. At six four, tatted and pierced, Tank was one of the most intimidating men Johnny knew, and Zeke was just as tough, although he was like a venomous animal, easy on the eyes but lethal. Their fathers had founded the Bayside chapter of the Dark Knights motorcycle club, and they and their brothers were all members. Johnny knew one call to Zeke or Tank would keep Aria surrounded by a number of badass bikers twenty-four-seven. But his sister wouldn't like that any more than what he'd arranged.

Johnny hated that his life impacted his family in this way, but that was the price of fame. "I know they'll keep you safe, but I'd feel better having a professional watching over you, too."

"*Fine*," Aria relented. "But where are you?"

"In Colorado. Harlow, guess whose place we're staying in? Beau and Char Braden's. Their place is an exact replica of Snow White's cottage just like in the movie. It's a trip."

"Really?" Harlow said excitedly. "I *love* them. Charlotte told me about their house and the inn. She's a riot. I swear she lives on Twix and energy bars. Beau is the kindest man alive, and he's *madly* in love with her. How did you end up there?"

"I pissed off his sister, Jillian, by canceling our meeting this morning. She was supposed to design my wardrobe for the tour, and she came up to chew me out when all of this was going down. Zoey said she wouldn't go anywhere without her, so I had no choice but to convince Jillian to come with us."

"I'm not surprised she called you out on canceling again," Harlow said. "You already put her off twice."

"That was nice of her to help, though," Aria added.

"It sure was," his father said. "John, what's the real story with you and Zoey's mother?"

"There is no story. She's just someone I must've hooked up with after a show. She left Zoey with Dick this morning and took off. Kane found out she was the one who tipped off TMZ. It sounds to me like she's all about the payoff."

"We need to talk about that," Kane said. "According to Dick, she wants nothing to do with Zoey, and if that's what you want, then we need to have legal documents drawn up and signed so she can't come back and use her as a weapon again. And while we're on the subject of legalities, the team has already uncovered major misappropriations of funds by Dick and several burned bridges with business associates that I'll need to fill you and your bandmates in on at some point. I have a feeling we'll be digging out of this for months, but we can take action now."

"I can't think about Dick right now—I need to focus on Zoey—but I want to hold his feet to the fire, so please talk to the guys and do whatever it takes to nail him. As far as Zoey's mother goes, I need to talk to Zoey and find out what she wants. But let's be honest. I don't know the first thing about parenting. Mom, Dad, I need some advice, but just so you know where we're starting from, as far as I can tell, her mother took all the money Dick gave her, and Zoey and her grandmother never saw a cent. Her mother is a snake, but will I do more harm than good if I close that door for Zoey?"

"Honey, there are lots of parents who can't raise their kids and have relatives do it for them," his mother said. "But any mother who would let her daughter go without and would drop her off with a stranger and then immediately seek money at her daughter's expense is doing her harm. I don't think that woman should be allowed anywhere near her ever again."

"I agree with your mother," his father said. "But I honestly don't know how something like that will affect Zoey in the long run. Maybe you should make that decision after talking to a professional who has experience dealing with issues like this."

"Yeah, that's a good idea. I'm flying blind here, you guys. I hope I don't mess her up."

"Oh, honey, you couldn't mess her up if you tried. You have too big a heart," his mother said.

"You didn't mess up me and Aria, and Lord knows you had every opportunity," Harlow said.

"But you had Mom and Dad. She doesn't have anyone but me."

"We didn't always go to Mom and Dad with personal problems," Aria said. "We went to you, too, and even when you were out touring, you made time for us, and you *always* knew the right thing to say. You still do."

Johnny was close to all his siblings, but he had a special bond with Aria. Everyone worried about her because of her anxieties, and sometimes their worry would make those anxieties worse. In those times, and others, she'd turn to Johnny. It wasn't unusual for him to fly home to check on her, even when touring, and fly back hours later.

"Maybe with you and Harlow, but that's because I know you. We grew up together. This is very different, and I can barely handle my own shit, as the situation with Dick surely proves."

"My ass it does," Kane said. "You have accountants and various managers, and every one of them missed what he was doing. This isn't on you, Johnny. You trusted a man who had us all fooled."

"Yeah, I get that, and I'm going to do everything within my power to do right by Zoey, but come on, Kane. What if I fail?"

"You've never failed at a thing in your life," Kane said.

"That's true," his father said. "And here's the thing about kids, John. Even kids who grow up in the best of circumstances test their parents damn near every chance they get. Some say it's a rite of passage. I think it's also done out of fear. They're growing up and seeing the light at the end of the tunnel. The elusive *freedom* teenagers dream about. Some run to it, others run from it, and many don't know how they feel about it. But very few try to understand what they're feeling, because most teenagers don't have the tools or the know-how to even understand that they're feeling *off*. That's when they act out. They shout and curse and take off to God knows where."

"I did all those things," Johnny said.

"All of you did," his father said. "If you ask me, kids need to know they're loved and need to trust that you're not going anywhere just because they turn into little jerks, and yes, I said *jerks*. Because kids are not all sunshine and rainbows."

"Hey, I was an angel." Harlow fluttered her lashes.

"Give it up, Harlow. You're not that good an actress," Kane said. "How many times did Dad call me to haul your ass back to the Cape from concerts in Boston or New York?"

"I never said I wasn't a naughty angel," Harlow said.

"Well, it doesn't matter what type of girl Zoey is," his mother said. "She's our family's new angel, and we can't wait to meet her."

His father nodded. "That's right, son. She's going to have a tough time, and she needs to know she has family looking forward to getting to know her."

"Absolutely," Harlow agreed. "She has the coolest aunt on the planet."

"*Thanks*," Aria teased. "But seriously, just make sure she's okay. We don't want to overwhelm her."

"It's too late for that. She's overwhelmed, and she's pissed, but Johnny will smooth things over and let her know she's safe." Kane held Johnny's stare. "Right?"

"Yes, of course." Johnny swallowed against the emotions welling inside him.

"Not to minimize the importance of what's going on with Zoey and what happened with Dick, but are we all going to pretend it's not weird that our brother brought a very beautiful woman with him to Colorado?" Harlow held up her phone, showing them a scorching-hot picture of Jillian. Her hair was sideswept, and she wore a curve-hugging, off-the-shoulder dark red minidress with sleeves that started with a puff just above her elbow and were tight from elbow to wrist. "*This* is Jillian Braden. Shall we take a minute to discuss how adorable they would be together?"

Holy hell. He'd already thought Jillian was gorgeous, but in that dress, she could make concrete go up in flames.

"She is beautiful," his mother said with a spark of hope in her eyes. "Is there something between you two?"

He glowered at Harlow, who was grinning, and said, "No, Mom, and I'm signing off now."

"Wait. I have questions," Harlow pushed.

"*Goodbye*, Harlow. Love you guys." There was a round of *Love yous* as he ended the call, feeling like a bit of weight had been lifted off his shoulders...and thinking about Jillian in that red dress.

AT A LITTLE after six, Johnny stood in front of Zoey's closed door, trying to figure out how to break the ice. Charlotte had brought sandwiches and a case of Diet Pepsi over for lunch, but Zoey had claimed she wasn't hungry. She had to be starved by now.

He knocked, and when she didn't respond, he said, "Hey, Zoey, it's me." *No shit.* Now he felt ridiculous. "I'm going to make dinner. Is there anything you don't like?"

Whoever said *silence is golden* was dead wrong. Zoey's silence only made him sadder. He may not know much about parenting, but he knew she was hurting, and his gut told him she needed a damn hug. But a hug from a guy she saw as the enemy wasn't the answer. He didn't even know what she'd been told about him by her mother or grandmother, much less what she'd read on the internet, which he also had to address with her. He wanted to open the door and at least clear the air, but barging in would do more harm than good.

He hated everything about this situation. *No.* That wasn't true. He didn't hate that Zoey existed, even if he hadn't planned on being a father, but he hated that he'd only just found out about her. He put his hand flat against her door, wishing he had the answers, and finally said, "I'll be downstairs if you need anything."

He made his way down to the kitchen and found Jillian staring into the refrigerator, wearing black leggings and a cream sweater cropped at her waist, giving him an incredible view of her sensational ass. His gaze moved up the swell of her hips to the sweet dip at her waist, and his fingers curled with the urge to touch her.

Fuck.

He forced himself to look away. This wasn't like him, even if she was sexy as hell. He wasn't into petite, mouthy women. He liked them leggy, with willing mouths that were eager to *please*, not *challenge*. He steeled himself to face her wrath as she closed the refrigerator.

She turned around with a Diet Pepsi in her hand. "Oh, *hey*."

"At least one female in this house is speaking to me."

Her eyes narrowed. "Are you hungry?"

"Why? Are you going to poison me?"

"That would not be worth the prison time. I have a fashion empire to run."

She was sharp *and* sexy, an alluring combination under any other circumstances.

She sipped her soda. "Listen, I'm stuck here, and I suck at holding grudges, so I'm calling a temporary truce. I can't exactly hate a guy in your situation, regardless of how self-centered you might be. But I *will* hold a grudge if pushed, so don't piss me off."

He held up his hands in surrender. "I'll do my best."

"Are you hungry?"

"Yes. But I'm worried about Zoey. She's been in her room all day, and she wouldn't even answer me when I knocked on her door."

"She's been through a lot. I'd imagine she needs time to decompress."

"I feel like I should do something. What if she's up there trying to find a way to escape?"

"She probably is. But she won't jump out a two-story window."

"You sure? I did at that age."

"She's not *you*. She's sad and angry, and I think she just needs a little time to digest what's happened. Forcing her to come downstairs will only piss her off more. But if she doesn't come out tomorrow morning, then you might want to gently step in."

"Okay. You're probably right."

"I usually am." She smirked. "Can we talk about dinner? There's nothing to eat, but we can order something at the inn and I can go get it."

"Let me take a look at what they have. I'm sure I can whip something up." He went to the fridge.

"You know how to cook?"

"Of course." He cocked a brow. "Don't you?"

"You don't have to sound so judgy. I never got the hang of the whole cooking thing." She shrugged. "I'm not a foodie, anyway. When I'm hungry, I grab a bowl of cereal or something to go from a local restaurant. Or I have dinner with my parents or one of my brothers. They're great cooks. There're a lot of options that don't require cooking."

"You sound a little entitled," he teased, scanning the items in the refrigerator.

"That's a sexist comment. Not every woman cooks. Besides, you can cook, but I bet you have a private chef at home that helps you keep that six-pack in shape."

He cocked a grin. "You thinking about me naked, Braden?"

"Dream on. Half the time you're onstage you're shirtless."

"For the record, it's hot up there, and I work hard for my abs. I don't have a personal chef. I don't like people in my space." He turned his attention back to the fridge. "They have a ton of fresh veggies."

"Yeah, but no dip." She sipped her soda.

He chuckled and shook his head as he opened the freezer. He tossed a package of chicken on the counter and went to the pantry, eyeing a box of pasta. "You're not gluten-free, are you?"

"No. Is Zoey?"

"Shit. Your guess is as good as mine." He made a mental note to ask Zoey if she had any allergies he should know about and forwent the pasta for a bag of rice. "Are you okay with stir-fry?"

"I'm fine with anything I don't have to make."

"That's too bad, because you're helping. It's time you learn to feed yourself. Help me find their cutting boards, will ya?" He began searching through cabinets.

She put her hand on her hip. "I'm perfectly capable of feeding myself, thank you. I just don't cook what I eat."

"Yeah, I get it. You're an adult who has her shit together and still goes to Mommy's for dinner." Why was that so fucking cute? He laughed as he set two cutting boards on the counter.

"That's…" She lifted her chin and smiled. "Accurate, and I'm okay with that."

Damn, that playful grin was a good look on her. So much better than the smirks and daggers he'd been getting. "Hey, we've all got our hang-ups." He put the chicken in the microwave to defrost and began pulling vegetables out of the fridge.

As he washed the vegetables, she said, "What are *your* hang-ups?"

"I like my privacy." He set three bell peppers on a cutting board and handed her a knife. "You know how to cut vegetables, don't you?"

She rolled her eyes and took the knife, but set it on the counter. "If I'm cooking, I need wine." She grabbed a bottle from the rack. "Want some? It's from my family's winery."

"Sure. Your family owns a winery?"

"Mm-hm." She filled two wineglasses and handed him one. "Hilltop Vineyards in Pleasant Hill, Maryland, where I live. It's been in my mom's family forever. My parents met there."

"That's kind of romantic."

"It's better than telling your kids you met on a dating app." They shared a smile. "My father says it was love at first sight, but my mom swears it was lust and only turned to love after my dad relentlessly pursued her. *That's* the romantic part, in my eyes, that my father refused to let her get away."

She said it with a hint of longing, and he wondered if she was one of those women who were looking to be swept off their feet. "Do you believe in love at first sight?"

"I never did. I was a firm believer in *lust* at first sight, but then three of my brothers, Beau, Jax, and Graham, fell in love so fast, and I realized my other two brothers, Nick and Zev, had probably loved their wives since first sight, which for Zev was in middle school. So now I'm on the fence."

"Sounds like the Braden men fall fast."

"Yeah, and I'll have five awesome sisters-in-law once Jax gets married."

"Beau said Jax is your twin. Where do you two fit in the lineup?"

"What else did he tell you?"

"Nothing I didn't already know. Tell me about your brothers."

"They're overprotective and awesome. Beau's the oldest. Then comes Nick. He's a freestyle horse trainer and performer, and as bullheaded as they come. He and his wife, Trixie, who is one of my closest friends, live near me. Zev comes after Nick, and he's married to his childhood love, Carly. Pay attention, Rocker Boy, because you'll be tested on names later."

Rocker Boy? "I've got it so far. Go on."

"Zev is a treasure hunter, and Carly is a chocolatier, but also a treasure hunter. They were like the Goonies when they were young, always exploring and searching for treasures. They split their time between Colorado and Silver Island, where they're recovering treasure from a sunken ship."

"Seriously?"

"Yup. What can I say? We're all pretty cool." She shrugged adorably.

"Are they in Colorado now? I'd like to hear their stories."

"No, they're still in Silver Island. They'll be heading this way at the end of October, I think."

"Bummer. So who's after Zev?"

"Me and Jax. Jax lives in Maryland, too, and he's engaged to an awesome friend of mine named Jordan. Jordan recently reunited with her sister, who disappeared twenty years ago, when she was four. It's a long story, but her sister is staying at a ranch near here and going through therapy while she puts the pieces of her life back together."

She took a long drink of wine.

"She was missing for twenty years? I can't imagine what her family went through."

"It's an awful story. She lost her parents, too. I can't imagine what she went through, although we rarely saw Beau and Zev for a number of years, but that's a story for another time."

"Why? We have time, and I'd like to hear it. You and Beau seem close."

"We are. I'll give you the condensed version, because I don't want to get sad right now. Beau lost his first love to an accident when she was in college. His girlfriend, Tori Raznick, Duncan Raz's sister, was like a sibling to the rest of us because we all grew up in the same close-knit community. She was also Carly's best friend. Everyone thought Beau and Tori and Zev and Carly would get married. But when Tori was killed, Beau and Zev blamed themselves. Beau took off, and Zev quit college and traveled, and they only came back a few times each year."

"That's horrible. You wouldn't know Beau suffered that kind of grief by looking at him."

"You would have before Char came into his life. He was broken for a decade, and I wasn't sure we'd ever get him back. But her love healed him, and eventually Zev ran into Carly at Beau and Char's wedding here at the inn, and he fought for her." Her eyes got watery, and she blinked several times and took a drink of her wine. "Anyway, they all were touched by the magic of the inn, and now they're living their happily ever afters."

Her emotions were as raw as they'd been visceral when she'd first stormed into his penthouse. He hated that she and her family had seen such heartache, but he liked knowing her passion extended to her family. "I'm glad, and I'm so sorry for your family."

"Yeah, well, thanks. Now back to my sibling lineup. My youngest brother, Graham, is an engineer like our dad, but he owns an investment company and specializes in eco-friendly businesses with his partner, Knox. Graham and his wife, Morgyn, a fashionista in her own right, just created a sustainable tiny house community in Seattle. Morgyn also repurposes used items and makes incredible clothing, jewelry, and home accessories. They travel *all* the time, and they live in a tiny house in Virginia and a treehouse in Maryland."

"A *treehouse?*"

"I know how weird that sounds, but Graham is all about nature, and his treehouse is amazing."

"You have an impressive family. They're all married except you and Jax?"

"Yes, but he's engaged, and he definitely fell in love at first sight. Jax is a bridal gown designer, and Jordan came to him as a client." She sipped her wine and went back to cutting the peppers. "I can't help but think that maybe I'm wrong about love at first sight, and it's just not going to work that way for me."

Her ability to change the subject could give a guy whiplash, but he didn't mind. Many people droned on about things. Jillian's matter-of-fact style was refreshing. "Does that bother you?"

"No. I'm good with lust." She took another sip, holding his gaze. "There's nothing like the excitement of it. When you see someone across the room, and you feel that instant rush of attraction, different from all others. It's like a burning ember, and it lodges in your stomach, growing hotter every time you think about them." She lowered her voice seductively. "And when you see them, it pulses through you, burning so hot you're sure you'll go up in flames."

Fuck yeah.

She licked her lips and set down her glass. "What about you?" she asked casually, as if she'd just recited the fucking alphabet. "Do you believe in love at first sight?"

He was still hung up on her body pulsing with desire. "I'm a lust guy, all the way. If not for my parents, I might not even believe in love." He took a drink, forcing his attention back to the task of cutting vegetables before he got himself in trouble. He needed to get away from the love-lust talk, which had never been a comfortable topic for him. "I'm curious about something. You're a successful designer, and you can obviously afford a private chef, so why don't you have one?"

"Let's just say there's a reason I live alone."

Soft hazel eyes flicked up to his, the early-evening light that cut through the window bringing out flecks of golds and greens, making them too damn entrancing to look away. Her expression was softer, too, bringing her delicate features into focus. Her chin was slightly pointed, giving her a youthful quality that didn't quite match her sexy, bowed lips but somehow also made her even more alluring. He had the overwhelming urge to take that adorable chin between his finger and thumb and tilt her face up further so he could lean in and taste her.

"I don't like people in my space, either," she said, pulling him from his thoughts.

His mind stumbled before he realized she was still responding to his question and not to their close proximity. As she went back to cutting the peppers, he silently cursed himself. What the hell was wrong with him? He hadn't been a player in years, and he sure as hell wasn't desperate. If he wanted to get laid, he could. Well, not in their current situation, but that didn't matter. He was selective about the women he slept with. But even when he'd been young and stupid and hadn't been as discretionary, he'd remained in control of his emotions. He'd gone out with his last long-term girlfriend for a year, and he'd never gotten lost in her.

So why was he getting lost in thoughts of *kissing* Jillian?

She bit into a slice of pepper. "These would be better with dip."

He glanced at her cutting board, which was a mess of seeds and odd-sized pieces of pepper, as if she'd massacred them. "As a fashion designer, shouldn't you know about symmetry?"

"It doesn't matter what it looks like. They're just going in my mouth." She took another bite.

He arched a brow.

"Ohmygod." She rolled her eyes. "Really?"

"Hey, you're the one with the dirty thoughts. I didn't say a word."

"You didn't have to." She picked up a big piece of pepper and made a dramatic show of chomping into it.

"Going for the biggest. I guess size does matter."

She laughed.

"I'll take that as confirmation." He didn't know why he was going down this path, but he couldn't help himself.

She smirked. "Worried you won't make the cut?"

"Why? You planning on trying to get into my pants?"

"*No.*"

"Ah, you're intimidated. That's understandable."

She swatted his arm. "You're too much."

"That's what they all say. Just relax your throat, and it'll go down easier."

"*Ohmygod.* You're a pig."

He snorted, which made her laugh, and her laugh was so cute, it made him laugh, too. After the day they'd had, it felt too damn good to stop.

"I've seen pictures of you in your skivvies," she teased. "You're not exactly packing a choking hazard."

"You want to put money on that?"

"*No.*" She shoved another piece of pepper in her mouth and bumped him with her hip. "Shut up and cut those vegetables."

Twenty minutes later they were still joking around as the rice simmered and Johnny stir-fried their dinner.

"You're not bad in the kitchen," she said, stealing another piece of chicken from the pan.

"I'm the very best kind of *bad* in any room. You, on the other hand, have eaten more than you've helped. You are not great in the kitchen."

She giggled. "You have no idea how *great* I can be in any room." She snagged a piece of broccoli and blew on it to cool it off, then popped it into her mouth.

"You blow *and* you're greedy? Not a bad combo."

She pointed at him, eyes narrowing. "Stop thinking about me like that." She stole another piece of chicken and blew on it with a taunting lift of her brows.

"I'm not sure I can now that it's out there." Their gazes connected and held, turning that taunt into something far more tempting. *Fuck.* This woman wasn't just alluring. She was dangerous. Like the perfect chorus that lures you in with unexpected notes, and soon you find yourself hoping it never ends. He didn't know what the hell was happening, but this was *not* what they were there for. He snagged the chicken from her fingers and popped it into his mouth, breaking their connection and forcing his attention back to the young girl upstairs. "*Mm.* This is done. Do you think I should have Zoey come down to eat or bring her a plate?"

"I don't know if you should push her or not," Jillian said matter-of-factly. "But I think she needs to know that you want to spend time with her."

He didn't know what was wrong with his brain, but it wanted to twist that into Jillian giving him a message about herself, which he knew wasn't the case. Shoving that ridiculousness aside, he said, "Of course I want to spend time with her. I just don't want to make it any harder for her." He filled a plate with rice and stir-fry. "I'll take this up and see if she'll talk to me."

"Wait. She needs silverware and a drink." She grabbed a Diet Pepsi, silverware, and a napkin and pulled a tray out of a lower cabinet. "Use this."

No, you're not the motherly type at all. He put everything on the tray and picked it up.

"Good luck, Daddy Bad."

He gave her the side-eye, then headed upstairs. He knocked on Zoey's door, and instead of waiting for a response he was pretty sure wouldn't come, he said, "I made dinner. I'd really like to eat with you."

"I'm not hungry" came from behind the door.

He touched his forehead to the door, wishing he knew what to say to make things easier for her. "I know this sucks for you, Zoey, and I'm sorry about all of it. But I'm not sorry you're here. I'm glad we finally got to meet, and I hope you'll give me a chance to get to know you." He set the tray on the floor. "I'm going to leave your dinner out here. I'll be downstairs if you'd like to join me or if you need anything else."

There was a faint "Thank you," and he took it as a good sign.

Twelve hours down, the rest of my life to go.

Chapter Five

JOHNNY PACED THE front yard the next morning, talking with his mother on the phone. He was so stressed he could barely think straight. He'd been up half the night talking with Kane and his bandmates about the mess Dick had left behind and the other half worried about Zoey. Then there was the too-fucking-sexy mouthy one that was unexpectedly sassy and fun to be around. He'd heard *her* downstairs at three in the morning and had nearly gone down just to distract himself from the mess he was in. But after the way he'd reacted to her when they were cooking dinner, he'd thought better of it and had stayed upstairs.

"How are things going?" his mother asked.

"I'm trying, but I don't know. I haven't seen Zoey since yesterday afternoon, when she locked herself in her room." He'd found her plate from dinner outside her bedroom last night. She'd eaten everything except the vegetables, but at least she hadn't starved. "I knocked on her door this morning and she told me to go away. What am I supposed to say to that?"

"Just let her know that you're there for her," his mother said.

"I *did*, but it's nearly ten, and she and Jillian haven't come downstairs. Am I missing something? Is there some kind of female rebellion going on?"

"Oh, honey. I know it's not easy, but a bedroom is a safe space, and Zoey needs that right now. Teens often hole up in their rooms.

You were on the road a lot when the girls were teenagers, so you didn't see how often they hid in theirs. As for Jillian, she's probably working. Don't forget, you disrupted her life, too."

Shit. He'd been so caught up in his own mess, he'd forgotten about that. Noises coming from inside the house caught his attention. "I think I hear them. I've got to run, Mom. I'll be in touch. Love you."

He pocketed his phone on his way inside and saw Zoey walking into the kitchen. He headed that way but stopped cold as Jillian came downstairs. Her hair was a tangled mess, her face was makeup free, and she was wearing a tight gray tank top with her initials over her left breast, no bra, and matching skimpy sleeping shorts with a thin line of lace at the hem.

She flashed a sleepy smile as she headed into the kitchen, and he tried to calm down his very interested dick. Could today get any worse? He gathered all his wits about him, hoping they worked as shields, and followed her in, determined not to look in her direction.

Zoey sat at the table, thumbing out something on her phone.

"Morning, Zoey," he said. "Do you want some breakfast?"

She shook her head but didn't look up.

He turned toward the fridge, but as if the universe had it out for him, Jillian was fishing around in there with her ass sticking out. She withdrew a Diet Pepsi and straightened. Her nipples pressed against the thin material of her tank top as she closed the fridge with her ass.

"Jillia—"

She held up her finger, silencing him, and leisurely opened the can, guzzling the soda. After she let out a long sigh, a smile crawled across her face. "Okay, now you can speak."

"Soda? Really?"

"Never mind. Please don't speak." She sat at the table.

Why did he feel like he was dealing with two teenagers?

Zoey's lips curved up, but she didn't look up from her phone.

He sat at the table and focused on Zoey, who was wearing another belly-baring shirt that looked far too small. He'd have to address her clothing at some point, but that was the least of his concerns. "Did you sleep okay?"

Zoey shrugged.

"Is there anything you need to be more comfortable?"

She didn't respond.

"Look, I know this is hard, and I'm sorry, but we're going to be here for a while, and we should get to know each other. Why don't you tell me something about yourself? I know you lived in New Jersey with your grandmother and in Pennsylvania with your mother. Do you have friends?"

"*No.* I *just* moved to Pennsylvania."

"What about in New Jersey?"

She shrugged.

"Were you in sports or cheerleading?"

"Gross," Zoey said, eyes still trained on her phone.

"What's gross? Sports or cheerleading?"

"Cheerleading."

"Okay, we won't sign you up for cheerleading. What do you like to do?" He felt Jillian watching them.

Zoey shrugged.

"Did you play sports?"

She didn't answer.

"Do you like music?"

She rolled her eyes.

"Who are you texting?"

"Nobody." Her fingers flew across the keyboard.

"I'm sure you read the garbage they're saying about us. Do you want to talk about it?"

She shook her head.

He blew out a breath, trying to keep his cool instead of taking the damn phone and making her talk to him. "Is it so bad that I want to get to know you?"

She glared at him. "I don't know *you*, and I'm not asking questions."

"So ask. I'll tell you anything. What do you want to know?"

She pressed her lips into a hard line and lowered her eyes.

When he opened his mouth to speak, Jillian nudged his leg under the table and shook her head, brows knitted. She inhaled deeply and said, "I'll be out of your hair in a minute so you can chat in private. I'm going to see Channing Tatum after I shower."

Zoey's eyes lit up. "Really? He's *here*?"

"Yeah. He's here all the time," Jillian said casually.

"Are you kidding? Can I go with you?" Zoey asked. *"Please?"*

Jillian finished her soda. "Sure."

"I need to get ready." Zoey popped to her feet and ran upstairs.

Jillian pranced over to the trash can in that skimpy outfit, and Johnny's traitorous dick tried to rise to greet her. He forced his gaze up to her face. "We're supposed to be lying low. If Tatum's in town, it'll be a media madhouse."

"Don't worry. Nobody will know we're here. I promise."

"*Jillian,*" he warned.

"Relax, it's not what you think. I would never put her in harm's way. We're not even leaving the property."

She headed for the stairs, and he grabbed her hand. Their eyes connected with a pulse of heat, just as they had on the plane and in the kitchen. It could have been frustration on her side. Lust and frustration could look a lot alike, and at that moment, he didn't trust himself to tell the difference. "I'm not messing around. If the media finds out we're here, her life will be a hell of a lot harder."

She cocked her head, looking more innocent than he knew her to be. "Put your daddy claws away and show a little trust."

"That's kind of hard to do after what's just happened to that young girl."

"And to you," she pointed out, giving his hand a squeeze. "I wouldn't purposely make her life, or yours, any harder. Okay?"

He nodded, although he didn't know why he felt like he could trust her.

"By the way, I read the gossip sites. Your brother is a master at setting up diversions, because you and Zoey have been spotted in the UK, on a boat to India, in the Caribbean, Florida, and about a dozen other places."

"Yeah, he's good at everything he does."

"*Hm.* I wonder if that runs in the family." There was a hint of seduction in her voice and a challenging taunt in her eyes.

He *knew* he should let it go, but he couldn't resist taunting her right back. Still holding her hand, he tugged her closer, that thrum of heat returning with a vengeance. He lowered his face a whisper away from hers. "I can see you're still thinking about my choking hazard."

"*Hardly.*"

"Your eyes tell a different story."

She lifted that adorable chin. "Dream on, Rocker Boy. Now, can I get my hand back, please, so I can shower?"

He released her hand, and as she walked away, he said, "Give me a holler if you need someone to wash your back."

She glanced over her shoulder with a coy grin. "I'm very flexible. I've got it. Thanks."

Conjuring images of her in compromising positions in the shower, he scrubbed a hand down his face.

I'm so fucked.

LEAVES CRUNCHED AND twigs snapped beneath the heels of Jillian's suede ankle boots as they made their way through the woods. If she'd known she was coming to Colorado instead of staying in New York, she'd have packed different shoes. If she'd known she was sleeping under the same roof as Johnny, she'd have brought her battery-operated little friend. At least she had her favorite rust leggings and black-and-tan sweater, even if she wasn't shopping in Greenwich Village as she'd planned. As for the other, her hand would have to do.

"Isn't it pretty out here?" she said, stepping over a log.

Zoey didn't respond.

At least she wasn't on her phone. Jillian took that as a win and glanced at Johnny, walking behind them and looking ridiculously hot in a blue Henley, jeans, and black boots. He lifted his chin in acknowledgment, that muscle in his jaw twitching like a heartbeat, as it'd been doing for most of the last twenty-four hours. He had so much on his plate, she couldn't imagine what was going through his head or what had been going through her own head when she'd flirted with him this morning. It was crazy, but she couldn't help herself after their playful banter and steamy innuendos last night. She'd wondered if that playful side of him had been a onetime thing. But he was proving not to be the arrogant ass she'd assumed he was. Their banter was fun, but that flash of unexpected heat that simmered low in her belly every time he looked at her was even more enticing. She hadn't felt anything like that in so long, she kind of craved it. If they were going to be stuck together for two weeks, she might as well have some flirty fun.

"I can't believe we're going to see Channing Tatum. Where are we meeting him?" Zoey asked as Jillian held up a branch for her to walk under.

"In a clearing. It's just a little farther."

"You must be really famous for him to come out here to meet you," Zoey said with awe.

"I'm not as famous as your father, but Channing doesn't care about fame."

"All famous people say that. Do I look okay?" Zoey fluffed her hair over her shoulder.

Jillian gave her a quick once-over. She wanted to tug Zoey's shirt down to her waist and wipe some of her eyeliner off, but she wasn't *her* daughter and not only had Jillian gotten her to eat toast with peanut butter before they'd left the cottage, but she was *finally* communicating instead of withholding words like she had a limited supply. Jillian didn't want to rock the boat, so she said, "You look great."

Zoey nodded with an *almost* smile, much nicer than her usual surly expression.

When they came to the thick bushes that bordered the clearing, Jillian parted the spiky branches and caught her thumb on a thorn. "Ouch." She put her finger in her mouth to stop the bleeding.

"You okay?" Johnny stepped in to hold the branches back, his dark eyes going straight to her finger in her mouth and lingering there.

"Mm-hm." *You like that, huh?* She could think of a dozen ways to toy with him if teenage eyes weren't watching them. She pulled her finger out with a smirk, but when those hungry eyes met hers, his wicked grin made her insides flame.

Damn it. He was better at this than she was.

"Okay, sweetie. Let's go." She hurried Zoey through the bushes, trying to ignore Johnny's chuckle.

Bandit darted past as they stepped into the clearing. Charlotte ran up from the direction of the chicken coop, wearing red rubber boots, shorts, and a sweatshirt, her long dark hair flying over her shoulders. "*Duncan!*" she shouted. "I'm sorry! Please come back!" She stopped in front of Jillian, out of breath. "Did you see which way Duncan Raz went?"

"No, but Bandit ran that way." Jillian pointed in the direction the dog had gone, as Beau came through the bushes farther down to their right, his serious eyes taking in the situation.

"Duncan Raz is here, too?" Zoey asked excitedly.

"Of course! But we have to hurry if we're going to catch him," Charlotte said anxiously.

Jillian nudged Zoey's arm. "You can go with her."

As Charlotte and Zoey ran off, Johnny glowered at Jillian. "*Seriously?*" He cursed and took off running after them, hollering, "Zoey, wait!"

As Beau sidled up to Jillian, she said, "I feel kind of bad for not telling them Channing and Duncan are chickens." Charlotte called her chickens chickendales and had named them after the cast of *Magic Mike*, and her favorite actor, Duncan Raz.

"Jilly," he reprimanded, shaking his head.

"They needed to get out of their own heads for a while, so I told them we were going to meet Channing Tatum, and Zoey lit up like a Christmas tree."

Beau's gaze remained serious. "I can't decide if that's brilliant or cruel."

"Let's go with brilliant, at least until they yell at me for it." She heard Bandit barking and knew they hadn't gone far.

He finally cracked a smile. "I got a call from Nick this morning, checking on you."

"Why? I filled him, and everyone else, in on the situation last night." She'd filled in her family and had also called Victoria to tell her she hadn't slaughtered Johnny, and she understood why Victoria hadn't been able to clue her in. While her family was sympathetic, they were glad she would be near Beau since they didn't know Johnny. She'd also fielded a dozen texts from her closest friends, who had known about the meeting she'd had scheduled with Johnny. They'd heard about Zoey and had wanted the scoop, but she'd honored Johnny's need for privacy and had simply said that Johnny was MIA and she didn't know anything more than the tabloids did, but she was going to stick around New York and work from her hotel, catching up with clients and spoiling herself with hours of shopping.

"You know Nick. He just needed to make sure you were really okay."

"I'm thirty. You'd think he'd ease up by now." As she said it, her thoughts turned to Zoey, and sadness tamped down her frustration. "Actually, I take that back. I'm grateful for Nick, and you, and everyone who loves me."

"Johnny and Zoey's situation sure brings perspective, doesn't it?"

She nodded. "It's like a blessing and a heartache for both of them. I feel so bad for Zoey. Fourteen is such a hard age, and she lost the woman who raised her. I can't imagine how hard that is, and then to be abandoned by her own mother? And Johnny's manager worked for him forever and totally screwed them both over. I can't even begin to imagine that kind of betrayal, by her mother or by his manager."

"Taking on a kid is a lot of responsibility, but he's a billionaire with teams of people at his fingertips. I think he can handle it."

"Do you *see* teams of people? Or even a bodyguard?" she said defensively, surprising herself. "There was a bodyguard in his building that he could have brought with him, but he didn't because he didn't want to make Zoey uncomfortable by having another man around that she didn't know. He's not as bad as I thought he was. He's really trying to do right by her."

He looked at her curiously. "That's good to know, but you seem on edge. Are you okay?"

"I'm fine. It's just hard watching them struggle. They have no idea how to communicate. I want to lock them in a room and make them talk."

"Don't get any ideas, Jilly. That's his daughter, and he has to handle things his own way."

"I *know*," she said. "I just feel like doing something fun would help, but he can't go anywhere."

"I know you're not keen on running around, but we have lawn games in the game shed. You can try those."

"Maybe I will, but what's a game shed?"

"A shed for games, obviously. I built it last spring. You can't miss it. It's behind the cottage."

Charlotte came over the crest of the hill carrying a big fat chicken. Zoey and Johnny trailed behind her wearing matching scowls.

"You know, I didn't see the resemblance between Zoey and Johnny until this very moment." Bandit trotted beside Zoey, pushing his nose into her hand. Jillian remembered something Nick had once told her about animals knowing who needed them most. She finally understood what he meant.

"Better brace yourself," Beau advised. "It looks like you're in for double trouble."

"I got him!" Charlotte said proudly.

"I knew you would, shortcake." Beau fell into step beside his wife and draped an arm around her shoulder, heading for the chicken coop.

"*Chickens?* Really?" Zoey said with disdain.

"*Chickendales*, actually," Jillian said with a smile.

"We heard." Johnny shook his head, and a laugh broke free.

"And don't ask me if I want to meet Jason Mamoa. I *know* he's a rooster," Zoey said as Bandit nosed her hand. "*Why* won't this animal leave me alone?"

"Maybe because he thinks you're cool," Jillian said.

Bandit barked, and she and Johnny shared a smile.

"Stupid dog," Zoey said, walking backward as Bandit continued trying to get her attention, following her and pushing his nose into her hand, her leg, wherever he could reach. She tripped and fell on her butt, and Bandit licked her face. "Ew! Stop! Help!" She covered her face, rolling onto her stomach and laughing. "Make him stop!"

They laughed with her, and the relief on Johnny's face was palpable as he pulled the pooch away by his collar. "A'right, Bandit, let her go." He offered a hand to Zoey, but she pushed to her feet on her own. "You okay?"

"*Fine.*" Zoey brushed dirt from her jeans.

"Do you want to take Charlotte up on the invitation to help her collect the chickens' eggs?" he asked.

"*Ew,*" Zoey said. "Since we're not going to see any famous people, can we go back to the house?"

Johnny splayed his hands. "Hey, what am I, chopped liver?"

Zoey rolled her eyes. "I mean *real* famous people."

"I'm about as famous as they come, sunshine. I bet plenty of teenagers would love to be here right now."

"Whatever." Zoey stalked away with Bandit on her heels.

Johnny sighed. "I feel like I do everything wrong."

"You were doing pretty well until your ego got in the way," Jillian said.

"Give me a break. I'm new at this."

"Lucky for you, I have a few other ideas to put her in a better mood."

"After chasing a chicken all over creation, I'm not sure I trust your ideas anymore," he teased as they followed Zoey into the woods.

Chapter Six

"WHAT'S TAKING SO long?" Zoey asked as they followed the narrow path through the woods.

"We're almost there." Jillian had decided to take them back to the cottage a different way, so they would walk by the creek with the hopes that Zoey might find it cool. Or at least not boring.

"I feel like one of the seven dwarfs following you through the woods," Johnny said.

"Hey, don't knock fairy tales." Jillian ducked under a branch. "Beau and Char gave every room at the inn a fairy-tale theme, and I wasn't kidding about the magic of the inn. It's real, and the fairy-tale theme made that magic even stronger. Char told me that three separate couples—complete strangers who were at the inn for separate events—fell in love here this year."

"I don't believe in fairy tales or magic," Zoey said as they descended a hill toward the creek.

"That's too bad, because the magic of the inn is all around you right now. You can't feel it or see it, but it's there. Just ask my brothers."

"Why your brothers?" Zoey asked.

"Because three of them found love here. Beau lost someone he loved a long time ago, and he turned into a whole different person. He was sad and angry, and he kept himself so busy, he rarely came home to see us, and Char lost her whole family and was raised here by her grandfather. I just realized that you two have that in common."

"I never knew my grandfather," Zoey said.

"But you were raised by a grandparent. That's what I meant. When Char lost her grandfather, she hid away at the inn, writing all day and night, and rarely left. Then a relative of ours hired Beau to do some repairs to the inn because it had gotten a little beat-up during a wedding they held here, and when Beau showed up, the magic of the inn took hold. He and Char rediscovered life together and fell in love." The creek came into view at the bottom of the hill, and Jillian picked up her pace.

"That's just a coincidence," Zoey said.

"I'd say that was true if my brother Zev and his first love, Carly, hadn't fallen back in love here, or if the magic of the inn hadn't wrapped itself around my brother Nick and my friend Trixie one special night and followed them back to Maryland."

"*Whatever.* I still don't believe in it," Zoey said.

"Well, I do," Jillian said as they reached the creek. "I keep hoping that if I come here enough, the magic will wrap itself around me, too, and maybe something wonderful will happen."

"That's weird," Zoey said.

Johnny held a branch back so Zoey could walk by and said, "That wasn't a nice thing to say."

"She believes in *magic*," Zoey said, as if it were the most ridiculous thing she'd ever heard.

Johnny picked up a stone, turning it over in his hand. "My sisters believed in magic when they were little, and a lot of their wishes came true."

Zoey kicked at the dirt, uninterested.

"Really? What kind of magic?" Jillian asked.

He looked at the creek with a thoughtful expression and tossed the stone into the water. "I don't know how to explain it."

"Try," Jillian encouraged, liking the warmer look in his eyes and hoping whatever he shared might help Zoey in some way.

"I can give you an example. My youngest sister, Aria, was four when my parents adopted her, and she'd had some rough times in foster homes. She had a lot of nightmares, and she'd get really upset. This went on for months. I was around Zoey's age, and it tore me up knowing how distraught she was. I wanted to fix it and help her feel better. I remembered what my father did for me when I was younger. If I was upset about something, he'd take me outside and pitch baseballs for me to hit. He'd tell me to channel all my negative feelings into hitting the ball. Like you, Zoey, Aria wasn't into sports, but she loved fairies and being told stories. So I took my father's idea of channeling negative energy into something I thought she would like, and one morning I walked her down to the creek near our house, which was similar to this, and asked her to find a smooth stone, one that wasn't too big."

Zoey was listening as intently as Jillian was.

He picked up another stone and turned it over in his hand. "Like this." He held it out for them to see. "Then I made up a story about a magical water fairy that lived in the creek, and I told her if she gave her nightmares to the stone and asked nicely, when she tossed it in the water, the water fairy would wash away her nightmares and grant her one wish. It took some doing, because she didn't want to think about the nightmares, but after some convincing, she'd close her eyes and think really hard. When she opened them and threw the stone in the water, her face was so full of hope, I remember thinking I'd do anything if it worked." He ran his thumb over the stone and tossed it in the water.

"Did her nightmares go away?" Zoey asked, hanging on to his every word.

He nodded, looking at her with a lift of his brows, as if he were surprised too. "The nightmares she gave to the stone never came back."

"Did she have other nightmares?" Zoey asked.

"Sometimes, but then we'd go down to the creek and send those away, too, and eventually her nightmares subsided."

Jillian was as caught up in him as she was in the story. She had a feeling he didn't share this side of himself often. She loved knowing he'd gone out of his way to help his sister and that he trusted her and Zoey enough to share what he'd done for her. But she was just as intrigued by the fact that Zoey hadn't asked about Aria's wishes. She'd only focused on casting away the nightmares.

"Does that mean you believe in a little bit of magic?" Jillian asked Johnny.

He looked at Zoey and said, "I met a daughter I didn't know I had, and she could have ended up anywhere, so yeah. I guess I believe in something like that."

Zoey's lower lip trembled, but she didn't say a word and looked down at the ground.

Johnny glanced at Jillian, hope and compassion thickening in the air around him. She wanted to go to him. To hug him and tell him he'd done well by sharing those pieces of himself and showing Zoey that she was in his heart. But something in the way he was holding her gaze told her she didn't have to say a word. He'd somehow felt what she wasn't saying.

"Can we go now?" Zoey asked abruptly.

Johnny tore his eyes away and cleared his throat. "Yeah. Let's get out of here."

THEY HAD A late lunch, and Zoey only picked at her food, but she'd remained with them at the table, which was nice, even if she didn't say a word and escaped up to her room right afterward. Johnny was quick to escape, too, taking his guitar outside. Jillian had wanted to talk to him about their morning, but he clearly needed space, so she took advantage of the time and set herself up in the living room to catch up on work. That way, if Zoey came downstairs, she'd be able to interact with her. She may not know much about Zoey, but she knew avoidance was a common teenage maneuver, and Zoey couldn't avoid what stood between her and the kitchen or the front door.

When Jillian finally came up for air, it was late afternoon. She plugged her phone into her laptop to charge and set both on the coffee table. Zoey hadn't come downstairs yet, so Jillian went in search of Johnny. She found him talking on his phone, rubbing the back of his neck as if the conversation caused him physical pain. Glad she wasn't on the other side of *that* call, she left him alone and went around back to find the game shed.

Beau was right. She couldn't miss the whimsical building, sided with horizontal boards painted the colors of the rainbow. The trim was bright white, the door orange. The colorful boards above the door ran vertically to the peak in the purposefully droopy roof that matched the main cottage. There were white-paned windows on the sides and front and window boxes bursting with pretty fall blooms.

She opened the door and flicked on the light, taking in shelves of games so neatly organized, she felt like she'd walked into an outdoor game store. There were horseshoes, Frisbees, croquet, volleyball, and badminton sets, and wiffle balls and bats. On the floor was a massive Connect 4 game, two cornhole games, and the biggest Jenga set she'd ever seen. She didn't have an athletic bone in her body. Jenga and Connect 4 were about her speed. But she had a feeling those games would bore Zoey.

As she looked over their options, she thought about Zoey and how her life had spun completely out of her control. It might help her feel empowered if she won a game.

And it might be fun to team up against Johnny.

With a sneaky grin, she collected the badminton set and headed out of the shed to set it up. She rolled out the net and put the poles together, but every time she got one side to stand up in the grass, the other side fell over. She was about to give up when a shadow fell over her.

She looked up, and, *Holy mother of hotness.* The rock-star god himself was gazing down at her. From that angle, with the afternoon sun glowing around him, he looked larger than life, and the amusement in his eyes gave him an annoyingly sexy new look. "You *could* give me a hand."

"But this is so much fun." He chuckled. "What is all this?"

"Badminton. Zoey's been in her room since we got back, and you sounded like you were chewing someone out on the phone, so I figured we could use a little fun. Is everything okay?"

"Fine," he said curtly. "You don't strike me as a badminton girl."

"I'm *not*, but I'm hoping Zoey is. You saw her this morning. She was *laughing*. There's a happier girl in there somewhere, and I want to find her. Or at least make her realize that our time here doesn't have to suck."

His expression turned serious, and she wondered if she'd said the wrong thing.

He studied her for a long moment before speaking. "Why aren't you pissed at me for dragging you out here?"

"Because I'm going to design your wardrobe, and that's a huge boon for my label. Besides, someone has to make sure you're not a total ass to Zoey."

His jaw tightened. "I bet she appreciates that."

"It's nice that someone does." She pushed to her feet, tossing her hair over her shoulder. "Are you going to help me or what?"

He looked down at her high-heeled boots. "Have you ever played badminton?"

"No, but how hard can it be?"

His expression softened. "You might want to put on sneakers."

"I didn't bring sneakers. I was supposed to be in New York, remember?"

"You're going to break your ankle in those boots."

"I can run faster in high heels than most women can in sneakers." She handed him the pole. "Now please make yourself useful and help me set this up."

He looked around. "Where are the stakes?"

"Stakes?"

"Yeah. The stakes to hold the poles in place. Didn't you read the directions?"

Oops. "I'm not exactly a *directions* girl."

"This ought to be fun. Let's go find those stakes, winger."

He headed for the shed, and she hurried to catch up. "Winger?"

"Yeah. You're winging it, aren't you?"

"Shut up. Not everything needs directions."

He gave her another amused glance.

"Whatever."

"Careful. You're picking up the vocabulary of a fourteen-year-old."

She rolled her eyes.

"Eye rolls, *whatevers*," he said teasingly. "It's a wonder how you get along in the adult world."

She shoved him playfully as they came to the shed, and their gazes collided with the heat of a Southern summer, obliterating the playfulness.

His eyes narrowed. "What was that for?"

"I was shutting you up."

He stepped forward, closing the gap between them, his dark eyes holding her captive. He was so big and broad and stood so close, her breasts brushed against his body. Her nipples pebbled with the contact, but it was the hunger in his gaze as it dropped to her mouth that made it hard to breathe.

"The next time you want to shut me up," he said low and seductively, "try using your *mouth*."

The wickedness in his voice stole the air from her lungs. She could do little more than stare as he stepped aside and went into the shed, leaving her mouth dry and her body hot.

She was still standing there when he came out with his hands full and a hammer hanging from his belt loop. "You going to stand there all day, winger, or help me set this up?"

His cockiness snapped her back to the moment.

He flashed an arrogant grin. "Let's go. I'll show you how it's done."

Damn it. How could one man be so infuriating and such a turn-on?

The bastard set up the net without reading the instructions, and ten minutes later Johnny went upstairs to get Zoey. Jillian stood at the bottom of the stairs, listening as he tried to coax her out of the bedroom with promises of fun. She had to give it to him, he sounded sincere about wanting to spend time with her, and he was incredibly patient. She couldn't hear Zoey's responses, but after his third attempt, she went upstairs to help.

He splayed his hands, looking defeated.

"I've got this," she said quietly, then louder, "Zoey, open this door and get your butt outside. *Now.*"

"*What are you doing?*" Johnny whispered harshly.

The door opened, and Zoey glowered at them, but she stalked out of her room and headed downstairs.

Jillian grinned at Johnny. "You're welcome."

JILLIAN RAN TOWARD the birdie and swung her racket, making another exasperated sound. The birdie sailed over the net.

"Nice hit, winger," Johnny said as he swatted the birdie back.

"Stop calling me that!" Jillian ran behind Zoey to hit the birdie and missed it. "Damn it!"

"Language," Johnny teased.

"I'll give you *language*," she panted out, laughing.

They'd been playing for what felt like hours but in reality was probably less than an hour, and Zoey had yet to move a muscle. She stood with the racket hanging limply at her side, kicking at the grass or staring absently in the opposite direction. Meanwhile, Johnny hadn't even broken a sweat, and Jillian was winded and sporting a bead of sweat on her upper lip from running all over trying to hit the damn birdie. It was not her finest moment.

Why was she doing this, again? *I must be a glutton for punishment.* But she wasn't giving up. One way or another, she was determined to get Zoey to crack a smile. She held out the birdie to her. "Want to serve?"

"No, thanks."

"Come on, Zoey. You might actually have fun if you play."

"I doubt it."

Time to pull out the big guns. Jillian lowered her voice. "We *could* beat him, you know."

She shrugged.

"Isn't there any part of you that wants to show him what you're made of?"

"I don't care what he thinks of me."

Sadness slid through Jillian. "You don't mean that. He's trying so hard to make this easier for you, and I know nothing will make it *easy*, but at least he cares enough to try."

Zoey lowered her eyes.

"He's not the jerk I thought he was," Jillian coaxed. "If you give him a chance, you might see that for yourself."

"If I play, will you stop bothering me?" Zoey asked bluntly.

That stung, and the fact that it did surprised Jillian. She wasn't thin-skinned, and it wasn't like she didn't show her own attitude from time to time. But if that one comment stung her, how many times had Zoey stung Johnny? "*Sure*, but do me a favor and watch your tone, because I'm trying hard, too."

A flicker of regret passed over Zoey's face, but she didn't say a word. She just took the birdie and hit it over the opposite end of the net from where Johnny stood.

Nicely done.

Johnny ran to the other side, swatting it over Jillian's head. She ran to get it, but Zoey batted it first, sending it sailing high over the net. Johnny hit it back *hard*, and Zoey jumped up, spiking it back to him. Johnny dove and missed, muttering under his breath.

"Yes!" Jillian cheered. She tried to high-five Zoey, but Zoey just stood there expressionless.

"Nice shot, sunshine," Johnny said.

Zoey's lips twitched like her face wanted to smile, but her brain wouldn't allow it.

Johnny hit the birdie, and Jillian ran, swatting it high but short. Zoey got to it just before it hit the grass, sending it over to Johnny. He hit it hard, and Jillian sprinted toward it, catching her foot in a divot in the grass. She shrieked as she fell to the ground.

"You okay?" Johnny called out.

"*Yes*. I just tripped." She tried to get up, wincing at a sharp pain in her ankle.

"Don't move." Johnny jogged over to her.

"Guess the game's over." Zoey dropped her racket and headed for the cottage.

"*No.* I'm *fine*. I can still play," Jillian called after her, trying to get up again and cringing in pain.

"Let her go," Johnny said. "She did good. She hung out with us longer than I thought she would, and *you* are anything *but* fine." He scooped her into his arms and pushed to his feet.

"*Johnny*," she shouted in surprise. "I can walk."

"Not until we check out that ankle."

"Don't be silly. I'm fine." She tried to wriggle out of his arms.

"Would you hold still?" He held her tighter, carrying her toward the cottage. "You're like a little angry bird."

"Did you just call me a video game?" she asked with a laugh, putting her arms around his neck.

"Yeah, I guess I did." He waggled his brows. "Want to get played?"

She started to laugh, but when she turned her face, his dark eyes found hers, smothering that humor in heat, making her acutely aware of the rest of him. She tried to ignore how incredible his muscles felt flexing against her and how rugged and potently male he smelled. Her mind tiptoed down a dark trail, wondering how good he would feel without so many clothes on. Would his chest hair tickle? How good would his scruff feel on her thighs?

He pulled open the door, jerking her from her thoughts. It had been way too long since she'd been with a man.

He carried her into the living room, and she heard Zoey's door close upstairs as he lowered her to the couch. His face was *right there*, his penetrating gaze making her nerves catch fire. He was close enough to kiss, and he wasn't moving away. He was gazing deeply into her eyes, pushing her hair out of her face with his fingertips, and tucking it behind her ear. Her pulse quickened.

"Are you okay?" he asked thoughtfully.

I'd be better if you kissed me. Where had this thoughtful person come from? He was so different from the arrogant rock star or the cocky kidder she was coming to know. She managed a nod, knowing she shouldn't be thinking about him that way, but what single female wouldn't? Not only was he gorgeous, but he'd just carried her inside like a white knight.

"A'right, let's get these boots off and take a look at your ankle."

Do we have to stop at the boots?

He eased off her boot, and she winced. "Too rough?"

"I like it rough" came out before she could stop it.

He laughed.

"*Ohmygod.* Forget I said that." Her cheeks burned. What was he doing to her? She wasn't a blusher.

"*Yeah*, there's not a chance in hell I'm going to forget that." He hiked a thumb over his shoulder as he rose to his feet. "I think I'd better go get you some ice."

"Yes. *Ice.* Lots of it, please." She flopped back on the couch and squeezed her eyes closed as he went into the kitchen. *I like it rough? What is wrong with me?* Her phone vibrated on the coffee table. She unhooked it from the charger and scanned the missed texts from her mother, Jax, Trixie, and her assistant, Liza.

Thank God. She could use a little girl talk. She quickly opened and read Trixie's message. *I'm sorry about Nick. I tried to get him not to bother Beau, but you know how he is. How are YOU?*

Jillian thumbed out, *Couldn't be better. I just twisted my ankle playing badminton, got carried inside by the hottest rock star around, and told him I like it rough.* She added a shocked emoji and a face palm emoji and sent it off. Trixie's response was immediate. Three laughing emojis, an eggplant, a peach, and *What's wrong with that? Rough is fun!* Another text popped up. *Wait. You're allergic to sports. Was it naked badminton? What about his daughter?*

Jillian typed, *I only played to try to get Zoey to have fun. Things are stressful between them. He's trying, but she's resisting. I hope they figure out how to communicate better than I can right now. He probably thinks I sleep around. What am I going to do?*

Trixie's response rolled in a second later. *HIM!*

Jillian thumbed out, *Maybe if circumstances were different, but he has a daughter and you know I'm not mommy material.*

Another text popped up. *Nick didn't do relationships, and look where we are now.* She added a diamond ring and a heart emoji. Jillian replied, *That is not in my future with Johnny Delicious.*

Her phone vibrated with Trixie's response. *My, my, how things change! Wasn't he Johnny Butthead just a few days ago?*

Jillian heard the freezer door close and typed, *I have to go. He's bringing me ice for my ankle.* She added a kissing emoji and sent it off. Her phone vibrated in her hand, and she quickly read Trixie's response. *Sweet and hot? Girl, you deserve a little fun. Go for it!*

"Everything okay?" Johnny asked, startling her.

She tucked her phone beneath her leg, knowing she probably looked guilty. "Yeah, just catching up with a friend."

His jaw tightened again. "I brought you a Diet Pepsi and some ibuprofen." He handed her a glass and the pills and set a bag of frozen peas on the coffee table.

She took the pills with a sip of soda. "Thanks." There was no hiding the surprise in her voice. This nurturing side had her even more curious about him. He'd been all over social media with gorgeous women on his arm for years after he was first discovered, but while he continued making headlines for his music, his personal life hadn't been splashed on gossip sites lately.

"I'm not a total jerk." He put a pillow on the coffee table and patted it. "Put your foot up." When she did, he gently placed the bag of frozen peas on it. "Okay?"

"Yeah, thank you. I just twisted it. It'll be fine."

"It's still good to ice it." He sat beside her and blew out a breath. "I'm sorry I got hurt and messed up your time with Zoey."

His brows slanted. "You've got to be kidding. If not for you, I wouldn't have any time with her. You're the one who got her out of the house to play. I have to admit, I was a little worried when you demanded she come out of her room. But it worked."

"It's called tough love," she said with a smile. "I understand why you're being careful with her, but sometimes teenagers need to be told what to do. Since I'm not her parent, I figured the worst that could happen was that she'd say no. I'm glad it worked."

"Me too. Thanks for making the effort. I appreciate it."

"It was fun. Was that story you told us about Aria true?"

"Yeah, unfortunately. She had a rough time of it as a kid. She still has social anxieties, but she's doing a lot better."

"That must be hard for her."

"It can be, but she's found ways to cope with it, and she has good friends who understand her limitations."

"That's good. Does she work?"

"Yeah. She's a tattooist and an incredible artist." He pushed up his sleeve, showing her the BAD INTENTIONS tattoo on his right forearm. "It's a good job for her. She can concentrate on her art without the pressure of talking with customers."

"I guess nobody wants to distract their tattooist," Jillian said. "It sounds like she's lucky you were there for her when she was younger."

"I'm still there for her and my other siblings, just as they are for me. I can't tell you how many times Aria has called and sounded a little off, or told me she needed me, and I flew out to see her for a few hours and make sure she was okay. I've done it while on tour a few times, and I was sure I'd be a zombie onstage the next day, but adrenaline is a lifesaver. But I'm the lucky one. My family is everything to me. They keep me grounded. Kane and my parents were my first real supporters, and Harlow and Aria were my first real fans. When they were little, they'd sing and cheer me on. I'm glad Aria still reaches out."

Jillian hadn't expected that, and it endeared him to her even more. "Then we have that in common. My family is everything to me, too."

He met her gaze, looking at her intently. "I assumed so, after the way you spoke about your brothers."

"Were the rest of you adopted, too?"

"No, just Harlow and Aria. My parents wanted a big family. It took them four years to have me after Kane, and they tried for another seven years before adopting Harlow. She was only a year old, and, *man*, I know I was young, but I remember when they brought her home like it was yesterday. Aria, too, when she joined our family four years later." He patted his chest over his heart. "I remember this pressure in my chest, and telling my father that I thought my heart had grown after he brought each of them home."

Lord help me. You just got even more attractive. "That's so sweet. What did he say?"

"He said I had a big heart, and that was just love showing itself, and I should get used to it because hearts were meant to love."

"He sounds like a good dad. This is none of my business, but do you feel any of that for Zoey?"

He was quiet for a moment before answering. "I feel so much toward her, I don't really know how to decipher it."

"Does that mean some of what you feel is negative?"

"Not toward her. She didn't choose her parents or ask to be here."

She could tell there was more to that and asked carefully, "Negative toward you?"

He was quiet again, making her even more curious. His phone rang, and he said, "Saved by the bell." He pulled it out, and his brows slanted at whoever's name he saw on the screen. He pushed to his feet and pointed to her ankle. "Keep icing."

Jillian wiggled her toes. "It doesn't hurt anymore."

"It's funny what a little ibuprofen and ice will do. Just ice it for a few more minutes before you go cruising around in your heels and aggravating it again."

"Yes, *Dad*."

He glowered at her.

"Might as well get used to it." She sank back against the cushions as he put the phone to his ear and walked out the front door.

She had a feeling there was a lot more *good* in Johnny Bad than she'd imagined.

Chapter Seven

JUST AFTER MIDNIGHT, Johnny lay on the bed staring at the ceiling, so damn frustrated he wished he could go for a run. Between Zoey's attitude, the sparks flying between him and Jillian, and overthinking his every step, he was going to lose his mind.

Jillian's ankle was feeling better by late afternoon, and she'd gone into town to pick up groceries before dinner. Johnny had given her a list of ingredients to buy so he could make his mother's macaroni and cheese topped with Tater tots, which had been one of his favorites as a kid. He'd thought Zoey would love it and had hoped it would help break the ice. But Zoey had just pushed it around on her plate and had barely eaten a thing. His and Jillian's attempts at conversation with her were met with silence or one-word responses. Jillian was doing everything she could to help them and had even gone so far as to offer to make Zoey something else for dinner. The feisty beauty didn't even know how to cook. It hadn't mattered anyway. Zoey had claimed she wasn't hungry and had disappeared into her room again. He felt bad for Jillian and for Zoey. He'd dragged Jillian into this, and he didn't like that Zoey was disregarding her efforts, but he couldn't fault Zoey for her feelings or her attitude.

He'd apologized to Jillian, but she seemed to take it in stride, and she'd spent the rest of dinner peppering him with questions about what he envisioned for his and his bandmates' tour wardrobes. How the hell was he supposed to go on tour with a kid in tow?

A kid who wouldn't even speak to him.

If he didn't turn his brain off, he was never going to get to sleep. He got up and paced, feeling like a caged lion. He'd tried to play his guitar after dinner just to get out of his own head, and he hadn't even been able to do that. Music had always been the one thing that had given him peace, but for the last few years, and especially since his mother's first bout with cancer, it just didn't hold the same magic.

Fucking magic.

He couldn't believe he'd told Jillian and Zoey the story about Aria and the magic water fairy. He hadn't thought about that time in years, and he wasn't even sure his family knew that story. But Jillian was going on about the magic of the inn, and for some reason, he'd wanted her to know that he believed in magic, too. How fucked up was that? But he'd noticed that while he'd told the story, he'd held Zoey's rapt attention, and he'd hoped that it might help break down her walls. But *that* would take more than a little magic.

Even so, he wasn't giving up.

He pulled on sweatpants, hoping some fresh air might clear his head, and headed out of his bedroom. He looked down the hall at Zoey's closed bedroom door, wishing he could make things better. He went downstairs, and—*Fucking hell.* Jillian was kneeling on the floor in front of the coffee table poring over sketches, wearing the same type of clingy tank top and sexy sleeping shorts she'd had on that morning, only this set was black. Music was playing low from her phone, and she was swinging her ass and wiggling her shoulders. He gritted his teeth. *Jesus.* She was every man's fantasy, and she was going to be the death of him.

He forced himself to look away and noticed about a dozen empty miniature Twix wrappers scattered around her on the floor, two soda cans lying on their sides, and a handful of crumpled papers. He took a step toward the door, and something crinkled beneath his foot. Jillian turned around with a Twix hanging out of her mouth. Her eyes trailed down his bare chest and abs and didn't stop there.

Are you fucking kidding me? What kind of torture is this? His dick twitched beneath the heat of her stare, and he cleared his throat loudly.

Her eyes flicked up to his, wide and doe-like. She blinked rapidly, as if she hadn't realized she'd been staring. "Oh, *hey*, hi," she rambled. "Can't sleep?"

"No. I guess you can't either?"

She shook her head. "I never sleep at night. That's when my muse speaks the loudest."

"Weird. Me too."

"Something we have in common." She pushed to her feet, her nipples straining against her top. She looked like sweet innocence and sinful temptation all wrapped up in one irresistibly sexy package.

He bit out a curse. "Is that the only kind of sleepwear you brought?"

"Yes. In several colors. It's one of my designs. Why?" She looked down at herself.

"There's not much to it. You might want to put on sweats."

She rolled her eyes. "I'm fine, thanks."

"Yes, you *are*," he said under his breath.

"What was that?" She looked up as she bit off a piece of her candy bar.

"Nothing. Are you going to share that, or what?"

She shoved the remaining piece of chocolate into her mouth, grinning around a cheekful of it.

You little vixen. "That was cruel." *And too damn cute.* "I can't believe you've been hoarding chocolate."

"I'm not." She swallowed the candy. "I found Char's secret stash."

He nodded at her sketches. "What're you working on?"

"I had some ideas for your tour wardrobe, but before I show you, I've been thinking about Zoey." She took his hand, leading him to the couch, and sat facing him, tucking her feet onto the cushion beside her like they were old friends. Her hair spilled over her breasts, and her eyes danced with excitement, a far cry from the fire-breathing dragon who had stormed into his penthouse or the lustful woman who had just eye-fucked him. "This afternoon, when you were telling us about Aria, Zoey *initiated* conversation. She was asking questions, which means you were getting through to her, and I remembered how much it meant to me when I was younger and my dad would take me out, just the two of us. He always knew when something was bothering me, and he'd talk *around* the subject, you know? Not too direct, and eventually his point would hit home, and I'd feel better. I know you can't take Zoey anywhere right now, but she might be more receptive to talking outside, where she doesn't feel trapped. You could go on a walk around the property or ask her to help you with a project? That's another thing my dad used to do."

"A project?"

"Yeah. He'd ask me to help him paint the shed, wash his car, or gather wood for the firepit. I wasn't a big help, but it got me out of the house and talking."

Who was this woman, and how did he get lucky enough to have her walk into his life at just the right time? "Those are good ideas. I've been trying to figure out how to get through to her, too. I've been walking on eggshells, afraid I might say or do the wrong thing. I know what it feels like to be with people but still feel alone."

"What do you mean?"

"Take touring, for example. You're on this high, and you're surrounded by people who think you're wonderful and will do anything for you. But at the end of the night, they love your music and who they *think* you are. But they don't know you. Zoey has us, and I know I'd do anything for her, and I think you've shown that you're willing to try to help, but we're still strangers to her. The difference is, after a concert, those people leave, and they move on to whatever is next on their entertainment list. But I'm not going anywhere, and whether I'm ready or not, I'm her father, and I need to learn how to act like it so she knows she can count on me, even if she hates me at first, and that means not walking on eggshells."

Her expression turned serious. "That's sad that you feel that way when you're on tour, but I get it. I think that's one reason I stayed in my small hometown around my family instead of moving to one of the fashion hubs, like New York or LA. Because after the hoopla is over, we're more than what we do, and family and the people we grew up with know that."

"You're lucky to have realized that from the start. That explains why you're so grounded."

She smiled. "I guess so. I think you're right about not walking on eggshells, but you should still be careful of her feelings, and for what it's worth, I don't think Zoey hates you. I think she's just hurting. She lost the one person she always felt safe around, and her mother might not have been around much, but now she's truly abandoned her. For all Zoey knows, you'll leave, too."

"I'd never turn my back on her. I'm all she's got, and she's my daughter. My blood. I'm her safe harbor now, whether or not I'm ready. I know I said some shitty things yesterday morning. I was frustrated and scared, but I'm going to find a way to fix it and make that up to her."

"I'm sure you will. Just remember, teenagers usually go one of three ways. Angel, avoidance, or attack. I doubt you're in danger of Zoey playing angel and pretending she's a perfect teenager to get what she wants, and she's obviously mastered avoidance. Which makes me think attack might be next on her list."

"She can't scare me away by getting angry, if that's what you mean, because I know whatever she dishes out can't be half as bad as what she's holding in."

Jillian tilted her head, smiling sweetly. "You're a much smarter guy than I gave you credit for."

"I'm not sure that's a compliment, but I also don't know how smart I am. I trusted the wrong person, and he screwed me over in more ways than just the lost time with Zoey. I mean, that's the biggest way, of course, but from what Kane's found out, Dick wasn't only embezzling; he was also burning bridges I had no idea were burned. He was out there jerking people around and using me as an excuse. Apparently they all think *I'm* an ass to work with."

"Uh, *yeah*. I had heard that long before your tour came up. I can't imagine the impact that alone has had on your business. I'd imagine you've paid premium prices for things along the way just because of that. Are you pressing charges?"

"Absolutely. Kane's taking care of that, but digging out from under Dick Waller's mess will be a nightmare." Thinking of Zoey, he glanced at the stairs and said, "Some things might never fully recover."

She put her hand on his. "Or maybe they'll be better than they would have been if you'd tried to build your career and be a father at the same time. You can't look back at the things you couldn't control and know how they would have turned out. It sounds like her mother is a real manipulator. From the little that I've heard about her, maybe Dick's misguided intervention stopped her from taking you for an even bigger ride. You never know what people are capable of."

"How could it have been any worse than what's already happened?"

"She could've convinced you to marry her when she was pregnant and stuck around for a few years, and then you could've lost half of everything you own, and who knows what else."

"Shit." He pushed a hand through his hair. "I didn't think of that. But she didn't want Zoey. She wanted money without the burden of raising a kid."

"It looks that way, but who knows? It still could've gone any number of ways. At least now you have Zoey, and ready or not, I think that's called a silver lining."

"You sound like my parents. They find silver linings in every situation. I just wish I hadn't been taken for a fool by Dick."

"You can't go backward, so why even stress over it? We've all trusted the wrong person at times. I know it's not the same thing as what you're going through, but I dated a guy when I was in fashion school, and he stole my designs right before a huge presentation."

"What did you do?"

"There wasn't much I could do. It was my word against his, and I'd spent my entire life manifesting this path for myself. I wasn't about to screw that up, so I let it go and designed something better. When we did our presentations, I pointed out all the flaws in his. I got an A and he got a B, and there *might* have been some soda thrown in his face along the way."

"Soda throwing? *You?*" he said with feigned disbelief. "The woman who practically accused me of being a pedophile?"

She wrinkled her nose. "Sorry."

"It's okay. You probably could have gotten that guy kicked out for what he'd done."

"Maybe, but that would have taken a lot of my focus away from my goals, and I figured a guy like that wouldn't last long anyway. It just pushed me harder to be a better designer, and he dropped out later that year. People can't hide their true colors forever, and as far as Dick goes, at least he followed your demands in one way."

"What way is that?"

"He hired *me*. He told me how much you wanted to work with me."

"He *what?*" *Could this get any worse?*

"Uh-oh. I guess I wasn't supposed to know that? Sorry, but I'm glad I did. It meant the world to me that you had noticed my work, and it weighed heavily into my decision to accept the contracts."

Fucking Dick. He debated going along with Dick's lies, but he couldn't lie to Jillian. Not after all she was doing to help them. And, more importantly, he couldn't lie to someone he liked, and he enjoyed spending time with her and talking with her. Besides being beautiful, she was funny and insightful, and she treated him like a regular guy. She spoke her mind, and even if it was irritating sometimes, it was a refreshing change from the women he usually met. Most of whom tried to seduce him every chance they got. Aside from designing his wardrobe, Jillian acted like she couldn't care less that he was a rock star, and he hadn't realized how much he'd missed that. She deserved the truth, even if it hurt to hear it.

"Jillian, I'm sorry, but I don't know what you're talking about. I had no idea what designer he hired. That's not a decision I was involved in."

"*Oh.*" Disappointment stole the light in her eyes, and he wished he could take it back. She squared her shoulders, the disappointment morphing into resilience. "Of course you didn't make that decision. You had more important things to tend to than worrying about what you'd wear when millions of people saw you onstage." There was an edge to her voice. "You've got things under control here. I think I'll head back to Maryland in the morning." She stood and began collecting her sketches.

Panic flared in his chest. He couldn't let her go. He didn't *want* her to leave, and it wasn't just because of Zoey. He grabbed her hand. "Jillian, wait." He pulled her back down to the couch. "I'm sorry. I didn't want to lie to you. I can't help that I had nothing to do with the decision, and I don't know when my tour will happen, but I'm glad you're designing the wardrobe. Please stay."

"You're just afraid to be alone with Zoey. You'll be *fine.*" She pulled her hand free and went back to gathering her things.

"*No*, it's not just that."

She gave him a deadpan stare, which was just as cutting as her words. "Well, it's not because of my designs. You probably don't even know what my work looks like, and I honestly don't know what I'm doing here after you canceled twice for personal reasons. Whatever *that* means. I can't believe I put off the launch of a new fashion line for an entire *year* just to work with you. That's the *last* time I let my ego get the best of me."

"I had good reasons to cancel," he said tightly.

"Apparently not good enough to share with the people who set aside other work to make *you* look good onstage. I guess that's the rock-star mentality, isn't it? Nobody matters but the king himself. Well, guess what? My time is *just* as important as yours." Her emotions bled through with a vengeance, and she clutched her papers, heading for the stairs.

Fuck. He had no choice but to tell her the truth or let her walk away. He pushed to his feet, steeling himself against the ache in his chest, making it harder to let the secret he'd kept to protect his family come out. "I canceled because my mother had cancer."

JILLIAN STILLED, HER hurt feelings obliterated by the pain in Johnny's voice.

"Nobody knows," he said gruffly. "We've managed to keep it under wraps, and I'd like it to remain that way."

She turned, the sadness welling inside her mirrored in his eyes. "I'd never say a word. Is she okay?"

"She's okay for now, or getting there. She's had it twice, and she's still going through treatments."

"Oh, Johnny. I'm so sorry." She set the designs on the coffee table and went to him. "Are you okay? I'd be a mess if that happened to my mom."

"I guess that's another thing we have in common." They sat back down, and he leaned his elbows on his knees as he'd done on the plane, wringing his hands. "To say I've been a mess is putting it mildly."

"That's understandable. You said she's okay for now? What does that mean?"

He sighed heavily. "It means exactly what I said. *For now.* She had neuroendocrine cancer the first time, which is rare and can go completely undetected until it's too late. It can occur anywhere in the body, and they usually find it incidentally. That's what happened with my mother. She had stomach issues and was losing weight but hadn't thought too much about it until she passed out in the kitchen. They did a battery of tests and found a mass in her lower intestines."

Jillian's throat thickened with emotion. "You must've been terrified."

"I've never been so scared in my life." He paused, jaw tight. "You hear about people getting cancer all the time, but when it happens to someone you love, it hits different. We'd been through it before. We lost our cousin Lorelei to leukemia when she was only eight, and that devastation came rushing back with my mom's diagnosis. Suddenly it was like, Mom could *die*." His voice was strangled.

She put her hand on his, her chest aching for him. "I can't imagine how that feels, but I heard about Lorelei. I know your cousin Brett. His wife, Sophie, grew up in Oak Falls with Graham's wife, Morgyn, and her sisters. I've met them a few times, and Sophie told me what Brett had gone through with his sister. It's awful. She was just a little girl."

He cleared his throat, nodding. "Your whole perspective on life and what's important changes when you lose someone, and when someone you love is diagnosed with what could be a terminal disease, it hits all over again. We've gotten lucky with my mother so far. They did surgery for the first cancer and were able to get all the cancer and clean margins. Everything looked good. She went through chemo, which was rough. She lost her hair and didn't feel great, but she kept her spirits up, at least in front of us. Her first PET scan was clean, and she was doing well. She encouraged me to reschedule the tour, and Dick was up my ass to give back to my fans, so we picked another date. But a few months later they found another mass, and I canceled the tour a second time. The second mass was in her colon. They biopsied it, and there was no sign of the neuro cancer, which is good, but she had colon cancer."

"*Oh my gosh*," she said softly. "That's awful."

"Yeah, it sucks," he said gruffly. "But they caught it early, and colon cancer is curable. She's been going through chemo again, and it's shrinking the tumor. If things continue to go well, she's scheduled to have surgery in January, and her doctors are hopeful that she'll be cancer free again. That's why she pushed me to stop putting the tour on hold. I didn't want to do it, but I could see how much stress knowing I'd put it off to be with her was putting her under. That's why we moved forward with another tour date for next summer, after her surgery."

"If the doctors are hopeful and she was pushing you to get back to your career, those are good signs, right?"

"Yes. But the neuro cancer can come back anywhere, at any time, without any signs, like I said, so assuming the surgery goes well, she'll continue going in for tests every so often and holding her breath until the results come in each time. We all will."

His pain was so visceral, Jillian squeezed his hand, feeling like she was finally meeting the *real* Johnny Bad. The one who began as a kind-hearted boy who went to great lengths for his sister, grew into a music icon, had nearly lost his mother twice, and was in the throes of not knowing if she'd be okay when Zoey showed up on his doorstep.

And I blew into your life in full-on bitch mode.

"I'm sorry about your mom and for what I said about your rock-star mentality. With all you're doing for Zoey, I knew it wasn't fair to say it even before you told me about your mom, but my feelings were hurt, and I acted like a jerk. You didn't deserve that. I'm sorry."

"Jillian, you shouldn't apologize to me. You're here because I forced your hand. You have every right to be mad, and you were kind of right about my rock-star mentality. There are different types of fame. Being in the spotlight changes everything, and I became famous when I was just a year older than Zoey." He exhaled loudly. "That seems like a lifetime ago. I felt like I was all grown up and knew more than anyone else, when I was just a stupid kid with good genetics and some talent. I had no idea how to manage any of it. Even as a teenager, I could snap my fingers and be anywhere in the world with people catering to my every whim and beautiful girls throwing themselves at me. I was an entitled asshole for a long time, putting myself and my career ahead of everyone else."

His emotions were so raw and honest, she wished she could go back in time and warn him of the things to come. "Including your family?"

Regret washed over his face, but he didn't look away. "I can't believe I'm telling you this, but yes. *Sometimes.* That said, being the main attraction gets old, and right before my thirtieth birthday, I was so tired of clubs and paparazzi and living up to everyone else's expectation of who I should be, I said *fuck it* and stopped living such a public life. Four and a half years later, I'm glad I did. I can't imagine going through everything my family is going through with my mom if it had been splashed all over the internet. We got lucky, and my breakup helped."

"Your breakup with Ramona Sisco, the model? Didn't you go out with her for like a year?"

"Something like that, but with our schedules, most of it was long distance. I don't even feel like I knew her all that well."

"Is that why you broke up?"

"No. As ironic as it is, she wanted to settle down and have a family, and I didn't."

She almost held her tongue, but she was so drawn to him, she wanted to know where he stood with Ramona. "Maybe once you get things under control with Zoey, you can revisit that relationship."

"No thanks. She was great but not the person I want to wake up next to for the rest of my life."

She probably shouldn't be happy about that, but she was. "You said your breakup helped. How?"

"We ended things a few weeks before I canceled the tour the first time, and that made it easier for the media to buy that I had personal issues. They assumed I was heartbroken and didn't go searching for some other reason, when in reality, I just wanted to be with my mother. I didn't know how much time I had left with her, and she was facing the worst battle of her life."

"But you're still dealing with her illness, and it doesn't sound like you've had time to breathe. Why did you agree to reschedule the tour instead of taking more time off? Was it just because your mom wanted you to?"

"Do you have x-ray vision or something? Most people would take my excuse at face value."

"Sorry. I probably should've been a detective, because that's how my brain works."

He laughed softly. "I'm glad you're not a detective, because I never would have met you."

He held her gaze, and she swore she felt threads of his confession winding around them, binding them together.

"The truth is, I felt guilty for letting down my bandmates, but that was nothing compared to the pressure I was getting from Dick. He was up my ass twenty-four-seven to do the tour. I know that was because he'd made promises he couldn't keep, and he wanted to skim more money off the top." His expression softened. "I'm really sorry for screwing with your schedule, Jillian. I'm kind of an asshole, but I'd like to think I'm not that *big* of one."

"It's okay. You've been through so much. I feel bad for calling you Johnny Butthead for the last year."

He laughed softly. "Seriously?"

"Maybe." She reached for the last Twix bar. She opened it and took a bite, processing all he'd confessed. "I'm really glad you trusted me enough to tell me the truth. It explains a lot, and I appreciate your honesty."

"I don't know what it is about you." He brushed his index finger back and forth over her hand, the intimate touch causing goose bumps. "I usually don't care what people think of me, but there's something different about you. I don't want you to think I'm an ass."

The way he was looking at her, like there was a deeper meaning behind his words, and the slow strokes of his finger, made her feel tingly in all her loneliest places. Just like when he'd first come downstairs and had caught her off guard. Seeing him shirtless, in low-riding sweatpants that showed off those enticing muscles that disappeared beneath his waistband, pointing like a slide to his...*Ohmygod. What is wrong with me?* He'd just confided his deepest secrets, and here she was, misreading his actions and thinking about doing dirty things with him instead of comforting him.

He was looking at her like he was waiting for a response, and now she was frazzled. "I don't think you're an ass, and I'm not great at the whole comforting thing, but after everything you've said, I feel like I should hug you or something."

"You're too cute for your own good." He spread his arms. "Don't let me hold you back."

She hugged him, breathing him in, wanting more of the man who had just bared his soul, and, for the first time ever, wishing she was better at the warm, fuzzy side of relationships.

He held her tighter. "Don't underestimate yourself. You're exactly what I need. You listen and offer suggestions, and you don't blow smoke up my ass."

"I have a knack for being brutally honest." She drew back and shoved the rest of the candy in her mouth before *And right now I really want you to kiss me* came out.

"How about sharing some of that chocolate? I could use a little something *sweet*."

Sweet rolled off his tongue as low and seductive as an invitation. He reached over and cupped her cheek, brushing his thumb over the corner of her mouth. His hand was hot, his eyes smoldering. Her nerves caught fire. Was she imagining this, or had she not misread him after all? She readied for a kiss, but as she started to close her eyes, he held up his thumb, showing her the chocolate he'd wiped off. Embarrassment swallowed her as he licked the chocolate from his thumb. Her breath rushed from her lungs. She'd never felt so foolish.

She got up to avoid looking at him, rambling nervously. "I'll get you a Twix. Although something tells me you have no trouble satisfying your *sweet tooth*." She stepped onto the hearth, and as she reached into the jar on the mantel, she sensed him behind her, felt his body heat seconds before his arms circled her waist and his scruff brushed her cheek, sending scintillating sensations racing through her.

"With a smart mouth like that," he said huskily into her ear, "and a body made for pleasure..." One hot hand slithered up her stomach, stopping just beneath her breasts, and the other spread over her lower belly. "I can't imagine you have trouble satisfying yours."

She closed her eyes, her body begging for more, her mind barely functioning. "How do you know what my body is made for?" came out breathily.

"A woman confident enough to walk around in a slinky outfit like this has no insecurities about the things she's capable of." His fingertips brushed the underside of her breasts, and she inhaled sharply. He kissed her neck. His lips were soft and tantalizingly warm, drawing a moan from her lungs. He continued to kiss her, his tongue gliding along her skin, alighting a throbbing ache between her legs. "Tell me I misread you, Jilly, and I'll stop."

His scruff abraded her cheek as his hands spread possessively over her lower belly, holding her tight against his hard body. She felt every blessed inch of him. The beat of his heart against her back and his hot breath coasting over her neck lulled her deeper into him. This was crazy. She'd never gotten this turned on by words and kisses. She'd been with enough guys to know they never lived up to what she wanted in the bedroom. She wanted white-hot passion, a little roughness, a little laughter, and a lot of dirty talk. As much as she hoped he wouldn't let her down, she knew he probably would. But she was so drawn to him, she didn't want to stop, and when those warm, perfect lips caressed her neck again, his hands an inch above her neediest parts, she felt herself go damp and couldn't hold back. "Just *touch* me already."

It was as much a plea as a demand, and he didn't waste any time. His teeth sank into her neck as one hand pushed under her top, the other into her shorts and beneath her thong, teasing her nipple and clit so mind-numbingly perfectly, she could do little more than hold on to him to remain standing as bursts of pleasure consumed her.

"*Oh God,*" she panted out. "Don't stop."

"We're just getting started." He growled against her neck, and his hand pushed lower, his fingers pressing into her slickness. "*Fuuck.* So wet for me. Give me your sexy mouth."

She turned her face, and he crushed his mouth to hers, kissing her rough and greedy as he squeezed her nipple and fucked her with his fingers. His mouth was unrelenting, his touch masterful. Overwhelming sensations burned in her core, spreading like wildfire up her chest and down her limbs, hot, sharp, and penetrating. She could barely breathe for the pressure mounting inside her. She went up on her toes, reaching behind her, grasping at his shoulders, trying to gain purchase, finally fisting her hands in his hair, earning the sexiest groan she'd ever heard.

"I can't wait to fuck you," he growled against her mouth.

His thumb massaged her most sensitive nerves in mesmerizing circles, his long fingers stroking over the hidden spot inside her that had her gasping sharp, fast inhalations.

"That's it, baby. Let's make you come." He sealed his teeth over her neck, sucking so hard, the edges of her vision went black and a surge of pleasure barreled into her. The world spun away, and there was no stopping her cries. He reclaimed her mouth, working his magic so exquisitely, she was lost in the titillating sensations ravaging her, soaring on a bolt of ecstasy that culminated in a crescendo of fiery explosions.

Her body clenched and rocked, and he swallowed her greedy sounds. As the world started coming back into focus, he withdrew his fingers, turning her in his arms, her body shuddering with lingering ripples of pleasure.

"That was…" She tried to catch her breath, searching her lust-addled brain for the right words.

"Incredible. *You* are fucking incredible."

He kissed her again, painfully slowly and impossibly deeply, and her already-weak knees gave out. He smiled against her lips, lifting her into his arms and guiding her legs around his waist. He pushed his fingers beneath her shorts, holding her bare ass, and groaned low in his throat. The sound, the heat of his hands, the way his fingertips grazed her wetness had her desperate for more. She didn't care that this was crazy or that they barely knew each other. She'd never been so full of desire and was sure it oozed from her pores.

He drew back, his eyes dark as night. "I need my mouth on you."

"Oh God, *yes*. But not down here."

"One step ahead of you, baby," he said as he carried her upstairs, stopping every couple of steps to take her in demandingly delicious kisses. "You're dangerously addicting."

His words burned through her. By the time they reached the landing, their kisses were messy and urgent. "My room; it's farther from Zoey's," she said, and they both looked down the hall toward Zoey's bedroom. Her door was open, and they both froze. His brows slanted, and he lowered Jillian to her feet, taking her hand, which was starting to feel like their thing, as he went to check on Zoey.

Zoey's bedroom was empty. "She's probably in the bathroom," Jillian said, and they headed down the hall toward the closed bathroom door.

"Zoey?" Johnny said. Answered with silence, he knocked. "Zoey? You okay?" He looked anxiously at Jillian.

"Zoey? Are you okay, honey?" When she didn't answer, Jillian's heart lurched. She tried the doorknob. "It's locked."

"Stand back." Johnny turned to use his shoulder.

"No, wait! Beau keeps keys on the doorframes."

He found the key above the door and opened it. The bathroom was empty, and the window was open. "Fuck."

They went to the window and saw a trellis beneath it. Jillian's stomach pitched.

"Damn it." Worry outweighed the anger in his voice. "I've got to find her."

"I'll get dressed and call Beau. He'll help us look."

Chapter Eight

"ZOEY!" JOHNNY HOLLERED, shining the flashlight from side to side, searching the woods with his heart in his throat and horrible thoughts going through his head. If anything happened to her, he would never forgive himself.

He heard Jillian and Charlotte calling Zoey's name in the distance. Beau took the truck out to search for her on the main road. There were miles of woods and pastures, and she could have gone any number of ways. Johnny had tried calling and texting Zoey's phone and had gotten a recording that the number was out of service. Her fucking asshole of a mother must have turned it off. He wondered when she'd done it and didn't remember seeing Zoey on her phone earlier in the afternoon.

Was that why she ran away? Her whole damn life had been stolen from her. She didn't need *another* reason. For all he knew, she could have arranged for someone to pick her up before the phone was turned off. That was farfetched, considering she didn't have a credit card to hire a ride, and she didn't know a soul in Colorado. But what did he *really* know about her besides what he'd been told by Dick and had learned over the last forty-eight hours from Kane? Kane had talked to her teachers and neighbors, and it sounded like Zoey was a tough but good-natured girl who was dearly loved by her grandmother, but she was a bit of a loner, with only a couple of friends she'd spent any time with, which made her even more at risk of doing something stupid.

Like getting into a car with a stranger.

Shit. His gut fisted. They'd been searching for forty-five minutes, and he headed back to the cottage to touch base with the others as they'd agreed to do in an hour.

As he came out of the woods, he saw Beau climb out of his truck and pull Charlotte into his arms. Jillian ran to Johnny, bringing an onslaught of guilt—Had Zoey seen them making out? Was that why she'd taken off?—and just as much gratitude that Jillian was there with him.

"We didn't find any signs of her," she said anxiously. "Bandit ran off and we thought maybe he'd seen her, but he was too fast and we lost him. Char thinks he was chasing a fox or something. Did you see any signs of Zoey?"

"No."

"Should we call the police?" Her eyes teared up. "I know that'll blow your cover, but it's *Zoey.*"

"I don't give a shit about myself," he snapped, and immediately regretted it. "I'm sorry. I just…She's *fourteen*, and she's out there all alone. I'll call out the fucking National Guard to find her if we have to, but let's see what Beau says." He looked up at her brother, heading their way. "Anything?"

"No, and we're so far out, the roads aren't heavily traveled. If she was out there, I'd have found her," Beau said.

"Unless someone else found her first," Johnny bit out, sickened by the thought. His hands curled into fists. "If someone took her, I'll fucking murder them."

"Hopefully that's not the case," Beau said sternly. "There's a lot of ground to cover here before we jump to any conclusions, but we have some trusted friends at Redemption Ranch, and they have eyes in all the seediest operations around here. We can get them to look for her, too. If someone did grab her, they'll find her."

"That's a great idea. Just in case," Jillian said.

"What's Redemption Ranch?" Johnny asked.

"That's where Jordan's sister, Sully, has been staying," Jillian said.

"It's not far from here. They rescue horses, giving them, and people, a second chance," Charlotte explained. "They hire ex-cons and recovering addicts and have a host of therapists on staff to help them find their way to a better life."

"More importantly," Beau said, "it's run by a Dark Knights motorcycle club family. The club has chapters all over the country, and the Hope Valley chapter has been keeping local communities safe for decades. They're effective and discreet."

"They found Sully because of the Dark Knights network," Jillian explained.

She'd been missing for twenty years. Johnny couldn't imagine Zoey going missing like that. Worry gripped him, and he grabbed the sides of his head. "How can this be happening?" He dropped his hands, pacing. "I had one job. To keep her *safe*. And I blew it. I should've brought bodyguards. I should've been with her every second, no matter how much she hated it."

Jillian took his hand. "Johnny, this isn't your fault. You can't be with her when she's supposed to be sleeping. We're going to find her."

"I don't think she would have left the property," Charlotte said. "It's scary for a young girl. When I was her age, I'd hide in the barn or an outbuilding before I'd try to get out to the main road. It's a *really* long, dark walk. Did you check near the chicken coop and the other outbuildings?"

"Yeah." Johnny paced. "They were the first places I looked."

"I wish we knew her better so we could figure out how she thinks," Jillian said.

"Me too." As Johnny said it, he remembered what Jillian had said about him finally getting through to Zoey down by the creek. "Wait a minute. The *creek*. Maybe she went there to make a wish. It's a stretch, and I don't even know if she could find it in the dark, but it's worth a shot." He looked at Jillian. "Do you think you can take me there?"

"Yes. It's not that hard if you know where you're going," Jillian said.

"Beau, can you and Char stay here in case Zoey comes back?"

"Absolutely," he said.

"Thanks. If we don't find her, then I think we should call your friends." Johnny squeezed Jillian's hand. "Let's go."

Their flashlight beams illuminated the forest as Jillian raced through the woods, saying things like, "Fat tree. Big bush. Boulder…" Johnny remembered her saying the same things as they'd made their way back to the cottage earlier in the day and realized she was spouting off landmarks on the path. Hope rose inside him that maybe Zoey had known that and paid attention, but on its heels was the dread of not finding her.

When they were deep in the woods, Jillian slowed, aiming her flashlight at the ground. She put her hand on Johnny's flashlight, pushing it down, too.

"What's wrong?" he looked around, his senses on high alert.

"We're almost at the creek," she whispered. "If she's there, we don't want to scare her or give her a reason to run."

"Good thinking." He turned off his flashlight and took her hand. He had so many things he wanted to say about what had happened between them, but it would have to wait. "You lead."

She held tightly to his hand, and with her flashlight pointed at the ground, they made their way toward the creek. *Please be there. Please fucking be there.* When the creek came into view, he scanned the water's edge, clinging to the hope of finding her. His heart thundered as he squinted into the moonlit darkness, scanning the rocky ground and peering between trees and bushes, but the longer he looked, the deeper the dread burrowed.

Steeling himself against the emotions clawing up his throat, he said, "She's not here. Where the hell is she?"

"Let's keep going." Jillian squeezed his hand, walking deeper into the forest, parallel to the creek. They walked for a long time, and suddenly she stopped and spun around, eyes glittering with tears as she pointed up ahead and to the right.

Two figures came into focus in the distance. A dog and a girl sitting on a boulder. Her knees were pulled up to her chest, arms wrapped around them, her face buried in the space between. Moonlight spilled over the hood of her sweatshirt, which was pulled over her hair, but Johnny didn't need to see beneath it to know it was Zoey. He felt it deep in his heart, and relief swamped him. He looked up at the sky, tears stinging as he pulled Jillian into his arms, holding her tight, relief coiling around them.

He looked down at her, whispering, "Do you mind if I do this part alone?"

"Of course not. Do you know how to get back?"

"I think so. I'll text if we get lost." He didn't think about what he was doing as he pressed his lips to hers in a kiss full of relief, gratitude, and other emotions he didn't have the bandwidth to decipher. "Thank you."

With a deep inhalation, he headed for Zoey as carefully as he could, twigs and leaves crackling under his feet. Bandit's ears perked up, and Zoey lifted her head, wide eyes scanning the forest.

"It's Johnny," he called out. "*Please* don't run. I just want to talk."

Bandit barked, standing guard at the edge of the boulder, but Zoey didn't move. Even though every ounce of him wanted to run to her, to haul her into his arms and hold her until she felt safe enough to never want to run again, he moved slowly, so as not to frighten her. As he approached the boulder, Bandit's tail wagged, and Zoey swiped at her eyes, gutting Johnny anew.

"Hey, sunshine," he said gently, petting Bandit as he did a visual sweep of Zoey to make sure she wasn't hurt. She was well covered in the ripped jeans she'd had on earlier, the hoodie, and sneakers. She appeared unharmed. "You scared the hell out of me. Are you okay?"

She nodded almost imperceptibly, her jaw set tight.

"Mind if I come up there with you?"

She shrugged.

He climbed onto the boulder, making sure to give her space as he sat down. Bandit took up residence beside her again, lying down with his body against her legs. It went against all Johnny's instincts not to get right to the heart of the matter, but he remembered what Jillian had said about not being too direct and decided to give it a try. The trouble was, he didn't know how to not be direct, and he wasn't great at small talk. He had a momentary thought that he and Jillian probably had that in common, too.

He pulled one knee up, resting his arm on it, hoping he looked casual and not like his heart was lodged in his throat. "You been out here long?"

She poked at the boulder with a tiny stone, and he noticed a handful of small stones beside her. He didn't know if she'd gathered them to make wishes or not, but it didn't matter. Just seeing the pile made him ache a little more.

"My sisters would be terrified out here all alone."

"I'm not scared," she said vehemently.

"I can see that. I think they'd be impressed with your courage. I know I am." He looked out at the creek. "Did I tell you that I have two sisters?"

She shook her head.

"Harlow is younger than me and older than Aria."

"The *actress*?"

"Yeah, but to me she's just my sister. I mean, I'm proud of her, but you know…I remember when she was a pest." He was going for a smile, but it didn't work. "She's the tougher of the two. Always has been. She ran away a few times."

Zoey's hand stilled, her gaze flicking up to him without lifting her face.

"It's true. She scared the living daylights out of our parents. I remember this one time when she was around eleven. She only ran around the corner to her friend's house, but she hid in the back of her friend's parents' SUV and fell asleep. The whole neighborhood searched for her all night, and come morning, someone saw her climbing out of the vehicle and brought her home. I've never seen my parents cry so hard."

She lowered her eyes again.

"I never understood why they cried instead of yelling at her for scaring them so badly. Until tonight." He paused, letting that sink in. She continued poking at the boulder with the stone. "If you'd told me you wanted to go out and sit by the creek, I would've come with you."

She glanced at him for only a second, as if checking to see if he was being honest, and went back to poking the boulder with the stone. "I wanted to be alone."

"I get that. I like my space, too."

"I *know*," she said angrily. "You made that clear yesterday."

Shit. "I'm not going to try to deny that or pretend to be someone I'm not with you. We won't get through this if we aren't honest with each other, and I don't want you to feel like you have to pretend with me, either."

She looked up, eyes watery again. "*Yes*, you *do*."

"What makes you say that?"

"You dragged me here without giving me a choice. You don't care what I want."

"I needed to keep you safe. I'm sure being splashed all over the internet as my daughter would be cool, or maybe you think it wouldn't be a big deal, but trust me—it would make your life *really* hard."

"You think my life isn't *hard* right now?" Tears streamed down her cheeks. "I don't *want* to be here, hiding from the world with some guy who doesn't want me around."

Her words cut him to his core. He forced himself to take a deep breath before responding. "I'm sorry. I said a lot of things right after you showed up that I probably shouldn't have, but I was as blindsided as you were. I had no idea you existed, and suddenly I was supposed to be your father. That takes time to process."

"How do you think *I* feel?" she said through tears. "I was *forced* to be with my mother, who was barely in my life when I was growing up and *never* wanted me. She moved me away from the only home I ever knew and dragged me from one guy's shitty apartment to the next just so she could party, and then she dumped me with *you*. I hope I *never* see her again." A sob fell from her lips.

He clenched his teeth against the anger rising inside him and reached for her, but she leaned away. He held his hands up in surrender. "I just wanted to give you a hug."

"I don't need a stupid hug."

"Then please tell me what you *do* need, because whatever it is, if I can manage it, I'll make it happen."

"You *can't*. Nobody can." More sobs tumbled out, and she wiped her tears with her forearm.

"I'd like to try, Zoey. Please give me a chance. I know I screwed up when we first met, but now that I've had time to get past the initial shock, I realized I was *robbed* of having any kind of relationship with you. That might be fine with you, but it pisses me off that we're starting now, instead of fourteen years ago. I probably would've sucked as a father when I was younger, but I promise you that I'll do everything I can not to suck as your father from here on out, because I *want* this, Zoey. I want you in my life, and I want to be there for whatever comes our way. But that only works if you want it, too, and if we're on the same team."

She wiped her eyes. "I don't want to spend my life hiding. I want to go to school like normal kids. Not some rich private school where kids are assholes."

"Then that's what you'll do. Eventually. It's going to take some figuring out, and like it or not, we need to keep you safe from weirdos, because your old man is pretty famous."

She looked down again, her chin trembling. "I wish my grandma didn't die, so none of this had to happen. I never even got to say goodbye to her." She swiped at tears. "My mother had her cremated and never picked up her ashes. Who *does* that?"

His chest constricted. He had so many questions about how that all went down. Had anyone comforted her, or did she have to face that alone and figure out who to call? Who called her mother to let her know Zoey was alone? Zoey was the only one with those answers, but he wasn't sure this was the best time to get them. "I'm sorry she's gone. I know you were the one to find her, and I can't imagine how awful that was. Do you want to talk about it?"

She shook her head.

"Okay, but if you ever do, that's what I'm here for. I'm grateful she was there to raise you, and I hope one day you'll tell me about her. I bet she thanked her lucky stars every day that she had you in her life."

She nodded, fresh tears streaking her cheeks.

"I know no one can replace her, and I know how difficult and scary this is for you. I'm scared, too."

Her brows knitted, like she was surprised to hear that.

"I want you to know that I've never backed down from anything because it was scary or hard, and I'm sure as hell not going to run from this or abandon you," he reassured her. "I have a big, loving family, and that means you have them, too. They're all looking forward to meeting you. My parents are your grandparents, and they're good people." He had a brief thought about his mother having cancer and Zoey already having been through enough loss. But he couldn't think that way. No matter how long his mother was in Zoey's life, he knew she would be a positive, loving influence, and when the time was right, he'd tell Zoey about the cancer. "I know you met Kane under harsh circumstances, but I promise he'll be the coolest uncle you could ever want. He's always been there for me, and I know he and my sisters will always be there for you, whether or not you want them there, because *that's* what family is supposed to do."

She was quiet for a long time, and he let that silence ride, knowing he'd given her a lot to think about. When she finally spoke, her chin trembled again. "What if I hate them?"

"I don't think there's even a chance you will. But if you do, we'll cross that bridge when we get there, and we'll cross it *together. You're* my family now, Zoey, my top priority. You'll never have to go through anything alone again."

Another sob rang out, and she covered her face. "Are you *sure* you want me?"

"*Yes.* And believe me when I tell you that no one is more surprised by that than me."

She laughed a little, and it was music to his ears.

"I know you feel stuck putting up with me, but I hope one day you'll be glad I'm in your life, and it doesn't matter how many times you run away or try to get rid of me. I'll always be here offering hugs you don't want, telling you not to do things so you don't end up hurting yourself, and how proud I am of you when you do something cool, because that's what fathers do. And I know I'm going to make mistakes, and you're going to get angry. You'll make mistakes, too, and I'll get angry, because we're only human, and that's how we learn. Hopefully you'll learn to forgive me for my faults, because I know I have many. But I think if we can learn to trust each other and talk about why we're mad or angry or sad, we'll eventually nail this father-daughter thing. At least that's my hope, because like it or not, it's you and me from here on out."

When she finally met his gaze, a sliver of hope accompanied the sadness in her eyes. "You're a rock star. You don't have time for me."

"I canceled my tour the second I found out you were my daughter. I will *always* make time for you. That's a promise."

"I don't like your music," she said flatly.

"That's okay. You don't have to. What kind of music do you like?"

"Pop, rap, and other stuff." Her brows knitted. "You suck at making mac and cheese."

"That's not surprising. I suck at a lot of things. Maybe you can show me how you like it."

"You're not mad?"

"Because you don't like my music or my cooking?"

She nodded.

"No, Zoey. You're your own person, and you've had fourteen years to decide who that is. I'm not going to try to change your likes and dislikes. I want to get to know you, and you may not like it, but I will continue to do everything I have to in order to keep you safe, and right now that means hiding out in a fairy-tale house."

She was quiet for a beat before saying, "I don't really hate your music."

"That's good, because you'll probably hear a lot of it." He was relieved that they were finally talking.

"And I don't hate fairy tales. They just remind me of my grandma." Her voice cracked. "And that makes me sad."

"I'm so sorry, sunshine. I can't move us to the inn. It's too risky. But I am sorry."

"It's okay," she said softly.

"Listen, I tried to call you tonight, and I got a message that said your cell number was no longer in service. I'm sorry. I should've thought to get you a phone before your mother had a chance to turn it off."

"It doesn't matter. I don't have anyone to text. The few friends I had are in New Jersey. I don't have their numbers."

"Why not?"

"My grandma couldn't afford to get me a phone."

"I'm sorry about that." That was more than a tough pill to swallow, given his wealth and all the money he was paying her mother. "You must miss your friends."

She shrugged.

"You were on your phone a lot when it was working. Did you look them up on social media?"

"Why bother? I don't live there anymore."

The hurt just kept piling up. "Well, hopefully you'll meet new friends when we go home. What were you doing on your phone if you weren't texting?"

"Looking at videos and stuff. My mother only gave me a phone so she could leave me places and call when she was coming to pick me up, so I could be ready."

His hands fisted. "What do you mean leave you places? What kinds of places?"

"She'd drop me off at McDonald's and give me money, or leave me with her weird friends, then go out with some gross guy and come get me a few hours later."

He fisted his hands against the venom eating away at him. "Did those friends…touch you?"

"*Ew.* No."

"*Good.* She will never have a chance to hurt you or put you in danger again. I'm sorry she did that, but I promise that I will *never* do that to you. If anything, you'll get sick of me hanging around."

"*Great*," she said sarcastically.

"Zoey," he said softly, "I don't have any practice at being a father, but I learned from the best. My father always put our family first, and I already do that, so now I'll start focusing on what else he did for us. But we don't have to fight all the time. You can tell me when I do or say something that bothers you. I might not like it, and I might not agree, but I won't get mad. Okay?"

She nodded. "I'm glad you're not still being a jerk to Jillian. I like her, and I looked her up on my phone before it was turned off. She makes cool clothes."

"She's a cool person, and I have a feeling you are, too." That earned a small smile. "What do you think, Zo? Can we give this Dad Bad and Mini Bad thing a try?"

Her brow wrinkled. *"Dad Bad?"*

"Give me a break. I'm new at this."

Another small smile softened her expression. "I'm not calling you Dad."

"That's all right. You can call me Johnny."

She nodded.

"Does that mean you're willing to give this a shot?"

"I guess."

"No more running away?"

She shook her head. "No more gross mac and cheese?"

"Hey, I like it, but I won't make it for you."

"Okay."

"I do need one favor," he said carefully. "I need you to apologize to Jillian and Beau and Char. You scared them, too, and they've been out searching for you."

She nodded sorrowfully. "I will."

He was glad she didn't fight him on it. "What do you say we head back?"

Bandit jumped down as he and Zoey climbed off the boulder, and the pup practically attached himself to Zoey's side, pushing his head under her hand.

"Why does he do that?" she asked with annoyance.

"I guess he's a fan of yours."

"I hate dogs."

"Why?"

She didn't answer, and Johnny's thoughts skipped back to when he was seventeen. He'd been up for a major gig overseas, but his ego had gotten in the way. He'd made outrageous demands and had lost the opportunity. He'd been gutted by the loss, and his mother had asked if he needed everything he demanded in order to be happy. Johnny had said he didn't but that he wanted it all. His mother had said, *Life is full of battles, and you can't win them all. So choose the ones that matter most, and remember, need and want are two very different things. One can lead to happiness, and the other can kill it.*

Johnny knew Zoey might suffer a lifetime from fear of abandonment, not feeling like she was enough, or any number of other issues caused by what she'd already experienced in her short life. He vowed to do all he could to help her, and as they made their way back to the cottage, he didn't push for answers about why she hated dogs, hoping they could find the road to happiness and navigate the bumpy ride together.

"GOOD NIGHT, SUNSHINE. I'm really glad you're safe and here with me."

"Please take *him*." Zoey looked at Bandit, who had refused to leave her side and was now lying at the foot of her bed.

"Come on, buddy." Johnny ushered the dog out of the room and closed the door, feeling like he'd been awake for days and put through a wringer.

When they'd gotten back to the cottage, Jillian had thrown her arms around Zoey, drawing tears as her fears had poured out in pure Jillian style. *Thank God you're okay! If you ever do that again, I'll have you fit with a tracking device and lock you in a room for a month.* Johnny had seen a hint of a smile on Zoey's face, and he wondered how a woman who claimed not to be the mothering type always seemed to do the right thing. Zoey had apologized to everyone, and after Jillian's bout of tough love, Beau and Charlotte were as gracious as he'd known they'd be. They'd embraced her, and though she'd stood awkwardly with her hands at her sides, just as she'd done with Jillian, they weren't dissuaded. They'd told her how happy they were that she was back safe and sound.

Johnny made his way downstairs to get a glass of ice water.

"Johnny." Jillian pushed to her feet from the couch and rushed over to him. Her hair was tousled, her eyes were tired, and she was still impossibly beautiful.

She'd waited up for him? Hell if that didn't loosen some of the knots in his chest.

"Is Zoey okay?" she asked.

"Seems to be." He pulled her into his arms as he'd done in the forest, more relief coming out in a sigh. He didn't bother picking that apart, either.

"Oh, *okay*," she said a little awkwardly and a little teasingly. "I guess we're huggers now."

Yeah, it's fucking with my head, too. "Mind sitting with me a minute?" They sat on the couch, and he pulled her closer, needing the connection. "This parenting shit is tough."

"No kidding." She yawned.

He didn't know how she was still awake. She was running on even less sleep than he was. He let his head fall back against the cushion. "Sorry the night was such a mess."

"I'm just glad she's safe. Are you okay?"

"Yeah. She scared the shit out of me. I can't believe how fast those feelings hit."

She rested her head on his shoulder and tucked her legs beside her. "Welcome to fatherhood."

"Nothing like diving in with both feet."

"Sometimes that's the only way to stay afloat. You're trying and you're learning, and you guys are getting there. It's going to take time."

"Yeah, I know. I made it clear that I'm not going anywhere, and I meant it."

"That's because you're a good man."

"Thanks." He closed his eyes, absently running his fingers through her hair, his mind strolling back to when they'd been making out. She'd felt incredible in his arms, as eager and hungry for him as he'd been for her, and that had only whetted his appetite. But there was something bigger than lust driving him to want a hell of a lot more. There was a pulse, a thrum of electricity between them every time they touched, and it felt deep and indescribable. Even now, as exhausted as they were, he felt that connection. He couldn't remember ever feeling like that. "We should talk about what happened between us."

"No, we shouldn't. You have more important things to worry about."

His chest constricted. "You're right. But I don't regret it, Jilly. Do you?"

She shook her head, yawning again. "It just can't go anywhere."

He kissed her temple, wanting to tell her that he'd felt more than just lust, and he had a feeling she'd felt their connection, too. But he kept it to himself and said, "Would you mind staying here with me for a little while, or do you need to go to bed?"

"I'm not tired," she whispered sleepily.

He closed his eyes, thinking of Zoey and Jillian and what his mother had said about needs and wants, the lines between them blurring as he drifted off to sleep.

Chapter Nine

JILLIAN AWOKE TO the sound of clanking in the kitchen and the feel of Johnny's hard chest beneath her cheek, his large hand resting on her butt. It took a minute for her to realize they were on the couch. If *he* was here with her, who was in the kitchen? *Oh God.* Zoey saw them sleeping together? "Johnny," she whispered, pushing at his chest.

"Hm?" He squeezed her butt.

"Get up. Zoey saw us," she whispered. The fact that Zoey had come downstairs without being asked meant she was making an effort, and that felt like a huge step. She didn't want to screw it up for them.

His eyes opened, and a too-freaking sexy grin lifted his lips. "We're fully dressed. I think it's fine." He glanced in the direction of the kitchen.

"Is it? I don't know if it is. I mean, who knows what she'll think, and you have to be careful not to—" Her words were silenced by a deep, delicious kiss, bringing back tantalizing memories of his hands on her, *in* her. *Holy crap. What are we doing?* She abruptly pulled back.

An amused glint shone in his eyes. "Now, if she'd seen *that*, there might be a problem. But she didn't, so chill."

"Don't tell me to *chill*, and don't kiss me like that." She spoke firmly but quietly. "We're not doing that anymore."

His eyes narrowed. "Yes, we *are*."

"No, we're *not*. That's not why I'm here. I'm not a groupie for you to use for your pleasure, and you're supposed to be learning how to be a father."

"I don't sleep with groupies, and that's *not* why I want you here."

"What if she thinks we had *sex*?" She whispered *sex*.

"Then I'd say we *should* since she already thinks we did."

"Ohmygod. Get *up*." She pushed to her feet.

He cocked a brow. "Already there."

She followed his gaze to the impressive bulge behind his zipper, and her stupid body threw a party. Why did she have to like him so much? She turned away so he wouldn't see the heat rushing up her neck and busied herself straightening her sweater and running her fingers through her hair. *Resist, resist, resist.*

He rose to his feet and leaned over her shoulder, whispering gruffly, "This conversation is *not* over." He slapped her ass and sauntered toward the kitchen, whistling.

She glowered at his back, her body begging for more. *Ugh. Stupid body.* She stalked past him into the kitchen, where Zoey stood at the stove in a pair of pajama shorts and a T-shirt. Bandit lay at her feet, tail wagging.

"Morning, Zoey. Did you sleep okay?" Jillian grabbed a Diet Pepsi from the fridge and loved up Bandit.

"Mm-hm," Zoey said.

Johnny sauntered in, raking a hand through his thick dark hair. "Something smells good."

"French toast." Zoey put a piece on a plate and set it on the floor for Bandit.

Jillian and Johnny exchanged surprised glances as Zoey transferred two more pieces to another plate. She held up the spatula, offering it to them.

Johnny took it. "Thanks." He started the coffee maker and petted Bandit, who was busy sniffing his breakfast. "So, you know how to make breakfast."

"It's not hard." Zoey took her plate to the table.

"Right. *Sorry.* Listen, about Jillian and I falling asleep on the couch—"

"It's fine," Zoey said. "I don't care what you do, and it's not like you were naked."

"Okay, then." His brows slanted. "*Wait.* Did you see your mother naked with guys?"

Zoey made a disgusted face. "Ew. *No.*"

He exhaled with relief. "Good. Just trying to make sure I'm asking the right questions."

"Don't worry. She never did anything like that in front of me," Zoey said sharply. "She just wasn't around much, and she rarely even talked to me."

"I'm glad she kept you physically safe," Johnny said. "But the rest of that stinks. Did your grandmother talk with you?"

She nodded. "All the time."

"Is she the one who taught you to cook?" Jillian asked.

"Mm-hm." Zoey ate another bite of her breakfast. "Can we talk about something else?"

"Sure," Johnny said. "Hey, Pepsiaholic, do you want French toast?"

Jillian sipped her soda. "No, thanks."

"Is there anything you'd like to do today, Zoey?" Johnny asked as he made his breakfast.

"Laundry." Zoey ate another bite.

"We can do that," he said. "Are you out of clean clothes already?"

She nodded. "I don't have that much, and I didn't have a chance to do laundry before being dumped at your manager's office."

Jillian looked uneasily at Johnny, irritation and empathy warring in his eyes.

"Why don't we get you some new clothes today?" he offered.

"I thought we were in lockdown," Zoey said.

"I can take you," Jillian offered. "Nobody's looking for me, and you can put your hair up in a ponytail and wear one of Beau's baseball caps. I'll even call you by another name just in case anyone gets suspicious. There are some really cute shops in town. It'll be fun."

"Her picture's been plastered all over the internet," Johnny reminded her.

"Oh, right. How about if she wears one of Char's blond wigs?"

Curiosity rose in his eyes. "Char has blond wigs? *Never mind.* I don't want to know."

"They're for her writing," Jillian explained. "She likes to act out scenes."

He smirked. "I bet Beau loves that."

"I think it's weird," Zoey said.

"Maybe so, but she writes one heck of a good book," Jillian said. "What do you think, Johnny? A blond wig and a baseball cap, and I promise to leave if anyone looks at us funny?"

His jaw tensed. "That'd help, but why can't we just order her stuff online?"

Zoey rolled her eyes. *"Boring."*

"It's hard to get the right fit online. Would you feel better if Beau went with us?"

"I'd feel better if this were a month from now," he said sternly, and glanced at Zoey, pushing food around on her plate. "You really want to do this, Zoey? It's a huge risk."

Her eyes lit up, and she nodded. "I promise not to talk to anyone, and I'll keep my head down and wear the wig and the hat. I won't try to run away, and I'll listen to Jillian the whole time. *Please?"*

He shot Jillian a serious stare. "If Beau is with you, it might raise more eyebrows since he lives here."

"Then we won't bring him," Jillian said.

"You'll be extra careful not to call her Zoey and to keep her close?"

"Of course, and it's not like we're in LA with paparazzi roaming the streets."

He looked at Zoey again. "You sure you want to risk this?"

"*Yes,* but I just remembered that I don't have any money, so forget it," Zoey said softly.

"How much do you need?" Johnny pulled out his wallet and started laying hundred-dollar bills on the table.

Zoey's eyes widened as he put down the ninth bill. "A lot less than that. I get my stuff at consignment shops."

"Not anymore you don't." He picked up the cash and held it out to her.

Zoey leaned back like the money was poisonous. "I can't take that. It's too much."

"I can." Jillian flashed a grin, snagging the cash. "This is enough to get her started."

"*Started?*" Zoey asked, astonished. "I couldn't spend that much in a year."

Jillian tucked the money into her back pocket. "Don't worry. I'll show you how."

"HOW ABOUT THIS?" Jillian held up a cute T-shirt.

Zoey looked like a different kid with the blond wig and baseball cap. She shook her head, just as she'd done to all the other clothes Jillian had suggested. To her credit, there wasn't that much to choose from that was appropriate for a fourteen-year-old. Most outfits were either too sexy or too childish.

Jillian put the T-shirt back on the rack and lowered her voice. "Are you afraid to spend Johnny's money?"

"It feels weird, but no. I just haven't seen anything I like."

"What do you like to wear besides crop tops?"

She shrugged.

"Is there a look you're going for?"

"I don't know. Edgy and comfortable."

"Okay. That's a start. How would you feel about crop tops that are a little longer and jeans that aren't quite so tight?"

Zoey looked down at her shirt. "I don't usually buy them this small."

"Oh. Did your grandmother buy you those?"

She shook her head. "All I have left from my grandma's house is a pair of shorts and a tank top."

"What do you mean, *all you have left?*"

"My mom was in a hurry when she came to get me after my grandma died, and she didn't give me time to pack anything. We drove forever to get to her friend's house, and the next day she gave me fifty dollars and dropped me off at a consignment shop, but it was a really small one, and they didn't have much in my size."

Jillian's heart broke for her, but she was also pissed at her greedy bitch of a mother. "What happened to the rest of your belongings?"

"I have no idea. I kept asking if we could go get them, but she said they weren't mine anymore."

"You lost *everything?*"

Zoey nodded. "All my clothes, shoes, notebooks. All my stuff. My grandmother's sewing machine that she taught me on and my jewelry box that she gave me when I was seven. It had a little ballerina inside it, and it played music when you opened it. I kept my pictures of us in it." She pulled her necklace out from beneath her shirt, touching the heart-shaped locket charm. "This is all I have left. The locket she gave me when I turned thirteen and this one picture of her." She opened the locket and showed Jillian a picture of a friendly faced woman with short brown hair who looked to be in her late fifties or early sixties.

"I'd like to have a talk with your mother," Jillian fumed. "Doesn't she know a girl's memories are sacred? If you ask me, that's cause for a riot."

"She didn't care. She paid someone to sell it all at an estate sale."

"Ohmygod. That's infuriating, and so freaking sad. I'm sorry, Zoey."

She shrugged. "Thanks, but whatever."

"Doesn't she know how important a girl's clothes are? They show the world how we feel about ourselves, and they have the power to make us feel pretty or tough or slouchy."

"I never thought of that. But it's true," Zoey said with surprise.

"Darn right it is. I might not know much about a lot of things, but I know fashion. Tell me what kinds of clothes you had, and we'll hunt them down."

"Really?" Excitement rose in her eyes.

"Yes, really. I don't mess around when it comes to fashion. Do you remember the name brands?"

"No, but I can tell you what they looked like."

Jillian pulled out her phone. "Good, and then we'll see if we can find something similar. Do you want to do it over an ice cream sundae?"

Zoey's eyes lit up. "I never turn down ice cream."

They spent the next hour eating ice cream and searching online for clothes similar to what Zoey had previously owned, and then they searched websites for stores within a forty-five-minute radius that sold similar items. As they drove from one shop to the next, buying her clothes as if they were on a scavenger hunt, Zoey's walls came down.

Two and a half hours, one café lunch, and just enough conversations and laughter to *almost* make Jillian forget just how much Zoey had been through, they walked into the last shop on their list.

"I can't believe we found so many clothes like the ones I had. You're like a fashion detective. My grandma would have loved you," Zoey said, making a beeline for the hoodies.

"Fashion has brought many women together. But why do you think she'd like me?"

"Because you don't waste time or second-guess. You make a plan and do it. That's how she was."

"I think I would have liked her, too." She pulled a gray cropped hoodie with navy stars on it from the rack. "Found it!"

"*Yes.* Thank you. This was one of my favorites." Zoey took it from her and held it up. "I cut a V in the neck, and then cut along these seams." She showed her the seams on the cuffs. "I took the string out of the hood, too, and replaced it with black and blue material that I braided together. I wrapped silver thread around them about an inch from each end to keep them from unraveling and then frayed them. It looked cool."

"You're really creative."

"My grandma showed me how to do some cool stuff. I embellished most of my clothes with studs or patches, and she taught me how to distress jeans and add tears to them, and to sweaters, too, without ruining them. I fringed almost all the hems. I love that look."

"Now I know I would've liked her."

"She was great," she said a little sadly. "She was a seamstress when she was young. That's where she learned to do it all."

"I'm glad she showed you. Now you'll always have a piece of her you can carry forward and give to your kids. You know what, Zo? I think we're going to need to find a sewing store, because that kind of creativity shouldn't be stifled."

"Really?" she asked excitedly.

"Absolutely. I'll teach you the tricks of the trade and what materials might work better than thread and regular fabric." That earned a wide grin.

"That's awesome, thank you. Do you think Johnny will mind?"

Jillian scoffed. "Just let him *try* to hold this fashionista down. We'll get him on board." She took her hand, dragging her toward the jeans. "Let's find those jeans you like."

They found a few pairs of jeans, and when Zoey was trying them on, Jillian chose a few more pieces that she thought would look great on her.

"What do you think?" Zoey came out of the dressing room wearing boyfriend jeans she'd rolled up to above her ankles, and turned in a circle.

"They look like they fit really well. Not too tight, but snug enough to look like they were made for you. How do they feel?"

"Really good. I like them."

"Then we'll get them. Do me a favor and try these on." She handed her a stack of clothes.

Zoey eyed the yellow-and-black plaid pants. "I'm not really into plaid."

"I know, but look at them with this top." She snagged the off-the-shoulder long-sleeved black top that had black embroidery around the edges of the sleeves and elastic around the bottom of the shirt, which should land just above Zoey's waist. "I think it will be to die for, and look." She lifted the top layer of the shirt and showed her the cami with a built-in bra beneath. "It's all one piece. So comfy."

Zoey rolled her eyes.

Jillian spun her around, giving her a nudge toward the dressing room. "Get in there. And the black skirt and oversize cable-knit sweater go together."

"A *skirt?*"

"Yes. This is what I'm best at." Especially now that she had a better sense of Zoey and her taste. "Trust me."

A few minutes later, Zoey came out wearing the plaid pants and black shirt. The sleeves hung to the middle of her hands, and the shirt was just short enough to show a sliver of skin above her waist, giving her the appearance of youthful rebellion Jillian knew she needed.

"*Wow*, you look incredible," Jillian said, and realized she needed to play it cool. "I mean, what do you think?"

"I kind of really like it," she said carefully, running her hands down the pants, and turned to look in the mirror.

"I was hoping you would. It's *so* cute, and it fits you perfectly. It's a little edgy and different, which is always good with fashion. Is it comfortable? It'll go great with your black sneakers, but we could get you black ankle boots if you want."

"The pants are soft and stretchy, almost like pajamas but nicer." She turned to look in the mirror. "I've never worn anything like this. Are you sure I don't look dumb?"

Jillian met her gaze in the mirror. "Clothes can't make a person look dumb. But they can make you look sharp, and you do. You look good in everything you picked out today, like someone who cares about what she wears. I know this outfit isn't what you're used to, but your fashion choices will change over time, and it's okay to add a few different pieces and try them out. You may not like them all when you try them on, and you don't have to buy them. But you might get lucky and find a few different things you want to buy. Some might become your favorites, and others you might only wear from time to time, but every girl should have choices to go along with her moods."

Zoey fingered the edges of the sleeves. "I love this shirt. And it goes with jeans, too."

"It sure does."

"Are you sure I'm not getting too much?"

"Honey, your dad wants to do this for you. He wants you to have what you need and feel good about yourself and be happy."

"Yeah, I guess."

"I say we take these and try on the skirt and sweater. I have a feeling you're going to like them, too."

"Don't hold your breath. I don't like skirts."

"I know." Jillian watched her disappear behind the curtain and had to hold in a squeal of delight.

"This skirt has shorts in it," Zoey said from behind the curtain. "And the sweater is super soft."

She came out in the outfit looking adorable, and a little embarrassed.

"What are you thinking?" Jillian asked.

"That maybe you should have held your breath."

Jillian squealed and hugged her.

Zoey laughed. "They're just clothes."

"They're never *just* clothes." She took Zoey's hands and smiled at the girl who was blossoming right before her eyes. "You are so cute. Johnny's going to have to lock you up to keep the boys away. Or girls. Either is fine, and you don't have to tell me what you're into."

Zoey laughed. "Boys."

"Me too. Well, men." She grinned. "I think we need to stop at the hardware store to get a lock cutter."

"You're so weird, you're funny." Zoey looked in the mirror.

"I'd rather be funny than funny looking like your dad when he's trying to figure something out." She furrowed her brow and tightened her jaw.

Zoey giggled. "Or when he's trying not to cuss, and he mumbles under his breath, then looks at me really quickly to see if I heard him."

"And then he cusses again and says, 'Sorry. I didn't mean that,' with that pleading look in his eyes." They both burst into laughter. "Okay, mini-fashionista, let's go pay for this stuff and hit the sewing and hardware stores."

"We're not buying a lock cutter."

They had a great time in the sewing store, and on their way out, they saw a flyer for an upcoming carnival, and Zoey talked about it the whole way back to the cottage.

Johnny came out the front door as they climbed out of the SUV. "I was starting to get worried."

"Sorry we took so long," Jillian said as Zoey grabbed her shopping bags. "We ended up going to two neighboring towns, but we got Zoey some great outfits, a few things to embellish her clothes with, and a pair of red Converse and flat-bottomed black ankle boots."

"Thank you for everything," Zoey said. "I've never gotten this much at once."

Johnny smiled. "I'm glad you had fun. I look forward to seeing what you bought."

"Okay." Zoey looked a little pensive. "I know you just bought me a lot, and I promise I won't ask for anything more, but we saw a flyer for a fall carnival coming to town next weekend, and I was wondering if we could go. Nobody knew who I was while we were out, and I'll wear the wig and a baseball cap, or whatever you want."

"I don't know, Zoey." He glanced at Jillian.

Jillian knew how risky it was for him to be out in public, and she'd warned Zoey. But Zoey had talked about the carnival nonstop for the last half hour, and she couldn't help at least trying. "You could let your facial hair grow and borrow a hat, a flannel shirt, and boots from Beau. We could even pad your stomach to give you more of a dad bod," Jillian suggested.

Johnny looked at her like she'd lost her mind.

"*Please?*" Zoey asked. "You could wear a wig, too, like a mullet or something that would make you look different, and you and Jillian could act like you're an old married couple and I'm your kid."

"Hey, I'm not *old*," Jillian said.

"And you *are* my kid," Johnny reminded her. "I don't know, sunshine. That's really risky. Let me think about it."

"*Fine*," Zoey said, deflated. "I'm going to put this stuff away."

When the door shut behind her, Johnny said, "Damn it. She probably thinks I'm an ass."

"She's just disappointed, and that's okay. Parents don't always have to give their kids what they ask for. We talked about it in the car. She knows you need to keep her safe. Have you spoken to Kane or your PR rep? What's going on with everything?"

"We're strategizing about when I should make a statement, but I don't want to do anything until we handle things with Dick and Zoey's mother."

"That makes sense. I have to tell you something." She took his hand, leading him behind the SUV.

"I like where this is heading." He pulled her into his arms.

"Would you stop?" She looked at him playfully. "Or at least table it for later. This is important."

"So is *this*. I didn't thank you properly for taking my daughter shopping."

His mouth came coaxingly down over hers. His tongue swept along the seam of her lips, and she opened for him, craving the kisses that had driven her mad last night, and *oh boy*, did he deliver. He held her tighter, taking the kiss deeper. She went up on her toes, seeking *more*. His hands slid down to her ass, crushing her against his erection, and they both moaned. He felt so good, she *almost* forgot where they were. Forcing herself to push away, she panted for air *and sanity.* "Johnny, we both know this can't go anywhere."

"It can go a lot of places." He pulled her close again.

She tried to ignore the butterflies swarming in her stomach. "You know what I mean."

"I know the timing sucks. I wasn't looking for this, and neither were you, but look me in the eye and tell me you don't feel something every time we're together."

She couldn't meet his gaze because she knew what it would do to her, so she looked at the sexy mouth that knew just what to say and made her panties damp with very little effort.

Big mistake.

"Tell me you don't like kissing me." He leaned closer and lowered his voice. "That you don't want to continue what we started last night and feel my mouth between your legs."

Desire whirled through her. She was starting to believe he wouldn't disappoint her in the bedroom.

"You can't say it, can you? There's something between us, and you know it, Jilly." He dipped his head, speaking into her ear. "Neither of us is looking for complicated entanglements, so why not enjoy each other while we're here?"

"Because you're"—*Making me crazy. I can't stop thinking about making out with you*—"the epitome of a bad decision."

He cocked a grin. "Is that a yes? Because we both know how much you like to be *bad.*"

"No, it's not a yes." She laughed because what else was she supposed to do? Pretending she didn't want him was ludicrous. Of course she wanted to strip him naked and do dirty things with him. *So why aren't I?*

That gave her pause.

"What do you say, Jilly?"

"I'll think about it." *God, what am I doing?* "Now will you listen to what I have to say before Zoey comes outside?"

"She's not going to come outside. She's mad at me, or disappointed, or maybe both. But I can absolutely listen to you." He spread his hands over her ass.

"*Without* holding my butt." She guided his hands to her waist, but he was still looking at her like he wanted to lay her out right there and devour her. "And stop looking at me like that before you get us both in trouble."

"I can't help how I look at you. It's not my fault you have a dirty mind."

She rolled her eyes. "Zoey told me something really upsetting."

His expression turned serious. "Go on."

"When her mother came to get her after her grandmother died, she didn't let her take any of her things, and she never got them back. Her mother sold everything at an estate sale. Everything Zoey has with her is *all* she owns, and she lost some really important things."

She told him everything Zoey had told her, and fury roared off him.

"That witch needs to pay for this." He pulled out his phone.

"Who are you calling?"

"Kane, to nail her ass to the wall."

Chapter Ten

THURSDAY AFTERNOON, JOHNNY ran along the five-mile trail Beau had showed him yesterday. It wrapped around the property far enough from the inn that he didn't have to worry about bumping into guests, and navigating the rough terrain was just what he needed to try to clear his head. He was used to his days being his own, hitting the gym, running, working on his music or jamming with his band, and generally having time to himself. But those times were over. A few days ago, that realization would have brought a multitude of negative emotions, but with one sentence, Jillian had changed everything. *You hold the power to step up and try to salvage how she feels about you and herself, or you can fuck her up beyond repair by making her feel even more unwanted.* The truth in her words had stopped him in his tracks, much like she was doing to him in other ways.

Thankfully, things had been getting better with Zoey since their talk two nights ago. She was still wary and guarded, but conversations were more than just a few words, and he'd even coaxed a few smiles and a bit of laughter out of her. But while the tension was easing with her, tension of a different kind was ramping up with Jillian. The feisty designer was pushing *all* his buttons. Seducing him to the edge of madness with taunting brushes of her body, furtive glances, and tantalizing innuendos, only to saunter away with an extra sway in her gorgeous hips, as if she hadn't left him aching for her. She was enjoying every second of it, too, and for some reason, that was even more of a turn-on.

She was the reason he was out for his second run of the day. If he saw her in those skimpy outfits she slept in one more time, he was liable to rip them off and bend her over the kitchen table. They were having a bonfire tonight with Beau and Charlotte, and if he didn't ease his pent-up sexual tension before then, he might spontaneously combust.

He ran faster, sprinting up the hill, his mind turning to Zoey. He felt a little guilty thinking of Jillian as often as he thought of Zoey. But his desire for her and his worries for his daughter weren't at war. They ran side by side. His thoughts of Jillian weren't only sexual. He enjoyed her taunts and playful banter as much as he valued being able to talk with her when he wasn't sure which way to go with Zoey. She obviously cared about Zoey, and she gave him solid advice without softening the blows when she thought he said or did something wrong, which should annoy him to some degree, but it only made her more intriguing. She cared more about making sure Zoey was getting the best version of him than she did about hooking up with him. He had a feeling Jillian Braden was one of a kind.

He ran up the hill, and the cottage came into view. It was funny, but he no longer noticed the frosting-like ceilings and the tree trunk they passed through to get to the kitchen. He assumed that was because his life had become so far from his norm, it eclipsed the oddness of living in a fairy-tale house. Or maybe it was because the surroundings didn't matter as much as the dynamics of the people did.

He slowed to a walk and took off his shirt, using it to wipe the sweat from his face. Zoey was sitting with her back against a tree, reading. Jillian had taken her to the inn to browse through the library, and she'd come back with a few books and a bright new outlook. It turned out that reading was one of Zoey's favorite hobbies. Bandit lay beside her in the grass. She still rolled her eyes at her new constant companion's attention, but yesterday she'd asked Beau to bring food over for him. She'd fed Bandit and given him fresh water twice today.

Maybe she didn't dislike dogs so much after all.

She looked up as Johnny approached and wrinkled her nose. "Sweat much?"

"It's good for you. You should come running with me sometime."

"No thanks." She looked cute in one of her new outfits. The cropped black-and-white sweater wasn't too tight or too short, and he'd noticed earlier that her jeans didn't look painted on, which he was thankful for.

"Did you find your missing T-shirt?" She'd mentioned that it, and a few socks, had gone missing when they'd done laundry.

She shook her head.

"They'll turn up. Are you still up for the bonfire tonight?"

"Yes." Her eyes lit up. She'd told them that she'd never been to one. "Jillian said we can make s'mores."

"That's what bonfires are for. I'm going inside to shower. Do you need anything?"

"No thanks," she said, eyes trained on her book again.

He gave Bandit a pet and went inside. After a quick stop in the kitchen to drink a glass of ice water, he headed upstairs. Jillian was coming out of her bedroom at the end of the hall looking beyond sexy in the cream off-the-shoulder sweater and black leggings she'd been torturing him with all day. Heat blazed between them, and from the grin spreading across her very fuckable lips, he knew she felt it, too.

"Mr. Bad," she said coyly. "Didn't you already run once today?"

"Yes." *And now I need to go for another run.*

She stepped closer, her chest almost grazing his skin. "Working off a little *tension?*"

Now he was the one stepping forward, backing her up against the wall for toying with him. "Why do you ask? Do you want to help?"

Her brows lifted. "I don't think so."

"The lust in your eyes tells me otherwise."

"I'm just a hot-blooded woman appreciating the male body." She licked her lips slowly and sensually. "I guess running twice a day is your secret to keeping yours tight."

Hot-blooded is right. "Speaking of *tight.*" He pressed his hips forward and palmed her hip, giving it a squeeze. "What's your secret?"

She lifted both hands, putting her fingertips on his chest as she went up on her toes, her eyes saying *let me show you,* as "Wouldn't you like to know" slipped from her lips, and she ducked out of his grasp, strutting away like she hadn't gotten him all worked up.

In the bathroom, he stripped off his clothes and stepped into a cold shower, grinding his teeth against the ache in his balls. He couldn't remember the last time a woman had had this effect on him. He was always in control, able to tamp down his needs by merely thinking of something else. Why her? A sprite of a woman who was everything he'd never wanted? Why now, when his life was in utter chaos? That should be enough to keep his thoughts out of the gutter, but nothing seemed to help. It didn't matter that he was focused on making sure Zoey was okay, spending whatever time she would allow with her. The three of them had made spaghetti and meatballs for dinner last night. Or rather, he and Zoey had made dinner while Jillian had put her hands in the raw meat mixture to form meatballs and immediately began jumping around on her tiptoes, making faces and cracking jokes about touching brains. They'd had fun, but that hadn't stopped him from wanting to haul Jillian into his arms every time she looked at him and fuck her senseless every time her hot little body brushed against him.

There was no escaping the *need* burning through his veins, and he knew there was only one way he'd make it through the evening. Fisting his dick, he closed his eyes and didn't even have to *try* to conjure Jillian's image. She was front and center, seductive eyes drawing him in, gorgeous breasts begging to be sucked, and that tight pussy waiting to be fucked. He stroked himself faster, squeezed tighter, replaying the dark fantasies he'd had last night of her lying on his bed, wrists bound, legs spread, as he feasted on her. Pressure built inside him, and he worked his dick faster, thinking of her writhing, *begging* to be fucked, and imagined driving into her hard and deep, until fire scorched down his spine, hips thrusting, teeth clenching as his orgasm tore through him. He grunted out a curse, pressing his hand to the wall as he jerked through the last of his release.

His head fell forward, and "*Jesus, Jilly*" tumbled out. *What the hell are you doing to me?*

JOHNNY FINISHED DRESSING and grabbed his phone just as it rang with a call from Kane. When they'd spoken about getting full custody from Zoey's mother, Kane had told him they were going after Dick today. The bastard had embezzled more than a million dollars, which meant grand larceny in the first degree. He'd get put away for a long time. Johnny felt a pang of disbelief. How had the mentor who had discovered him and groomed him for success taken such a bad turn?

"Hey, Kane. How'd it go?"

"About as well as you'd expect. Dick was arrested an hour ago, and it's already all over social media."

"Fucking prick deserves everything he gets." Johnny rubbed the back of his neck, pacing the room.

"Damn right he does. He knew what he was doing before he ever took you on. That's why your team didn't catch it. He's been paying fake companies that he owned under an alias for everything from travel consultants to promotional outlets, and our guess is that he was doing it to other clients before he even discovered you. We notified his previous clients, and I have no doubt they'll be taking action, too. It's a fucking mess, but we've got him. I'll fill you in once some of the smoke clears."

"Thanks, man. I don't know what I'd do without you." Kane had been asking to take over management of Johnny's career for years, but Johnny hadn't wanted to mix business and family, and he'd felt loyal to Dick for discovering him. He'd trusted him, even though Kane had always been skeptical. Big mistake. "I should've let you take over years ago."

"No use beating a dead horse. Focus on what's in front of you, not what's behind you."

"I'm trying. Any news on Zoey's mother?"

"Yeah, she followed some two-bit group to LA. I picked up the custody papers today, and I'm flying out to get them signed tomorrow. Don't worry. I've got eyes on her until then. How are things going with Zoey?"

Johnny had already filled him in about Zoey running away and her outing with Jillian. "She's coming around. We've got a long way to go, but I think we're on the right path. I'll tell you what. This has given me a new appreciation for Mom and Dad. I feel bad for all the shit we pulled as teenagers."

"You can say that again. How are you holding up?"

"I'm a'right."

"You sure? You're a *father*, Johnny, for the rest of your life. An overnight Daddy, and not the fun kind."

"Dude, really?"

Kane laughed. "I'm just trying to lighten the mood. You sure you don't want Mom or Harlow to come out and help you? I'd suggest Aria. If anyone knows what it's like to have been shuffled from one house to the next, it's her, but it's a long-ass drive to Colorado from Cape Cod."

"It's funny you say that. Aria called this morning to see how things were going, and she actually offered to drive out with Zeke."

"Really?"

"Yeah. It meant a lot to me, but we're doing okay. Jillian's really good with Zoey. She sets boundaries and knows how to get her talking. She even gets her to smile sometimes. Usually that comes at my expense, but it's all in fun. Zoey trusts her, and that's everything, right?"

"That counts for a lot. What about you? Do you trust that hot little number?"

"Yeah, man, I do, even though she drives me insane. She's mouthy and calls me on my shit all the time."

"You could ask her to leave now that you're settled."

"Nah. I don't want her to leave. I'm glad she's here."

"Aw, hell, Johnny. What am I hearing in your voice?" Kane asked sternly. "You want to fuck her, don't you?"

Johnny forced himself to remain silent, refusing to give his brother the satisfaction of an answer.

"Did you forget that's how you got into this mess? By trusting the wrong woman?"

"Bullshit. I got into this mess because I was a horny nineteen-year-old who didn't give a damn who I stuck my dick into. There was no trust or mistrust there. It was probably a drunken night. She could've been anyone. The only wrong person I trusted was Dick. He did this to me, and you know it. If he hadn't screwed me over, this would've been handled right from the get-go. Not that I know what *right* would have meant, but it sure as hell would be better than the way things went down."

"Just be careful," Kane warned. "You don't know Jillian."

"I'm being careful and I'm getting to know her. Besides, you said you checked her out and you didn't find anything I should be worried about."

"I didn't, but I assumed she'd be gone once you were settled. Any woman would bend over backward to be with you, and the last thing you need is to try to juggle a new girlfriend and a new relationship with your daughter."

"Well, Jilly's *not* bending over backward or any other way for me, and trust me, I want her to."

Kane laughed. "Now I get it. You want what you can't have."

"Shut the fuck up. It's not that. Okay, maybe it is a little. I mean, the chase is always fun, but I really like her. You know she didn't want to be here, but instead of bitching, she's done everything she can to help bridge the gap between me and Zoey. You should've seen her playing badminton with us."

"Since when do you play badminton?"

"I don't, but Jillian's trying to get Zoey to come out of her shell, and that was one of her attempts. It's working, but Jilly twisted her damn ankle. It's better now, but the woman has *no* athletic ability, and she can't cook worth shit. She lives on Diet Pepsi, and I'm pretty sure she never sleeps, but she's working on the wardrobe, just like she said she would. She showed me some of her designs earlier, and they were really good." He felt himself smiling, remembering how passionate she was as she'd gone over her sketches, showing him different styles for him and each of his band members. She'd really captured all their personalities, which was surprising, considering he'd been little help.

"So she's actually *working?*"

"Yeah. She's not a slacker, Kane. She's like the Energizer Bunny in heels. Kind of no-nonsense, but at the same time, she knows how to get under my skin with one look. She's down to earth but classy. Not model or actress snobby, more like she's had to fight her way to the top and *knows* she belongs there, and I fucking love that confidence."

"You've really thought about her. I don't think I've ever heard you talk like that about a woman."

"She's unlike any woman I know. She's tough and you know she's mouthy, but there's something about her that drives me wild."

"I'm going to say it again, Johnny. Be careful. Your life isn't your own anymore, and you can't afford to get caught up in any more messes."

"No shit." Although, he could think of a few fun ways to get tied down with Jillian, but that would involve silk scarves and didn't need to be shared with his brother. "I like hanging out with her. We're not here for much longer anyway. I spoke to Shea earlier. She's lining up interviews for early next week so I can get my face in front of the camera and make a statement about Dick and Zoey, but she was waiting to hear how things went with Dick, and I don't want to do anything until this shit with Zoey's mother is settled."

"I'll give her a call."

"Great. After I make a statement, Zoey and I can head back to New York and figure out our lives." It felt weird, even after just a few days, talking about him and Zoey without Jillian in the mix. "Jerry's been looking into schools, but Zoey wants to go to public school."

"That's not a good idea in the city. It makes her and, in turn, *you*, too accessible."

"I know. One thing at a time. Listen, I need a couple of favors." He and Kane talked business for a little longer. "Thanks, bro. I've got to jump off to get dinner ready. We're having a bonfire with Jillian's brother and his wife tonight, and I want the girls to have something real in their stomachs before they pig out on s'mores."

"Let me get this straight. You're playing mother hen to Zoey *and* Jillian? I'd say Jillian's a hell of a lot smarter than you are. Does she make you wear an apron, too?"

"Shut the fuck up." Johnny laughed.

"Wait until I tell Harlow."

"Bye, asshole."

JOHNNY HADN'T BEEN to a bonfire since he'd lived at home with his parents. He'd forgotten how relaxing and fun they could be. Hell, he'd forgotten how great it was not to spend every minute in a concrete jungle. He sat beside Zoey, who was making s'mores and feeding bits of a graham cracker to Bandit. Beau and Charlotte were sitting across from them, sharing a story about the bonfire they'd had at the inn after their wedding. Jillian was on Zoey's other side, licking chocolate off her fingers, her hazel eyes locked on Johnny. He'd thought it would be safer not sitting next to her, since taunting him had become her new favorite pastime, and the last thing he needed was to have a hard-on with an audience. But her seductive glances were even more potent, and her body more alluring, with the flames reflecting in her eyes and her bare shoulders shimmering in the moonlight. There was surely some kind of sin in lusting after a woman while in the presence of her brother and his own daughter, but he was powerless to stop. And from the way Jillian was watching him, the conversation had turned to white noise for her, too.

"Then Bandit stole Brindle's breast pump, and all hell broke loose," Charlotte said.

"That was hilarious," Beau said. "When our baby is born, we're going to have to make sure Bandit doesn't get any ideas and take off with it."

Charlotte gasped, and Jillian startled, jerking her attention away from Johnny. "*What?* Did you say *your* baby? Are you pregnant?"

Charlotte looked nervously at Beau. "We weren't supposed to *say* anything until Amber's wedding, when the whole family is together."

Beau winced. "Sorry, babe. It just slipped out."

"You're having a *baby?*" Jillian exclaimed.

Beau's and Charlotte's smiles were all the confirmation Jillian needed to squeal and jump to her feet. She ran around the fire and hugged them. "Congratulations! I'm going to be an auntie!"

"Congratulations," Johnny said, feeling a whisper of guilt, knowing if he'd been told about Zoey before she was born, he wouldn't have radiated with joy the way Beau was. He vowed again to do everything within his power to make sure she never felt unwanted again.

"Congratulations," Zoey said, taking a bite of her treat. "Our neighbors in New Jersey had a baby. It was cute, but it cried all the time. I hope yours doesn't."

"Me too," Charlotte said. "But if it does, we'll just keep loving it."

Johnny noticed Zoey's brows knitting as she processed that. Was she trying to figure out why her mother didn't love her like that?

"I can't wait to throw you a baby shower," Jillian said. "This will be *so* fun, but don't worry. I won't say anything until you tell everyone else."

"So you *like* babies?" Johnny asked. "You gave me the impression you didn't."

"Jillian loves babies as long as she can give them back," Beau said.

"Exactly." Jillian held Johnny's gaze. "I don't do puke or diapers, but I can be the doting aunt who makes sure the baby is fashionable at all times and loves it to pieces."

"Until it needs a diaper change," Johnny teased.

Jillian's lips quirked, and she sat up taller. "That's right."

"I'm with you on that," Zoey said.

Johnny leaned against Zoey's side and said, "Well, we don't have to worry about you having a baby until you're thirty, because you're not dating until then."

"What*ever*," Zoey said.

"Don't worry, Zoey," Jillian said. "My father and brothers used to tell me I couldn't date until I was thirty, too. I'm sure he'll let you when you're a little older. Maybe fifteen or sixteen."

"*What?* That's way too young," Johnny said.

"Twenty, at least," Beau added.

He and Beau shared a nod, and the girls rolled their eyes.

"The truth is," Beau said, "we got lucky with Jilly. She was always into fashion more than dating."

That piqued Johnny's interest. "Really? I pictured her as the most popular cheerleader dating the high school quarterback."

Beau scoffed. "Jilly didn't have time for that nonsense. She's been focused on fashion practically since she could speak. She and Jax held their first fashion show in our backyard when they were four."

"Four? That's adorable." Johnny eyed Jillian, imagining her as a bossy little thing strutting down a runway.

She glanced at him, her proud grin turning seductive.

You naughty girl, trying to get me riled up in front of your brother.

"Jax wanted to design a dress for Jilly when they were four. Our mother hooked him up with a seamstress, and our father built them a runway," Beau explained. "After that, Jilly and Jax were unstoppable.

While other kids were playing sports, hanging with their friends, or working with tutors, they spent time with the seamstress, learning everything they could. They used to make the costumes for school plays, and even as teenagers, whenever someone had an event, they'd come to Jilly and Jax months ahead of time to see if they could design something. You're sitting next to the original girl boss."

"That's *so* cool," Zoey said.

"You should see the clothes she designed with Jace Stone, one of the owners of Silver-Stone Cycles. They have an entire Leather and Lace line for women bikers." Charlotte went on to describe the fashion line.

He imagined Jillian wearing the sexy lingerie and other outfits Charlotte was describing. *My girl likes leather and lace.* The thought startled him, and he quickly corrected himself. *My girl for now.*

Jillian's gaze smoldered, as if she could read his mind and *liked* it. But as if she'd suddenly remembered they weren't alone, she abruptly broke their connection, leaving him craving more.

"Enough about me," Jillian said a little breathily. "This is Zoey's first bonfire. What do you think of it so far?"

"It's fun, and the s'mores are delicious," Zoey said. "Can I have another?"

"One more. I don't want you up with a stomachache all night," Johnny said, and realized he sounded very much like a parent, which felt good. Jillian's approving smile made him feel that much better.

"Yes," Zoey whisper-cheered, and reached for more marshmallows.

"I grew up on Cape Cod, and we used to have bonfires in our backyard and on the beaches all the time when I was a kid," Johnny said. "Anyone who wandered by was welcome to join us."

"It sounds like your family is a lot like the Bradens," Charlotte said. "They have a way of making everyone feel welcome, and every time they're together they have a big dinner or a barbecue or bonfire."

He thought about how Jillian had treated Zoey from the moment they'd gotten off the plane, and Charlotte's comment rang true.

"I love our bonfires and barbecues," Jillian said.

"You love it when anyone else will cook for you," Beau teased.

"Yes, I do," Jillian said. "There are benefits to living close to family."

"Where do you live?" Zoey asked.

Jillian's eyes brightened. "In Pleasant Hill, Maryland. I bet you didn't know that's where Duncan Raz is from."

"The person or the chicken?" Zoey asked.

Johnny chuckled.

"The person," Jillian said.

"No *way*. Do you know him?" Zoey asked.

"Very well, actually." Jillian looked sympathetically at Beau. "He lives someplace else now. But you know what? Your dad will appreciate this. When Duncan comes home to visit, he doesn't have to worry about paparazzi, because there are none there. And the people who live there respect Duncan and his family, so he's not overwhelmed by fans wanting autographs."

"Sounds too good to be true," Johnny said.

"Jilly's right," Beau said. "The community is small but not intrusive. It's a great place to live. When Char and I got married, we kept my house in Pleasant Hill so we could split our time between here and there."

"We have a thing for small-town life," Charlotte said.

"How small is it?" Zoey asked.

"Small enough that when you go to a bookstore or a café more than two or three times, the people who work there get to know you by name. But it's big enough that if you go out at night, you don't know everyone. And there's always something to do." Jillian focused on Zoey. "You know that carnival you wanted to go to? Pleasant Hill has festivals and parades for every season, and they decorate the whole town for them."

"The pumpkin festival is coming up on Halloween weekend," Beau reminded her.

"What do you do at a pumpkin festival?" Zoey asked.

"It's a lot of fun," Jillian said. "There's a parade, and the cafés and bakeries sell pumpkin-flavored treats. There are hayrides at a local farm, and all the stores have sidewalk sales. Artists come from all around and set up booths in the park to sell their stuff. My brother Graham's wife, Morgyn, is going to have a booth this year."

"What does she make?" Zoey asked.

"Lots of really cool things. She repurposes clothes and jewelry and antiques and just about anything you can think of. You'd love her clothes, and she makes it all herself."

"That sounds amazing," Zoey said.

"It is," Charlotte said. "I'm sorry we're going to miss it this year."

"That's right. We'll miss you. Everyone else will be home for the weekend for Nick and Trixie's Halloween party," Jillian said. "Zoey, that's another reason I like where I live. Not only do our parents and our brothers Nick and Jax live there, but our other brothers, Graham and Zev and their wives also spend time there, and our cousins live in the next town over."

"You have a *huge* family," Zoey said. "Are you the only girl?"

"I sure am, which is probably a good thing. I don't know if I could handle a sister like me."

They all laughed, even Zoey, who was especially animated tonight.

"I thought you lived in New York," Zoey said.

"I love visiting the city, but I like living in Maryland," Jillian said.

"Why? I mean, other than family," Zoey said as she roasted a marshmallow.

Johnny was surprised by how interested Zoey was in Jillian's life, but he was glad they were connecting, and he liked learning more about the feisty designer.

"Maryland isn't as chaotic as the Big Apple," Jillian said thoughtfully. "But what makes it really special is that I can drive ten minutes in one direction and spend time in town with all the shops and restaurants, but if I go in the opposite direction, there are farms and horses as far as you can see."

"I would *love* to live around horses," Zoey said.

Johnny took note of that.

"You'll have to come visit." Jillian glanced at him. He winked, but she quickly averted her eyes and said, "Nick has several horses. He's a freestyle horse trainer and showman, which really means he does crazy stunts on horses, and his wife, Trixie, has a miniature horse therapy business. She has the *cutest* miniature horses."

"*Really?* I've never seen miniature horses," Zoey said, putting the marshmallow on her graham cracker.

"Like I said, you can visit anytime, but Beau and Char have horses, too," Jillian said.

"Here?" Zoey asked hopefully.

"Yes. We have four. They were a wedding gift from a relative of Beau and Jilly's who lives here in Colorado," Charlotte said. "Do you ride?"

"My grandma took me riding a few times, and I was really good at it, but we couldn't afford lessons."

"I bet you're good enough for a trail ride," Beau said. "Jillian knows all the best trails."

"Good idea." Jillian's gaze shifted to Johnny. "I *love* riding."

I bet you do.

"*You* ride?" Zoey asked with disbelief.

"Why do you sound so surprised?" Jillian asked.

"I don't know," Zoey said. "Because you always wear heels and nice clothes. I can't see you getting dirty."

"Clothes can be washed, and getting dirty can be fun." She slid a playful smirk Johnny's way, and he couldn't help but chuckle.

"Can we go riding?" Zoey asked.

He hadn't ridden a horse since he was a kid, but he'd do just about anything to keep that smile on Zoey's face. "You bet."

"*Yes.* Thank you!" Zoey exclaimed, but her smile faded as she turned to Beau. "What if I forgot how to ride?"

"Char has plans to write tomorrow, but I could give you a lesson," Beau offered.

"You wouldn't mind?" Zoey asked.

"Not at all," Beau said. "I'll come over around ten. By the time we're done, you'll know all you need to."

Johnny felt an odd streak of jealousy, wishing he knew enough to be the one to show her how to ride.

"Thanks," Zoey said. "What are your horses like? Do I need riding boots? I only have sneakers."

Again, he'd like to jump in and say he'd buy her boots, but he couldn't even go to the damn store.

"What size do you wear?" Charlotte asked.

"Seven and a half," Zoey said.

"Perfect. You and Jilly can both borrow a pair of my boots," Charlotte said. "And you'll love our horses. They know these trails by heart, and they're sweethearts, real easy to ride…"

Zoey remained interested as they talked about the horses, the trails, and the other things Beau and Charlotte liked to do around the inn. They talked about music and asked Johnny how he got started. Zoey seemed interested in that, too, and asked him a couple of questions. He began to wonder why he was rushing back to New York when she was just beginning to loosen up and they were finally starting to connect. Zoey's happiness was everything. He wanted to encourage it, not cut it short.

As he pulled out his phone to text Shea, he glanced at Jillian, catching her watching him again. This time she didn't look away, the curve to her lips more seductive than playful, confirming his decision to stay was the best one yet. He thumbed out a text to Shea. *Don't rush the statement. I want as much time here as possible. It's good for Zoey. Thanks.*

As the night wore on, his and Jillian's connection became more intense. He worried the others might notice and tried to temper the heat by not looking at her, but he was too drawn to the trace of wickedness in her eyes and her sexy smile, which carried a hint of challenge. There was no dousing the flames between them, but if anyone else noticed, they didn't let on.

Conversations died down, and Zoey and Charlotte slowly ran out of steam. Beau kissed Charlotte's temple. "I think it's time I got my shortcake home."

Charlotte looked at him adoringly as she and Jillian pushed to their feet. Not for the first time, he noticed Jillian looking longingly at Beau and Charlotte, just as she had when they'd held hands, kissed, or whispered privately.

"This was fun," Jillian said, drawing him from his thoughts as she hugged Charlotte. "We'll have fun raiding your closet for riding boots."

"Don't you always?" Charlotte teased.

"Thanks for hanging out with us," Johnny said as he put the grate over the firepit. "I enjoyed getting to know you both."

"We enjoyed it, too. I'll get the horses saddled up for you tomorrow," Beau said.

"Can I help?" Zoey looked at Johnny as she pushed to her feet. Bandit rose to all fours beside her.

"I was going to suggest we meet him at the barn instead of at the house so you could give him a hand," Johnny said. "Is that okay, Beau?"

"I'd like that," Beau said.

Zoey's smile was a mile wide.

"Congratulations again on your pregnancy," Johnny said.

"Thanks." Charlotte smiled at Zoey. "It was fun getting to know you." She hugged her, and to Johnny's surprise, Zoey returned the embrace. "No more midnight wanderings, right? I wouldn't be able to stand it if anything happened to you."

Johnny braced himself for Zoey to shut down, but she smiled a little sheepishly and shook her head.

"Right. I won't." Zoey turned to go inside.

"I'll walk you in," Johnny offered.

Zoey gave him an irritated look. "I'm fourteen. I don't need to be tucked in, and I just said I won't run away again." She quickly added, "Thanks, though."

"Right, sorry. G'night." As he watched Zoey and Bandit walk inside, he turned to Beau. "Is it okay that Bandit has stuck by her all this time?"

"It's more than okay." Beau slung an arm around Charlotte. "She needs him more than we do right now."

"I need a handbook for raising a teenage girl."

Beau laughed. "You and every other parent. Have a good night."

JILLIAN'S PULSE QUICKENED as Beau and Charlotte disappeared down the lane, leaving her alone with Johnny. The desires she'd been grappling with for two days crackled like live wires between them, the other night sounds magnifying in the quiet. She didn't want to deny her feelings for him, even though she knew she should. They'd already crossed a line that couldn't be uncrossed, but she couldn't stop thinking about the other night, and she wanted more. More of his hands and that evocative mouth. She wanted to feel *him* everywhere, and that lust was unstoppable, sneaking out in a dangerous game of cat and mouse. She should be wary of such strong desires, but she loved every second of it. She was still staring absently in the direction Beau and Charlotte had gone, but she could feel the heat of him coiling around her, hot, tight, and titillating.

He sidled up to her, setting those live wires ablaze. "What's going on in that gorgeous head of yours?"

A full-on war. "That I should go to bed, too," she said unconvincingly as he stepped in front of her. She kept her eyes trained on his chest to keep from looking into his eyes, fearing that if she did, her clothes would melt off. All of them in one fast *whoosh.*

He took her chin between his finger and thumb, lifting her face so she had no choice but to meet those devastatingly dark eyes. "That sounds good to me."

"Johnny." The word sounded as confused as she felt. "I work for you, and I don't need to be the designer who everyone thinks got the job because I screwed the rock star."

"I'd never let that happen."

"You know you can't control the media."

"But I *can* control who works for me." His lips quirked. "You're fired until we leave this place."

She laughed softly, and he pulled her into his arms. Her entire body flooded with awareness of his muscular frame, heightening her desires.

His fingers tangled in her hair. "Tell me you haven't been thinking about me." He brushed his lips over her cheek. "Tell me you don't want me, and I'll back off."

His hand skimmed up her side, causing shivers of heat, and brushed the side of her breast. She struggled against the desire vibrating inside her. "It would be a lie."

"Good." He kissed the edge of her mouth. "Because I can't stop thinking about you, either." He tugged her head back by her hair, sending scintillating sensations skating through her core. His mouth hovered a whisper above hers, his warm breath sweeping over her lips. "How many times have you thought about my mouth on you?" He dragged his tongue along her lower lip, and her breath rushed from her lungs. "How many times have you thought about me fucking you?"

She felt herself go damp, and a whimper escaped. She was *never* like this. Not with anyone, and she didn't want to fight it. He licked the shell of her ear, sending tingles rippling through her, and she closed her eyes, reveling in the luxurious feel of unstoppable lust.

"I'm so attracted to you, I can't think straight," he confessed gruffly, and bit her earlobe. She inhaled sharply, and he kept her there, with his mouth beside her ear, speaking low and gravelly. "This isn't me just wanting to get off, Jilly. There's something about you that makes me lose my mind. I haven't been with anyone since Ramona, and I've had plenty of opportunities, but I want *you*, Jilly, and I know you want me."

She tried to process that, and she knew he could be lying, but when he framed her face with his hands, gazing deeply into her eyes, the honesty staring back at her was inescapable.

"If I was just Johnny, and you were just Jilly, and my life wasn't a mess, and nobody knew who we were, what would you do right now?"

Her resolve snapped, and before she could think twice, she said, "Drag you into the shed and *fuck* you."

His smile registered for only a second before he captured her mouth in a feverish kiss that unleashed everything she'd been holding back. She tore at his shirt as they stumbled toward the shed, consumed by his kisses, his tongue sweeping and plunging, as if he couldn't get enough. His hands moved swiftly over her, groping her breasts, her ass, diving into her hair and *fisting* as her back hit the shed. He stilled, his eyes blazing, concern and lust intertwining. "Sorry."

"Rough is *good*," she reminded him, pulling his mouth back to hers.

He yanked the door open without breaking their kiss, and they stumbled inside, knocking into the shelves as he kicked the door closed. Moonlight spilled through the windows, illuminating balls and rackets as they tumbled to the floor, making Jillian and Johnny laugh as they stripped off each other's shirts. He deftly unhooked her bra and threw it to the floor. He tore his mouth away, biting and sucking his way down her neck and over her breast. His teeth brought a thrilling mix of pain and pleasure.

He leaned back, his gaze sweeping over her breasts. "You're so fucking sexy."

Jillian grabbed his hair as he sucked her nipple into his mouth, tongue swirling, teeth grazing her sensitive skin. Needy noises fell from her lips, but she was too lost in the pleasures consuming her to care. When his other hand pushed into her leggings, finding her clit like a heat-seeking missile, she gasped, "*Johnny*—" and went up on her toes as he took her to the edge of madness. She writhed and whimpered, pleading for more. He rose, taking her in a mind-numbing kiss as his fingers pushed inside her, and his thumb took over where his fingers had been, working her fast and toe-curlingly perfectly, catapulting her into ecstasy. She cried out into their kisses, hot sparks of pleasure exploding inside her. He continued his tantalizing touches as she rode out her pleasure, and then he kissed her softer, whispering against her lips, "I cannot wait to get my mouth on you."

"*Yes*," she panted out.

He tasted and nipped his way down her body, taking off her boots and stripping her bare between nips and touches. He grabbed her hips, pressing a kiss just above her sex, and dragged his tongue along her wetness. *Holy cow.* She gripped his shoulders, already on the edge again.

"*Fuck*, you're sweet."

His naughty praise wound through her. *Finally*, a man she didn't have to hold back with. "Just get busy," she said with a laugh, hungry for more.

He licked her again. One slow slide of his tongue, and her head fell back against the wall with a sigh.

"Oh, no, you don't," he said gruffly. "Watch me, Jilly. Watch me make you come."

She couldn't have been more wrong about him disappointing her. She looked down at him as he guided one of her legs over his shoulder and flicked his tongue like he'd been born to pleasure her, his dark eyes watching as his fingers invaded her again. *Sweet baby Jesus.* It took everything she had to keep her eyes open, but when he stroked that hidden spot so perfectly, the pleasure was too intense, and her eyes fluttered closed.

"Eyes on *me*, gorgeous," he demanded.

She opened her eyes. "Needy, aren't you?"

"I believe you mean *greedy*." He continued licking her until she was writhing and moaning, clutching his hair in her fists. He drew back, looking up at her with a devious grin, his lips wet with her arousal. "When you're lying in your bed thinking about *me* and you reach between your legs to relieve the pressure, I want you to see *my* face looking back at you, *my* mouth making you come."

His words turned her on as much as his touch. But she'd never admit that to him when it was so much fun to push his buttons. "How do you know I'm not picturing someone else while you're doing it right now?"

His gaze hardened. "Even if you are, you won't be when I'm done with you."

She added confidence and control to the list of sexy things about him as he feasted on her, teasing and taunting, rendering her unable to think past the sensations consuming her. She grabbed his thick hair with both hands, riding his mouth as he lit her on fire with every lick, suck, and scrape of his teeth. He did something with his fingers and tongue that sent her racing up to the edge and *held* her there. Her body quivered and quaked, her consciousness ebbing.

"Johnny—" A string of desperate pleas flew from her lips, but he didn't relent. Her legs trembled, his every touch alighting more flames, until she was breathless and shaking, and then he was pushing to his feet, leaving her bereft. *"Why'd you—"*

"We're finishing *together*," he growled.

"Hurry." She couldn't wait and tugged at the button on his jeans.

He shoved them down, and his erection sprang free. She reached for his thick length, but he lifted her into his arms, lowering her onto his cock. She cried out at the exquisite intrusion, her body stretching as he filled her. The raw, guttural sounds coming from him and the feel of his muscles flexing against her had her clawing at his shoulders, frantic for more. He gritted out, "So tight. That's it, baby, squeeze my cock," and reclaimed her mouth in a fiercely possessive kiss. It was freeing to finally be with a man who didn't hold back. She gave in to her desires as their bodies took over, urgently thrusting and riding for all they were worth. They ate at each other's mouths, fingernails digging into skin, heat scorching with every pump of his hips. She'd never felt so animalistic. She felt him *everywhere*. In the air swirling around them, the perspiration beading her flesh, and in the carnal desires drawing out, "*Harder...Yes...Don't stop.*"

He was right there with her, growling into her mouth. "So good, so...*Fuck.*" There was a bite to the curse, and he stilled. "We don't have a condom."

Her lust-addled brain tried to slow down, but she was too far gone. "We're *not* stopping. You'll have to pull out."

"You're not on birth control?"

"No! I'm not having sex with anyone. Why would I be on birth control?"

He looked down at their joined bodies, and they both laughed. His mouth crashed over hers, hard and demanding, as she rode him like she'd been waiting her whole life to do it. How could he feel so good? She didn't want to stop. He tore his mouth away with a groan. "*Fuck, Jilly. Fuck.*" In the next breath, she was lifted up and set on her feet, and he was turning her around. She reached for the wall as he drove into her from behind, both of them crying out with the intense pleasure. He thrust hard and fast, fucking her so exquisitely, she could barely breathe.

"Jesus, *Jilly.*" Her name sounded harsh, like a curse. "You feel too good. I'm close."

"Me too. *Don't stop.*"

He growled. "You're killing me." Hips thrusting, he reached around her stomach, touching her exactly where she needed it to spiral out of control. Her inner muscles clamped around his cock, hips bucking wildly.

"*Fuckfuckfuck—*" He pulled out, and she felt his warm come on her ass, his knuckles grazing her skin as he pumped his cock. His hips jerked against her, and he let out a long, low, "*Damn,*" as he came down over her back. "What're you doing to me?" he panted out. "I've never forgotten a condom."

Her head was too foggy, her body vibrating with such immense pleasure, she could only smile.

"Christ, Jilly. We're dangerous together." He bit her shoulder, and another needy sound fell from her lips. "Did I hurt you?"

"No," she panted out. "Can't talk yet."

He pressed a kiss where he'd bitten her, sending a chill down her spine, and held her until her legs stopped shaking. "Let me get my shirt, and I'll clean you up."

He cleaned her gently, and it was such an intimate thing to do, it took her by surprise. She'd expected sex with Johnny to be good. *Great* even. But not so all-consuming that she knew she'd relive his touch, his growly demands, and the way he felt inside her for weeks.

When he was done cleaning her up, he gathered her in his arms, pulling her against his nakedness. He felt oddly familiar, and insanely good, as if they'd been there before.

"Where's that snark?" he whispered. "You okay?"

"*Mm-hm.* Recovering. It's been a while."

"How long is a while?"

"Let's just say that your hookup hiatus has nothing on mine."

His brows knitted. "The way you toyed with me, I wouldn't've guessed that."

"It's also been a long time since I've flirted like that."

"Come on…?"

"What? I don't usually want to have sex with guys I don't know very well."

"You know more about me than most people do." He kissed her lips. "I'm honored to have broken your sex-fast with you."

"Shut up." She laughed and touched her forehead to his chest.

He lifted her face, gazing intently into her eyes. "I'm not done with that snarky mouth of yours."

He kissed her again, slowly and sweetly and so freaking tenderly, butterflies swarmed in her belly. *Nonono. No swarming.* Their lives were heading in two very different directions, too far apart for her to get wrapped up in him.

He brushed his nose along hers, whispering, "We're in a *shed*."

She laughed. "I guess now I have an answer for the strangest place

I've ever had sex. And *no*, I don't want to know your answer."

His expression turned serious. "It's not what you think."

"You don't know what I think."

"You think it's me and a handful of women in a hot tub, or back-stage, or in a limo."

"I didn't think of any of those things, but thanks for the imagery. I told you I don't want to know." She tried to push out of his arms, but he tightened his hold on her.

"It was in a shed behind Snow White's house with a gorgeous designer who drives me out of my fucking mind."

She rolled her eyes, but she couldn't help swooning a little.

"Seriously," he said gruffly. "I've had a lot of sex, but not in creative places."

"I *don't* want to know." She moved out of his grasp. He watched her step into her thong and started getting hard again. Heck if her body didn't throw a little celebration.

He must've seen it in her eyes, because he arched a brow and said, "What do you say we work on stockpiling answers for those most-creative-place questions? I bet we can find a number of unique places around here."

God, he was *too* addicting. She needed to try to keep her head on straight. "Don't act like I'm a sure thing," she said, trying to convince herself more than him.

He hauled her back into his arms, and her entire body flamed. "Does that mean you're going to try to resist me again? Because I kind of get off on winning you over."

He was a little too good at winning her over, too, but she liked knowing he got off on it.

"You could at least acknowledge that you like me," he said, sliding his hands down to her butt.

"I never said I didn't."

He lowered his lips to hers, kissing her so deeply, every part of her begged for more. He brushed his lips over hers, whispering, "And you like having sex with me."

She forced herself not to agree, using all her willpower to summon her snark as she stepped out of his arms. "It was pretty good." She grabbed her sweater. "Now put that viper away before I do it for you."

He waggled his brows. "I'd like to burrow in your den, baby."

She laughed. "Get dressed. You've had enough burrowing. We've got to clean this up, or Beau will slaughter me." She picked up a croquet ball. "I'll never look at lawn games the same again."

He chuckled, and as they dressed, he said, "I hate to ask you this, but do you think you can run into town tomorrow and get some condoms? Magnum XL."

"You didn't bring any?" There was no masking the shock in her tone.

"I was a little sidetracked when I was packing, and shouldn't you be offended if I *had* brought them?"

"Um…*yes*." She laughed and finished dressing.

After they tidied the shed, they grabbed the marshmallows and other accoutrements they'd left by the firepit and headed back to the cottage to put everything away. When they headed upstairs, Johnny put a hand on her lower back. Why did she have to like that possessive touch so much? They both glanced at Zoey's door, which was closed.

"I think we *all* had a good night," he whispered.

She nodded in agreement. "She's loosening up, trusting you more."

"She trusts *you*." He drew her into his arms again. "That seems to be going around."

Her heart stumbled, and she thought about the secret he'd kept for so long about his mother and how long he said it had been since he'd had sex, and the fact that they'd just had sex in her brother's shed and she'd trusted *him* to pull out. She barely recognized the brazen woman she'd become tonight. *Yeah, that whole trust thing is going around all right.*

"Tomorrow night. Midnight. You and me in the barn, and don't even try to pretend you don't want to meet me there." Dark promises glimmered in his eyes. "Prepare to be ravaged and *wow*ed."

He lowered his lips to hers, kissing her so passionately, she felt herself getting lost in him again. When their lips parted, he sauntered into his room without a backward glance, closing the door behind him, while she tried to remember how to breathe.

Chapter Eleven

ZOEY BEAMED AS she rode Ginger, a chestnut mare, across the field to Beau with Bandit trotting beside them. Beau had shown her how to post, to lead and guide the horse, and to trot. She'd been at it for almost an hour, and her smile was enough to make Johnny wish he owned horses. She'd bounded down the stairs this morning like a different kid, and she'd talked about how she was looking forward to riding throughout breakfast. Her bright mood had lifted a weight from Johnny's shoulders. He knew it may not last even throughout the day, but he was soaking in every second while it did.

Jillian sauntered over, gorgeous in a tight black sweater and skinny jeans tucked into riding boots. He'd thought last night might take the edge off his desire for her, but it had only made him want her more. He'd heard her downstairs after he'd gone to bed, and it had taken everything he had not to go down and coax her back into his arms. When she'd finally stumbled downstairs this morning, hair a mess, wearing slinky pink sleeping shorts and a matching tank, he'd sworn she'd bent over a little further to get her Diet Pepsi out of the fridge just to drive him wild. That could've been all in his head, but then she'd said she didn't want any breakfast and ate off his plate, as if they were a couple who shared. The look in her eyes wasn't that of a couple, though. It was the look of a challenging seductress, and the sexy innuendos she'd been tossing him all morning sure weren't in his head. She kept him on his toes, knowing he had to keep himself in check when Zoey was around. Not that he minded the juggling act. He was as determined to help Zoey feel safe and like she was never a bother or intrusion as he was to spend more time with Jillian.

Helping Zoey was an uphill battle, but he was going to make sure they made it to the top together. That was why he was bringing his guitar on the trail ride. He needed something to distract him from Jillian's taunts and hoped music might bring him and Zoey closer together.

"She'd probably love to take riding lessons when you get back home," Jillian said as she stepped beside him.

"I was thinking the same thing. I bet there's a lot of things she wants to do, and I look forward to finding out what they are and trying to make them happen."

"For a guy who didn't want to be a dad, you're catching on pretty quickly. Is that why you packed a picnic lunch? Because she said she'd never been on a picnic last night during the bonfire?"

"You were so intent on driving me crazy, I didn't think you heard that conversation."

"I never miss a thing," she said with a smirk. "I would've helped pack lunch if you'd asked."

He grinned at her. "I'm not sure Twix and Diet Pepsi are enough sustenance for any of us."

She laughed, looking so cute and happy, he had the urge to hook his arm around her neck and pull her into a kiss. The weirdest thing about that was that it felt natural, and it definitely wasn't. He hadn't wanted to put his arm around anyone in a long time. He'd had a good enough relationship with Ramona, but he'd never felt like they were a real couple. They'd been on a hamster wheel, catching up when they could. Ramona had been safe. She wasn't with him for his status, and he didn't have to worry about her sleeping around or causing unnecessary drama. He'd enjoyed hanging out with her, and the sex wasn't bad, although a little vanilla for his taste, but he hadn't thought about her when they weren't together, as he did with Jillian.

"Why are you looking at me like that?" she asked.

"Because I want to kiss you right now and I can't." He'd scoped out the barn and was already making plans for their midnight tryst.

Her eyes widened, the heat in them undeniable. "Darn right you can't. Don't say that. Someone might hear you and get the wrong impression."

He glanced from side to side. "Who's going to hear me? The seven dwarfs? The deer?"

"Just keep it to yourself, please."

"That's not what you wanted last night."

She glowered at him. "Chalk that up to a momentary slip in my rational thinking, and *stop* looking at me like that."

"Then maybe you should stop looking so beautiful, and don't smile or lick your lips or *breathe*, for fuck's sake."

She laughed. "It'll be hard not to breathe while I'm riding a horse."

"Even harder when you're riding me later."

Her eyes widened. "I told you I'm *not* a sure thing, Mr. Bad."

"But you want to be."

She futilely tried to hide her smile and crossed her arms, lifting that adorable chin and turning her attention to Zoey, all of which did nothing to stop the sparks flying between them.

He was beginning to wonder if anything could.

JOHNNY HAD TRAVELED extensively, holing up in gorgeous hotel rooms all over the world without ever venturing too far. That was one thing that sucked about fame. Privacy was nonexistent unless it was demanded and protected like Fort Knox. He'd never felt like he'd missed out by not exploring those places. But as he rode a white horse named Sugar along a rocky dirt trail behind Jillian and Zoey, taking in the serenity of their surroundings—untamed grasses, stately trees, and gnarly bushes—with the crisp fall air kissing his skin and the clear blue sky smiling down on them, he wondered how much he'd missed. That thought led him to think about the time he'd missed with Zoey. Was she a happy kid when she was younger, like she was today, or had she always had a surly streak?

She and Jillian were talking loudly as they crossed a meadow. Jillian was pointing out different places along the trail, like where Beau had once showed her a fox's den, and another trail that led through a heavily treed area. Zoey glanced over her shoulder at Johnny, her smile radiating happiness. The warmth spreading through his chest must be the *love like no other* Dion and Chad, two of his bandmates, both divorced, had talked about with regard to their own children. They said they missed their kids every day they were apart. Johnny hadn't thought too much about that. People got divorced all the time, but even after just a few days with Zoey, he couldn't imagine not seeing her every day.

She and Jillian began talking about the ways in which Zoey had been making subtle changes to her new clothes, like cutting her skinny jeans to crop them, fraying hems, and somehow making small holes in the sweater she wore without unraveling it, giving it an edgier look. He'd thought her clothes had come that way. He was glad she was finding a way to express her creativity.

A little while later he was settling into the bumpy sway of the horse as they waded through a creek. Zoey squealed with delight, and Jillian looked back at him with a knowing expression. He lifted his chin in acknowledgment, glad she'd mentioned Beau and Char's place in the middle of all the chaos the morning they'd met. If she hadn't, he'd probably have whisked Zoey out of the country and holed up in a hotel, where she'd have been so bored, she'd probably have run away every damn day. This place, and having Jillian with them, was more of a blessing than she could ever know.

They crossed a pasture and made their way up to the crest of a hill with glorious views of pastures, trees, and mountains in the distance. Jillian looked at them and said, "This is a beautiful spot to have lunch. Okay?"

"Looks good to me," Johnny said.

He and Jillian dismounted, and as she tied their horses to a tree, he set down his guitar and helped Zoey off her horse. "What'd you think, sunshine?"

"It's so peaceful. I wish I could go riding every day," Zoey said.

"You probably can while we're here," he said as he tied her horse to a tree.

"Really?" Zoey's eyes lit up.

"We'll have to clear it with Beau and Char, and you'll have to be with one of us. I don't want you going off on a horse alone."

"I won't. I promise."

"And if we're going to ride every day, then we should probably help Beau with caring for the horses while we're here. Feeding, watering, whatever they need."

"Okay. I will. *Jilly!*" she hollered. "Johnny said I can ride every day while we're here!"

"That's *great*." Those vixenish eyes landed on him. "You know, I think I'd be up for daily rides, too."

She enjoyed torturing him far too much. *Watch out, winger. Two can play at this game.*

"Really?" Zoey asked excitedly.

Johnny held Jillian's gaze and said, "Sounds like she's a *sure thing* to me."

JILLIAN CHIDED HERSELF for leaving that door wide open. She kept forgetting that Johnny was better at innuendos than she was. She went for a change in subject. "Boy am I hungry. Who's up for lunch?"

"I'm always up for a good meal." Johnny smirked. "Or a midnight snack."

The image of him on his knees, growling out demands, popped into Jillian's mind, and she felt her cheeks burn. Why did she have to like his dirty side so much? And don't even get her started on how seeing his relationship with Zoey blossom was making her all warm and fuzzy inside. She didn't know what to do with warm and fuzzy. It was as alluring as the white-hot lust coursing between them.

He flashed a wolfish grin and opened the saddlebags to get their lunches.

They sat in the grass eating turkey sandwiches, chips, and apple and carrot slices. Jillian was impressed that Johnny had packed little containers of peanut butter to dip the apples in, and he'd even remembered napkins and drinks.

"I feel like I'm in grade school. You packed a perfectly healthy lunch. You must've been a mom in your former life," Jillian teased.

"My mom never packed me lunch. She never even cooked for me," Zoey said flatly.

"I'm sorry. I didn't mean to bring that up," Jillian said, feeling bad for saying it. She wondered how many times Zoey had heard kids at school, or people around her, talking about their mothers in a positive way, and whether she'd made comments to them or had kept that hurt to herself. If she had kept it to herself, that meant she trusted Jillian and Johnny enough to tell them how she really felt, and that was something, wasn't it?

"It's okay. My mom was useless, but my grandmother was awesome." Zoey bit into her sandwich. "Maybe Johnny was a grandmother in a former life."

Johnny nudged Zoey's foot with his. "Does that mean you think I'm doing okay as your dad?"

Zoey looked at him for a long time, her expression giving nothing away. Jillian hoped she'd say something nice. Was this what it was like for all parents? At the mercy of their kids' attitudes? Hoping for kindness and often getting snark in return? She thought of her own parents, who must be gluttons for punishment, having so many kids so close together.

"I guess you don't suck at it," Zoey finally said.

Jillian exhaled with relief.

"I'll take that." Johnny finished his sandwich and reached for his guitar. "Mind if I play?"

Zoey shook her head and ate an apple slice. "You don't act like a rock star."

"No? Why not?" He strummed his guitar.

His guard was coming down, too, and it was nice to see him relaxing a little.

"I don't know," Zoey said, eating a chip. "I thought rock stars partied and did drugs all the time."

"I used to party a lot, but not anymore. I drank more than I should back then, but drugs have never been my thing. I don't like anything that messes with my head." Johnny's brows knitted. "Have you tried drugs?"

Zoey shook her head. "I knew kids in school who smoked weed, and it made them act spacey." She looked at Jillian. "Have you done drugs?"

"No. I tried smoking pot once, but I didn't like how it made me feel. It slowed me down too much," Jillian said, glad Johnny had been honest with Zoey.

"What about your band?" Zoey asked Johnny. "Do they party a lot?"

He continued strumming his guitar and looked her in the eyes. "Are you asking because you hope you can party with them, or are you just curious?" He sounded very fatherly.

Zoey's expression turned to one of disgust. "I don't want to party with a bunch of old guys."

Jillian stifled a giggle.

"Fair enough," Johnny said.

"So, do they?" Zoey pushed.

"Adrian, our drummer, was into drugs for a while, and they nearly killed him. He got clean a few years ago and hasn't touched them since. Chad, our other guitarist, smokes weed, but he doesn't touch other drugs. He's divorced, and he usually smokes when he's missing his kids, and Dion, our keyboardist, can drink anyone under the table, but he doesn't touch drugs. He's also divorced, but he tends not to drink when he misses his kids."

Zoey seemed to think about that for a minute as she ate her sandwich. "How did you meet them?"

"Adrian and I have been friends since we were kids. My manager tried to get me to play in a boy band a couple of years after he started managing my career, and Dion was part of that band. He and I got along great and I gave the band a shot, but I hated it. I wanted to keep doing my own thing. Dion and I remained friends, and I introduced him to Adrian, and we all started playing together. We eventually formed Bad Intentions, and a couple of months later we heard Chad playing in a bar, and we all clicked and started jamming together. It wasn't long after that when he joined the band. They're good guys. Like family. You'll meet them once we're back home."

Zoey lowered her eyes and pulled her knees up to her chest. "What if your friends don't like me?"

"Then they'll miss out on knowing a great kid," he said earnestly. "But it won't change a damn thing between you and me, and that's a promise."

"But you *need* your band," Zoey said softly, eyes clouded with worry. "You don't *need* me."

"No, sunshine, I don't *need* my band. I don't need anyone in my life other than family, and that *includes* you."

"But you just said *they're* like family," she insisted.

"Yes, they are *like* family. That means I love them *like* they're my family, but it's different from how I feel about you or my parents or my brother and sisters. It's hard to explain. You know how you felt about your grandmother?"

She nodded.

"That's what I feel for you," he said softly but firmly. "I realized how strongly I felt it the night you ran away, and I knew I didn't want to go a single day without you in my life. I know it'll take time for you to trust that I'm a man of my word, but as I said before, *you're* my daughter. My *family*. We're a team now, and I will never leave you behind. Not now, not ten years from now, not *ever*, and I hope one day you'll realize that you don't have to worry about that anymore."

"But you *just* met me," she said emphatically.

"That's right. It's hard for me to comprehend, too, but what I feel is real. I feel it in here." He patted his chest over his heart. "You've already claimed a piece of my heart that will *always* be yours. And if I thought you'd let me, I'd give you one of those stupid hugs right now, because I don't want you to be sad or to worry about where you belong. I want you to know that wherever *I* am is where you belong."

Zoey's worry hung over them like a dark cloud, but Johnny's sincerity showed in his eyes, his face, his *energy*.

Zoey inhaled deeply and wiped her eyes. "Now I feel stupid."

"Why?" Jillian and Johnny said at once.

"Because I want to trust you," she said to Johnny. "But I'm afraid."

This time Johnny didn't hesitate to move over and wrap his arms around his daughter. "It's okay to be afraid. That's not stupid. It's because of everything you've been through. But I'm not going anywhere."

As he held Zoey, Jillian met his gaze, nodding encouragingly. She hurt for both of them, but she knew this was exactly what they needed. For Zoey to feel safe enough to share her deepest worries and for Johnny to share what had become his truth. She knew in her heart that he would go to the ends of the earth if that's what it took to make sure Zoey never had to worry about where she belonged again.

A little while later, as Zoey went to pet the horses, Johnny sat on a rocky outcropping playing his guitar. One of the horses pressed her muzzle into Zoey's chest. Zoey smiled and scratched the horse's big head.

"She loves those horses," Jillian said as she lowered herself beside Johnny.

"Yeah. I'll have to get her one."

"Slow down, Daddy Big Bucks. Where would you keep it? You live in a penthouse. You might want to start with lessons."

"I don't do anything halfway." He winked. "Do you think she's okay?"

"I think she's going through all the emotions you'd expect her to. She needs to trust that you're not like her mother and you're not going to abandon her. She'll come around, but it could take a long time. Years, even, to fully trust. What her mother did will probably affect every relationship she ever has."

He glanced at Zoey, his brows slanting. "I hate that her mother made her feel so unwanted. Childhood is supposed to be about having fun with friends and family and figuring out who you are. Not having a mother who is in and out of your life like you don't matter and then being left with strangers while she parties. At least she had her grandmother, and that's the only saving grace. I think she learned what love and stability are from her grandmother. But I agree, trust might always be an issue."

"I talked to Jax this morning, and he suggested talking to a therapist."

"I've been thinking about that, too. Beau gave me a couple of numbers, including Dare Whiskey at Redemption Ranch. He said he works closely with teens."

"Jax mentioned him. He said all the therapists at the ranch are good."

"I know. Beau told me. I'll give Dare a call."

Zoey looked over, and Johnny called over to her. "Are you okay?"

"Yeah." She petted Spice, a beautiful dark brown horse. "What if you change your mind? Where will I go?"

A lump lodged in Jillian's throat.

"I will never do that to you," he reassured her.

"But maybe that's because we're *here*, and when you're with your band you won't want a kid anymore." Zoey said it in a very grown-up fashion, as if she'd been thinking it over and had come to that painful conclusion.

"It's not because we're here," he reassured her. "You can ask me a hundred times in a hundred different ways. Here, in New York, or anywhere else, and the answer will always be the same. It's you and me, kid. Forever." He started playing the theme song from the show *Friends*.

Zoey smiled. "You're such a *dork*."

"But he's *your* dork," Jillian said as he sang.

"Come on, sing with me," he urged.

"No." Zoey was smiling so big, it made Jillian feel a little better.

Johnny arched a brow at Jillian. She jumped to her feet and began dancing like they did at the beginning of the show, singing the chorus with Johnny. He pushed to his feet, playing the guitar and singing louder.

"Come on, Zo!" Jillian ran over and took her hand, pulling her away from the horses to dance with her.

Zoey blushed a red streak, and Johnny joined them, singing to Zoey about how he'd always be there for her. She covered her face, turning around, and he followed, making her laugh.

"What's the matter? You don't like my song?" he asked.

"It's from a hundred years ago," Zoey complained, but she was grinning from ear to ear.

"Looks like I'm going to have to teach you to play, so you can teach *me* to be young and hip. Because you know, I'm just an old rock star."

Johnny started playing one of his rock songs, singing louder, and Jillian grabbed Zoey's hand, dancing until Zoey finally relented and danced with her. They laughed and did silly moves, making faces at Johnny as he played one song after another, until Jillian and Zoey fell into each other's arms, laughing and out of breath.

ZOEY'S GOOD MOOD carried over for the rest of the day, and later that night, after dinner, Jillian was working on designs and texting with Trixie, when Johnny came through the front door looking ridiculously sexy after his run. His hair was finger combed and a little sweaty, and his shirt was stuck to his body, leaving very little to the imagination.

"Where's Zoey?" he asked.

"Eating ice cream in the kitchen with Bandit."

His eyes filled with wickedness, and he sauntered over, putting one hand beside her head on the back of the couch and leaning in so close their lips almost touched.

Jillian's heart raced. "What are you doing?"

He gathered her hair in his other hand. "Taking a taste of what's going to be *mine* later." He yanked her head back and crushed his mouth to hers in a penetrating kiss, setting her entire body on fire. He tore his mouth away, eyes full of dirty promises as he straightened to his full height and said, "See you at midnight," and sauntered toward the kitchen.

Jillian shuddered with anticipation. She closed her eyes, trying to calm her racing heart. She heard Zoey ask him if he'd meant what he'd said about teaching her to play guitar. She opened her eyes, listening for Johnny's answer.

"Of course," he answered. "I'd like that. We can get started after I shower, if you want."

"Okay, thanks."

The smile in Zoey's voice told Jillian they'd turned a corner, at least for now, and she filled with happiness for the man and the girl who were weaseling their way into her heart.

Chapter Twelve

JOHNNY WAS A man on a mission. He wanted to make tonight special for Jillian, and he'd been stealthily preparing all day. He'd asked Beau if he could borrow a few things from his workshop that he'd seen the other night when he'd been searching for Zoey, and Beau had said to help himself. After their trail ride, while Zoey had gone to her bedroom to read and Jillian had gone into town, Johnny had gathered supplies and taken them down to the barn.

Shortly before midnight, he checked on Zoey one last time and found her fast asleep in her room with Bandit lying at the foot of her bed. He had a feeling she had a month of sleepless nights to catch up on. He'd enjoyed showing her the basics of how to play guitar. He'd thought she might get frustrated, but her face had pinched in concentration, and she'd been determined to learn, asking, *Is this right?* and, *Like this?* She'd asked if he could teach her to read music, and they'd practiced for nearly two hours. She'd asked if they could do more tomorrow, and when he'd said he'd like that, he could tell she wanted to hug him, but she'd held back, and he hadn't pushed.

He looked down the hall at Jillian's closed door and heard her talking. To herself or someone on the phone, he didn't know, and he didn't stick around to find out. He hurried downstairs to grab a bottle of wine and opened it. He borrowed one of the bottle toppers he'd found, filled the ice bucket, and put the wine in it as he headed outside. He'd barely gotten off the porch before thoughts of Zoey stopped him. He went back inside and wrote a note to Zoey in case she woke up.

Z, Jilly and I took a walk. Jilly's number is in my phone. Text and we'll come right back. He thought about how to sign it. *XO? Love?* He went with the safest option and simply signed his name. He put the note and his phone on the kitchen table and headed back outside.

When he'd gone running earlier, he'd retrieved a number of battery-operated lanterns from Beau's workshop and had set them out along the darkest parts of the path to the barn. As he made his way there now, he turned them on for Jillian.

He pushed through the trees and stepped into the clearing, greeted by the sounds of the babbling brook that snaked along the left side of the barn. Moonlight sparkled like diamonds in the creek where Charlotte's grandfather had created rocky waterfalls, and wildflowers poked out between long blades of grass at the water's edge. This place *was* pretty magical. Just being there, away from prying eyes and the fast pace of the Big Apple had lessened the stress of the situation, allowing Johnny to focus on the scared girl who needed him and the burgundy-haired firecracker who acted like there was nothing she couldn't handle.

Except cooking, diapers, and puke, he mused.

Jillian might not need him in the sense that she could forage for food and take care of herself, but he had a feeling that beneath that tough exterior was a woman who might enjoy being taken care of if she ever gave anyone a chance.

He went to the water's edge and picked some of Jillian's favorite flowers, and then he made his way into the barn and went to work. He lined up hay bales to form a bed and spread the blankets and pillows he'd carried down earlier over them and placed the flowers on the blanket. He wished he could take Jillian out on a real date. Yet another unfamiliar urge. He pushed away the impossibility and swept the area around the hay bales all the way down to the concrete floor. He put the ice bucket beside the makeshift bed and placed the candles he'd found in the cottage in metal buckets. After lighting them, he hung the buckets from hooks in the rafters to keep the flames away from the hay.

When he was done, he stepped back, taking it all in. He'd never done anything like this before. He'd had money since he was old enough to want to spend it, and he'd never had to impress or wine and dine any woman. Once he'd been discovered, girls of all ages had thrown themselves at him. It felt good making an effort for Jillian, and it looked kind of romantic, with the flowers and the candles, which made him a little nervous. *Jesus.* He couldn't remember ever being nervous about being with a woman. Even the first time he'd had sex, he'd done what he'd always done, just barreled into it knowing he'd nail it.

He hadn't.

He'd come way too fast, but that had only driven him to hone that skill and become the best fuck possible.

He reached into his back pocket for his phone to check the time and remembered he'd left it for Zoey. Taking a deep, calming breath, he paced, the smell of the horses bringing memories of their afternoon. It had been a good one, and tomorrow he was going to call Dare. He wanted so badly to do everything right for Zoey and knew that no matter how hard he tried, he was sure to come up short. But maybe loving her was more important than always saying and doing the right things.

A horse made a noise, pulling him from his thoughts. It had to be close to midnight. Where was Jillian? He went outside, pacing the grass. Why was it that minutes felt like hours when he was waiting for something? As time passed, his gut knotted, and he wondered if she was standing him up.

He thought she was just as into him as he was into her. Had he completely misread her taunts? Had she been flirting with no intention of continuing what they'd started?

He walked back into the barn, reassessing all that he'd done, and suddenly he felt like a fool. They'd *fucked*, and that was all it was. Hadn't she said as much? So why was he getting carried away? She was probably up at the cottage working in a skimpy outfit, not even thinking about him. Or worse, thinking about how she'd gotten the better of him.

Silently cursing himself, he took down the buckets and blew out the candles.

"Hey, thanks for putting out the lanterns."

His pulse ricocheted at the sound of Jillian's voice. He turned around, and those knots in his gut loosened at the sight of her sweet smile. She looked beautiful in a sweater and jeans. "Hi."

"Sorry I'm so late. I was on the phone with my sisters-in-law about my friend's wedding, and every time I tried to get off, someone needed one more thing."

"And here I thought you weren't coming."

"Didn't you get my text?"

He shook his head. "I left my phone with a note in the kitchen for Zoey in case she woke up."

"That was smart." She peered around him, brow furrowing. "What is all this?"

"Nothing," he said gruffly, feeling ridiculous.

She glanced in the buckets he was holding. "Are those *candles*? Did you light them for us?"

"Yes, *okay*?" He set the buckets down. "I lit candles, I brought wine, made a bed, and picked flowers, and yes, I'm a fucking idiot. Go ahead and give me shit. I wanted to do something special for you because you're a gorgeous, classy woman, and you're worth more than a dirty fuck in the barn."

She got a little dreamy eyed. "That might be the sweetest thing anyone's ever done for me." She stepped forward, hooking her finger into the waist of his jeans, and dreamy went out the window, replaced with a hint of sin. "But I was kind of excited for a dirty fuck in the barn." She lifted her other hand, dangling a string of condom packets from it.

"Baby, I can make that happen." His mouth came roughly down over hers, taking the kiss he'd been dying for all day. She tasted sweet, kissing him like she'd been dying for it all day, too. She went up on her toes, moaning into their kisses, unleashing the incessant desire he'd been wrestling with. They devoured each other, urgent and ravenous, teeth gnashing as they made their way to the blankets. He pulled off her sweater, revealing bare flesh and peaked nipples. "You *dirty* girl. Your tits are insane." He sealed his mouth over one taut peak, teasing and sucking, reveling in the greedy sounds spilling from her lips.

"God, Johnny...So good." She pushed at his shirt, and he reached over his back, tugging it off.

Her eyes flamed, and she slicked her tongue over his nipple, then bit down hard.

"Fuuck." Heat streaked straight to his cock. "I need that sexy mouth on me."

She was already fumbling with the button of his jeans. He shoved them down, and she fisted his length, giving him a tight stroke. Her eyes flicked up to his as she bent at the waist and swirled her tongue around the head. She licked him from base to tip, slowing to tease, taunt, and kiss, all while holding his gaze. She *was* his dirty girl, and he couldn't get enough of her.

"Suck it, baby. Let me fuck your mouth."

She took him in deep, and he groaned at the feel of her hot, wet mouth, his hips pistoning forward. She continued stroking and sucking so perfectly, he tangled his hands in her hair, steeling himself against the pressure stacking up inside him. Her eyes remained trained on his, lips stretched around his cock. Watching her taking him deep was the sexiest thing he'd ever seen. But he wanted *more.* He needed to *claim* her, to mark her as *his,* and he knew his dirty girl would be up for anything. "You're so fucking beautiful. I want you *naked* and on your knees."

The lascivious grin forming on her lips nearly did him in. "Do you?" She swirled the tip of her tongue around the head of his cock, while stroking him tight with her hand. "What if I want *you* naked and on your knees?"

Tightening his grip on her hair, he tugged her up to her feet. "You and I both know there's no *if.*" He crushed his mouth to hers, fucking her mouth with his tongue as he'd just done with his dick. They both went a little wild, tugging off boots and tearing at pants, until they were naked. He reclaimed her mouth, teasing between her legs with his fingers. "So ready for me. I can't wait to fuck you again, but first…" He caressed her cheek and brushed his thumb over her lower lip. "I need this mouth. On your knees, sexy girl, and don't give me any sass. I'll be on mine soon enough."

She sank down to her knees, and he fisted his cock, dragging it over her lips. "Lick me." Her tongue slid over his aching dick. "That's it. Touch yourself while you do it."

Her eyes flamed as she reached between her legs. "Someone gets off on control."

"Are we going to pretend you don't?"

Her eyes narrowed as she dragged her tongue along his cock, moaning with every stroke. He pushed just the head into her mouth, and when she closed her lips around it, he said, "*Open your mouth.*" She opened wide, still working her pussy. "That's it. I want to *watch* you lick it." He withdrew, pushing just the head in again, and began pumping his hips, never going deeper, as she licked, stroking herself *and* him, eyes pleading for more. *So fucking gorgeous.*

She pulled back, eyes blazing. "Stop teasing and just *do it,* or you're done seeing me on my knees."

"Now you're learnin'." He pushed into her mouth, and she grabbed his hips, pulling him in deeper. "Christ, you're good at this," he hissed. He pumped as she sucked and stroked, and *holy hell.* He was going to lose it. "I want to come in your mouth, baby."

She drew back, challenge brimming in her eyes. "Only if I can come in yours."

"Damn right you will." He lifted her to her feet, kissing her hard and deep, leaving them both a little breathless. "Now sit your pretty little ass on the edge of that blanket." He smacked her ass, earning a seductive glare as she sat on the hay bed.

He tossed the condoms beside her and stepped between her legs. She wrapped her fingers around his length, guiding him into her mouth, and proceeded to drive him out of his mind. "That's it, baby. *Jesus*...So damn good." He pushed his hands into her hair, losing himself in her. "Your mouth is *mine*," he growled. She quickened her efforts, and he was right there with her, thrusting faster, unable to hold back the stream of curses and demands. *"Suck harder. Squeeze...Aw fuuck."* His jaw clenched and his legs flexed, pressure mounting like a turbulent wave, barreling down his spine, exploding with violent thrusts and gritted-out curses. She didn't pull back, didn't try to escape the flood of his desire, and when she tickled his balls, he groaned at the intensity of the pleasure ravaging him.

When the last aftershock jerked through him and she released his dick, he cradled her face in his hands and tried to catch his breath. He looked down at the incredible woman who was taking him to unimaginable heights. Her eyes were soft and hazy, as if she were as drunk on him as he was on her, tugging at something deep inside him. He caressed her jaw, wanting to spend a month getting to know every dip and curve of her body, learning all her erogenous zones, and exploring those often-overlooked spots that made her gasp or giggle. He wanted to see her on her own turf, on her own terms, and know what she was like in her beloved small town, with the family and friends who he was sure adored her.

He had no idea where that had come from. He'd never met a woman who could *own* him before, but he knew it wasn't the magic of the inn he had to worry about. Jillian Braden worked her own brand of magic. He tried to combat that surge of emotions by regaining control.

"Spread those legs, sexy girl. It's your turn."

JILLIAN HAD NEVER gotten off giving a blow job before, but between Johnny's dirty demands and knowing *she* made him lose control, she was on the brink of orgasm *before* he even sank to his knees and started making good on all his sinful promises. She tried to keep her emotions in check and not think about his efforts to make tonight special, but the look on his face when he'd told her what he'd done was as ingrained in her head as the look in his eyes right before he sank to his knees.

She closed her eyes as he devoured her to perfection. If it were possible to die from pleasure, she was pretty sure her life was at risk. His teeth grazed her clit, and she came undone like a wild animal, clawing at his shoulders, begging him not to stop. He pushed his fingers inside her, and all thoughts fell away, obliterated by the tantalizing sensations and sheer *need* coursing through her. "*Johnny*," she pleaded, and he quickened his efforts, expertly sending her spiraling into ecstasy. He stayed with her, feasting as they rode out the last of her climax.

Then he pressed feathery kisses to her inner thighs and tasted his way up her body, his handsome face coming into focus above her.

She reached up and stroked his scruffy jaw, panting out, "Am I dead? Is this heaven?"

He grinned. "If it is, I want to die a thousand deaths."

God, even the things he said got to her.

The taste of him still lingered in her mouth as he lowered his lips to hers. The taste of *her* was just as ripe as their tongues tangled, revving her up anew.

"You still up for a dirty fuck?" He kissed the edge of her lips. "Or did I wear you out?"

She was giddy at the prospect. "You mean you can go again?"

"Baby, we're just getting started." He rocked his hips, brushing his hard length against her, sending shivers of lust racing through her. "Scoot up, baby girl. This Bad boy is ready to ride."

She moved up to the head of the makeshift bed, her heart pounding with anticipation as he tore open a condom packet with his teeth and sheathed his length. She'd never been this into any man, and with Johnny, she couldn't get enough. Her body tingled with anticipation as he crawled over her, those dark eyes eliciting all sorts of naughty thoughts.

His cock pressed enticingly against her entrance as he said, "I thought about fucking you all day."

His voice was gravelly and so full of emotion, the truth came easily. "Me too."

His mouth came down over hers as their bodies came together. With his weight bearing down on her, the pressure was even more intense, more gratifying than last night, which she hadn't thought possible.

"*Christ, Jilly.* Nothing has *ever* felt so good."

For me either.

His mouth claimed hers, demanding and rough, and *oh*, what a thrill it was! They pumped and rocked in perfect sync. He lifted her legs at the knees, holding them by his hips, driving in so deep her toes curled under. How did he know what she liked? What she needed?

"So tight," he growled. "So damn good." He rocked his hips at an angle that sent sharp, excruciating pleasure searing through her like lightning. She cried out with the intensity, and he broke the kiss, worried eyes drilling into her. "Too hard?"

"*Never.*"

A rough chuckle tumbled out, and he reclaimed her mouth, their bodies grinding and rocking. She clung to him, her nails digging into his flesh as he pushed his hands beneath her and grabbed her ass, pounding into her like they'd never get another chance. *This* was what she always craved. A man who wasn't afraid to take what he wanted but would still give her what she needed.

"Hold on, baby." He held her tight and rolled onto his back without breaking their connection.

She didn't miss a beat, riding him like she had in her fantasies. He groped her breasts, squeezing her nipples between his finger and thumb so hard the pain turned to pleasure. Their moans and pleas filled the barn, bodies growing slick with sweat despite the chilly air. Desire burned beneath her skin, pulsing and billowing, until she felt like she was going to explode. His hand zeroed in on the sensitive nerves at the apex of her sex, and her eyes slammed shut. Holding on to her sanity by a thread, she wanted—*needed*—him to come with her. She reached behind her, taking hold of his balls, and he bit out a curse, his hips shooting up, sending tides of pleasure crashing over her. *"Johnny—"* flew from her lips as he surrendered to his own powerful release, gritting out her name like a prayer.

They rode out their passion until she collapsed, boneless and sated, onto his chest. His arms circled her, his fingers threading into her hair as he kissed her cheek, his heart hammering against hers. She wanted to stay right there, close her eyes, and sleep in his arms, which was exactly why she rolled onto her back beside him.

"Wow. That was…" Better than any sex she'd ever had, but she kept that to herself, because couples admitted things like that, and that wasn't them. They were just having fun, and she needed to remember that. Plus, she really liked teasing him.

"Spectacular?" he offered. "Hot? Mind-blowing?"

Yes, yes, and yes. "Let's go with *not as bad as last time.*"

He laughed as he went up on his elbow, smiling down at her. His fingertips trailed down her stomach, light as a feather, bringing rise to goose bumps. "We're combustible, and you know it."

"So?" she teased, loving the feel of his fingers playing over her thighs.

"Has it ever been that way with anyone else?"

"Don't ask me that."

"Why not? I told you the truth when I said nothing had ever felt so good. Just be honest with me."

His fingers slid up to her breasts, circling her nipples, and her hips rocked greedily, as if she hadn't just had several of the best orgasms of her life.

He cocked his head, expecting an answer.

"No, *okay?* It hasn't. But unlike you, I haven't been with a hundred guys."

"I haven't even been with *one* guy."

She pushed at his chest, earning another chuckle. He held her gaze as he traced her collarbone and ran his fingers along her shoulder and down her arm, alighting every nerve ending. She needed a distraction before she staked him down to that hay bed and had her way with him again. Grasping for something, she said, "Do you think Beau will mind that we've defiled his outbuildings?"

"After the last two nights, I think they've earned the name in-and-out buildings."

She laughed, and he leaned down and kissed her, quick and sweet. "I like you, Jilly Braden." With a quick lift of his brows, as if to say, *There you have it.* He sat up and turned around to take care of the condom.

How could one sentence make her feel so wanted and special?

The flowers he'd put on the bed were crushed and scattered all over the blanket, and several petals were stuck to his broad back. "We crushed the flowers you picked," she said with a pang of regret and sat up, brushing them off him.

"I guess I'll have to pick more." He tied off the condom and put it on the floor, turning a sexy smile on her. "Turn around. Let me see your back."

He gathered her hair to one side, pressing a kiss to the shoulder he'd bared. She closed her eyes, soaking in the intimate touch.

"I love your hair." He began picking pieces of flower out of her hair.

"You like *pulling* my hair." She glanced over her shoulder, and he flashed a wolfish grin, making her belly flip-flop. "I think I need some of that wine you mentioned." She leaned past him to grab the bottle, and he caressed her ass, then leaned down and bit it. *"Hey!"* She futilely tried to glower at him, but that bite had sent a tantalizing thrill through her.

"What can I say? I like your ass, too."

"I hope you're not going to bite every part of me that you like."

She pulled the side of the blanket over her lap.

He leaned in close. "How do you know you won't like it?" He pressed his lips to hers and sat back with a knowing grin.

She rolled her eyes, but now she was thinking about *that*, too. She held up the bottle. "Did you bring wineglasses?"

"*Shit.* I knew I'd forget something."

"That's okay. We don't need them." She took out the bottle topper and tipped the bottle to her lips, taking a long swig, and handed it to him. As he drank, she looked around. He'd not only picked her favorite flowers and made them a bed, but he'd put *several* blankets on top of the hay. He'd made sure she was comfortable. He'd also stacked the other bales along the wall and swept the floor around them. She glanced at the blown-out candles and buckets, and her heart took another hit. "Thank you for going to so much trouble tonight. I don't want to sound ungrateful, but why did you?"

"Because I like you." He handed her the bottle.

His words struck her with the same impact they had the first time. She tried to drown the butterflies in her belly with a gulp of wine. "You like having sex with me."

"*Obviously.* But I also like being around you and talking to you. I like your sense of humor and how you're always looking out for Zoey and trying to help us."

That made her a little too happy, and she took another drink. He was making it hard to keep her feelings in check. "Well, I'm here. I might as well help."

"That's not why you do it. It's who you are. If you weren't a caring person, you wouldn't have come with us in the first place." He reached for the bottle.

"It wasn't like I had a choice."

"I doubt there's a person alive who can make you do something against your will. What I'm trying to figure out is why you're still single."

"Not every woman is pining for a man."

"True, but you're too passionate not to want more than a dirty fuck in a barn, and I see the way you look at Beau and Char, like you want a love like theirs."

She didn't think he'd paid that close attention to anything other than her looks, but she'd never felt more *seen*. "I guess I haven't met the right guy yet. I'm not an easy person to have a relationship with. In case you haven't noticed, I'm stubborn and opinionated, and my success can be intimidating to guys."

"There is a certain subset of weak men who are intimidated by strong women. I get that."

"I'm not just strong. I work *a lot*. It's not uncommon for me to work at my office until eight or ten, then go home and work all night and catch a few hours of sleep in the morning."

"Your schedule sounds like mine. When I'm working on new songs, I'll go days with only an hour or two of sleep, just grinding it out."

"I wondered about that. Being with Zoey will be a big adjustment."

"Yeah, no kidding. That's one reason the whole family thing wasn't on my radar."

"I totally get that, and so many people don't. It's a stumbling block for most guys my age. They're usually looking to be taken care of and want to start a family, and I'm not exactly wifey material. I can be *great* in the kitchen." She wiggled her shoulders. "Just not at cooking, and thank God I have a housekeeper, or I'd have to move every time my house got dirty. Even if I did cook and clean, I've got too many career aspirations to take on a family anytime soon."

"You make it sound like you've given up on having a relationship. Most women want one, even if it comes with stipulations."

"I want a relationship, but I'm not going to change who I am or set aside work to go looking for one."

"If anyone understands that, it's me. So what else is important to you?"

She took another swig of wine. "Why do you want to know?"

"Because I want to know what makes you tick. Come on, Jilly.

Don't play games. You know my secrets. You've told me *why* relationships are difficult for you, but what do you want in one? What do you want in a partner?"

He'd been honest with her, so she went for it, even if it made her sound selfish or unrealistic. "If you must know, when it comes to love, I'm greedy. I want the magic of the inn that lasts forever and goes the extra mile. I don't want to settle for a guy who *puts up* with my late nights. I want someone who will cheer me on, and I'd do the same for him. Someone who will push me when I'm not pushing myself hard enough, because he knows I can do better, but at the same time, who knows when to back off. And I want sparks that last. I want to see love *and* lust in my husband's eyes and know that in fifty years, it's still going to be there, and he'll still want to drag me into a closet and make out when we're at a dinner party or when our families are over for Thanksgiving. I don't want to go a single day questioning his love for me. I want to feel it twenty-four-seven."

"People fight, Jilly. I'm pretty sure no matter who you end up with, you'll see anger in their eyes at some point."

"Of course. But I think when you truly love someone, you should want them to be happy and fulfilled. You will and *should* fight with them *and* for them. But fighting shouldn't make you question if they really love you. I want that to be a given. I think couples should show their true selves. The good, the bad, and the ugly, so the other person knows what they're getting into, because just like the right clothes, hair, or makeup come off at some point, so does that sparkly outlook that new relationships often have. Which is why speaking your mind is so important. I won't last with a guy who walks on eggshells when I'm angry or stubborn or who expects me to be strong *all* the time or judges me for being vulnerable. I want a guy who's confident enough to fight for what he believes in, but he should also be smart enough to know that he won't always have the right answers, and sometimes he has to compromise. A guy who will admit when he's wrong, even if he gloats when he's right. In fact, he *should* gloat when he's right, because I know I would."

Johnny laughed. "You do enjoy a challenge."

"I do, and I love smart, witty banter and dirty, sexy banter. I want it *all*."

"It doesn't sound like you're asking for much. A guy who's crazy about you, who'll support your creative endeavors and let you cry on his shoulder when you're having a shitty day."

"Yes, and know that I'll let him bitch a blue streak when he has bad days without taking it personally."

"Right, but you also need a guy who will tell you to cut the shit if you're going too far."

"Exactly," she said with awe. "I can't believe I left that out. How'd you know that?"

"Because you're describing my parents' relationship. If I were ever to settle down, I'd want all of that, too."

That was so unexpected, it took her a minute to get past how enticing it was. "So, do you do things like this for all the women you like?" She didn't want to care, but she held her breath in anticipation of his answer.

"Hardly." He took a drink. "I've never even planned a date."

"No way. What about with Ramona?"

"She didn't like the places I suggested, so if we went out, it was all her doing. This will sound bad, but women have always thrown themselves at me. I never had a reason to go on a date or plan anything. They just wanted a piece of me, and for a long time, I was happy to oblige." He took another drink. "But as I said, I stopped doing that years ago. I'm not proud of the way I was, but it helped me become the man I am. And thank God I sowed those wild oats before Zoey came around. If I hadn't grown up, I'd be a dick of a dad."

"And now I've thrown you right back into the man-whore game," she said more lightly than she felt.

"Like hell you did." He set the bottle on the floor and crawled over her, pushing her back down to the blanket. "Did you miss the part about me not being like that anymore and actually *liking* you?"

She grinned. "I heard it, and I like you, too."

"Good." He nipped at her lower lip. "Because I can't get enough of you, Jilly, and I can think of several more creative places to christen and add to our answer list."

Tingles of anticipation prickled her skin as he kissed a path along her jaw.

"What other naughty lists can we conquer?" he asked huskily.

Her mind sprinted down a dark path of all the dirty things she'd *ever* wanted to do, and the idea of doing them with Johnny was intoxicating. She couldn't believe she felt safe enough to even entertain the idea, but she couldn't deny that feeling of safety any more than she could deny the desire for him that had seeped so deep into her being, she was sure it had taken root in her bones. "I *might* have a little fantasy list we could work on."

His eyes flamed. "Baby, you just might be my perfect woman."

As he trailed kisses down her neck, the giddy girl inside her wanted to cling to that comment and hope for more. But the rational adult in her knew better. Hoping for something real with a man whose life was anything but conducive to hers would only lead to heartache. So she forced a reminder for both of them. "Don't go falling for me, Johnny. You're on the family track, and as much as I like Zoey, that's a hard pass for me."

"Don't worry, sweetheart. I'm in no danger of falling. I'm just here for the encore, and you haven't come nearly enough yet."

Chapter Thirteen

JILLIAN STRETCHED, FEELING like she'd slept for days, and grabbed her phone to check the time. *Nine thirty. Nope. Not days.* But she had slept for about four hours, which was a lot for her, *and* she'd missed a text from Johnny. Her pulse quickened. She'd woken up to a steamy text from him yesterday morning after their midnight barn rendezvous, telling her how he couldn't wait to get her alone again and a litany of dirty things he wanted to do to her. All of which she'd happily let him do last night when they'd added another creative place to their answer list and had snuck into Beau's workshop for their midnight tryst.

She opened and read his message, which he'd sent at 6:02 a.m. *I can still taste you.*

Those five little words sparked fires beneath her skin. Smiling like a giddy girl, she got up to brush her teeth, hoping for another good day with him and Zoey. Yesterday had started with a trail ride, and to keep the happier mojo going, Jillian had talked them into playing more lawn games, which she still sucked at. They'd shared a lot of laughs over her lack of athletic ability, and her dirty rock star took every opportunity to drive her crazy throughout the day, stealing kisses whenever they were alone and whispering sexy innuendos. He'd surprised her again last night when she'd gone upstairs to shower after dinner and had found a wildflower on her pillow. It appeared her bad boy had a romantic side.

It was time to have some fun and turn the tables.

Wearing another one of her favorite sleeping tank tops and shorts, she headed out of her bedroom. On the way downstairs, she heard Johnny talking, and he sounded so serious, she stopped midway down, giving them a moment of privacy.

"I don't feel like going horseback riding today." Zoey sounded sad. "I think I'll just go up to my room."

A knot of worry lodged in Jillian's chest. Last week, on the flight there, she'd felt like Zoey and Johnny were sitting at the bottom of a pool holding their breath, waiting for someone to rescue them. But since the night Zoey ran away, Johnny had stepped up and become Zoey's hero, at least in Jillian's eyes. He'd swooped that scared girl up and hadn't just carried her up to the surface, but he'd *forced* her to remain there by giving her reasons to breathe, and every time Zoey started to go under, he was there to catch her and remind her that she wasn't alone anymore and never would be again. Even more unexpected was that each time Zoey faltered, Jillian held her breath, too, wanting to dive in and save them both.

Zoey came out of the kitchen with Bandit on her heels. Her eyes remained downcast as she passed Jillian on the stairs.

"Good morning," Jillian said, wondering what had happened, but her greeting went unanswered. She headed into the kitchen and found Johnny sitting with his elbow on the table, forehead in hand. She touched his shoulder. "Is everything okay? Zoey seemed really down."

He looked up with a tortured expression. "I told her that her mother signed custody over to me." He shook his head. "I thought that was what she wanted, but she looked destroyed."

Jillian's heart broke for both of them. "I'm sure when she said it, she meant it, and she probably still feels that way. But even though her mother has done nothing but hurt her, hearing she signed custody away without fighting for her would be devastating for anyone, and she's just a young girl." She moved between his legs to hug him where he sat. His arms circled her, pulling her close, and he rested his forehead on her chest, breathing deeply, the weight of his heartache palpable.

"It's going to be okay," she said, hoping she was right. "You did the right thing. She needs honesty, and she needs protecting."

"I just hope I didn't fuck things up between us."

"I'm sure you didn't. Why don't I go talk to her?"

He pulled her down onto his lap. "I'm sorry you're stuck in the middle of this with us."

"I'm not stuck. I can leave anytime." As she said it, she realized how true it was, and that she had no desire to leave. "We'll figure this out." She kissed him. "I'll be back."

He held her for a long silent moment, and she knew he was wrestling with too many emotions. When his grip loosened, she kissed him again and got up. She grabbed a Diet Pepsi from the fridge, and as she headed for the stairs, he reached for her hand, giving it a gentle squeeze, which was becoming a familiar touch, and said, "Thank you."

She smiled and headed upstairs to see how Zoey was. She knocked on her closed door. "Zoey, can I come in?" When she didn't respond, Jillian opened the door. Zoey was sitting against the headboard with her knees pulled up, her face a mask of hurt. Bandit sat dutifully beside her.

Jillian didn't ask permission as she stepped into the room and closed the door. "I heard what happened." She sat on the edge of the bed, petting Bandit. "It's okay to be sad."

"I'm *not* sad. I'm glad," she said sharply. "Now she can't bother me anymore."

"That's true, but she's still your mother, and that has to hurt."

Zoey looked away, her chin trembling.

"Do you want to talk about it?"

"*No.*" Zoey climbed off the bed, and Bandit jumped down behind her. She crossed and uncrossed her arms, hurt billowing around her. "Why did she even have me if she was just going to throw me away?"

Jillian went to her. "I can't answer that, but it's her loss, Zoey.

You're an amazing person."

"Well, I can answer it," she snapped. "*Money.* That's all she cares about. She *never* loved me."

Tears stung Jillian's eyes. "But your grandma did, and Johnny does, and so do I."

"But *why?*" Her shoulders slumped, arms hanging loosely at her sides, tears spilling down her cheeks.

Jillian could practically hear her heart shattering and somehow knew that she wasn't asking why they loved her but why her mother didn't. "Because there's something wrong with *her.*" She pulled Zoey into her arms, her own tears falling. "This is *not* your fault."

Zoey sobbed.

"You're good and kind and lovable, Zoey." That made her sob harder, but Jillian wanted to be sure she heard it. "This is *not* your fault. You are lovable."

She held her tighter, crying with her, *for* her, and for Johnny and all they were facing. She held her until Zoey had no more tears to cry, and then she continued holding her, whispering reminders that she was loved and special.

A long while later, they sat on Zoey's bed talking, with Bandit stretched out between them. "I am glad she's not coming back," Zoey said. "But it does hurt."

"I know, honey, and I'm sorry."

"When my mother used to come see us, she'd talk about herself and hardly say two words to me, and then she'd be gone the next morning. At first I was sad, but as I got older, it just made me mad. My grandma used to tell me it wasn't my fault, too. My mother wasn't very nice to her, either, but at least she let her raise me."

"Some people aren't meant to be parents. But that doesn't mean that you're not meant to be loved and to be a mother one day. You are not your mother. You were raised by a woman who loved you very much."

"My grandma told me that, too." She was quiet for a few minutes, petting Bandit. "I don't really want to talk about this anymore. I'm hungry. Are you?"

"I could eat. I was thinking about going to the inn and raiding their pastries. Want to come?"

Zoey nodded, eyes brightening. "I'll get the hat and wig."

"I need to shower first. Give me fifteen minutes?"

"Okay."

Jillian hugged her and went to her bedroom. Before showering, she texted Johnny. *I think she's going to be okay, but you should probably ask Dare for a therapist for her in New York.* His reply was instant. *Already made the call. He's finding me one. Thank you.*

JILLIAN AND ZOEY found and devoured chocolate croissants at the inn and then went to visit Charlotte. They found her staring out the window of her sunny pink and white office, watching Beau chop firewood.

"Are you ogling my brother again?" Jillian asked as they walked in with Bandit in tow.

Charlotte spun around in her shorts, sweater, and purple Uggs, eyes wide and happy as she bent to love up Bandit. "I'm desperate for inspiration."

"You just like my brother's butt." Jillian knocked on the window and waved at Beau. He lifted his chin in acknowledgment.

"You guys are so weird," Zoey said.

"And you look adorable as a blond," Charlotte said. "I love the sporty baseball cap. I'm going to use it for my heroine."

"O-*kay*," Zoey said, as if that were an even weirder thing to say, and looked around at the framed book covers of Charlotte's books touting #1 *NEW YORK TIMES* BESTSELLER and the literary magazine covers they'd graced, hanging on the walls.

As Zoey meandered over to the bookshelves, Charlotte said, "I'm so glad you're here. I'm writing this scene and I'd love your help."

"*My* help?" Jillian asked.

Charlotte eyed Zoey. "Yeah, you know how sometimes we brainstorm together? I thought we could work out a scene or two."

Her imploring look told Jillian this was a ploy of some kind. "Okay."

"The heroine I'm writing about is a woman who just found out she has to raise her niece, and she has no time for a relationship, and the hero owns a gallery several states away. He's a total workaholic, and they're thrown together unexpectedly on a...?" Charlotte's brows knitted.

"Business trip?" Jillian suggested.

"Yes, exactly. It's a conference at one of those resorts that has cabins. I wrote a great bonfire scene, and sparks were flying between them. Now I can't wait to see what they do next, but since they work together, I'm not sure if they should hook up. What do you think?"

"Aren't you the writer?" Zoey asked with her back to them.

Jillian realized her sneaky friend was trying to find out the scoop about her and Johnny, and she shared an amused glance with Charlotte.

"Yes, but I've written so many books, sometimes I need new ideas," Charlotte said.

"Sounds hard," Zoey said, and went back scanning the shelves.

"What do you think, Jilly?" Charlotte asked.

"Oh, it's *hard* all right." Jillian couldn't help herself, and Charlotte stifled a laugh. "If they have chemistry, they probably can't keep their hands off each other."

"*That's* what I was thinking." Charlotte's eyes danced with excitement. "My heroine manifests everything she wants in life. She visualizes it and makes it happen. She did it with her career, her friends, and she's spent years dreaming about finding a great partner. When I started writing this story and met the hero, I thought, *This is him.* I felt it in my gut, even though she didn't."

No, I sure didn't. "Char, you can't manifest everything," Jillian said.

"Yes, you can. You of all people know that," Charlotte said.

"Why do you have these?" Zoey stood in front of the bookshelves, dangling a pair of pink fuzzy handcuffs from her fingers.

Charlotte snagged the handcuffs. "I use them when I'm coming up with…crime scenes."

"The cops in your books use fuzzy handcuffs?" Zoey asked.

"No, but Char wanted them to match her office," Jillian said.

Zoey looked nonplussed and went back to looking at the books.

"Okay, so we're hooking up!" Charlotte clapped. "But where? It's cold. They can't take their clothes off outside, and they don't want her niece to know about them."

Jillian couldn't hide her smile. "Do they have an equipment shed? There must be someplace where they keep snowboards and toboggans."

"*Ohhh.*" Charlotte's brows lifted.

"*Gross.* Don't have them hook up in a shed," Zoey said. "Don't they have a car?"

"It's a clean shed," Jillian said, then caught herself.

"They don't have a car of their own," Charlotte said.

"So? What's wrong with a rental?" Zoey asked, picking up a literary magazine from a shelf and paging through it.

"Yes, that would work," Charlotte said.

Jillian wondered if Charlotte realized in their scenario that would mean using *her* SUV. "You should make him romantic. Have him leave flowers that he picks for her on her pillow."

Charlotte's eyes widened. "I *love* that."

Me too.

"There's one other thing I need help with," Charlotte said. "When I'm writing about them, I can feel how much the hero likes her, and I think the heroine is developing feelings for him, but it's a little harder to tell with her."

"I'd be careful with her," Jillian warned. "Feelings can be dangerous, especially for a single parent. She has to do what's right for her niece, and if their lives are so far apart, I can't see how it can lead to more. You'd better spin some magic in those pages."

"Look where we are." Charlotte waved around them. "Magic is everywhere."

Zoey set the magazine down and pulled a book from a shelf. "Nice Girls? What's this series about?"

Jillian plucked it from her hands. "Girls who aren't the kind of *nice* you should be reading about."

"Then why is it called Nice Girls?" Zoey asked.

"It's a marketing thing," Jillian answered. "I think it's time for us to go. We'll stop at the inn's library on our way out and look for more appropriate books for you." She guided Zoey toward the door with Bandit trotting behind them and tossed Charlotte a wink.

"Good luck with your book," Zoey said over her shoulder.

"I don't need luck," Charlotte called after them. "I'm manifesting!"

WHAT A DAY.

Johnny had spent most of it catching up on the nightmare that was his business with Kane and Mick and worrying about Zoey. She'd come back from the inn in a better mood, and she'd lain low all afternoon, spending most of it in her room with Bandit. Jillian had filled him in on what had transpired with Zoey earlier, and it had slayed him to hear that his daughter had broken down, but he was glad Jillian had been there for her. He wondered if she knew how much she was helping them pave the way to a better place and helping him transition from unencumbered rock star to responsible father. He had a long way to go, but she'd definitely helped him get this far.

He'd been relieved when Zoey had come down later and offered to help him make dinner. He'd asked if she wanted to talk about her mother or her feelings, and she'd said she'd rather not, so he'd let it go. She'd been more like herself as they cooked, and she'd been more talkative while they ate dinner. He was pleased when she'd asked if they could practice guitar.

Teaching her to play was becoming one of his favorite things. They were sitting on the front steps and had been practicing for forty-five minutes. Now that she knew the chords, she was practicing "Love Me Do" by the Beatles, an easy song for beginners. "You're really getting the hang of the open chords."

"Thanks." She kept her eyes trained on the fretboard. "I still mess up sometimes switching between them."

"Everyone does."

"How did you learn to play?"

"My mother taught me. She played a lot when I was growing up, and I loved listening. Her father taught her when she was eight, and the song you're playing is the first one she taught me. She's a huge Beatles fan."

"Really?" Zoey smiled. "How old were you?"

"Seven, and she'll tell you that I'd been bugging her to teach me practically since I first learned to talk."

"Were you good at it?"

"I had a hard time switching between chords, like you do sometimes, and C major was a pain."

"Tell me about it."

He chuckled. "You're doing great. Just keep practicing, and you'll be able to play anything you want. What's your favorite song?"

She shrugged and stopped playing. "I don't really have one."

"One day you will have many, and we'll make sure you know how to play them."

"Do you think I'll ever be as good as you?"

"I think you'll be great at whatever you put your mind to. Is there anything else you've always wanted to learn?"

"I wanted to ride horses, and I like changing things on my clothes, and playing guitar is fun. But I can't think of anything else."

"Okay. Just know that I'm happy to support whatever you want to learn, and I'm sure there will be tons of things that interest you over time."

She sat with the guitar in her lap, running her fingers over the edge of it. "Did you always want to be a rock star?"

"I've always loved music, but when I was young, the only thing I wanted was to learn to play my mother's favorite song. Once I learned that, there was always another song I wanted to learn, and eventually playing other people's music wasn't enough. So, yeah. I guess I wanted to be a musician even before I knew I did."

"What's your mom's favorite song?"

"'I Want to Hold Your Hand' by the Beatles." As he said it, he remembered why it was her favorite song. "She used to say that holding hands is the simplest, purest type of connection, and with the right person, it's one that never fades."

She was quiet for a minute and looked like she was thinking about what he'd said. "Can you teach it to me before I meet her?"

"We can try, but it's not that easy."

"That's okay. My grandma always said if things were easy, life would be boring." She handed him the guitar. "Can we try tomorrow? I'm kind of tired. I want to go read."

"Of course." He touched her hand and realized his mother was right. "I'm sorry today was a rough one."

She nodded and stepped toward the door. But she stopped and stood with her back to him for a beat. When she turned around, he could tell she wanted to say something.

"What is it, sunshine?"

"I'm glad she can't come back for me, even if it hurts. Thank you for doing that."

"I'll always have your back. You can count on it."

She nodded and headed inside.

Johnny let out a breath he hadn't realized he'd been holding and looked out over the yard. When the door opened again, he turned, expecting to see Zoey, but it was Jillian, as beautiful as ever in a sweater, skinny jeans, high-heeled boots, and a warm smile.

"She sounded less choppy playing tonight," she said as she sat beside him.

"Were you spying on us again?" He was only teasing. He knew she listened when Zoey practiced, because she opened the window to hear her while she worked in the living room, and she always commented later on how well Zoey was doing or how patient he was with her.

"It's not spying when you can see me through the window. I like listening to her play and hearing you encourage her. But I went to put my things upstairs when she stopped playing, and when I came down, I passed her on her way up, and she hugged me. Is everything okay?"

"Yeah. I think we're heading to a better place. She thanked me for getting her mother out of her life."

"Oh, Johnny," she said thoughtfully. "That's huge."

"Yeah. It's really *us* now. She's officially mine, and that would've scared the hell out of me a week ago. But it feels really good. It feels *right*, like this is how things are supposed to be." He set the guitar on his leg. "She asked if I always wanted to be a musician. I never realized I did until I answered her."

"What do you mean?"

"I wasn't like you. From what Beau said, you've wanted to be in fashion from the time you were four. Music was always part of my life because my mom had always played the guitar and she taught me when I was seven. But it wasn't like I knew at that moment that it was what I wanted to do forever. It just kept building. I wanted to play more songs, then I wanted to write songs, and then it was like I couldn't *stop* writing them. They bled from my veins. I was thirteen or fourteen before I was sure this was what I wanted to do. But the last couple of years something's been missing, and I haven't felt the drive I used to."

"You've been going through a lot this last year."

He nodded. "You can say that again. Is that what it's like for you with designing? You're so motivated, you couldn't stop if you wanted to?"

"Pretty much. It's like I'm starving and designing feeds my soul."

"So you can cook for yourself." That earned a soft laugh. "I'm really sorry you had to put off the launch of your new line for me. What's that line like?"

"Wanderlust?" She smiled so big, it lit up the night. "Wanderlust is about women letting their *real* selves shine through. It's outlandish and forgiving and free flowing. The pieces are romantic, but not to lure men or partners, or even for society's sake. They're designed for the women who wear them to feel empowered to be themselves and feel good *for* themselves. And the pieces are affordable for women from most walks of life. I'm really proud of the line."

"It sounds impressive. What inspired it?"

"Mostly my sisters-in-law and my mother. They're a mix of all these wonderful attributes. They're resilient and vulnerable with a hint of feminism and hippie spirit. They're tough, but also sweet and romantic."

"That sounds a lot like you, minus the hippie spirit."

"You're just getting to know me. How do you know I'm not a secret hippie?"

He laughed. "I could be very wrong, but something tells me you wouldn't enjoy living in a van or at a Woodstock type event."

She wrinkled her nose. "Maybe you know a little about me."

"You need to get that line out there."

"I will when the time is right." She bumped him with her shoulder. "I have a tour wardrobe to design for four wild musicians."

"This musician is very thankful for that." He was in no hurry to leave Colorado, because that would mean leaving Jillian, but the day was coming, and he had to take care of a few things. He leaned closer, lowering his voice. "I don't suppose I can be greedy and ask you to add one more thing to your very full plate while we're here?"

"That depends." A spark of heat rose in her eyes. "Is it something I'll enjoy?"

"I think you will, but if I'm wrong, you can always punish me later." He waggled his brows. "We're set to go home next Sunday, and I don't have Zoey's room ready. Think you can help me pick out a few things?"

"Help you spend your money on a girl who deserves it? Now, *that's* a project I can get into."

"I had a feeling you might." He reached for her hand, and as he ran his thumb over the back of it, he realized how much he felt every time they'd held hands and how that connection had been there from day one, on the plane, when he'd first reached for her hand. His mother was onto something. He picked up his guitar. "Do you mind if I play my mother's favorite song for you?"

"Why your mother's?"

"I think you'll figure that out." He gazed into her eyes as he started playing, and a hint of something akin to bashfulness came over her beautiful face. That was new, and, *man*, he liked it. As he sang about holding her hand and wanting to be her man, she swayed to the beat, that bashful smile drawing him in.

She sang the chorus with him, laughing a little, and when he strummed the last chord, she bumped him with her shoulder again and said, "Be careful, Rocker Boy. A girl could fall for a guy like you."

He laced their hands together. "My plan is working."

Her eyes narrowed. "I said *a girl*, not me."

The emotions in her eyes betrayed her vehemence. He lifted her hand to his lips, kissing the back of it. "Don't worry, winger. I know you're just my midnight plaything."

Chapter Fourteen

DAYS PASSED WITH sunny skies perfect for horseback trail rides, picnics, and lawn games, barbecues with Charlotte and Beau, guitar lessons, and feeding and grooming the horses, which Zoey was enjoying. Chilly evenings led to midnight rendezvous with Jillian and Johnny ravenously bound together. He didn't miss a single opportunity to be close to Jillian, cornering her in the pantry while making dinner and in the barn for quick-and-dirty make-out sessions after their morning rides, when Zoey would head back to the cottage. Jillian had begun anticipating his steamy kisses and seductive glances and had found reasons to walk into the kitchen when he was cooking or sought him out when he was on the phone, just to drive them both wild. All of this was new to her, the unstoppable desire, the teasing, even having so much leisure time, much less wanting to play games or have sex all night instead of working. Not that her life back home or her usual schedule were boring. She spent her days designing and catching up with friends when she could over texts and lunches, and most nights she worked until the wee hours of the morning.

Okay, maybe her schedule was a *little* tedious, considering most of her friends were now coupled off and she rarely had time to go out in the evenings. Even so, she was surprised at how much she enjoyed hanging out with Johnny and Zoey instead of working and how much more inspired she was when she did work on designs without being solely focused on it. It didn't make sense to her, but she was loving the change.

The tension between Johnny and Zoey was easing, and that was bringing out different sides of all three of them. He and Zoey were up bright and early each morning, cooking breakfast, packing lunches, and getting to know each other better. By the time Jillian came downstairs, the horses were saddled up out front and ready to ride, and Bandit, Zoey's four-legged sentinel, was ready for duty. In the afternoons, Zoey disappeared to read, either out front or up in her room, Johnny spent hours dealing with the fallout from Dick's wrongdoings, and Jillian caught up with her girlfriends and work. As much as she loved their days together, evenings were becoming her favorite time. Usually Johnny would make dinner, and Zoey would wander in at some point and end up helping. After dinner, Jillian worked, while Johnny and Zoey practiced guitar. She loved listening to them. He was so patient with Zoey, and even when Zoey was snarky, there was a smile in her voice now. That's not to say things were perfect. They both had a lot to deal with, and there were times when they butted heads. But they were figuring out how to move past those times together, and Johnny was talking with Dare and asking his parents for advice and doing all he could to do right by her. He often sought out Jillian to talk things through, and every time, the heartache or joy in his voice was inescapable. She knew he was proud of the progress they were making.

But all this togetherness left Jillian in a quandary. She didn't know what to do with her feelings for Zoey any more than she knew what to do with her growing feelings for the man who was surprising her at every turn. She'd found wildflowers on her pillow on more than one occasion, and yesterday she'd found one between the pages of her sketchbook. Johnny continued sending steamy texts, but he'd started sending sweet texts, too. Like when she was showing Zoey the designs she was working on for his tour and he'd texted, *The two of you together are becoming my favorite sight.*

She had a hard time concentrating after both types of texts. One left her desperate for their sexy trysts, and the other left her longing for more.

Their private time had also taken a surprising turn. Every night, after wearing each other out, they lay together talking and kissing until they had no choice but to reluctantly head inside, leaving her both sated *and* counting the minutes until she'd see him again. They'd continued adding to their *creative places they'd had sex* list, which was another thing she couldn't believe she was doing. Having sex in a barn? Her friends would never believe it. But other than her brief chat in code with Charlotte, she'd kept the details of her relationship with Johnny private, and she liked it that way. He'd been scouting places during his runs for them to meet, and he was thoughtful with his choices, although some nights they couldn't hold out. They'd ended up having sex in the back of Charlotte's SUV—*Sorry, Char*—and against the side of Beau's workshop, and one night, against the side of the cottage. But the nights they made it to his chosen destination were unforgettable. Sunday night he'd taken her to a secluded spot surrounded by wildflowers, not far from the house, and she lay in his arms afterward listening to his stories about touring and his family, and last night he'd taken her to another creek he'd found on the other side of the inn. After he'd turned her legs to butter, he'd handed her a stone to make a wish. In her heart, she wished they could stay in Colorado forever and never return to real life. Who wouldn't want to spend their days horseback riding and going on picnics with two people who were quickly becoming her favorites and their nights in the arms of a hot, beautiful man with a secret penchant for romance?

But that wasn't the wish she made when she'd tossed the stone in the water.

She'd wished for his and Zoey's relationship to continue to flourish through all the trials and tribulations they were sure to encounter once they headed back to New York. She'd had a moment of sadness, thinking about going their separate ways, but like a big girl, she'd stuffed it down deep and carried on.

It was Thursday afternoon, and Johnny and Zoey were practicing guitar out front. Jillian had taken over the living room to work on ideas for a young-teen fashion line she'd been toying with since taking Zoey shopping. After an hour or so, she heard them arguing about school. Last night Johnny had shared with Jillian that he thought it was best for Zoey to go to a private school, at least for a little while, and he'd known he'd get pushback from Zoey.

"It's not fair." Zoey stalked into the living room with Johnny and Bandit on her heels and plopped onto the couch, crossing her arms. Bandit planted himself by her feet. "How would you like it if I made you spend six hours a day with people you had nothing in common with?"

"How do you know you have nothing in common with kids you haven't met yet?" Johnny asked.

"Seriously?" Zoey was appalled. "Look at my life, and then look at *anyone* else's. Do you think any kid in a private school has ever had to buy all her clothes for fifty dollars? Do you think any of them have parents who didn't want them?"

"*Mothers*, not parents," he corrected, the hurt in his voice tangible.

"That's what I meant. *Sorry.*" Zoey's sincerity was genuine.

Jillian chimed in to try to ease the tension. "Zoey, a lot of celebrities' kids have issues and not just with their parents, but with drugs, insecurities, friends, and who knows what else." She could tell Zoey didn't believe her, and she added, "You know who Drew Barrymore is, right?"

"*Yes*," she said sharply.

"She got emancipated from her mother when she was fourteen, and I'd imagine she went to private school."

"She's *ancient*," Zoey snapped.

"Maybe to you, but she was your age when that happened," Jillian said gently. "My point is, everyone has something they're dealing with that makes them feel like an outsider to their peers. I would bet that every kid in whatever school you go to is going through something they feel like nobody else could possibly understand. That doesn't diminish how hard and heartbreaking it has been for you, but what you've gone through does *not* have to define who you are, unless you let it. *You* have the power to define yourself by showing people who you are through your actions."

Zoey crossed her arms and lowered her eyes.

Jillian moved closer to her on the couch, speaking gently. "Will it be scary? Heck yeah. But you had a grandmother who adored you, and you have a father who loves you and would move heaven and earth for you."

The anger eased in Zoey's eyes, but it morphed to worry. "The kids won't like me."

"Some might not, but others will," Jillian said. "Nobody is liked by everyone. I wasn't liked by everyone when I was your age. I was bossy and not into boys, and I was all about becoming a fashion mogul. A lot of kids laughed at me, and some thought I was, for lack of a better word, bitchy or snobby. That hurt more than I let on at the time. But that's how I learned to pay attention to how I presented myself and how I treated others. I realized pretty quickly that there was a difference between being confident and being arrogant." She took Zoey's hand. "I'm sure more changes feel overwhelming, but even after knowing you for only a little while, I can see how resilient you are. You can get through anything."

Zoey didn't respond.

"But it's exhausting being strong, isn't it, Zoey?" Johnny said.

Jillian was surprised by his comment, but he'd told her he'd spoken with Dare before dinner, and she assumed that was where his perspective had come from. *Go, Dare.*

Zoey lowered her eyes.

He crouched by Zoey. His scruff had thickened from not shaving, giving him a rougher appearance, which made him even more handsome, but it was the love for Zoey in his eyes that took Jillian's breath away as he gazed at his daughter and said, "I understand because I had to be who everyone else wanted me to be for years, and it was exhausting. I don't want to do that to you, but I'm not willing to risk your safety. So why don't we make a deal?"

"What kind of deal?" Zoey asked skeptically.

"Try private school for a month. If you hate it, we'll figure something else out. I can't guarantee I'll send you to public school, but if you try, at least we'll see what you like or don't like, and then we can figure out our next step together."

Zoey was quiet for a beat, as if she was thinking it over. "Together?"

"Yes," he said firmly. "Like everything else we've been working through. You and me, having conversations and making a decision that works for both of us."

She was quiet again, and when she finally met his gaze, she said, "*Fine.*"

He held out his hand, and she rolled her eyes. "Shake on it, girl. I've got your word, but I want it sealed with a handshake."

"You're so weird," she said with a smile, and shook his hand.

That smile took the tension out of the air.

"Weird but cool." He winked. "I'm going upstairs to change, and then I'm heading out for a run. Want to tag along on my run this time?"

Zoey looked at him like he'd lost his mind.

"I'll take that as a no." Johnny cocked a brow at Jillian.

"Don't look at me," Jillian said. "I'm allergic to exercise. Besides, I want to get Zoey's opinion on these ideas." She waved to the sketchbooks.

"Mine?" Zoey asked, and Johnny looked just as confused.

"Yes, yours. I wasn't thrilled with the clothing options for girls your age, and based on the modifications you've made to your outfits, I don't think you are, either." She was impressed with the changes Zoey had made to her clothes. They weren't tacky or childish. They were well thought out and well executed, even with limited tools. "I've been playing with a few ideas for a young-teen fashion line, and I'd really like your opinion because while I'm a great designer, I haven't been fourteen for a few years."

Zoey's eyes lit up. "Really?"

"Yes, thirty is a far cry from fourteen."

"I mean about the fashion line," Zoey said.

Johnny arched a brow. "Are you serious about this, Jilly?"

"Yes. I take fashion very seriously for any age. Don't you have a run to go on?" she teased. "We have girl business to get to."

He pushed a hand through his hair and shook his head. "You're really something."

"And you're really distracting." She shooed him up the stairs, earning a smile from Zoey.

Jillian gathered her sketches and sat beside Zoey on the couch. "Okay, we're going for edgy and cool with a side of class."

"I'm not sure what that means."

"It means we want girls to look good without showing too much skin. When people see girls in these outfits, we want them to think, *Wow, she knows how to dress cool and protect her assets*, not *Holy cow, she might as well wear Saran wrap*."

Zoey laughed softly, then studied each sketch. "I love the gray jeans with the zipper pockets and the black jeans with the lace through the hole. This shirt with the zippers on the sides is cool, too." She went on to comment about cropped tops, sweaters, and different types of pants. "I don't wear dresses, but I love this one." She pointed to a forest-green minidress with black stitching. It had a fitted bodice and a loose skirt, and Jillian had paired it with chunky black shoes.

"Good. I was thinking it could be worn with this." She paged through the sketches and pulled one of a cropped denim jacket with a funky dark floral design on the back.

"I like it, but can you make it with black denim? And it needs a black choker."

"That's something to think about, but we don't want the outfit to look too harsh. What about a light brown choker or a gold choker with a small heart charm?"

"That'd be cool." Zoey examined the next design, taking in the black-and-white color-block miniskirt and oversize white sweatshirt with frayed hemlines and an oversize breast pocket, accessorized with colorful bracelets and black high-tops. "This one is awesome. Can you put skulls along the hem of the sweatshirt?"

"Maybe. What do you like about skulls?"

"They're cool, and they show you're not afraid of anything. You can make them really small and add some color so they're not creepy. That way the person wearing it knows what they are, but people across the room would just see a little color."

"Give a girl a confident edge without being flashy," Jillian said, mulling it over. "I like that. How do you feel about boyfriend jeans?" She turned the pages, showing her several designs of boyfriend jeans, some long, some rolled up above sock height, with oversize cropped sweaters and shirts and some fitted tops and wide belts.

"I'd wear every one of those, but can you put some tears in the jeans?" Zoey asked, and then she went on to make other suggestions, like putting holes in the tops, and they negotiated different styles.

Zoey's input was fresh, and her excitement was like nothing Jillian had witnessed before with her.

Zoey turned the page to one of Jillian's favorite outfits, inspired by Zoey's love of horses. Slim black knit pants with a wide-sleeved, cropped-at-the-waist, herringbone-patterned gray top and black riding-style flat-bottom boots. She'd drawn it with and without a horse on the edge of the left sleeve.

"I love the horse, and the pants, *and* the boots," Zoey said excitedly. "Can you show me how to make this outfit?"

Happiness bubbled up inside her. "Would you like to make it together?"

"That would be amazing."

"We can't make it while we're here, but I think we can probably figure out a way to make it happen after you're settled in New York with school and everything." Jillian knew she and Johnny could never make things work long-term, but that didn't mean they couldn't remain friends.

"Thank you!" Zoey threw her arms around her just as Johnny

came down the stairs.

He stood stock-still, the affection in his eyes mirroring the warmth in Jillian's heart. So why did she feel like she was standing on a runway naked?

"*Johnny*," Zoey said excitedly. "You have to see these!"

"Yeah? Are they any good?" he teased, eyes lingering on Jillian as he crossed the room.

"They're awesome," Zoey said, and she showed him the designs, explaining the modifications they'd discussed.

As he looked at the sketches, Jillian found herself hoping he liked them. It was hard to tell by his serious expression.

"This is what you've been working on all week?" he asked.

"Some of it. I was working on your tour wardrobe, too, and a few things for other clients," Jillian said. "But I'm really enjoying designing for a younger crowd."

"These are great, Jilly. I'd love to see Zoey in them. Do you think you could design a line of clothes for my Baddies that I can sell at shows?"

"That's a cool idea," Zoey said.

Jillian gave him a scrutinizing look. "Are you serious?"

"Hell yeah. We have T-shirts and sweatshirts but nothing unique. You can call it the Bad Intentions line."

"That fits, but if *that* doesn't brand a girl a certain way, I'm not sure what would," Jillian pointed out.

"I like it." He held up the designs. "And you can call these Mini Baddy wear," he suggested.

"I don't think parents of teen girls would appreciate their daughters being called Mini Baddies. I was thinking something a little more generic, with a nod to you and Zoey, since I probably wouldn't have come up with the line without you guys. What do you think of Rocker Girls, with a *z* for Zoey instead of an *s*?"

Zoey's eyes widened. "*Really?*"

"Do you like it?" Jillian asked.

"I *love* it!" She hugged Jillian again.

Johnny was watching them with such happiness, Jillian's heart stumbled, bringing reality crashing in. Pulling away from Zoey's embrace, she said, "Okay, enough of this mushy stuff. We have work to do." She pointed at Johnny without looking at him, because she couldn't afford to get swept away by a man who had to be temporary. "And you have a run to go on."

JILLIAN AND ZOEY worked together coming up with new ideas and searching online to make sure someone hadn't already designed something too similar, while Johnny went for his run and took a shower. They'd just finished cleaning up when he came downstairs looking delectable in jeans and a black Henley, his wet hair finger combed away from his face.

"I'm ready to make dinner for my girls. Who's helping?" He eyed them expectantly.

My girls? Jillian's stomach flip-flopped.

"Have you thought any more about the carnival?" Zoey asked hopefully. "It starts tomorrow night."

Jillian had thought she'd given up on that.

"I'm sorry, sunshine, but I don't think it's a good idea," he said gently. "It's too risky."

Zoey's smile faded. "I understand. I'm gonna go read." She headed upstairs, her fingers grazing Bandit's fur as he walked beside her.

Johnny waited until she was upstairs to say, "I hate disappointing her."

He looked at Jillian with so much regret in his eyes, she ached for both of them. "I know, but she understands you said no."

"I hope so." He reached for her hand. "Looks like you're my sous-chef tonight."

"As I recall, you were not thrilled with my help the last two times we cooked together. You said I wasn't great in the kitchen, remember?"

He tugged her into his arms with a coy smile, those mischievous eyes getting her all tingly as he said, "But you're phenomenal in the pantry," and lowered his mouth to hers, reminding her just how much he'd liked it.

Chapter Fifteen

JILLIAN TIPTOED DOWNSTAIRS at midnight and hurried into the kitchen to make sure Johnny hadn't forgotten to leave a note for Zoey, as had become her habit. He never forgot, and tonight was no different. She had that warm, fuzzy feeling again, knowing that Zoey was always on his mind. She made sure the back door was locked and slipped out the front. As she turned to lock the door, strong arms circled her from behind.

"Where do you think you're sneaking off to?" Johnny's voice was pure seduction.

"To see my secret lover." She shivered with anticipation as he turned her in his arms, caging her in against the door with his big body. He laced their fingers together and lifted her hands above her head, holding them there, his eyes drilling into her.

"I'm too damn addicted to you." His mouth came passionately down over hers, and she bowed off the wall, aching to touch him. He took the kiss deeper, rubbing his body against her, making her crave so much more. But he broke the kiss on a groan, leaving her breathless, and brushed his nose along her cheek. "*God*, Jilly. I could kiss you for *hours*."

"Then do it." She tried to free her hands, but he held them too tight, and then he was kissing her again, deep and lustful. She rose onto her toes, but he broke away again, uttering a curse. "Let me touch you," she pleaded.

"I can't." He dipped his head beside her, inhaling deeply. "You always smell so damn good."

She smiled. "Are we playing some new kind of game where you're in total control and I try to take you to your knees?"

"*Fuck*. Don't talk for a minute."

She giggled and arched against him. "I guess I shouldn't mention that I was looking forward to going down on my knees tonight."

"*Christ.*" He released her hands and walked away, raking a hand through his hair.

"John—"

He held up his hand. "Give me a second. I have other plans for us tonight, and I can't go like this." He grabbed his crotch. "*Fuck.* I should know better than to get started with you when I can't finish."

Confused, she said, "Don't our plans include *that?*"

"Not tonight, baby." He went to her, his movements full of restraint, and he brushed his lips over hers. "Just know I'll make it up to you." He reached for a bag she hadn't seen and pulled out two hoodies, handing one to her. "Put this on."

"Aren't you supposed to be taking *off* my clothes?"

"Don't remind me. Please put it on."

She held up the hoodie, which had COLORADO written across the chest, and realized he was wearing a matching hoodie. As she put it on, she said, "Are we role-playing? I've always wanted to do that."

"Jesus, woman. *Stop.* Come on." He took her hand, leading her back inside and upstairs.

She whispered, "We can't use a bedroom. Zoey might hear us."

He touched his lips to hers in a tender kiss and stopped in front of Zoey's door. He put his finger over his lips, indicating for her to be quiet as he opened the door. Jillian opened her mouth to ask what he was doing, but he shushed her again. Zoey was sleeping next to Bandit, her arm around the dog's middle. Bandit lifted his head as Johnny walked in.

"It's okay, buddy," Johnny said softly, and bent to kiss Zoey's head. "Wake up, sunshine."

"What are you doing?" Jillian asked. "It's after midnight."

Without answering, he gently shook Zoey, rousing her. "Sweetheart, wake up."

Her eyes fluttered open. "What…?"

"I need you to get up, Zo." He helped her sit up. "Put this on." He handed her a matching hoodie to theirs.

She pulled it on. "Is something wrong? Did the paparazzi find us?" she asked nervously as she and Bandit climbed out of bed.

"No, but we have someplace we need to go."

"Now?" Jillian and Zoey asked in unison.

"Yes. Sorry. I can't say any more yet. Just put on jeans and sneakers and let's get out of here."

He and Jillian left her alone to change, and when they closed her door, Jillian started to worry. "Should I call Beau?"

"No. He knows we're leaving, and we'll be fine. We just have to go now," he said as Zoey came out of the bedroom.

THEY HEADED DOWNSTAIRS and outside. Johnny opened the passenger door for Jillian and the back door for Zoey. When Zoey climbed in, Bandit jumped in beside her.

"Bandit, out," Jillian said, but Bandit didn't budge.

"He can't come?" Zoey asked with panic in her voice, her arm circling the dog.

Beau had warned Johnny that Bandit might not leave her side if this went down as he'd planned. "I'm sorry, sunshine, but we have to drop him off at the inn."

He drove down to the inn, where Beau was waiting. Beau opened the back door, his serious eyes landing reassuringly on Zoey as she petted Bandit. "Don't worry, honey. He'll be here when you get back. Come on, buddy." He patted his leg, and Bandit jumped out of the vehicle. He glanced at Jillian and Zoey again. "You're in good hands. Johnny's got your best interest in mind."

Jillian looked curiously at Johnny as they drove away, and he hated making them worry, but some things were better left unsaid.

He drove down the mountain and through town. As they neared the dark fairgrounds, Zoey looked longingly out the window at the peaks of the tents, the massive Ferris wheel, and the outlines of other rides visible against the night sky.

"I have to pull over and get something out of the back." He pulled onto the road that led to the fairgrounds.

"I wouldn't go down there," Jillian said. "Beau said they've closed all the roads around the fairgrounds until Friday so they can test the equipment without worrying about people climbing the fences."

Thank you, Beau.

"It's not safe to pull over on the side of a road." Sure enough, there was a roadblock up ahead, but it was one Johnny had arranged, just like the roadblocks on all the other roads around the fairgrounds. What Jillian and Zoey couldn't see were the Elite Security professionals standing guard around the fences and the plain-clothed guards that would be staying close enough to them to keep them safe if anything were to go awry.

The guard waved him through, and he glanced at Jillian, catching a grin working its way across her face, a hint of curiosity in her sharp hazel eyes. He winked and turned his attention back to the road.

"Why'd they let you through?" Zoey asked.

"Who knows," he said casually, and made his way through the main gates, driving past the security guards. He parked near the entrance and got out of the vehicle, walking around to the passenger side and helping Jillian out.

"What are you up to, Daddy Bad?" she asked quietly with that dreamy look in her eyes as she stepped out.

"Making my little girl's dreams come true. I might be hamstrung by my fame, but I don't want that for Zoey, so I pulled a few strings." Thanks to Beau and Dare, who apparently knew every influential person in town, and Johnny's cousins' security teams, he was able to pull off one magical night for the young girl who deserved a lifetime of them.

He opened Zoey's door and held out his hand. "Come on, sunshine. You wanted to go to the carnival. Let's go see what it's all about."

She looked at the dark fairgrounds as she took his hand and stepped out. "But they're not even open."

He kept hold of her hand as they walked over to the entrance. "For you they are."

As if his words held magic, vibrant neon lights burst to life, illuminating the rides, tents, and kiosks, lighting up the entire fairgrounds. Zoey's jaw dropped, her eyes filling with tears as she turned to him. Her trembling lips moved like she wanted to speak, but no words came.

"They can't turn on the music. The lights are enough of a risk, but I wanted—"

She launched herself into his arms, laughing and crying at once. "Thank you. I can't believe you did this. Thank you so much."

He hugged her, emotions clogging his throat. "I don't want to be one of those dads who raises an entitled kid, but I have a feeling I could give you the world, and you'd never take it for granted."

She wiped her tears. "I won't. I promise." She turned to Jillian, who was wiping her own tears, and said, "Did you know?"

Jillian shook her head, her gaze soft and wondrous. "This was all Johnny's doing. I'm just as surprised as you."

If he had any lingering doubts about the risk of making such a public gesture for Zoey, the look in hers and Jillian's eyes made it worth whatever trouble might come his way.

"I had a little help, but enough about that. Funnel cake awaits." He slung his arms over their shoulders and headed into the carnival.

They made their way through the carnival, eating funnel cakes and cotton candy, playing games, and riding rides. They raced down the super slide, drove the bumper cars with reckless abandon, rode the carousel, the giant swings, and even the Zipper. Johnny was pretty sure he left his stomach at the top of that ride, and Jillian swore she nearly puked. Zoey was as fearless as he was, taking on the roller coasters without hesitation and squealing with delight on the Scrambler, both of which she dragged Jillian onto, despite Jillian's pleas for her life.

As they came off a rocket-ship ride, Zoey clutched the giant stuffed bear Johnny had won for her and pointed at the WATER GUN FUN game. Red, blue, and yellow flags waved along the top of the sign, and stuffed animals and other prizes hung on the walls. "Can we play that?"

"Only if you feel like losing," Johnny teased.

"I bet you haven't touched a water gun in twenty years," Jillian said. "Come on, Zoey!" She and Zoey ran ahead, giggling.

A few minutes later they stood with water guns in hand, aiming at their respective bull's-eyes, egging each other on as their horses wobbled across the track. Zoey's and Johnny's horses were neck and neck, and Jillian's was behind.

"You're going to lose, sunshine," Johnny said.

"Dream on," Zoey said, her face intent.

"Go, Zoey! Show him who's boss," Jillian cheered.

Johnny glanced at Jillian, taking an extra second to admire how cute she looked in the baggy hoodie, with her face pinched in concentration. He tore his gaze away, and his stream of water strayed from the target. "Shit."

"Language!" Jillian and Zoey hollered, laughing.

"Go, Zoey, go!" Jillian yelled as Zoey's horse neared the finish line.

Johnny's horse inched up on Zoey's, approaching its shoulders. His horse was almost past Zoey's when hers lurched to the finish line. The buzzer sounded, and she and Jillian dropped their water guns and jumped up and down, squealing and hugging each other. It was the best damn sight he'd ever seen.

Zoey did a happy dance as she picked up her giant bear and said,

"I can't believe I won!"

"You're a mini Bad, all right." He tousled her hair. "Good going, kid. Pick a prize."

Zoey beamed, and as she looked over the prizes, Jillian sidled up to him, her smile as bright as the summer sun. "How does it feel to lose to a fourteen-year-old?"

He leaned closer, speaking directly into her ear. "I'd lose a hundred times over if it earned her smiles."

"Don't pretend you let her win," she whispered.

"I didn't let her, but I was *distracted*." His arm slid down her back, and he squeezed her butt.

Jillian glowered at him, looking so damn cute, he nearly kissed her.

"I'd like that one, please." Zoey pointed to a stuffed unicorn with rainbow wings. The attendant handed it to her, and she turned to Jillian. "This is for you."

"*Me?* Why? You won it. You should keep it," Jillian urged.

"I have this." She wiggled her giant bear. "And I want you to have it. I've never had a friend like you, which kind of makes you a unicorn, and sometimes Johnny calls you winger, so it fits with the wings."

She handed the unicorn to Jillian, and Jillian hugged her. "I've never had a friend like you, either. Thank you."

Johnny fought the urge to put his arms around both of them and cleared his throat to try to push away those feelings. "What's next?"

"The mirror maze!" Zoey yelled, and they headed in that direction.

They navigated the maze and about a half dozen more rides. As they came off a spinning teacup ride, Zoey said, "Let's go on the Ferris wheel!" and ran toward it.

"She's loving this, isn't she?" Johnny couldn't remember ever feeling as happy as he did right then. He put his arm around Jillian, pulling her close, and pressed his lips to hers.

She froze, her eyes darting up ahead to Zoey.

It took him a second to realize what he'd done. *Fuck.* She stepped out of his arms, and every ounce of him wanted to drag her back. "Shit, sorry. I lost my mind."

"Better find it fast," she said with a grin.

As they followed Zoey toward the Ferris wheel, he wasn't sorry. He *wanted* to be with Jillian, to hold her hand and laugh with her, to kiss her whenever the feeling hit, and make love to her until they lost themselves in each other. But Zoey was about to go through even more changes when they left Colorado, and it would be unfair of him to try to split his attention between her and Jillian.

"Hurry up, slowpokes!" Zoey turned around, waving them over.

"Race ya, Rocker Boy!" Jillian took off running, and then they were both laughing again.

He caught up in three strides, wrapped his arm around her tiny waist, and ran the rest of the way carrying her like a football as she flailed and Zoey cracked up.

"Want to all ride together?" Johnny asked as he set Jillian on her feet.

"I want to ride alone," Zoey said.

"Embarrassed to be seen with your old man?" he teased.

"*No,*" she said, full of teenage attitude. "There's nobody here to see us. I just want to ride by myself."

"Okay, then. After you, sunshine." He waved her toward the seat.

As she settled in and the attendant secured the bar in front of her, Jillian bumped Johnny with her hip. "Guess you're stuck with me. Think you can handle it?" She flashed the secret smile she *knew* drove him wild.

He leaned closer, speaking low and seductively. "Baby, if my daughter weren't on this ride, I'd give you something to *handle* right up there at the top."

Her eyes flamed. "Any chance you can rent out another carnival for just us?"

The attendant motioned them into their car, and Jillian sauntered past with a bounce in her step, casting a *gotcha* glance over her shoulder. *Christ*, she knew exactly how to get under his skin.

WHEN THE RIDE started, Johnny put his arm around Jillian, pulling her closer and gazing into her eyes with the mischievous smile she adored. "Ever kissed a guy on a Ferris wheel?"

"Maybe," she said coyly.

"Seriously? I thought you were too busy with fashion to be into boys when you were younger."

"I was, but I didn't live in a bubble. I just had to hide my secret flirtations from my brothers. I went to a fair with my friends when I was thirteen, and Ronnie Templeton was there. He was in the same grade as me, and all the girls liked him. He had shaggy brown hair and the cutest dimples. He asked me to ride with him, and when he kissed me, his braces cut my lip. I had to lie to my parents when I got home and tell them I tripped."

"And what happened with Ronnie?"

"I told him I was swearing off boys with braces and that maybe I'd go out with him when he got his braces off."

"And did you?"

She shook her head. "He had a girlfriend by then, and I was onto bigger, better things. Have you ever kissed a girl on a Ferris wheel?"

"No, but I'd like to. Want to be my first?"

A little giddy at the prospect, she thought, *No, I want to be your first and your last.* But that wasn't reality, so she'd take what she could get. "What about Zoey?"

"She can't see us if we kiss while we're on the way up. We'll be below her."

"You've really thought this out."

"I've had *days* to think about all the places I could steal kisses."

The way he said it, low and hungrily, made her want it even

more. She waited with bated breath as he pulled her tighter against him, taking her hand in his other hand as their car made it to the top. The ride down seemed to take forever. The minute they were behind Zoey, his big hands cradled her face, but he didn't rush to kiss her. His thumb brushed over her lips, and he said, "I want to remember this moment."

Her heart skipped as his gaze moved over her face for a second before his warm lips touched hers. He kissed her slow and deep, like they had all the time in the world, and when he threaded his fingers into her hair, angling her mouth beneath his, taking the kiss deeper, that world fell away, and all she felt was their kiss and his hands and the heat of his body against her. She felt like she was floating on a cloud, and she never wanted to get off.

When he drew back, the sounds of the ride creaking and Zoey yelling, "Woo-hoo!" jerked her back to reality. But she didn't move, could barely breathe for the way Johnny was looking at her like she was something precious, something to be treasured.

"Best first kiss ever," he said, and he took out his phone, putting his arm around her again and pulling her closer, kissing her as he took a selfie, another of them laughing, and a third of him kissing her temple. "Let's do one for Zoey." They made funny faces as he took a few more. He pocketed his phone and took her hand as their car started the upward ride, and then he kissed her again, roughly and ravenously and oh so *Johnny*.

When they'd ridden all the rides and were on their way out of the park, Zoey asked to play one last game. They went to play the game where you throw a basketball into a net. Zoey went first, and she made one basket out of four. Johnny was as cocky as ever, swooshing the first two, but the third and fourth bounced out.

"Let me show you how it's done." Jillian handed Johnny her stuffed unicorn and stepped up to the counter.

"I thought you were allergic to sports," Johnny said.

"I am, but it's fun to try."

"Want me to get you a stepstool?" he teased, winking at Zoey.

"I'm going to make you eat those words, Mr. Bad." Jillian aimed the basketball just like her father had shown her. She hadn't played in years, but she had a good memory. The first ball rolled around the rim. *"Go in, go in, go in!"* It dropped outside the hoop. "Darn it."

"That's okay. You'll get it this time," Zoey said.

"Come on, Jilly." Johnny clapped his hands. "Show Zoey there's nothing you can't do."

Jillian loved their support. As she lined up her shot, her father's voice whispered through her mind. *Fingers facing the basket, hands not too close.* She took her shot, again with her father's lesson playing in her mind. *Straight line to the basket, release pushing through the elbow, wrist snaps down.* The ball sailed to the basket and dropped into it, vibrating on the way down.

She squealed and jumped up and down, and Zoey hugged her.

"Way to go, winger!" Johnny pulled her into a quick embrace, whispering, "That's my girl."

Did he know what that claim did to her? Even if it was just for now?

"Two more!" Zoey cheered as Jillian grabbed another ball.

"Come on, Jilly," Johnny encouraged.

She lined up the shot, her nerves tingling. She drew in a breath, blowing it out slowly, and took the shot. The ball arced up and swooshed the net. More squeals and cheers rang out. She couldn't believe it. She'd never gotten two baskets in a row. Her hands were sweating as Johnny and Zoey cheered her on, and she lined up her last shot.

"I'm so nervous I'm gonna puke."

"Gross," Zoey said.

Johnny laughed. "You've got this, baby."

Jillian didn't know if he realized that he'd called her baby, but Zoey didn't even flinch, so she must've thought he was just excited. She threw a silent prayer up out to the universe as she took her shot and closed her eyes.

"Yes! You did it!" Zoey yelled, and hugged her.

Johnny threw his arms around both of them and said, "I think we've got a secret pro baller on our hands."

"I can't believe I made it!" Jillian bounced on her toes, elated. "What did I win?"

The attendant handed her a plastic bag with two goldfish in it. She stared at it. "A *fish?*"

"Two," the guy said.

"*Um.* Thanks…?" She giggled as they left the booth. "Unless this fish has a death wish, I think you'd better take care of it." She handed it to Zoey.

"I might forget to feed it." Zoey handed it back.

"Well, I can't even remember to feed myself." Jillian turned to Johnny. "You're so good at taking care of us, will you please adopt Winger and Rocker Boy?"

Johnny took the bag of fish and arched a brow. "Winger and Rocker Boy? How do I tell them apart?"

"*Obviously* Winger is the cute, sassy one whose scales sparkle, and Rocker Boy is the big broody one trying to act cool."

Zoey laughed.

It was after three o'clock when they finally walked out of the park, and Zoey couldn't stop raving about how much fun she'd had. She was smiling so big, carrying that enormous bear, her eyes dancing with new light.

"What was your favorite part about the carnival?" Johnny asked.

"*Everything,*" Zoey exclaimed. "The rides, the games, the food. Funnel cake is my new favorite food, but I didn't like the corn dog. It tasted like rubber."

"Worse than my mac and cheese?" he asked.

"Much," Zoey said with a smile. "But I think my absolute favorite part was being there with you guys. You're so funny, the way you tease each other. It seems like you've known each other forever, and that made it even more fun. This was the best night of my life. Thank you so much." She threw her arms around Johnny, the big bear squished like a third person in their embrace.

A kernel of longing formed in Jillian's chest. She wanted to be in that circle with them. How on earth was she going to leave them at the end of the week and go back to her normal life?

"I'm glad you had fun, sunshine. This was one of my best nights, too." He looked at Jillian, eyes warm and affectionate. "How about you, Jilly? Did tonight make it into your top ten?"

She'd thought nothing could surpass the first time she'd seen her designs worn by someone famous, the day she'd opened her own boutique, or the first time she'd done Fashion Week. But their steamy nights had surpassed them all, and tonight even outdid those.

She looked at the two people who had become vitally important to her and welcomed the warm, fuzzy feelings she'd miss so much when they went their separate ways. She wanted to bathe in those feelings, soak them in until they were a part of her. Her heart was fuller than it had ever been, and she knew she'd relive the memories of their time together forever. But that was all they could ever be: the best memories of her life, with a man who drove her batty and a surly girl who was every bit her father's daughter.

They were looking at her expectantly, and she didn't *want* to answer. Once she did, they'd get into the SUV and drive back to the cottage, and then morning would come, and they'd be one day closer to leaving.

Johnny arched a brow, and she did what she had to. She stuffed those feelings down deep, and when they bobbed to the surface, she pretended not to feel them and said, "Tonight was right up there at the top. Unforgettable."

Chapter Sixteen

JILLIAN FISTED HER hands in the sheets, squirming at the feel of Johnny's thick scruff against her inner thighs, his fingers playing her like she was his favorite guitar. He shouldn't be in her bedroom. It was too risky. Zoey might hear them, but his talented tongue was making it hard to care. *"Ohgodyes. Don't stop."* She dug her heels into the mattress as fire burned deep in her core, blazing through her like the rising sun, setting every part of her on fire, eclipsing her thoughts until right and wrong no longer existed. *"I'm close. I'm gonna c—"*

The shrill ring of her phone broke through her reverie, and she bolted upright, scrambling to cover herself with the blanket, gasping as she realized she was alone. She was shaking, on the verge of orgasm, trying to get her sex-addled brain to function. *Shit. Shitshitshit.* How could a dream do that to her?

She grabbed her ringing phone, seeing Beau's name on the screen, and tried to pull herself together. "Hey," she said, embarrassingly breathy.

"Hi. You okay? You sound like you're out running."

"Yeah. Running. In place. In my room." *Ohmygod, really?*

"Seriously? Johnny must really be getting to you."

Squeezing her thighs together, she closed her eyes. "You can say that again. What's up?"

"I'm at Cutter's helping him with some renovations this morning, and I just got off the phone with Char. She woke up feeling nauseous, and I'm stuck here for a few hours. Would you mind gathering the eggs and taking them up to the inn?"

"Sure, no problem. Is there anything else I can do to help? Is she okay?"

"Yeah, she'll be fine. It's just morning sickness. It comes and goes. She hates it, because it interferes with her writing, which puts her behind schedule, but hopefully it won't last too long."

"*Ugh.* I can't imagine how frustrating that is. I would lose my mind if I couldn't work when my muse was showing herself."

"It's not ideal, but it'll be worth it."

"I still can't believe you guys are going to have a baby. Mom and Dad are going to be ecstatic. Everyone will. Are you over the moon about becoming a dad?"

"Yes, and equally terrified, but it's all good."

"You've made a good impression on Zoey. She really enjoys helping you with the horses, and she loves you and Char. I know you'll be an amazing father, like someone else is turning out to be. But you know that, and I have a bone to pick with you. Since when do you keep such big secrets from me?"

"Since I know you can't hold your tongue to save your life, and Johnny didn't want Zoey to find out about the carnival." She rolled her eyes.

As if he'd seen her, he said, "Don't roll your eyes at me. You know damn well you're not great at keeping secrets."

Little did he know that she was keeping the biggest secret of all.

"Bandit did not like being left behind. Did Zoey have a blast?" he asked.

"Thank you for letting him wait by the front door. Zoey was so excited to see him when we got home, and she loved *everything* about the carnival. She cried when she realized what Johnny had done, and she rode every ride and played all the games. I know she'll remember last night forever, and you should've seen Johnny. He was like a proud peacock that he'd made her so happy."

"You really like them, don't you?" Beau asked.

"As much as I can like a cocky rock star and an attitudinal teen." She didn't know why she felt the need to cover her emotions with snark, but it just came out.

"That sounds like a hell of a lot to me. Even with all the chaos they're dealing with, you've seemed less intense than usual. You seem happier."

"I'm on a two-week vacation, being paid while I ride horses and have barbecues and bonfires."

"And play lawn games?"

She heard the knowing tone in his voice and tried to play it off as no big deal. "Just making life easier for Zoey."

"Uh-huh." He wasn't buying it any more than she was. "Want to talk about the elephant in the room?"

"No," she said with a sigh. "It'll probably trample me. I want to go take a shower and see those handsome little chickens. Don't worry about Char. I'll stay with her after I get the eggs if she's having a rough time."

"Thanks, Jilly, and for what it's worth, I think Johnny's a good man."

She'd caught Beau and Johnny *bonding* on several occasions, like when Johnny had helped Beau carry supplies from his workshop to wherever he'd been working, when they went running together, and when they manned the grill at the barbecue the other night and chopped wood for the bonfire. She finally understood Charlotte's fascination with watching Beau chop wood. Jillian could watch Johnny chop wood for *days*.

"I'll keep that in mind and try not to stab him when he drives me crazy. Thanks for lending us the sweatshirts."

"I didn't. Johnny had them delivered along with a new suitcase for Zoey and a massive basket of baby gifts and Twix bars for me and Charlotte. The man's got a big heart and a load of class."

She was momentarily stunned by Johnny's thoughtfulness. *Big-hearted, thoughtful, and he satisfies me sexually and challenges me in too many ways to count.* The man was damn near perfect. *Perfect for a woman who is ready to be a mom.* A spear of pain accompanied that thought.

"Are you still there?" Beau asked, drawing her from her thoughts.

"Yeah, sorry. I've got to go shower. Channing Tatum awaits."

Ten minutes later, she stood beneath the warm shower spray, trying to recall her dream so she could finish the dream Johnny had starred in. But every time she closed her eyes, she remembered they were leaving Sunday, and those sexy thoughts went right down the drain.

She finished showering, dried her hair, put on a little makeup, and dressed in black skinny jeans and a clingy beige top. She looked at her New York–appropriate designer boots. Chicken poop and Isabel Marant boots did not go well together. She headed into the closet to borrow a pair of Charlotte's rubber rain boots. Her options were vast—red or blue with a floral print, green with ladybugs on them, yellow with tiny green umbrellas, or rainbow striped. She snagged the red boots, and as she put them on, she worried about her shirt and snagged one of Beau's flannels. He had a great selection, too, and she was pleased to find a tan, white, and black one that went with her outfit.

She put it on and rolled up the sleeves on her way downstairs.

The clink and clatter of dishes floated out of the kitchen, along with Johnny's and Zoey's happy voices, drawing her forward like metal to magnets. She paused before passing through the tree trunk, taking a moment to drink them in. They were standing by the stove with Bandit lying by their feet. Zoey's back was to Jillian. She was wearing the sweatshirt Johnny had given her last night and a pair of the boyfriend jeans they'd bought, rolled up at the ankles. Her hair was pulled up in a ponytail, and she was teasing Johnny about making guitar-shaped pancakes. Johnny looked delicious in a gray Henley and jeans. His feet, like Zoey's, were bare. She longed to walk over and be a part of their little family, to drop a kiss on Zoey's cheek and say *good morning* as Johnny bent to drop one on hers.

Oh boy. Where had *that* thought come from? It was far too domestic.

She and Johnny were good together there in Colorado, but anything more was a fantasy. She wasn't what they needed long-term. But this was exactly how she wanted to remember them, even though she knew Zoey's attitude would rise and fall for the next few years like a battering storm and a sunny day that were often at war, and Johnny would be in a constant state of trying to keep up without making things worse. Would Zoey end up in private or public school? Would she like living in the city and make friends who were good influences? Would Johnny ever tour again? How was he going to manage the ups and downs that lay ahead? Would he get in touch with Ramona after all and be the man she'd hoped for?

Jillian's stomach clenched with jealousy.

She pushed those thoughts to the side, unwilling to let them cast shadows on their last few days together. She pulled out her phone, taking a picture of them as Johnny's voice whispered through her mind. *I want to remember this moment.* Her stomach tightened even more painfully. How had she gotten in so deep?

Johnny glanced over, a smile tugging at the lips she knew by heart, as he nudged Zoey with his elbow and said, "Who is that?" nodding in Jillian's direction.

"Maybe she's sleepwalking," Zoey said conspiratorially.

"Very funny," she said as she walked into the kitchen. "Char isn't feeling well, so I'm collecting the eggs this morning."

"She spoke nicely before ten o'clock," Johnny whispered. "It's definitely an impostor." He handed Zoey the spatula and stalked predatorily toward Jillian, eyes narrowing.

"*Johnny,*" Jillian warned, walking backward, her pulse quickening. "What are you doing?"

He lunged, catching her by the waist, and she squealed as he lifted her over his head, like he was helping a child pretend to fly, and demanded, "Who are you? What did you do with *our* Jilly?"

She and Zoey cracked up, but she schooled her expression and said, "You'd *better* put me down."

He acted like he was going to put her down, but he stopped and pressed her back against the wall, feet dangling above the floor, and held her in place with his body, his eyes gleaming with as much playfulness as desire.

"Johnny," she warned. Why did he have to feel so good?

"What do you think, Zoey? Should we tie her up?"

Zoey laughed and transferred the pancakes to plates, putting one on the floor for Bandit.

"Don't you *dare*." Jillian meant it as a warning, but she was thinking about how being tied up by him would be extremely enticing if circumstances were different, and she was unable to suppress her grin.

"Prove you're *our* Jilly or face the consequences," he challenged.

She could think of several consequences she'd like to face with him and said, "Tell me about these consequences."

Zoey snort-laughed, and Johnny shook his head, his smile breaking free as he lowered her to her feet and pressed his entire body against her, whispering gruffly in her ear, "Don't think I won't spank you."

"Don't make promises you can't keep," she whispered back. His eyes flamed, and she pushed at his chest. "Outta my way, Rocker Boy. I need a drink."

Zoey was already pulling a Diet Pepsi from the fridge and handed it to Jilly. "I like your flannel."

"Thanks. It's Beau's."

"The boots could be cooler," Zoey said.

Jillian laughed. "They're Char's."

"It sounds like you need to add boots to your Rocker Girlz fashion line," Johnny said.

"That would be awesome," Zoey exclaimed. "Can we, Jilly?"

"We can definitely look into it. Jace Stone and I designed leather boots for our Leather and Lace line, so I've already ironed out the process."

Johnny cocked a brow. "Good, then we can make them for the

Baddies, too."

She hadn't been sure he was serious about that. "Do you really want to create a Bad Intentions fashion line? It's not an overnight endeavor. You don't just throw fashion lines together and toss them out to the public willy-nilly. I hope I didn't give you that impression, because there's a lot of planning, strategizing, marketing, designing, and about a dozen other things that go into launching a fashion line."

"He does want to," Zoey said. "He told me."

They'd talked about it? Did they talk about her, too?

"I think it's a smart business move, and there's no one else I'd rather get into bed with." He smirked. "Unless you'd rather not get tangled up with me."

The double entendre had her thinking about her dream, and she sat down and squeezed her thighs together. Did she want to get tangled up with him like that? Could she handle it if they weren't secret lovers? If he moved on and was with Ramona or someone else?

The thought made her chest ache.

"I think the line is a great idea, but you have a point." She hoped she sounded businesslike and not as torn as she felt. "Why don't we table making a decision about being tangled up like that until we see how things pan out after we leave here?"

Johnny's jaw clenched.

"Does that mean we can't make that outfit together for a while?" Zoey asked. She carried hers and Johnny's plates to the table. Johnny's was piled high.

Jillian was hit with another pang of longing. She couldn't remember *when* Zoey had started giving him extra food because Jillian always picked off his plate. "No, I meant a decision about a Bad Intentions fashion line. We can make your outfit whenever your dad feels like you're settled in enough for us to get together." She tried to ignore the way the conversation made her feel like an outsider, even though that's exactly what she was.

Despite the fact that she'd just put him off, Johnny motioned to his pancakes, offering her his fork. She shook her head, realizing how much she was going to miss that, too.

"I need to talk to you guys about that." Johnny's voice had a regretful edge to it. "Not the clothes but settling in. I got a call from Shea this morning. She set up several interviews for me on Monday in New York, so I can address the rumors. Zoey, I don't want you around the chaos of the sets, so Kane is coming to stay with you while I'm working. He's sending his plane tomorrow morning, which will give us time to settle in, and I'll only be gone a few hours for the interviews."

Jillian's stomach sank. *We're leaving tomorrow?*

The thought had no sooner taken hold before Zoey said, "I thought we were here for two weeks. It's only Friday."

"I know, sunshine. I'm not thrilled about leaving early, either, but it's important that I get the truth out there, and we're at the mercy of the shows' availability."

She looked frantically at Jillian. "Are you coming with us?"

Sadness swamped her as reality sank its claws in. The pleas in Zoey's and Johnny's eyes were at war, but she knew he was doing what was best for Zoey. "No, honey. I have to get back to work, too, but you can text me anytime. Your dad has my number."

Tears welled in Zoey's eyes. "Can't we just stay until Sunday? I don't need to get settled in."

"I don't think it's a good idea," Johnny said. "I want to make sure you're comfortable before I have to leave for the interviews."

"Then you can *cancel* Kane. I'm *fourteen*. I don't need a babysitter." She swiped at tears.

"I know you can take care of yourself," Johnny said without a hint of placation. "But I'd feel better if you were with someone I trust, just in case you need anything. I'm sorry, Zoey, but Kane's coming to stay for the hours I'll be gone."

She pushed to her feet, chin trembling. "*Whatever*. I'll be outside." She stormed out, and Bandit chased after her.

"*Damn it.*" Johnny's elbows hit the table, and he rubbed the back of his neck with both hands, stretching it up, then down. He blew out a breath and sat back, looking as frustrated as he did defeated.

"You're doing the right thing," Jillian managed, knowing he needed to hear it, but it came out halfhearted, because she felt the same way Zoey did. She wanted to dig her heels in and beg him to stay through the weekend, but that wouldn't help the situation. It was better to just rip the bandage off. "Change is hard, but one day she'll realize it was the right decision."

"I hope so," he bit out. "I don't want to leave early any more than she does. Shea wanted me to go back last Monday to make a statement, but I couldn't leave when Zoey was finally opening up to me, and you and I were just beginning to get to know each other better. I fought Shea on leaving tomorrow, too. The last thing I want to do is upset Zoey when it feels like she's finally *thriving*, and Jesus, Jilly. I *don't* want to leave you, but Shea said I've been silent for too long, and if I don't speak up now and clarify things, it'll be harder for Zoey when she goes to school."

Jillian nodded lamely. He was doing the right thing for Zoey. The three of them had known each other for less than two weeks. She'd dated guys longer than that and hadn't thought twice about them after they'd stopped seeing each other. This should be a blip on her radar screen.

So why did it feel like her lungs had a hole in them?

He pushed to his feet. "I'd better go find Zoey."

She wanted to offer to go with him, but why prolong the inevitable? Instead, she pushed to her feet and headed for the bathroom, needing a minute to pull herself together.

He grabbed her hand, drawing her into his arms. "Our timing sucks. I need to focus on Zoey right now, but leaving here doesn't have to be the end of us."

She closed her eyes, breathing him in and allowing herself a moment to wonder if she was wrong and she *could* be what they needed. It wasn't like Zoey was an infant who needed to be changed and fed and coddled. Jillian wanted to be selfish, to tell him he was right, maybe they could make it work. But it wouldn't be fair to Zoey if they tried and it didn't work out, and she couldn't be selfish where Zoey was concerned.

She looked up at him and said what she knew she had to. "I think it does. Our lives are too far apart and going in different directions. You need to be there for Zoey as she finds her way in her new life, but you also need to deal with your band and your business and all the messes Dick left behind. Kane might be managing it, but you're still the star. You've got to figure out if you're going to tour and how to manage being a rock star with Zoey in your life. You don't need to worry about trying to remember to call or text a girlfriend who's hundreds of miles away. I've got big things on my plate, too. If you're putting off your tour, then I'm going to resurrect Wanderlust, and I'm excited about the young-teen line, and I want to get that going."

"Jillian…"

The anguish in his voice made it hard to stick to her resolve, but she knew she had to. "Think about it, Johnny. You just found out you're a father, and you and Zoey are all over social media. If we become a couple, we'll be all over it, too, and if we don't work out, that's another nightmare for you and Zoey to deal with. That wouldn't be fair to her or you." She swallowed against the lump in her throat. "We're like star-crossed lovers, and star-crossed lovers don't get happy endings."

He held her tighter. "Eventually all this will settle down, and Zoey and I will figure things out, and then you and I can give *us* a shot."

"Yeah. *Maybe.*" She hoped so, but she wasn't holding her breath. Once he got back to his life, thoughts of her might slip away.

"I wish I hadn't canceled the tour a year ago, so we'd've been together when I found out about Zoey."

Struggling against the emotions threatening to choke her, she did what was best for Zoey. She stepped out of his arms and severed any lingering hope for herself as much as for him. "That wouldn't change the fact that I'm not cut out to be a mom, and you are definitely meant to be a dad. You'd better go check on Zoey."

She hurried into the bathroom so he wouldn't see the tears spilling down her cheeks.

JOHNNY CHEWED ON that comment as he went to find Zoey and was relieved that he didn't have to look very far. Bandit greeted him at the barn door. "Hey, buddy." Zoey was petting Spice.

He glanced at the hay bales as he walked in. He'd put them back where he'd found them after his and Jillian's first midnight rendezvous. He'd never forget a second of that night. Hell, there were so many moments he'd never forget from this trip, including this one. He looked at his daughter's slumped shoulders and knew he'd been the one to cause her sadness.

Dare had told him that one of the most difficult things a parent could do was to forget they were a parent and try too hard to be their child's friend. Right now Johnny wished he could be her friend and talk about how much her dad sucked for making her leave early. But while that might be what she wanted to hear, it wasn't what she needed.

He went to her and pressed a kiss to the top of her head. "Hey, kiddo, can we talk?"

She didn't reply.

He petted Spice. "It's going to be hard to leave the horses, huh?"

She looked away.

"I know this transition won't be easy, and it's probably scary as hell starting over again, but I promise you that I'm going to do everything within my power to make it easier for both of us." He paused, giving her a chance to respond, but she continued looking the other way. "Sunshine, I don't want to be the kind of dad you can't talk to."

"I'm sick of losing the things I love." She turned on him, anger and hurt coming out in droves. "First it was Grandma, then Charlie, now *Jillian*. And I'll never see the horses again, or Bandit, or Beau and Char. I won't even meet their baby." Tears spilled down her cheeks. "It hurts so bad, I wish I never met *any* of them."

He pulled her into his arms, wishing he could take her sadness away. "You're not losing anyone, sweetheart." His mind raced. Who was Charlie? Would she ever let herself love someone again? How could he take her pain away? He tried to collect his thoughts as he said, "Who is Charlie?"

"My *dog*." Sobs took her to the floor, and she pulled her knees to her chest.

Confused, he sat down beside her. "You had a dog?" Why didn't Kane tell him about that?

"He wasn't really mine. He was our neighbors', but they left him outside all the time. I fed him and he slept on our back porch. They were going to take him to the pound because her husband was allergic, but when Grandma died they said I could have him."

"Okay, where is he?"

She shrugged. "My stupid mother wouldn't let me take him."

Her fucking mother deserved to rot in hell. He ground his back teeth together, trying to will his anger away. "I'm sorry, sunshine. That sucks, and I know it feels like you're losing Jillian, but you're not." *At least I hope we're not.* "You two are designing Rocker Girlz with a *z*, remember? But Jilly has a life and a business in Maryland she needs to get back to, and I promise you can keep in touch with her. We can ask Beau and Char if it would be okay for you to keep in touch, and once things settle down, we can plan another trip out here so you can see Bandit and ride the horses."

"Can Jillian come?" Her voice cracked.

"I can't answer for her, but when we're ready to plan the trip, we can ask her." He put his arm around her. "Leaving is going to be hard for me, too, but sometimes we have to do hard things and make difficult choices in order to move forward."

"I *hate* it."

"I do, too," he admitted.

They sat in silence for a few minutes, and Zoey rested her head on his shoulder. "Will you miss Jillian?"

His chest tightened. "More than you could ever know."

Bandit barked and ran out of the barn. Johnny heard Jillian talking to the dog, and then there she was in Beau's flannel shirt, which made him wish he had a flannel shirt to give her, holding an empty basket, looking like an angel in rubber boots and an empathetic smile.

"I got worried that maybe you'd both run away," she said as she walked into the barn, glancing at the hay bales, her cheeks turning a pretty shade of pink.

"I told you I wouldn't scare you like that anymore," Zoey said softly.

"Then I guess I can cancel the tracking device I just ordered." Jillian knelt in front of Zoey and put down the basket, glancing at Johnny. "Are you guys okay?"

He noticed her eyes were red-rimmed, too, adding more regret to the already-mile-high pile. "We're getting there."

Jillian took one of his hands and one of Zoey's and said, "We have today, and I know it's not as much time as we'd like, but I was hoping we could spend some of it together." She gave Zoey's hand a little shake. "I think Channing and Jason would like a proper goodbye from you."

"What do you say, sunshine? Want to go see the *Magic Mike* crew one more time?"

"I guess, but I'm not touching the poop-covered eggs."

"That's your dad's job." Jillian lowered her voice. "Why do you think I invited him?"

Zoey smiled, and Johnny helped her to her feet and hugged her. "I love you, kiddo."

She didn't say she loved him back, but she hugged him, and that was enough for now. He closed the doors as they left the barn and followed Jillian and Zoey toward the chicken coop.

He couldn't hear what they were saying, but when Zoey reached for Jillian's hand, his heart nearly stopped. He found himself pulling out his phone and taking a picture of them. The need to gather memories was new to him, but when Jillian had told him about Zoey's mother leaving all of Zoey's pictures behind, he'd been determined to make up for it with a lifetime full of new memories.

As he followed them through the woods, their whispers and giggles leading the way, he thought about what Jillian had said earlier. She was right that he was meant to be a dad. He was getting the hang of it, and although it was the hardest thing he'd ever faced and he'd never felt so ill prepared for anything in his life, he was learning from the struggles and savoring the little victories. But she couldn't be more wrong about not being cut out to be a mom. She might not be the kind of woman who baked cookies or doted on people, but Jillian Braden's affection was as fierce and as strong as a lioness's, coming out in tough love, gentle nudges, and sexy sass.

If only she could see it.

Chapter Seventeen

I'M DOING THE right thing.

That's what Jillian told herself Friday evening when she was supposed to be packing, after telling Johnny that she thought it was better if they didn't sneak out tonight. It was one of the most heart-wrenching decisions she'd ever made, and she'd been an emotional wreck all day, missing Zoey and Johnny already despite having spent every moment by their sides. She'd managed to keep her emotions to herself for the most part, and she didn't want him to see her break down. She knew without a shadow of a doubt that if she was close to him tonight, if he held her in his arms, loving her the way only he could, she'd lose it.

This wasn't the time to be weak. Johnny needed to focus on Zoey, not worry about Jillian. When she'd taken Zoey to the inn this afternoon to return the books she'd borrowed, Zoey had been reduced to tears at the mere sight of Charlotte. It had broken Jillian's heart. The girl who had gone fourteen years living in a little bubble with her grandmother had developed lifelong bonds in less than two weeks while her life was in shambles. If that wasn't a testament to Zoey's ability to love, Jillian didn't know what was.

She wanted to be there to see what other incredible things Zoey would realize she was capable of. To see her face when she first walked into her new bedroom and watch her relationship with Johnny flourish. She wanted to help them both along the way. But now wasn't the time to long for impossibilities.

Jillian was determined to get through this without having an emotional meltdown. She took a deep breath and drew her shoulders back, mentally slipping into her girl-boss armor, and sent a group text to her family, letting them know she'd be home tomorrow. Then she focused on the miserable chore of packing.

She picked out slacks and a blouse to wear on the flight and carried the rest of her dress clothes to the bed to put them in her garment bag. Her fingers slid over the gorgeous designs she'd put her heart and soul into creating and had chosen carefully for her two weeks with Johnny in New York. She was supposed to spend her days getting to know his style, coming up with ideas, getting his feedback, eating at fabulous restaurants, and maybe taking in a show with one of her cousins or clients. She never would have imagined she'd end up horseback riding, playing lawn games, finding herself elbow deep in slimy-meatball concoctions, and falling for a surly teenager whose smiles lit her up inside and her cocky, misunderstood rock-star daddy, whose mere presence drove her wild, much less sneaking out to have sex in filthy places like two destitute lovers who would give their left arms for another hour together.

As she emptied her drawers, each piece brought back a memory. The pajamas she'd worn the first night they'd hooked up and the glorious way those first few kisses had awoken parts of her she hadn't even known existed. The sweater she'd worn the night they'd ravaged each other in the shed and the lace panties he'd taken off with his teeth after one of their barbecues with Beau and Charlotte.

This was *not* helping.

Her phone rang, and Trixie's name appeared on the screen. She was thankful for the distraction. "Hi, Trix."

"Hey. I saw the group text. You're coming home tomorrow?"

"Yup. We leave in the morning," she said as cheerily as she could, unwilling to give in to the ache in her chest. She'd never believed in faking it until she made it, but it suddenly became her new mantra.

"And...?"

Jillian ignored the knowing lilt in Trixie's voice. "And it'll be great to get back to my studio and catch up with the girls at the boutique and back to my normal client schedule. I can't wait to get started." It was true, but it also *wasn't*, because if staying in Colorado with Johnny and Zoey for another two weeks was an option, she'd move heaven and earth to clear her schedule and stick around.

"That's *great*," Trixie said curiously. "And what about you and Johnny?"

Jillian had confided in Trixie the other night about hooking up with Johnny, although she hadn't given her any sordid details. "What about us? We both knew this was temporary, and it's not like I need a busy rock star with a kid complicating my life. I'm barely going to have time to breathe when I get home. I didn't get much done while I was here." Which meant she'd be working long hours, which was perfect. The less downtime the better. Her mind did *not* need time to wander. "I started working on ideas for a young-teen fashion line that I'm excited about and really want to fit in at some point."

"How? By giving up sleep altogether?"

"You know me. I'll find a way."

"That's what I'm worried about," Trixie said softly. "Jilly, I got the impression you really liked Johnny and you were getting attached to Zoey."

"What's not to like? I'm pretty sure the man could make a dead woman come, and yeah, our chemistry is off the charts, and he makes me laugh, and he's the only person who has ever tried to teach me to cook, but he also annoys me. He's always pushing breakfast on me and making snarky comments." It wasn't a total lie. He was good at one-upping her, and he could get her hot and bothered with a single glance. That was annoying in the very best possible way, but Trixie didn't need to know that.

"Yeah, you're right. It's not like that kind of chemistry is rare or anything. I'm sure you can find dozens of guys you click with on that level right here in Pleasant Hill. You'll be swatting them away like flies."

"Exactly." Trixie's sarcasm wasn't lost on Jillian, but once again, she chose to ignore it. "And Zoey's great, but she's a teenager, and you know how attitudinal they are. With everything she's been through, there'll be endless drama." She felt guilty talking like that. But she was in self-preservation mode, and she couldn't afford to step out of it, because the alternative might take her to her knees. "But that's enough about them. Amber's wedding is next month, and I haven't gotten her a gift yet. Do you want to go shopping with me Sunday?"

"Sure, but, Jilly, this is *me* you're talking to. You don't have to hide your feelings. I grew up with a house full of brothers, just like you. I know what it's like to be tough and hold everything in so nobody knows you're hurting, and the problem with that is that it makes it hurt even worse."

Jillian went to the window, and her gaze caught on the colorful shed, and just beyond, the place where Johnny had come out of the woods with Zoey the night she'd run away. Swamped with too many emotions, Jillian relived the fear and relief of that night, and she closed her eyes, willing tears not to fall.

"Come on, Jilly," Trixie urged. "You know I'll keep your secrets."

She trusted Trixie explicitly, but she didn't trust herself to get her feelings out without falling apart, and once she unraveled, she wasn't sure she'd be able to put herself back together again. "I appreciate that, but I can't, Trix. I just...*can't*."

AFTER PACKING, JILLIAN set out to clean the cottage top to bottom to distract herself from the things she couldn't afford to think about and to avoid being alone with Johnny.

Unfortunately, Johnny insisted on helping, which meant he stealthily slid his hand along her ass while he vacuumed and stole her away to a bedroom closet for smooches. She'd finally told him to pick a floor, to which he'd responded, *I'd like to take you on every floor in the place.* That was too enticing, so she'd gone downstairs to clean the first floor and warned him not to follow. She'd then sent Zoey upstairs to help her father, leaving Jillian alone to work her fingers to the bone. She'd scrubbed every surface until it shined like glass. That was a feat in and of itself, since she didn't even clean her own house. She left that to her amazing housekeeper, whom she paid handsomely and who was now going to receive a raise and be paid like a queen.

She'd showered, worked, read, and had even walked a few laps around the yard, but hours later, as the clock neared midnight, she lay in her bed, a bundle of nerves. Her phone chimed, and she told herself not to look at it, but she wasn't that strong.

She read Johnny's text. *It's 12:01, and you're not here.* Her heart thudded faster as she thumbed out, *I'm not allowed out after midnight.* His response was immediate. *I'll sneak you out the window if I have to. I hear there's a great trellis by the hall bathroom.* She smiled despite her heartache as another text rolled in. *I miss you, and I know you miss me.*

More than he'd ever know, and she was hoping to keep it that way.

She texted, *You're making this harder.* He sent back a devil emoji, a heart-eyed emoji, and a winking emoji. She typed, *One emoji would have done it. Show-off.* Her thumb hovered over the arrow, but she felt a stab of longing. He always went above and beyond, like the night in the barn and all the sweet messages he'd sent, the flowers he'd left, and the dozens of other things he'd done for her and Zoey.

A lump formed in her throat, and she deleted the message and set down her phone, feeling so torn she wanted to cry.

But she refused.

She threw off her covers and headed into the bathroom to take another shower, hoping it might take the edge off so she didn't burst into tears. She flipped on the light and stumbled over her own feet at the sight of a handful of wildflowers lying on the vanity. How had he sneaked those in there? There was a note sticking out from beneath the stems. *I'll be waiting* was written in Johnny's messy handwriting, signed with a single heart instead of his name. She closed her eyes against a rush of tears. Her phone chimed again from the bedroom, and that simple sound opened the floodgates.

What the hell? She'd gone thirty years without crying over a guy, and suddenly she was like Niagara Falls? She turned on the shower and stripped off her clothes, hoping to stop the tears falling like rivers down her cheeks as she stepped beneath the warm water. But what was meant to relax her had the opposite effect, drawing more tears, and she was too emotionally exhausted to do anything more than let them flow.

She'd always considered herself strong, but for the first time in her life, as she wrapped her arms around herself, she wished she were stronger. She closed her eyes, letting the water wash away her tears. As she stood trembling despite the warmth of the water, their time together played out like a montage in her head, doing nothing to halt her tears.

The door to the shower opened, and she looked up through the blur of tears as Johnny stepped in and wrapped his strong arms around her, cocooning her against his naked body. He rested his cheek on the top of her head, his heart beating as frantically as hers. He was warm and familiar and everything she wished she didn't need.

"You shouldn't be in here," she said shakily. "It's too risky with Zoey right down the hall."

He cradled her face between his hands, eyes full of emotion. "Just let me have this."

He kissed her so tenderly, she melted into him, filling with relief, gratitude, and emotions so all-consuming, she was afraid to pick them apart. His hands moved along her shoulders, down her arms and back up again, causing ripples of desire and a wealth of those warm fuzzy feelings that had once been so foreign. Her body hummed with anticipation as his hands, familiar and arousing, slid down her back. She snaked her arms around his waist, holding his deliciously firm butt as he palmed hers, keeping their bodies flush as he intensified the kiss. His hard length pressed enticingly against her belly, and her heart begged for more. She broke the kiss, bending to take his thick cock in her mouth.

"Christ, baby." His words were full of emotions so much bigger than lust. She worked him faster, wanting more of that. He tangled his hands in her hair, hips pumping as she moaned around his length, earning a low groan. She stroked him tighter, faster, licking and sucking, and felt him swell impossibly thicker.

He groaned out, "*Fuck*," and pulled her up by the hair, crushing his mouth to hers. His fingers found her clit with mind-numbing precision. She clung to him, her back against the wall, her thoughts fracturing as he took her right up to the edge of release, her body quivering, pulsing, begging for more. Her head tipped back with something between a moan and a whimper, and he dropped to his knees, shoving her legs apart as his mouth covered her sex. He feasted with teeth and tongue, bringing his fingers into play. She closed her mouth to keep her needy sounds from escaping, clawing at the wall, at his hair, his shoulders. He pushed his fingers inside her, crooking them repeatedly, and took her clit between his teeth, sending her orgasm careening into her. She squeezed her eyes closed as she rode the waves of pleasure. And then he was kissing her again, rough and greedy. They both broke the kiss, demanding "I need you" in unison. He spun her around, driving into her in one hard thrust, and he didn't slow down. He pounded into her as roughly as he'd kissed her, *freeing* and *possessing* her at once, taking her right back up to the edge of madness. He fisted his hand in her hair, tugging her head to the side, and curled over her back, hips still pumping as his other hand snaked around her waist and dove between her legs. "You're mine, Jilly. *Mine*." He crushed his mouth to hers, working her clit faster, sending bolts of pleasure shooting through her, until it filled her with scintillating electric pulses.

As she came down from the peak, he growled against her lips, "I need *more* of you." He pulled out and turned her around, lifting her into his arms. She sank onto his cock as his hips shot up, burying him to the hilt, and they both cried out just as he recaptured her mouth. Her back hit the cold, wet tiles, the perfect leverage for him to send her soaring again. Riddled with so much pleasure, she could barely breathe, her inner muscles clenched like a vise around him.

"*Fuck. Fuck, baby.* I need to—" He pulled out, and her feet touched the floor as he fisted his cock. Warm spurts hit her stomach as he reclaimed her mouth in a passionate kiss that had her going up on her toes. He finished with a guttural, gratified sound and wrapped his arms around her, pressing his body to hers, his essence binding them together. His warm breath coasted over her shoulder as he kissed her there. "I want to be inside you all the time."

His words were as titillating as his touch. "That might be embarrassing when you're onstage."

He nipped at her neck. "Tough." His sexy smile cut right to her heart. "Like I said, you're *mine. Mine.*"

These two weeks were like a cruel joke. Right person, wrong time. She pressed a kiss to the center of his chest and forced the truth, for both their sakes. "You know that's not possible."

He took her chin between his fingers and thumb, tilting her face up and gazing deeply into her eyes. "Tonight it is."

A LONG WHILE later, they lay on their sides in Jillian's bed, her head resting on Johnny's arm, their legs intertwined. He knew he should go back to his room, but he didn't want to move. They'd ravaged each other twice just as frantically as they had in the shower, though fully protected, and it still wasn't enough. He wasn't craving more wild sex. He just wanted more of *her.* She was so unguarded when he'd stepped into the shower, her emotions so raw, he wished she'd told him how she felt instead of just trying to box him out. But why would she when tomorrow would change everything? She was too strong for her own good sometimes. Seeing her so sad reminded him of how small a part of their lives they'd shared. He wanted so much more. He wanted to hold her like this, like she was *his*, for her to trust him with all those other parts of herself she was so used to masking. He knew he was doing the right thing as far as Zoey was concerned, but damn it, he wanted it all.

He ran his fingers through her hair, thinking about all the changes he'd gone through since they'd gotten to Colorado. His business life was still a mess, and yet he was happier and more fulfilled than he'd been in a long time. He looked forward to spending time with Jillian and Zoey and seeing what each day held regardless of the emotional roller coasters that went along with his and Zoey's situation. He had no doubt he was a more patient father because of Jillian's influence, and he was actually coming up with new music. *Good* music, which he'd worried he might never do again.

He looked at the woman who had made such a big impact on his and Zoey's life in such a short time and wondered what it would be like if circumstances were different.

Jillian reached up and pressed her index finger between his brows. "What's this about? If you're not careful, you'll need Botox before I do."

She always knew how to make him smile. "I've just got a lot on my mind. Tomorrow's going to suck." He nuzzled against her neck. "I want to stay right here and hold you tonight."

"Zoey has enough trauma to work through. She doesn't need to find us tangled up in the sheets."

"I didn't say I was staying. I said I *wanted* to." He kissed her softly. "But I'm not leaving this bed until I've worshipped every inch of your body and loved you the way you deserve to be loved."

He rolled her onto her back, and her eyes narrowed. "That's an awfully big word to be throwing around when we're leaving tomorrow."

"I'm just differentiating what we're about to do from the fantastic fucking we've been doing."

She grinned up at him. "You mean you've been withholding other sexual talents? Because you have already surpassed every man who came before you." She wrinkled her nose. "No pun intended."

"And now I'm going to ruin you for all the rest of the men on the planet." He rained kisses down her neck and along the swell of her breast.

"And just how do you plan on doing that?"

He dragged his tongue around her nipple as he pushed two fingers into her slick heat. Their eyes collided with the darkest of hungers and the greediest of needs.

"With everything I have."

Chapter Eighteen

JILLIAN HAD THOUGHT saying goodbye to Johnny and Zoey would be the most difficult thing she faced today. But watching Zoey put on a stiff upper lip when she said goodbye to Beau and Charlotte nearly did her in. That stiff upper lip had lost the battle when she'd said goodbye to Bandit. She'd sunk to her knees and wrapped her arms around his neck, crying a river and reducing Jillian and Charlotte to tears, too. Jillian had cried more in the last two days than she'd probably cried in years, but she was determined to be done with that nonsense.

She was the one keeping a stiff upper lip on the flight home.

Gone was the need for each of them to sit in different areas, replaced with the desire to be close. Jillian's seat faced them. They'd tried to make small talk when they'd first settled into their seats, but conversations felt stilted by the things they were trying not to say. They'd been in the air for hours, and the silence was even more deafening than it had been on the trip to Colorado when they'd barely known each other.

Zoey was listening to music on Johnny's phone, staring absently out the window with the fish tank tucked between her feet on the floor. She was wearing the hoodie Johnny had given her with the hood pulled over her head. If Jillian could pull it off, she'd be hiding behind a hood, too. But her father was picking her up at the airport, and if he saw her dressed like that, he'd immediately know something was off. Johnny vacillated between glancing at them and tipping his head back, eyes closed. She knew he had to be exhausted. They'd dozed in and out of sleep until dawn, when he'd finally, reluctantly, gone back to his own room.

When the DC runway came into view, Jillian's stomach knotted. She was getting off there, and Johnny and Zoey would continue to New York without her.

She glanced at Johnny, with his thickened scruff, tousled hair, and sun-kissed cheeks, and she didn't even have to try to memorize the face she'd once seen only as arrogant. It was seared into her heart.

He winked and managed a small smile, but his fingers curled around his leg like a death grip told her that he was struggling, too. *We're doing the right thing.* That was her new mantra. It had to be if she was going to live up to her promises of seeing Zoey again to design her outfit without completely falling apart.

A nest of bees swarmed in her belly as the plane landed, minutes passing like hours until it finally came to a stop. Johnny and Zoey were both looking at her like they didn't want to move either, but there was no point in pretending this would end any other way. Mustering all the positivity she could, Jillian said, "I guess this is it."

They all stood at the same time. Jillian wanted to throw her arms around Johnny, kiss him one last time, and feel his warm lips against hers. But she stood stock-still and tried to keep it professional, because that was a hell of a lot easier than coming undone. "I'm really glad I went with you. I'll be in touch about the tour wardrobe as I make progress on the designs, and you can let me know my deadline once you figure things out."

He took her hand, just as he had on the flight out and a hundred times since, and drew her into his arms. "I will," he said tightly.

She closed her eyes, soaking in the feel of him, his familiar scent, and the rapid beat of his heart against her.

"This isn't over," he whispered, and kissed her cheek, giving her hand one last squeeze before letting go. "Thank you for coming with us and showing me who I could be and what life could be like if I wasn't arrogant and self-centered."

Thankful for the humor, she laughed softly, willing her tears not to fall. "Zoey's going to have to keep you in line." She turned to the young girl who made her question how much she really knew about herself, wanting to pull her into her arms and tell her how much she loved her. But she didn't want to make it any harder for her. "Think you can handle that, Zo?"

Zoey's gaze flicked to Johnny, her lower lip trembling. "I'll keep him in line." She threw her arms around Jillian. "I'm going to miss you."

The words she'd meant to hold back tumbled out. "I love you, and I'm going to miss you, too. You're an amazing person, and I know you're going to have the greatest life with Johnny and your new family."

Zoey held her tighter, so much like her dad, her tears wetting Jillian's cheek. "Aren't we going to see each other again? To make the outfit?"

"Yes, I hope we will, but don't feel pressured. I'm sure you'll make lots of new friends and you'll want to hang out with them, and you'll be busy spending time with your grandparents and aunts and uncle. I want that for you, Zoey. I want you to be happy."

"But I want to see *you*, too," Zoey said with a thread of panic.

Jillian drew back, the sight of Zoey's tears nearly bringing her own, but she fought them off with everything she had. "I will *always* be here for you, but what's most important is that you keep doing the things you love, like playing guitar with your dad and riding horses and staying open to learning new things along the way, because I know you're going to do great things. Promise me you will."

Zoey nodded tearfully. "I promise."

Jillian turned to Johnny, the ache in her chest deepening as she said "Bye" one last time and walked out of the plane, leaving two of the biggest pieces of herself behind.

Tears brimmed, but she refused to let them fall. She would get through this like she got through every hard thing she'd ever done in her life. She straightened her spine and squared her shoulders, holding her head up high despite the ache in her heart, and reminded herself that she was Jillian Braden, the woman who had single-handedly built a fashion empire—and had no fucking idea what to do with the emotions swamping her.

Her father was already loading her luggage into his trunk when she came off the plane. He smiled and waved. It didn't matter what she was facing. The sight of his warm smile always comforted her. *That's* what she wanted for Zoey. That sense of safety, of knowing that when she saw Johnny, he would ease whatever pain she felt, and Jillian knew the only way Johnny could be wholly present for his daughter was if he wasn't also trying to be there for her.

"There's my girl." Her father hugged her tight. "How was the trip?"

"Great. Thanks for coming to get me." *Don't cry. Don't cry. Don't cry.*

He opened her door, and after she got in, he settled into the driver's seat, brows knitted. "Are you okay? You sound a little down."

"Yeah. I just got a little too attached to"—she stopped before saying *them*—"Zoey. I didn't expect it to be so hard to leave her."

As he drove away off the tarmac, he said, "Beau mentioned how close you'd gotten. I wondered how you'd handle leaving."

"Apparently not so well, and I don't get it. I haven't even known them for two full weeks, and it's not like I'm someone who gets attached like that. Why her? She's a teenager, and I'm not great with kids. One minute she's got this attitude like nothing can hurt her, and my brain goes to tough love, and in the next breath, all her vulnerabilities come out and she's crying and all I want to do is make it better."

"She sounds pretty special."

"She *is*," she relented as he drove away from the airport. "And you should've seen Johnny. He was totally freaked out when I got there, which was right after he found out about Zoey, but then he worked *so* hard to build a relationship with her. The poor guy came to *me* for advice. Can you imagine? What do I know about raising kids? I was barely a kid when *I* was a teenager. I was so focused on becoming the next great designer, I hardly paid attention to kids my age. I probably didn't help him much, but he figured it out. He got through to her, and anyone can see how much he loves her. They tease each other a lot, but he knows when to bring the hammer down and just how gently to do it."

"It sounds like Johnny *Butthead* ended up being pretty special, too, and honestly, he sounds a lot like you."

"We do have a lot more in common than I ever would have thought. I really misjudged him. He was dealing with a lot of family stuff before he found out about Zoey, and then his entire life imploded, but, Dad, he became a father she could be proud of, and count on, like you."

"Kids and the people we love have a way of grounding us. I bet you'll miss him, too."

She nodded, her throat thickening again. "But shouldn't I be able to just walk away without feeling like my heart is being ripped out?"

"That's the funny thing about love, honey. You meet thousands of people in your lifetime, and you might get attached to a handful of them. But when the *right* people come into your life, the ones who are meant to stay there forever, that kind of connection is bigger than we are. We can't escape it, and most of the time we don't understand it, but that's what makes it so special. That kind of love is everlasting."

"But I don't make connections like that. I'm too busy, and I don't even know how to make people feel warm and welcome the way other girls do. I'm like, *You're having a hard time? Okay, let's figure it out and move on.* Warm and fuzzy are like foreign objects to me."

"Is that really how you see yourself?"

"Yes, and you know it's true."

He shook his head as he drove away from the airport. "No, I don't. You can be tough, and you speak your mind, which is something to be proud of, but you do it because you care deeply about people and you will fight for their happiness, even if it means telling them if they're screwing up."

"I think that makes me hard to be with."

"Maybe for some, but that just means they're not your people. You don't take love lightly, and you don't waste your time on people who aren't worthy of it. That's something Zoey could learn from. But for those who are worthy, baby girl, you give *everything* you have. You may not coddle or dote, but you don't need to. Your love comes through in the things you say and in the way you give of yourself."

"Do you really mean that?"

"Absolutely. You've been on the move since the day you learned how to walk. When we realized fashion wasn't just a phase for you, your mother and I said, *Watch out world. This girl is going to do incredible things, and nothing will stand in her way.* You've proven us right. You haven't slowed down since you did your first fashion show in our backyard. But from what I hear, you spent the last two weeks playing games and living life, not hunkering down designing from ten in the morning until two the next morning. Is that true?"

"Yes. I was trying to help Zoey and Johnny connect."

"The fact that you slowed down and enjoyed life for what is probably the first time since you were four tells me just how special they are, and from the sounds of it, you probably had a lot to do with why Johnny was able to become the father Zoey needs. Morgyn would tell you there's a reason the universe brought you to his penthouse that morning, and I'm inclined to believe there was a little magic at work that day, too."

Jillian gazed out the window, thinking about what he'd said. She *was* fighting for Zoey's happiness, and for Johnny's as a father, and she knew she was doing the right thing. As if his ears were burning, her phone vibrated with a text from Johnny. She held her breath as she opened and read it. *We miss you already.* A picture of him and Zoey popped up. Zoey's eyes were damp, and Johnny's were so full of emotion, Jillian's tears broke free.

WHEN JILLIAN WALKED off the plane, Johnny felt like his heart was being ripped out of his chest. But there was no time to think about that when his daughter was in tears beside him. He drew her into his arms, promising things were going to be okay. Zoey insisted she was *fine* with an anything-but-fine tone and too many tears. Eventually, sending a text to Jillian helped Zoey feel a little better, but she'd been silent the rest of the trip home.

It was just as well, because he was struggling with missing Jillian, too.

As they were driven through Manhattan, Johnny looked at the skyscrapers towering over the congested roads and people rushing along crowded sidewalks while staring at their phones. The sounds of traffic were suffocating even in the back of the vehicle. He didn't have to open the window to know he missed the crisp, clean air, the serenity of nature, and fuck it all to hell, he missed his snarky, fire-breathing beauty most of all.

He spotted paparazzi camped out in front of his building. He fucking hated this part of fame, and he despised it even more now that he had Zoey to protect. "Zoey, there are paparazzi around our building. They might holler and run for the car. But don't be scared. They can't get to you or see you, okay?"

She nodded, nervously looking out the tinted windows as they turned the corner, slowing as they approached the vehicle-elevator entrance. The paparazzi spotted them and ran toward the car, cameras to their eyes, shouting. "Are you *sure* they can't see us?" The worry in Zoey's voice was palpable.

"Yes." The elevator door opened, and the driver pulled in, the shouts of the paparazzi fading as the elevator door closed behind them.

"Don't they have anything better to do than wait around here for two weeks?" Zoey snapped. "Why didn't you just get out and tell them to back the heck off?"

"Because they get paid for the pictures they take, and that would only give them the chance to sell pictures of me losing my temper, which would end up with twisted headlines aimed to piss us off. Like JOHNNY BAD ATTACKS PHOTOGRAPHERS WITH DAUGHTER IN CAR. IS HE FIT TO BE A FATHER?"

"They suck," she said angrily. Then, softer, "You're a good father."

He had no idea those four words could mean so much coming from her. "Thanks, sunshine. You're a good daughter, too. The best."

As the elevator rose, Zoey clutched the seat, frantically looking around. "What's happening?"

"This is an elevator. It'll bring us to the garage in the penthouse, so we can avoid the paparazzi."

"Whoa. You must be *really* rich."

He smiled. "We have a buck or two."

She lowered her eyes, fidgeting with the hole in her jeans. "Thank you."

"For what?"

"Keeping me safe and making Jillian come with us to Colorado."

He put his hand over hers, giving it a reassuring squeeze, wishing he'd asked Jillian to come with them to New York and, at the same time, knowing they both had too much on their plates to make it work. "There's nothing I won't do for you, but Jillian could've gotten out of going with us. I'm pretty sure she went because she wanted to be there for *you*."

"I'm gonna miss her." Her voice sounded strangled, tugging at him even more.

"Me too, sunshine. We'll see her again—don't worry."

When they arrived in the garage, Johnny grabbed their luggage and thanked the driver, while Zoey carried the fish and the stuffed bear he'd won for her, and they headed through the service hall into the penthouse.

"Welcome home, sunshine. Let me show you around." He set down his bags and carried Zoey's as they headed down the hall. Zoey glanced tentatively at the eat-in kitchen and massive dining room. He'd bought the penthouse more than a decade ago, when his financial adviser had told him to sink his money into real estate. It had become his sanctuary, his escape from the rest of the world, but Zoey looked so uncomfortable, gazing at the pretentious hand-carved table for ten, and he realized how intimidating it must look to her. Now it felt off to him, too.

"Do we have to eat in here?" she asked.

"Of course, and the butler will walk you to the table every night," he said as seriously as he could, trying to lighten the mood.

She gave him a deadpan stare.

"Think about it, sunshine. You've eaten dinner with me for two weeks. Do I strike you as the kind of guy who eats in a formal dining room?"

She shrugged.

"The answer is no. I've only eaten at that table a few times when my family was in town and when my bandmates and their families came over for dinner. I usually eat at the kitchen table or on the couch if I'm watching a game. This is your home, and I hope you'll be comfortable here. Let's go check out your room."

"*My* room?"

"Yes, but there's no maid, so you'll have to keep it clean."

"That's fine. I cleaned the whole house with my grandma."

"Really?"

She nodded. "That's how I earned my allowance."

Dare had told him it would be good to keep any routines Zoey had been used to with her grandmother, but Johnny hadn't even considered giving her allowance. He'd assumed he'd just give her money when she needed it, but he'd been given an allowance before he'd been discovered, and it had helped him learn how to manage money. *If only I'd continued managing my finances. Maybe then Dick wouldn't have gotten away with so much.* He shook that joke of a thought off. There was a big difference between managing a few bucks and managing millions. Music was his thing. Finances and business were Kane's.

"Tell me about your allowance."

Zoey looked around. "Are you going to make me clean the whole place? Because the fourteen dollars my grandma gave me isn't enough for that."

He chuckled. "I was kidding about the maid. A wonderful woman named Terri comes every other week. I only expect you to clean up after yourself, not after me. But I like the idea of an allowance. Let's think about how that should work."

"I can keep my room clean and do my laundry and help with dinner dishes."

"That sounds fair to me."

They walked into the elaborate living room near the main entrance, and she went to look out the floor-to-ceiling windows. "Wow. You live on the water."

He was caught up in the memory of Jillian coming off the elevator in that sexy white dress, ready to tear him apart. God, how things had changed. He cleared his throat to try to clear his head and turned to look out the windows. "*We* live on the water. That's the Hudson River. Do you like the water?"

She nodded. "I love beaches. My grandma and I used to go to Cape May and stay with her friend John for a week every summer. But he was really old, and he died two years ago. That was the last time we went."

"I grew up at the beach in Cape Cod, which is in Massachusetts. I—*we*—have a house there, so we'll be sure to go."

"Is it as big as this place?" she asked with a bite of distaste.

"No. It's a small three-bedroom cottage."

"Sounds cool." She looked at the black and white leather couches and brushed-stainless-steel and glass tables with an uneasy expression. "Am I allowed to sit in *here*?"

He set down her suitcases. "Sunshine, this is your home. You can use, sit in, lie down in, and spend time in any room you'd like, but I'd rather you didn't go into my recording studio without me, because there's expensive equipment in there."

"You have a recording studio *here?*"

"Yeah. If you ever wake up in the middle of the night and I'm not in my room, I'm probably in the studio." He pointed across the room to a glass floor on the far-left side of the room. "That glass opens with a push of a button, and there are stairs below it that lead down to the recording studio and a guest bedroom. I'll show it to you after we put your stuff in your room."

Her eyes widened. "The floor opens? That's so cool."

"Yeah, so are you." He picked up her suitcases—the old one and the new one he'd gotten for her new clothes. "Come on. I'll show you your room."

"One sec." She walked over to the fireplace and placed the fish tank on the mantel. "Is this okay?"

"Sure. You don't want them in your room?"

She shook her head. "I thought you might want to see them, too. You know, to remember that night with Jillian."

That was a night he'd never forget. "Thank you."

He led her down the hall to her bedroom. "I hope you like it. Jillian helped pick everything out, because, you know, I've never been a teenage girl. We can change anything you don't like." He flipped on the light and stepped aside so she could walk in first.

She didn't say a word as she walked in. Her gaze trailed over the boulder-gray dressers and white desk and chair, to the reading nook with a round pink chair and a squarish teal one, to the wall just beyond, where her name hung in enormous brushed-silver letters. She looked down at the multicolored throw rug beneath her feet and then across the room at the bookshelves, which Jillian had had stocked with books and other things she'd ordered that she'd thought Zoey would like.

"Jilly picked out books, an ereader, journals for you to write in, and sketch pads for your clothing designs."

Zoey pressed her lips together, looking like she either wanted to smile or cry, and continued walking around the room. She put her stuffed bear in the pink chair and touched the pink-and-teal curtains as she gazed out the window at the view of the water. She didn't look at Johnny as she made her way to the bed and ran her fingers along the fluffy white comforter with colorful butterflies, flowers, and skulls on it. Her gaze swept over the teal headboard and over the bright throw pillows with teal and pink accents that Jillian had insisted Zoey needed. *A girl's bedroom is her refuge. She'll go there to cry into pillows when boys break her heart, and she'll flop onto those same pillows in fits of laughter with her friends.* He'd told her he'd kill any boy who broke Zoey's heart, and she'd laughed at him, telling him he'd better table those urges. If only she were there with them now. She'd know just what to say to make things easier for all of them.

Zoey looked up at the three swooping strings of lights he'd had hung on the wall above the headboard and scrambled onto the bed to get a better look at the pictures hanging from them. He got the chills as she reached up and touched the photos of her and her grandmother. Tears spilled down her cheeks as she looked at the other pictures of her and Jillian on horseback and playing yard games and of Zoey and him playing guitar and laughing while making dinner—*thank you, Jillian.* She laughed softly at pictures from their last barbecue with Beau and Charlotte and touched the pictures of her and Bandit reading beneath a tree and sleeping on her bed at the cottage.

She turned, her eyes sweeping over the jewelry box on the nightstand, bringing more tears. She sat down and pulled the wooden jewelry box into her lap. Her head bent, tears flowing as she opened it, and music began playing, the tiny ballerina inside spinning.

He sat beside her and put his arm around her.

"You found it," she whispered.

"I always want you to remember the woman who raised you and loved you and the people and things that are important to you, so I had Kane track down what he could from when you lived with your grandmother. I was also able to get your grandmother's ashes. We have them, sunshine."

She gasped and looked at him through a rush of tears. "Where?"

"They're in an urn in my safe, and when you're ready, you can decide what you want to do with them. We can have a funeral or scatter them someplace special. Whatever you want."

"Is it weird if I want to keep them?" she asked in a shaky voice.

"Not at all. It'll be nice for you to always know she's nearby."

She cried through a smile, and he pulled her against his side, holding her as sobs she'd probably been holding in for weeks tumbled out. When her tears finally slowed, she wiped them away and said, "Thank you. Thank you so much."

"I have one more thing to show you." He got up and reached for the doorknob to the ridiculously large walk-in closet and dressing area he'd had transformed into an ample closet and sewing room, knowing she couldn't see into the room from where she sat. He opened the door, revealing the brightly lit sewing room with long white countertops with drawers and shelves beneath lining two walls. Pegboards filled with various sewing accoutrements and corkboards for Zoey to pin her sketches on hung above the counters. There was a drawing table with a silver and pink chair, a sewing mannequin, and against the opposite wall from the door was her grandmother's sewing machine. "Jillian designed this room for you. You don't have to use it, but with how much you enjoy messing around with clothes, we thought you might like it."

She set the jewelry box on the nightstand and went to the doorway.

"Ohmygod." Tears flooded her eyes as she ran across the room, touching the ancient sewing machine and tracing her name, which was etched into the antique table that held the machine. "How'd you find it? I thought it was gone forever."

"The Rileys, your neighbors who owned Charlie, bought the sewing machine and jewelry box from the estate sale. They said if you ever came back, they thought you'd want them. We tried to find Charlie, but he'd already been adopted from the shelter."

"You tried to get *Charlie?*" she asked incredulously, swiping at tears.

"I tried to adopt Bandit, too, but Beau wouldn't give him up. He said it was a good way to get us back there to visit."

Zoey laughed and cried and threw her arms around him again, hugging him tight. "Thank you so much. I can't believe you and Jillian did all this for *me.*"

"We love you, sunshine. I guess that means you like it."

"I *love* it." She wiped her eyes with her sleeve. "Can I borrow your phone to call Jillian? I want to thank her."

"I don't think so," he said casually, walking back into her room.

"But you *said* I could still talk to her," she complained. "I want her to know how much I like everything."

He opened the nightstand and pulled out the phone he'd gotten her. "You can. On your *own* phone."

There were many more hugs and *thank you*s, and then she called Jillian on video chat.

"Zoey! How are you? Are you home?"

The sound of Jillian's excited voice brought back the bone-deep ache he'd been trying to ignore.

"Yes, and I just saw my room! And the sewing room! Thank you! Can I put you on video chat?"

He wanted to jump into their conversation, to see Jillian's beautiful face and tell her how much he missed her, but he knew there would be no masking his feelings. He left the room instead, giving them privacy and giving himself time to pull his shit together.

He went through the motions of making dinner, glad when Zoey offered to help. He thought she'd be a good distraction from his thoughts, but she couldn't stop talking about how much she missed Jillian.

"I know you miss her, too," Zoey said as they set the table.

He thought it best not to respond and retrieved two glasses from the cabinet.

"She asked how you were."

"Yeah? That's nice." He set the glasses on the table.

"Don't you want to know how she is?" Zoey asked, annoyed.

He faced the girl who he worried might not ever open herself to love again and realized that by keeping his feelings to himself, he was teaching her how to turn her back on her own feelings. "Yes, Zoey. I do want to know how she is, but I got a little too used to seeing her. It's just going to take me some time to get used to not seeing her."

"Well, she said she's fine, but I know she misses us. I could tell."

"I think we'll all miss each other for a while."

They had a nice dinner, and Zoey was relieved that he'd put off seeing her new school until next Monday in order to let some of the hype over their return to town and his upcoming interviews pass. After they finished eating, he said, "We're going to see my family at my parents' house in Boston next weekend."

"Okay," she said a little nervously. "Will Kane be there?"

"Yes. So will Harlow and Aria, and everyone's looking forward to meeting you. I don't want you to worry about whether they'll like you, because I know they will. But there is something I need to tell you." He moved his chair so he could take her hand in his. "I don't want to scare you, but I will be honest with you, even when it's hard."

"Now you *are* scaring me."

"I'm sorry, but you need to know this. My mother has cancer, but she's doing great, and the doctors think she's going to be just fine. She's going through chemo, and it's shrinking the tumor so she can have surgery to remove it in January. But she's lost a lot of her hair, and she might get tired easily when we see her."

Sadness washed over her features. "Last year a girl in my school's mom got cancer, and she lost her hair and had to have surgery, and she was fine afterward."

"That's good, and that's what we anticipate will happen with my mom."

"Is *she* scared?"

"She's a really strong person, and I think she has faith that she'll be okay, but I'm sure she gets scared sometimes."

"What about you? Are you scared?"

"Cancer is a scary word, but I'm holding on to the hope that the doctors are right and she'll be okay."

He went on to tell her about his mother's first bout with cancer, and he answered all her questions and hopefully waylaid her worries. "I know it's a lot to digest, especially after losing your grandmother."

"I wish my grandma had died from cancer and not an aneurysm. Then at least I would have known something could happen to her."

"I understand how that might have made it easier. But it also might have made it harder. Watching someone you love in pain is difficult."

They talked for a while longer, and after cleaning up from dinner, he showed her his studio. She was mesmerized, asked a million questions, and she wanted to practice guitar more than ever. He gave her one of his guitars to use. She was really getting the hang of it, and Johnny loved that she was so into music.

After she went to bed, Johnny caught up with his family, his assistant, Jerry, and his bandmates. They had a lot of decisions to make about the business and their tour, and they scheduled meetings with Kane and Victory for later in the week at the apartment, so he wouldn't have to leave Zoey.

Midnight found him pacing the living room, his thoughts running in circles, still plagued with missing Jillian. He'd wanted to text her a hundred times and tell her how much he missed her and how badly he wanted to make things work between them, even if it meant waiting six months or a year. But she hadn't responded to the text he'd sent after she'd gotten off the plane, and not responding was a message in and of itself, wasn't it?

He walked over to the mantel and watched the fish, remembering Jillian's expression when she won them. "What do you two think? I should let her go, but I can't." He wanted to ask Jillian to wait for him for however long it took for him and Zoey to get settled into their lives, but that wasn't fair. He didn't want to be the guy who let her down or forgot to text or call. But the need to connect with her, to let her know how he felt, was visceral. He pulled out his phone and sat on the couch, thumbing out, *It's 12:01. Wish you were here*, and stared at the screen. His thumb hovered over the arrow as her voice whispered through his mind. *Don't go falling for me, Johnny. You're on the family track, and as much as I like Zoey, that's a hard pass for me.*

"Too fucking late."

He deleted the message, but he couldn't shake the need to reach out, and finally texted, *Thanks for helping with Zoey's room. Is it good to be home?* He got up and paced, waiting for a reply, which came just a few minutes later. *I'm glad she loves it. The stuff from her grandma's meant the world to her. Good job, Daddy Bad. It's nice to be home, although I miss having a personal chef.* He read the message several times, overthinking the fact that she'd written *a personal chef* instead of *my personal chef.* The three dots danced again like she was typing, and his fucking pulse sped up as he waited for more, but the dots stopped, then disappeared altogether, leaving him feeling gut punched.

But he *knew* her. She wasn't done with them any more than she'd been done last night when he'd found her crying in the shower. The question was, would those feelings last for however long it took him and Zoey to find their footing?

As if she were sitting on his shoulder, her voice tiptoed through his mind again. *We're like star-crossed lovers, and star-crossed lovers don't get happy endings.*

Whoever thought up that bullshit needed to have their head handed to them with a two-by-four. *It's 12:01, and I wish you were here* sang through his mind like a lyric, and he found himself stringing more words together, emotions he'd been holding in, and tapping his foot to an unfamiliar tune.

Holy hell. This is a song.

A really fucking good song.

He headed across the room, pushed the button, and hurried down to his studio.

Chapter Nineteen

"YOU LOOK LIKE hell," Kane said when he arrived early Monday morning.

"Good to see you too, bro," Johnny said sarcastically as Kane pulled him into an embrace, clapping him on the back.

"I was going to ask how it's going with Zoey, but if your appearance is any indication, I guess it's not going well. You look like you've been out partying all night."

"You know me better than that. I've been working on a song the last two nights."

"Really? So pining after a hot piece of ass does it for you?"

Johnny glowered as he lowered his voice. "Talk about Jillian like that again, and we're going to have trouble. And watch your mouth. Zoey's right down the hall."

Kane smirked. "Guess that means you finally got a piece."

"Are you *looking* for a black eye, asshole? Because I'd be happy to mess up that pretty face of yours."

"I'm just checking the seriousness of this thing, that's all. I'm glad Jillian finally bent over backward for you."

Johnny lunged at him, and Kane sprinted around the couch, laughing. Johnny caught the back of his shirt and spun him around, cocking his fist as Kane's leg swept across his ankles, taking them both to the ground. They landed with heavy thuds and matching groans and immediately began wrestling and cracking up.

Zoey walked by and said, "Get a room, perverts."

They rolled onto their backs, laughing.

"Your father needed his butt kicked," Kane said as they pushed to their feet, and Johnny realized why he'd goaded him into a fight. His brother always knew when he needed to blow off steam.

Zoey crossed her arms, eyes narrowing. "What're you fighting about?"

They both mumbled, "Nothing."

"Who started it?" she asked.

They pointed at each other, laughing again.

"Watch it, Kane. You're *old*. My dad can definitely take you."

Johnny was stunned at her use of *dad*, and the way Kane was looking at him, it appeared to have struck him just as hard. "Damn right I can." Johnny raked a hand through his hair.

"Thirty-eight is not old, kid," Kane insisted.

"Well, it's not *young*." Zoey crossed her arms, and a small smile broke free. "But I guess I need to give you a break since you went to all that trouble to track down my stuff. That was really nice of you. Thank you, but my money's still on Johnny."

Kane laughed, low and measured. "As well it should be. Welcome to the family, kid. You're going to fit right in."

BY THE TIME Johnny went to his last interview, he'd had enough of the same questions about Dick and how the situation with Zoey had come to light, enough of feeling like he had to defend himself and of fighting crowds to get into his waiting car. But he managed to keep his calm, because every move he made and every word he said would affect the way the world viewed his daughter, and in turn, they would affect Zoey's relationships with teachers and kids at school. Not to mention how his daughter viewed him. Zoey had asked if she could watch the interviews as they were aired, and he said she could as long as she was with Kane. He trusted Kane explicitly, but he wished Jillian was with her, too. Kane would make sure Zoey understood where Johnny's responses were coming from, but Jillian had a way of explaining things that made it easy for Zoey to see the bigger picture and the ramifications of situations, and she usually did it without saying more than a few words. He wondered if she was watching the interviews and if she missed them as much as they missed her.

"Is there anything else you'd like to say to your fans?" the host asked, drawing him back to the moment.

"Yes." He looked directly into the camera, and this time he didn't hold back. "This is an important time for me and my daughter, and I have one request for fans and the media. I grew up in the spotlight, but that was *my* choice. Zoey didn't choose to live a life where her every move would be scrutinized or remarked on in the headlines. My daughter is *not* a love child. She wasn't a secret baby, and she sure as hell isn't a mistake. She's a bright, caring, fourteen-year-old who has lost someone she dearly loved, and she is dealing with major life changes. While I ask that you respect our privacy and refrain from spreading misleading information about my family, I give you my *word* that I will take action against anyone who goes against my request."

ON THE RIDE home, Johnny pulled out his phone to check his messages, hoping for one from Jillian. He scrolled through texts from his parents, sisters, bandmates, Victory, Shea, and about a dozen others, with the exception of the one he'd been hoping for.

He was responding to them when a new message bubble popped up, with Jillian's name on it. His heart raced like a fucking teenager with a crush as he opened it. *You nailed it. Way to protect your girl!* She added a pink heart emoji.

He thumbed out, *Nobody messes with Mini Bad. Say you're my girl and I'll protect you, too.*

Her reply was instant. *Johnny…*

He cocked a brow, texting, *I'm sure you meant to type "Oh, Johnny" to be read in that breathy voice you use when I'm buried deep inside you.* Another message popped up. *I'm at work!* He couldn't resist getting under her skin and typed, *And I bet you're thinking about me bending you over the desk.* She replied with a shocked emoji. He laughed, and another message appeared. *Well, NOW I am, and I have a client meeting in ten minutes. Thanks a lot.* He thumbed out, *Just keeping your man on your mind* and added a flame emoji. She sent an eye roll emoji and, *I'm going now. Try to be good.* "You walked right into this one, baby," he said as he typed, *Why be good when you love it when I'm bad?*

When he got home, he found Zoey and Kane at the dining room table playing cards. His brother's jaw was tight, while Zoey was grinning. She popped to her feet and ran to hug him. "Thank you for what you said. That was pretty badass."

There was something great about being called badass by his daughter. "I guess you heard the last interview."

She nodded. "We watched them all."

"I've always got your back, sunshine."

"Well, tonight I've got *yours.*" She whipped a wad of cash out of her back pocket. "Dinner is on me!"

He eyed the cash, then Kane. "Where'd that come from?"

"I won it playing poker," she said proudly, and walked over to Kane, patting his shoulder. "Thanks for hanging out with me, loser."

"You bet, swindler."

She grinned a mile wide. "I have to go text Jillian and tell her I kicked Kane's butt!"

As she ran to her room, Johnny called after her, "I'm not sure you should be so proud of gambling."

"Whatever!"

She closed her door, and Johnny turned to Kane. "You taught my daughter to play poker?"

"No, sir. She *played* me. Her grandmother taught her to play when she was ten, and apparently her gambling grandma also taught her the tricks of the trade, because she whooped my ass."

Chapter Twenty

LATE THURSDAY MORNING, JILLIAN was poring over designs, trying to concentrate, when a text rolled in from Zoey. *Can you talk?*

How could one text make Jillian's whole world feel more balanced?

She'd been feeling *off* all week. She'd claimed to be too tired to have dinner with her parents Saturday night and again on Sunday, only to find her mother on her doorstep Monday evening with dinner in hand. She was pretty sure her mother hadn't bought her excuse of being too tired to chat, but there was no use spilling her guts when it wouldn't get her anywhere. She'd been trying to catch up with clients and lose herself in work all week but to no avail. The only designs she was feeling inspired to work on were the ones for the young-teen line, which made her feel closer to Zoey and Johnny, and that wasn't good. She really needed to stop losing herself in thoughts of them and focus on her clients. Especially since other than the dirty texts she'd gotten from Johnny on Monday, she hadn't heard from him at all. Zoey, on the other hand, had texted or video chatted daily to say she missed her and give her updates on her life.

Jillian glanced at the clock. It was eleven forty-five, and she was meeting Trixie and Jordan for lunch at noon. She'd managed to get out of shopping with Trixie on Sunday and had put off seeing her and Jordan earlier in the week, but yesterday Trixie had threatened bodily harm if she didn't agree to meet them for lunch today. It was just as well. Jillian needed to get her head on straight, and she hoped seeing her friends would do the trick.

She texted Zoey, *Sure. I'm on my way to lunch.*

She grabbed her bag and sunglasses as she answered Zoey's call and headed out of her studio and downstairs to her boutique. "Hey, Zo. How are you?"

"*Okay.* Johnny is teaching me to read music, and I'm getting really good at it."

"That's great. Maybe you can play something for me sometime." She poked her head into Liza's office, mouthed, *I'm going to lunch,* and headed out the doors that separated the offices from the boutique, waving at Annabelle, the cute blonde who ran the shop, on her way out the front door.

"I'm not *that* good yet," Zoey said.

"I bet you're better than you think." She put on her sunglasses and headed down the brick-paved sidewalk toward her childhood friend Emmaline's café, where she was meeting Trixie and Jordan.

"Johnny says I have a knack for it, but he has to say that. He's my dad."

Jillian warmed at her use of *dad.* She told herself not to ask about him, but that was like trying not to drink Diet Pepsi. "How is your dad?"

"Okay, I guess. He's been working a lot from home. He's in a meeting right now with Kane and Victory. She's really nice. She told me she's your cousin, and oh my gosh, she is *so* pretty, but it's weird that she's so tall and you're so short."

"*Petite,* Zoey, not short. It sounds better."

"Okay. Anyway, I met the guys in his band last night, and they're really cool and pretty funny."

"I'm glad you like them." She felt a pang of jealousy. *He's back to his normal schedule, so why am I having such a hard time?*

"Me too. They let me watch them work on a song in the studio. It was cool. I thought they just thought up the lyrics, like it was easy, and when they went into the studio, they just played and recorded it.

But in some parts of the songs, they didn't even know what they were going to sing or how the music should go, and they all figured it out together. One person would say something, and Johnny would go, 'That's it!' then say something completely different, like the lines came to him out of nowhere."

"Their comments probably inspired him. I think it's that way with every type of art. Like when you decide what to do to your clothes. You see a picture or think of how you want to look, and you just know, right?"

"I guess. But it was cool to watch, and Johnny's been working in his studio every night after I go to bed. I can't wait to hear the songs when they're done."

"Me too," she said, wishing she were there to see him in action and share in that side of his life with them. "Have you been out at all?"

"Not really. There are still photographers hanging around. Not as many, but I don't like it. It's creepy knowing people are watching where we live."

"I'm sorry, but that'll probably stop as soon as the next big story comes out. I don't think they'll hound you forever. Are you still nervous about meeting Johnny's family this weekend, or are you feeling better about it?" Earlier in the week, Zoey had told her that Johnny had told her about his mother's cancer and that she and Johnny had been practicing playing "I Want to Hold Your Hand" so she could try to play it for his mother.

"That's why I wanted to talk to you. I'm nervous, but Johnny and Kane have talked about them so much, I'm kind of excited to meet them."

"You should be. That's good, Zoey."

"I guess, but I also feel kind of guilty. It feels like I'm doing something wrong being excited to meet another grandmother. I don't really know what I believe as far as if my grandma can see me or not, but I don't want her to think I could ever love anyone more than her."

For the millionth time, Jillian wished she were there with her. "Zoey, love isn't a competition. I didn't know your grandma, but when you love someone, you want them to be happy, and I think your grandma is watching over you, and she's proud of who you are and how you're handling things. I bet she's *hoping* you'll love the rest of your family as much as you loved her."

"Really?" Zoey asked in a thin, hopeful voice.

"Absolutely."

Zoey sighed loudly. "I wish you could go with us to meet them."

Me too. "You don't need me, honey. There's nothing you can't handle, and you'll have your dad with you."

"I'm also not sure I can handle the school visit next week."

"Sure you can. I know meeting new people is scary, and you worry because you grew up in a different place without knowing your father, but your grandmother's influence is one of the reasons you're so wonderful. Just be yourself, honey. Don't try to be whoever you think they want to meet."

"I won't. I hate fake people."

"Me too. Remember to hold your head up high. You're Johnny Bad's daughter, and you had an amazing grandmother. Those kids will be lucky to be your friends."

"What if they ask about my mom?"

Jillian crossed the street and stopped on the sidewalk in front of the café. "What do you want to tell them?"

"That she sucked, and I'm glad I don't have to see her anymore."

"Then that's what you do, sweetie."

"Seriously?"

"You do know who you're asking, right?"

Zoey giggled.

"To be on the safe side, maybe you should ask your dad what he thinks, too, but I think you're going to be fine. You're the coolest teenager I know, and if anyone gives you a hard time, I'll show up and knock some sense into them."

Zoey laughed. "The paparazzi would love that. FASHION DE-

SIGNER'S FISTS FLY AT LOCAL HIGH SCHOOL."

"Listen to you making up headlines. You sound like your father," she said with a smile.

"We've been doing it a lot. It's fun. Did you see all the stupid memes going around about people *volunteering as tribute* to be my stepmom?"

"What? *No.*" She'd made a point of staying off social sites since she'd gotten home. She didn't want to read whatever was being said about Johnny and Zoey. "You mean like that girl said in *Hunger Games?*"

"*Yes.* It's so stupid."

"I'm sorry. That must be uncomfortable to see." Jillian felt a stab of jealousy, wondering if Ramona had reached out to Johnny.

"I don't really care. It's not like Johnny's going to marry a stranger. I'd better go. I'm working on an idea for shorts that I thought you could use for the Rocker Girlz line."

"Really?" Jillian loved that.

"Yeah. I'll show you when I'm done if it doesn't suck. Thanks for making me feel better."

"Anytime. Love you" came as easily as it did with her family.

"Love you, too."

Jillian ended the call and navigated to her social feeds, searching Johnny's name. Pages of posts and tweets from single women offering themselves up to him appeared. Jealousy spiked sharp and hot inside her.

"Who are you plotting to kill?"

Jillian looked up as Trixie and Jordan approached. "Every single woman on the planet." She pocketed her phone. "*Volunteer as tribute?* What kind of bullshit is that?" She glowered at Trixie, whose long dark layers fell over her shoulders. "And why didn't you tell me?"

"Because every time I brought up Johnny, you hung up the phone," Trixie snapped. The logo for her miniature horse therapy business, Rising Hope, peeked out from the T-shirt she wore beneath an open flannel shirt, which she wore with jeans and cowgirl boots, her standard attire in cold weather.

"Why didn't you want to talk about Johnny?" Jordan asked. She was a Kate Bosworth lookalike, and she was dressed for work in a navy A-line skirt, white blouse, and cute jacket. "I thought you were working on his wardrobe."

"Yeah, getting it *off* his body," Trixie quipped.

Jordan's eyes widened. "You and *Johnny*? How did I not know this?"

"Because it was nothing," Jillian huffed, trying to shake off the sharpness of the lie.

"Yeah, and I hate orgasms," Trixie said sarcastically, opening the door to the café. "We have to talk over lunch because Jordan's on her break and I have to meet the farrier this afternoon."

They found a table near the back of the café, and Jordan spoke in a hushed voice. "I thought you were in Colorado for Zoey and designing Johnny's wardrobe. What happened?"

"I *was* there for Zoey, and I did *start* designing his wardrobe. I don't know what happened. I met him right after he'd fired his manager and found out he was a father, and after he lost his shit over it all, he made up his mind to put Zoey *first*. It was pretty amazing watching him go from furious prick to *holy shit I'm a dad and I need to do the right thing*. And as I got to know him and he got to know Zoey, he was thoughtful and funny and worried about this teenage girl whose very existence had sent his life spiraling in ten different directions but whose own life had been blown to smithereens. We kind of came together to help her, and I can't even tell you how it happened. One minute we're hanging out and he's cooking us dinners and breakfasts, and the next we're going at it in Beau's shed."

"His *shed*?" Trixie asked with astonishment.

"I can't picture you doing that," Jordan said.

"Neither could I—until we did. And it was *my* idea. I wanted him so badly, I would have dragged him in there if he didn't go willingly." *And he's so good at the dirty stuff. He takes charge and does all the things I always wished a guy would do. He pulled my hair and took me from behind and talked dirty.* She warmed all over just thinking about their nights together, but she kept all that to herself and said, "I couldn't get enough of him, and don't tell Beau, but we did it in his shed, his barn, his workshop, at the creek. No place was off-limits as long as Zoey was asleep."

"Holy cow," Jordan said.

Trixie's eyes sparked with mischief. "Was there champagne involved in the barn?"

"No, why?"

"You don't want to know," Trixie said quickly. "But it was *so* good."

"You *too?*" Jordan whispered, "Geez, and I thought Jax and I were creative. We did it in the pool and on the balcony at a hotel."

"*Stop.*" Jillian put her palm up. "This is not an open forum for sexual discussions involving my brothers."

Jordan and Trixie laughed as Emmaline sidled up to their table.

"Hey, girls." Emmaline touched Jillian's shoulder. "It's about time you moseyed on in here, Jilly. How was New York? I've missed seeing you."

"Oh, you know. There's never a dull moment in the city that never sleeps."

"It's the perfect place for a girl like you, who's go, go, go all night long," Emmaline said.

"You can say that again." Trixie smirked.

Jillian glared at her, then smiled at Emmaline. "I need your strongest latte, please."

"Okay, one Baby-Mama Tribute coming up," Emmaline said.

"Ohmygod. Are you kidding me?" Jillian looked at her incredulously.

"*Nope.* I'm shamelessly capitalizing on the Johnny Bad baby-mama drama," Emmaline said.

"They're real people, you know, with real feelings," Jillian said.

"Sorry, Jilly," Emmaline said. "I know you're working with him, but they're selling like hotcakes, and a girl's got to make a living."

"I'll take one, too," Jordan said sheepishly.

"Make that three," Trixie said. "And we should order lunch or we'll get to talking and forget."

"Do you want your usual, or are you feeling naughty and want to chow down on something super yummy that's really bad for you?" Emmaline waggled her brows. "We're trying out a new heavenly glazed croissant with bacon, lettuce, and tomato, smothered in ooey-gooey cheese."

Jillian threw her hands up. "You're killing me. Give me the naughty-bad thing. It's the only naughty-bad action I'm going to get."

"You and me both," Emmaline said. "I swear the dating pool around here has been pissed in. What about you Trix? Jordan?"

They ordered the same, and Jillian said, "You're going to have to roll us out of here."

"I don't mind," Emmaline said.

As she walked away, Trixie said, "Roll me into Nick's bed. He'll work it off me."

Jillian pressed her hands together and looked up at the ceiling. "Please make it stop."

They all laughed.

"Why does Emmaline think you were in New York?" Jordan asked quietly.

"Since we had to keep Johnny's whereabouts a secret, anyone who isn't family thinks I was in New York working and shopping. But, you guys, I seriously need help before Liza calls my family to stage an intervention."

"Why? What's going on?" Jordan schooled her expression.

"Remember how I said I wanted Lady Fate to wave her wand and work her magic on me? Well, I was wrong. I found my Daryl Magnum, and now I don't know what to do."

"Who's Daryl Magnum?" Jordan asked.

"Only the hottest book boyfriend on the planet," Trixie explained. "He's the hero in Char's book *Crazy, Sexy, Sinful.*"

"Johnny's better than Daryl because he's real, and like an idiot, I fell for him and Zoey, which is totally weird, right? Single dads have always been a no-go for me. No questions asked."

"Travis Helms could testify to that," Trixie said about one of her close friends.

"Exactly. I mean, Travis is a tall, dark glass of champagne, but he's also a single dad, and even though his daughter is freaking adorable, I have never wanted to jump that fence. Which is why *this* has thrown me for a loop. I'm even having trouble concentrating at work. Poor Liza probably thinks I've lost my mind. She's used to me being as sharp as a tack. I never even procrastinate, and now I'm like, *Plan the release of my line? Yeah, that can wait.* What the hell is *that* about? And the worst part is, it's not just Johnny I'm thinking about. It's his *daughter.*" She told them about Zoey and how she was meeting Johnny's family in a few days and starting a new school and how badly she wished she could be there for her.

"I love that you connected with her," Jordan said.

"Me too, but it's really messing with my head. She's a great kid, and she's been through hell. It's hard to have gone through so much with them, and then to sit back and know I can't do anything more than talk with her over the phone. She's got a great eye for teen fashion, too, which I wouldn't have guessed when we first met, but that was because her bitch of a mother had left all her clothes, and everything else she owned, behind." She gave them a recap of what had happened. "When we were shopping, she was really particular, and once we got to the heart of the matter, I realized why. Her grandmother didn't have a lot of money, so she'd buy cheaper things and modify them herself." She told them what Zoey had done to her clothes and about the Rocker Girlz line she'd inspired. "I'm so excited over the new line, it's all I want to work on, and you know I have other pressing work. The Wanderlust line is waiting for its launch, and I have clients lining up, but all I can think about is seeing Johnny and Zoey and making Zoey's horse top with her."

"I don't know what that is, but I need one," Trixie said.

"It's a sweater in the Rocker Girlz line, but I could make an adult version." She showed them pictures on her phone of the designs she'd come up with. Emmaline brought their lattes, and she showed her a few of the designs, too, which she loved. When Emmaline walked away, Jillian said, "Zoey and I are working on some of the designs together."

"Collaborating with a teenager? That's interesting," Trixie said.

"It sounds like you and Johnny are good together and you and Zoey obviously get along well, so what's the problem?" Jordan asked.

"The problem is, he's the right guy at the wrong time." Jillian took a drink. "He and Zoey are going through huge changes, and she needs her father's attention while she navigates getting to know a family she didn't know existed, starting a new school, living in a new city, and basically starting over on every level. And he needs to fix his business and figure out how to make rock-star life and daddy life work together. The last thing he needs is to try to juggle another new relationship with someone who lives hundreds of miles away. And I have things I need to focus on. I'll never be the kind of girl to follow him around the country on a tour bus, playing Mommy. Our lives are just too different."

"So, that's it?" Jordan asked. "You fall for a guy who you think is *the one*, and you just let him go?"

"I'm obviously not doing a great job of letting go, but I know I have to. Think about it. If we tried and it didn't work, where would that leave Zoey? You know how difficult new relationships can be, and I'm sure long distance is a thousand times harder. Plus, I'm not an easy partner. I'm a night owl, not a lunch-packing mommy."

"Who gives a damn about packing lunches?" Trixie said. "She's a teenager. She can pack her own lunch. It's more important that she's loved and supported."

"I agree with Trix," Jordan said.

"What does Johnny say about all this?" Trixie asked.

"That he has to focus on Zoey, and he doesn't want it to be over, but I haven't heard from him since Monday, so I think he's realizing it's not doable."

"Well, if he's going to give up on you that easily, then he's not good enough for you anyway," Trixie said adamantly.

"Trixie...?" Jordan shook her head.

Trixie sat back and crossed her arms. "He's a fool if he lets her go."

"But after everything she just told us, don't you feel like he deserves a little slack?" Jordan asked sweetly. "Maybe it *is* too much for him right now, but that doesn't mean it has to be over forever. You never know what the future will bring. Look at me and Jax. I wanted to be with him for eight months, but I couldn't figure out how to do it because my personal life was a mess. But I never once stopped thinking about him, and look at us now. I might never have found Sully if it weren't for him."

"I hate when you're right," Trixie said as Emmaline brought their lunches.

As Jordan and Trixie *ooh*ed and *aah*ed over the scrumptious-looking sandwiches, Jillian chided herself for complaining about her personal life when Jordan had finally been reunited with her sister. This wasn't who Jillian was. She basically had the equivalent of a *Johnny hangover*, and she was looking for someone to give her a remedy.

She'd never needed anyone to save her before, and she didn't need them to now. She was *done* pining for him and feeling sorry for herself.

Maybe Jordan was right, and she'd get lucky, and like Jordan and Jax, her and Johnny's time would eventually come. *Or maybe he'll reconnect with Ramona or get together with one of the million women vying for his attention.* Her chest tightened, and she pictured his handsome face and the way he'd looked at her when he'd stepped into the shower—*Just let me have this*—and the longing in his honest dark eyes when they said goodbye on the plane. Maybe he *was* just busy, and she was being too needy, which was another thing she'd never been before.

It was time to pull up her very expensive lace panties and do what she'd done all those years ago when Beau and Zev had gone away. She mentally packed up her feelings in an iron-clad suitcase and pictured herself sitting on it to get it to close as she locked it down tight, hoping it wouldn't burst.

"This is too good for words," Trixie said around a mouthful of food and eyed Jillian's untouched sandwich. "Are you going to wallow over the MIA orgasm king or eat something that'll make you moan just as loud as he does?"

"I doubt that, but you can relax. I'm done pining." She picked up the sandwich and sank her teeth into it. The savory ingredients melted in her mouth, and she did, in fact, moan. "This might be better than orgasms."

Trixie and Jordan looked at her like she'd lost her mind, and they all cracked up.

"Work with me here. I'm trying to get off the Johnny train." Jillian sipped her latte, which also earned a moan for its scrumptious flavor. "Jordan, I'm sorry for hogging the conversation. Jax told me about your trip, but what was it like for you, seeing your sister again after all these years?"

"It was surreal. Sully is beautiful and sweet, and I'm loving getting to know the person she's become." Jordan's voice was laden with emotions. "She doesn't remember our family. There's a chance she could get her memories back over time, but even if she doesn't, I'm thrilled to finally have her back in my life."

"I'm so happy for you." Jillian leaned in to hug her.

Jordan nodded, and Jillian could tell she was a little choked up.

"She's got a hot cowboy looking after her," Trixie added lightly.

Jordan smiled. "That she does. Callahan Whiskey, but he goes by the nickname Cowboy. He's super nice and protective, and she seems really happy." She sighed. "I still can't wrap my head around the fact that she's alive and safe."

"Miracles do happen," Trixie said.

"Yeah," Jordan said. "She's braver than I could ever be."

"There's no doubt Sully must have a level of strength that's beyond anything we can fathom, but we're all strong in our own rights, and I'd like to think that if it came down to it, we'd save ourselves, too." Jillian was reminding herself of that as much as she was reminding them, and as she said it, she realized what she needed to do in order to move forward and filed it away for later.

"I'm not that strong," Jordan said.

"Yes, you are," Jillian insisted. "You got out of a long-term relationship that was holding you back but had also given you a touchpoint of stability after you lost your entire family. Walking away from that took courage. We're all strong. Look at Trixie. She deals with Nick every day. That can't be easy."

Trixie rolled her eyes, but she earned a smile from Jordan, which was what she was hoping for.

"I'll have you know that my hubby, the man who didn't do parties, is not only throwing the first annual Braden Halloween Bash since I'm missing my family's barn bash for the first time ever, but he's going all out. He wanted me to be Catwoman, so he's dressing up like Batman."

"No way," Jillian said with a laugh. "You got my brother to wear *tights*?"

Trixie sipped her drink, shaking her head. "Black jeans, but I *might* have gotten him sexy Batman underwear and a promise to role-play after the party."

Jordan told them that she and Jax were dressing up like the Phantom of the Opera and Christine, and it only made Jillian miss Johnny more. But she tucked those feelings away, and they talked right up until the second they had to leave. They said goodbye with promises to get together and go shopping for Amber and Dash's wedding present next week.

Jillian headed back to work, feeling more in control than she had all week, and she strode directly into Liza's office. "We're launching Wanderlust in February."

Her ever-efficient assistant looked up from whatever she was doing on the computer, her keen green eyes narrowing behind her black-framed lenses. "February?"

"Mid-February, actually, and I want to go all out. Billboards in every major city. I want Wanderlust everywhere people look. Times Square, Chicago, LA, and on every handheld digital screen available." She paced. "We need a runway show, but we're doing this one right. This line is about freedom from everything that holds women back, and we need to show that from the moment it hits the public. When women see this line, I want them to think, *This is for me.* Forget our usual models. We need real women of all sizes, shapes, and color. Differently abled women. Women who have muffin tops and jiggly arms. Short women, tall women, tough women, meek women. I'm going to ask my sisters-in-law to model, too, since they were such a big part of the inspiration."

"That's a very different show than consumers are used to. You know what our marketing and PR reps will say about that."

"I didn't get ahead in this business by falling into line. We don't follow trends, Liza. We create them."

"Yes, we do. I'm just making sure you know what's coming. I think April would be a more realistic launch date," Liza said firmly. "Digital advertising is booked months in advance. If there are any slots left, they'll be at a premium around Valentine's Day, and distributors and buyers need time to do their jobs."

Jillian stopped pacing. "We'll do it in March. Everyone works better with a fire under their ass, and we have marketing contracts in place. Use them."

"It would be a shame if this leaked to the press early," Liza said coyly, pushing to her feet.

"Yes, it would," Jillian said sarcastically. "Who wants to deal with that free press?"

Liza came around the desk, towering over her at five foot ten. Her long silver hair was gathered over one shoulder of her stylish gray shift, and the green in her silk scarf made her eyes *pop.* "It's about time you got your head out of your bum." She held out her hand.

"Welcome back, boss lady. Let's do this."

JILLIAN WORKED LIKE a fiend and was so happy about finally being able to concentrate, she was afraid to break her stride and worked in her studio above the boutique until well after eleven.

But as she drove down her quiet street and parked in front of her home, she lost some of that gusto. She loved her house, with its painted white brick, black trim, and glass front door with two sidelights. It was unique, classy, and homey, with French doors instead of windows on the right side below a high-peaked roof and tall windows and an arched entryway on the left with a massive six-window dormer on the second floor that showered her studio with natural light. The interior boasted clean lines and splashes of color, arched doorways, a stone fireplace, a guest suite below her studio, and a master suite and two more guest rooms on the second floor.

It was everything she could want, but ever since she'd gotten home from Colorado, she'd had a hard time readjusting to the silence. She missed the sounds of Johnny playing his guitar and Zoey plucking away as she learned. She missed their laughter and the banter that seemed to belong to the three of them, like they were part of a secret group who knew just how to wheedle and tease each other.

She headed inside and ate a bowl of cereal, then went upstairs to her studio to work. She flicked on the lights, and as she went to her drawing table, her gaze caught on the stuffed unicorn Zoey had given her and the framed picture beside it of the three of them in Colorado, which Beau had taken. The excitement of *being* Jillian Braden, fashion designer extraordinaire, on the cusp of an exciting launch, took a back seat to thoughts of Johnny and Zoey.

After rereading the same notes too many times to count and retaining none of what she read, she gave up and headed back downstairs. She poured herself a glass of wine and flopped onto the couch, but she was too frustrated to relax and headed back upstairs to take a bath. She snagged the novel she hadn't had time to read in Colorado from the dresser and set her phone in the holder beside the tub. As the tub filled, she added her favorite bath bomb, and once it was full, she stripped off her clothes. She sank into the warm water and closed her eyes. Johnny's face appeared, bringing a longing deep inside her as she remembered his most recent text. *Just keeping your man on your mind.*

"You do that a little too well," she said softly.

Thoughts of him and Zoey were *always* there. Constant reminders of what she really wanted. Just like her fashion goals had been from the moment she realized she was meant to be a fashionista. She didn't know why he would imply he was her man and then go three days without even sending a text, but she didn't chase guys, and she wasn't about to start.

Liking someone this much sucks. With a sigh, she grabbed her book, hoping a hot fictional man would take her mind off her very real, and too far away, rock star.

She opened her book, and several wildflowers fell out from between the pages, landing in the water. A smile stretched across her cheeks as she took in the pretty flowers floating like dozens of little reminders of what they'd had. Why did that make her heart hurt even more?

She set the book beside the tub and took a picture of the flowers in the water with her phone. She texted it to Johnny with a pink heart emoji. His response rolled in a minute later. *You might be great at fashion, but your sexting skills need some help. Angle the phone the other way so I can see all the parts of you I want to devour.*

Her pulse quickened, and she couldn't help teasing him. *You have a line of women volunteering as tribute. I bet any of them would be happy to send you dirty texts.* Her phone rang, and his name flashed on the screen. A dozen thoughts raced through her mind as she put the phone to her ear. "Yes, Mr. Bad?"

He groaned. "Your voice fucking kills me."

Kind of like that groan does to me. "Can't say I'm sorry about that."

"*Jesus*, Jilly. There's only one person I want volunteering to send me dirty texts, and it's the same woman I want sucking my cock and fucking me."

Her body caught fire at his words, and suddenly those three days without hearing from him didn't matter. But she loved getting him riled up, and she needed to know where they stood without asking as much. "Then why are you calling me? I think you have Ramona's number."

"You're lucky you're not here right now, because I'd bend you over and teach you a lesson for that."

He had no idea how much she wished he could.

"I don't want *her*," he growled. "I want my mouthy girl who's not afraid to tell me to get on my knees."

God, how she missed him, but she had to know if he wanted *her* or if he was just getting off because she'd sent the picture. "Where is this coming from? Are you watching porn?"

"Who needs porn when the image of you lying naked beneath me is burned into my mind? I tried to go cold turkey to make it easier for both of us, but *fuck*, Jilly. All it took was that picture, and now I can't stop thinking about being beneath you in that tub as you ride me, with one of your perfect tits in my mouth."

She closed her eyes as a rush of heat consumed her. "I like where this is going."

"I knew you would," he said huskily. "Five days is too long without seeing you, touching you. Touch yourself, baby. Touch your pussy for me."

She slid her hand down her stomach and between her legs, gasping as it moved over her clit and between her swollen lips.

"That's it, sexy girl. Are you ready for me?"

"*So* ready for you." She heard a familiar noise. "Was that your *zipper?*"

"Hell yeah, it was. These jeans are coming off."

The worked-up woman in her screamed, *Yes!* But the rational adult pushed her bossy self to the forefront and said, "Where are you? What about Zoey?"

"She's sleeping, and I'm in my recording studio. It's soundproof, and I *need* to see you."

He switched to a video call, and she had a momentary thought about whether she could go through with it if he was watching her. But the idea of watching *him* had her answering, and the sight of his sun-kissed face, emotions radiating from his smoldering eyes, nearly did her in. When his tongue swept over his lips, she craved the feel of them.

"*God*, Jilly. I've missed your face."

Her heart stumbled.

"Put your phone somewhere so I can see all of you."

Her nerves tingled. "Only if you do, too."

"You're getting a front-row seat, baby, and I expect the same."

He set up his phone beside a leather couch, tugged off his shirt, and stretched out on the leather, completely naked. His thick erection made her mouth water. She propped her phone in the cradle and angled it so he could see her. She felt a little embarrassed, but at the same time, she'd never wanted anything more than she wanted this with him.

He stroked his cock. "You're so fucking gorgeous. Touch yourself, baby."

She slid her hand between her legs, and she tried to hold his gaze, but her eyes kept moving to his hand wrapped around his cock.

"Pretend it's me touching you. Touch your tits with your other hand."

She did, and a needy sound escaped.

"I fucking love the sounds you make. Tease your clit like it's my tongue doing it."

She obeyed, and pleasure seared through her core. "I wish it was you," she panted out. "I can make myself come in seconds."

"Not tonight you can't," he said authoritatively. "I want this to last. I want you to think of my fingers as you push yours into your pussy." His eyes implored her.

She did as he asked, breathing heavily. "If you'd given me warning. I could've gotten a toy."

"Aw *fuck*." He gripped his cock at the base. "Now that's got to happen."

"I'm *not* getting up right now."

A cocky grin spread his lips. "Something to look forward to, then. How does it feel to fuck your fingers?"

"Good. *Tight*." She met his gaze, wanting to drive him just as wild. "Can you feel my mouth on your cock?" He made a guttural sound that was so hot, she moved her other hand to her clit. "I want to lick all of you," she said, loving the wickedness in his eyes as he stroked himself faster. She opened her mouth wide, running her tongue all the way around, and he moaned. "I want to suck you until you come."

"*Fucking hell*," he said through clenched teeth. "I want to eat you until you come and then suck your clit until you beg me to fuck you."

She whimpered, pressure mounting inside her.

"I want to see you fuck yourself with that toy while I bury my cock in your ass."

"Ohmygod," she said in one long breath, squeezing her legs together.

"My dirty girl likes that, huh?" His eyes narrowed. "Open those legs wide, baby, and let me watch you fuck yourself."

Her knees fell open. "I need *you*," she panted out, desperate for him. "I want to feel you inside me."

"Is your toy safe for the tub?"

"Uh-huh."

"*Get it*," he demanded.

She didn't even hesitate this time, needing it as much as he wanted to see it. She climbed from the bath and ran into her bedroom, grabbing the biggest vibrator she had, because nothing else compared to him, and was back in the tub seconds later. His grin was as devious as she felt, which turned her on even more.

"Go up on your knees, like you're riding me."

She did.

"Turn it on." As she did, he said, "Eyes on me, baby, and put it in slowly." He stroked himself faster, watching her do it. "You're so damn hot. I want to see you fuck it slowly. Imagine my hands on your hips as I lower you onto my dick."

"Squeeze your cock tight as I do it," she commanded, and he did, the sight of it intensifying her pleasure as she fucked herself painfully slowly, the pressure and the vibration taking her higher. "I need to lie down."

"Not yet. Look how beautiful you are. Squeeze your nipple and pretend it's my mouth sucking it."

She did, needy sounds falling from her lips. She closed her eyes and fucked herself faster, the thick vibrator taking her right up to the edge. She gripped the side of the tub, opening her eyes, watching him stroke himself. *"Fuck it."* She lay down, quickening her efforts.

"Think about my mouth on your pussy, licking, sucking, *biting.*"

Her breaths came in sharp, fast bursts. "So close."

"That's it, baby. Think of us fucking in the shed that first time. Can you feel me pounding into you from behind?"

"Uh-huh" was all she could manage.

"I'm so fucking close. I want to come on your tits."

"*Yes,*" she pleaded.

"Come with me, baby. Imagine me on top of you in the tub, fucking you so good that your nails cut into my flesh."

"Oh*god*—" She cried out as a stream of curses left his lips, and she forced her eyes open, watching him come, his eyes blazing as she shattered into a million needy pieces.

She went limp and withdrew the toy with a whimper. She lay panting in the lukewarm water, enveloped in a sense of *them* and surrounded by wildflowers. Her eyes fluttered open, and she found him lying with his head back, breathing hard, one hand on his chest.

"Johnny."

He turned, a slow, sated smile crawling across his face, his emotion-filled eyes reeling her in. "Hey, baby. That was amazing."

"What are you doing to me?" she asked softly, not really expecting a response.

"My situation may take a long time to figure out." He shrugged casually, as if the answer were obvious. "I'm just keeping my girl satisfied so her eyes don't wander."

Johnny Bad, you just might be worth the wait.

Chapter Twenty-One

JOHNNY GLANCED AT Zoey as he drove through the gates of his parents' small private estate Saturday afternoon. She was staring out the passenger window, fidgeting with a tear in her jeans. She'd barely said two words during the nearly five-hour drive. She'd been so nervous, she'd changed her clothes five times that morning into nice sweaters, pants, and skirts she and Jillian had bought. She'd looked cute as hell in everything, and he'd told her to wear whatever she was most comfortable in, because they cared about her, not her clothes. She'd settled on a pair of jeans she'd been working hard on modifying the last few nights with black skull-patterned fabric she and Jillian had bought during their shopping spree. She'd made holes in the thighs of the jeans and had sewn the fabric on the inside so it showed through. She'd rolled up the jeans, and she wore them with a long-sleeved black knit shirt that had a boatneck and was cropped at her waist and her red Converse.

As he parked in front of the stone manor-style house, wishing he could ease her worries, he said, "Hey."

She turned worried eyes to him.

He reached for her hand, giving it a reassuring squeeze. "It's going to be fine."

"I'm so nervous. They're going to see how nervous I am, and Harlow is a movie star. I don't even know how to talk to her."

"I'm one of the biggest rock stars around, and you have no problem talking to me. Just play it cool. Harlow is no different from me. She's just a lot prettier."

"But you're my dad."

Damn, that made him grin. "Yeah, I am. Listen, when I was not much older than you and nervous about playing in front of people, my dad told me to picture the audience picking their noses. If you do that with Harlow, she'll seem a lot less like a movie star. And I'm sure everyone else is just as nervous as you are, because they want *you* to like *them*. Hell, Zo, *I'm* nervous."

"You are?" she asked anxiously. "Why? Don't you think they'll like me?"

"I know they'll love you, and I'm ninety-nine percent sure you'll love them, but you're my kid, so it's still nerve-racking. Here's what you need to know. It's going to be a little overwhelming at first. I come from a family of huggers, except for Aria. She'll probably stand back a little."

"Because of her anxiety?"

"Yes, and don't take that personally. But if after an hour it's still too overwhelming, just say the word and we'll leave. We don't have to stay overnight."

Her eyes widened. "You would do that after driving all this way?"

"The last thing I want is for you to be uncomfortable or feel stuck. We can always try again another time."

She let out a long sigh of relief. "Okay. Thanks." She looked up at the house. "Their house is gigantic."

"It's hard to find a small house on a private lot around here. But I think you'll like it. It doesn't feel stuffy inside, and they have a big backyard with a pool. Come on. Let's go meet the troops."

He got out and came around to open her door, but she was already out of the car, and as they walked up to the door, she reached for his hand. That was a first, and *man* it felt good to know she trusted him to take care of her. "You've got this, sunshine."

As they made their way up the walk, the front door opened, and Kane stepped out, wearing dark slacks, a white button-down, and a big-ass grin. He called over his shoulder, "Better hide your money! Swindler's here, and she brought her old man."

Zoey laughed.

Johnny gave him an appreciative nod.

"You and I are playing a rematch later," Kane said, wrapping her in his arms. "I missed you, kid."

Harlow ran out the door. "*Zoey!* I have been dying to meet you."

Zoey froze, eyes wide.

Harlow's smile faded, and she looked at Johnny, whispering, "Did I say the wrong thing?"

"No." Johnny had seen that look on fans' faces enough times to know Zoey was starstruck. He nudged her and tapped the side of his nose.

Zoey blinked several times. "Hi. You're Harlow."

"I *am*, and I *love* your jeans," she said enthusiastically.

"You *do?*" Zoey asked with astonishment, giving Johnny a *holy cow, she likes them* look.

"*Yes*. Where did you get them?" Harlow asked as their parents and Aria came out the front door.

"I made them," Zoey said a little bashfully. "Well, not the jeans, but they didn't have tears or anything when I got them."

Harlow looked impressed. "Seriously? Girl, I need you to take a peek in my closet. I have jeans that could use some help."

"Really? You want *my* help?" Zoey beamed at Johnny.

"She knows talent when she sees it, sunshine," Johnny said as their parents and Aria joined them. His mother looked casual and pretty in tan slacks and a white sweater, and his father wore his usual attire of jeans and one of his many V-neck sweaters. Aria wore a gold hoop in her nose, distressed jeans, and a gray long-sleeved Wicked Ink shirt with the sleeves pushed up to the elbows, revealing her slender tattooed forearms.

Johnny put his hand on Zoey's shoulder and said, "Mom, Dad, Aria, this is Zoey. Zoey, these are your grandparents, Jan and Bruce, and your aunt Aria."

His mother smiled warmly. "Hi, sweetheart. We're so excited to finally meet you. Johnny has told us wonderful things about you." She gently hugged Zoey.

"Are you sure he was talking about *me*?" Zoey asked.

Harlow laughed. "You're going to fit right in."

"You're definitely Johnny's daughter," his father said, hugging Zoey.

"He and Kane told me a lot about you guys, too," Zoey said.

"Well, that could go either way for us, couldn't it, John?" His father pulled him into an embrace.

"I only told her the good stuff."

"I told her the rest," Kane said, earning another grin from Zoey.

"There's nothing bad to tell." Aria stepped closer. "Hi, Zoey. I like your jeans."

"Thank you. Your tattoos are cool."

"Thanks."

"I like your nose ring, too. Can you pierce my nose?" Zoey looked at Johnny. "Can she give me a tattoo while we're here?"

"No, she cannot, and you're not getting your nose pierced today, either." Johnny shook his head, and everyone laughed.

"She gave you a tattoo," Zoey pointed out.

Kane chuckled. "Yeah, Johnny. She gave you one."

Johnny glared at him.

"I'm not allowed to give you a tattoo until you're eighteen," Aria said. "But I can draw some cool stuff on your arms or your sneakers if you want."

"Really? Okay, on my sneakers!" Zoey exclaimed. "Then it won't wash off. Thank you."

"Why don't we go inside and we'll show you around and get to know each other?" his mother suggested. "Aria and I were just about to bake cookies, but we realized we don't know what kind you like."

"I like all kinds of cookies, and I love baking," Zoey said. "I used to help my grandmother bake all the time."

His mother's eyes softened. "We are so sorry that you lost your grandmother, and I know it might be too soon for this, but we're excited to be your grandparents, and you can call us Grandma and Grandpa if you want, or Bruce and Jan, or whatever you're comfortable with."

"Thank you," Zoey said softly, looking a little choked up. Johnny put his hand on her back.

"Would you like to help us bake?" his mother asked.

Zoey looked at Johnny. "Can I?"

"Of course."

"I'm helping, too! Come on, Aria." Harlow took the girls by the arms, hurrying them toward the house.

"Harlow Elizabeth, do *not* eat all the chocolate chips," their mother called after her.

The girls giggled as they ran into the house.

"You're not going to win that one, Mom," Kane said.

"Remember last Christmas when Harlow ate the entire bag of chips your mother was going to use in the pumpkin bread? She was sick for the rest of the day." His father shook his head. "You'd think she'd learn."

Kane patted Johnny on the shoulder. "Your daughter will never be the same after today."

"Aria will keep Harlow in line," his father said.

"I have a feeling Zoey can fend for herself," his mother said, and she hugged him. "I've missed you, sweetheart."

"I've missed you, too, Mom. How are you feeling?"

"I'm doing fine, honey. I rested all morning."

"Okay, good. If it's too much with all of us here, just let me know what I can do to help."

"Thank you, baby." She patted his cheek. "Fatherhood looks good on you. Zoey is a sassy little gal, isn't she?"

He exhaled, feeling like he'd been holding his breath for hours. "She really is. But she's not loving living in the city."

"Not everyone does," his mother said. "Give her time to settle in, and in the meantime, just keep doing what you're doing. As long as she knows she's loved and wanted, the rest will eventually fall into place. And if she really hates the city, there's always the Cape. I'd better get in there before they all end up with bellyaches."

His father pulled her into a quick kiss, and as she headed inside, he said, "What do you think, boys? To the man cave?"

"Only if you want your ass whooped in pool," Kane said.

"I'll take that over getting my ass whooped by a teenage girl in poker," their father said.

Johnny laughed. "You're never living that down, Kane."

They went inside, and as his father and Kane headed downstairs, Johnny said, "I'll be right there." He went to check on Zoey and heard her telling the others about their mornings in Colorado.

"Jillian doesn't cook, and she's *not* a morning person, so Johnny and I made breakfasts and packed lunches, and every morning we rode horses. He always packed Jillian extra food because she's not a big breakfast eater. Sometimes she even ate some of *his* lunch. He acted like he cared, but I know he didn't."

"My brother rode horses?" Harlow asked.

"Yeah. It was fun. They were always teasing each other, and me and Jillian talked the whole time we were on the trails."

"You must miss her," Aria said.

"I do, like crazy. But I talk to her every day. She's letting me help with a new clothing line…"

I miss her, too, sunshine. As Zoey brought them up to speed, he thought about Jillian.

He'd called her last night to tell her he'd received a package from Beau with Zoey's missing shirt and socks that Bandit had apparently taken off with. Jillian had gotten a kick out of that, and she hadn't been kidding about how dedicated she was to her work. She'd still been at her office when he'd called at ten, and she'd gone on for forty minutes about finally planning the launch of her Wanderlust line. He loved sharing in her excitement, but he wished like hell he'd been there with her. They'd talked about Zoey and awkwardly tiptoed around the fact that it might be months before they could see each other in person. It didn't matter that they'd just spoken the night before after their sexy bathtub time. He liked hearing her voice, and he got to learn little things about her that he hadn't known before, like that her favorite color was burgundy, like her hair, because it reminded her of fall, which was her favorite time of year. And that she loved pickles but only put up with cucumbers, and if she could do any part of her life over again, it would be the day Beau and Zev had left home, so she could try to keep them from leaving and get those ten years back to do over with them. He felt so much for her, he wondered how he could have gone his entire life without ever feeling like that.

He pulled out his phone and texted her. *The eagle has landed, and she seems to like the nest.* He typed, *We miss you*, but immediately deleted it, not wanting to make it harder for her.

Her response rolled in as he headed for the stairs. *Yay! I knew everyone would love her. She's a great kid. It must be wonderful to see your family.* He leaned against the wall at the top of the stairs and typed, *It is.* Fuck it. It was already hard, and holding in his feelings sucked, so he thumbed out, *But I wish you were here. I miss you.* He waited, assuming those three dancing dots would disappear, but a reply popped up. *You can show me how much tonight.* She added three flame emojis. He typed feverishly. *We're staying at my parents' house. I may not have that kind of privacy.* Her response was immediate and began with a frowning emoji. *Too bad. I got a new toy called the Lickmaster. I'll let you know if it lives up to its name.*

"I'm not fucking missing that." He typed furiously, *Midnight walk it is. Do NOT start without me.* How was he supposed to go weeks or months pretending that every time Zoey said Jillian's name, he didn't ache to be with her and to see her stumbling out of the bedroom, bleary-eyed and beautiful at ten in the morning? Or that he wasn't dying to hold her? Hell, even to hold her hand and see that spark in her eyes that could go from snarky to sexy in a single second?

This was crazy. He was a fucking rock star. He could snap his fingers and have anything he wanted—except the one woman who set his heart on fire.

He tried to push those thoughts away as he headed downstairs to join his father and brother. Kane was getting beers from the fridge by the bar, and his father was racking billiard balls.

"Everything okay with Zoey?" Kane handed him a beer and grabbed a pool cue.

"Seems to be. They're gabbing in the kitchen. She sounded happy. I didn't want to walk in and throw things off."

"That was smart. How are you holding up?" their father asked as he grabbed a pool cue. "How are the guys taking the tour delay?"

"I'm okay, and the guys are good. They know Zoey has to come first, and thanks to Kane, the rest of Dick's shitstorm is getting straightened out. But it looks like I'm going to be busy making amends to a lot of important people once Zoey's in school and I've got time for meetings. I'll tell you one thing, Dad. I have a greater appreciation for you and Mom than I ever did before. Every decision I make has an effect on Zoey in one way or another."

"You got that right," his father said. "How is she settling in at home?"

"I think she's okay at home, but how can I know for sure? Sometimes I feel like everything I say and do is wrong, and other times I feel like I won the lottery because she smiled or agreed with something I said."

"Welcome to fatherhood, son." His father clapped him on the back. "In my experience, girls are a little harder to read than boys. If we did something you and Kane didn't like, you both let us know. You'd argue or fist your hands like you were going to explode. We played a lot of baseball back then. But when the girls were Zoey's age, it was a whole different story. I think Harlow spent about a year saying *whatever* or *nothing* to anything we said, and Aria stayed in her room drawing all the time. If we asked if something was wrong, she'd just shake her head without even looking up. Eventually Harlow realized that dealing with parents was a way to hone her acting skills. That was *fun*. And Aria just bloomed like this beautiful quiet lily, allowing us in bit by bit, sharing her art, and through that, showing us what she wanted or didn't want."

"I wish I'd known Zoey when she was younger," Johnny said as Kane walked around the pool table to take his shot. "Sometimes she gets this troubled look in her eyes and she won't tell me what's wrong. It doesn't last long, but I wonder if I'll ever really know all the things she's thinking or feeling, or if she'll just pretend to be who she thinks I want her to be."

"That little girl is *not* a people pleaser," Kane said sharply. "And that's a good thing. You want her to be strong because there are a lot of dicks out there, and she needs to be able to handle herself."

"Yeah, that's what Jilly said last night."

"The designer you told us about?" His father arched a brow. "You're still talking with her about Zoey?"

"Among other things," Johnny admitted. "We got close while we were away, and Zoey really likes her."

"Is that a bad thing? You sound a little stressed about it," his father said.

"It's a good thing for Zoey."

"He's into Jillian, but he has to focus on Zoey and getting his life back in order," Kane said. "It's your shot, old man."

Their father looked over the pool table. "Want to talk about that, John?"

"We just spent so much time together, I feel like a part of me is missing. But talking about her will only make it worse, so I'd rather not. But I'd like to hear any advice you have about how to handle Zoey."

"She obviously respects you," his father said as he took his shot. "I saw that when she checked with you before running off with the girls. Just keep those lines of communication open. Fourteen is a rough age. I assume she's already gotten her period, so you've got to make sure you have feminine products on hand and talk to her about sex and all that."

"*Shit.*" Johnny paced. "I didn't think about that. How will I know what to buy? I can't ask her if she uses pads or tampons. It'll embarrass her."

"She'll be more embarrassed having to come to you with blood-stained underwear, and she might try to deal with it on her own, like Aria did. You don't want her getting caught stealing," his father said as Kane lined up his shot. "I suppose you could have your mother or sisters talk to her."

"No. She's *my* kid. I should be able to talk to her about that. It's a natural process, nothing to be ashamed of."

"Don't forget the birds and the bees." Kane smirked.

"She's fourteen. I'm sure she knows about sex. Don't they cover that in school?" Johnny stopped pacing.

"Don't tell me you're going to be one of those fathers who rely on school to teach your daughter about life," Kane said sternly.

"Shit. You're right. Any advice on that, Dad?"

"I handled you boys. The girls were your mother's domain."

"I'll talk to her, and I'll call Dare and ask him if there's anything I should watch for, given all she's been through."

"Just stock up on one of every kind of feminine product," Kane said. "And make sure you have chocolate on hand for when she's PMSing."

Johnny paced. "*Jesus.* What else am I missing?"

"You've got to meet her friends. Get to know everyone she's hanging out with," his father said. "Kids are sneaky. You'll have to follow up, talk to the other parents, and if something feels off, it probably is."

"Should we talk to him about when she starts dating?" Kane asked.

"No, *asshole*," Johnny snapped. "She's not *ever* dating. Dating leads to sex, and—"

Kane and his father cracked up.

Johnny stopped pacing and crossed his arms. "This is not funny."

"If you could see your face right now, you'd be laughing, too," Kane said.

"*Shit.* You suck." He paced again. "I mean, you're *right*. Those are important things I need to think about, but *stop* laughing already."

His father clapped him on the shoulder again. "All kidding aside, John, you're Zoey's Mom *and* Dad now, so you might want to have a chat with your mother about what you need to know. But I can give you a few real tips. Finding a common interest is helpful, something you can bond over."

Music and Jillian came to mind.

"Kids appreciate honesty," his father said, drawing his attention. "She'll know when you're bullshitting."

"Females have a built-in bullshit detector that guys don't come equipped with," Kane interjected.

"It's true," his father agreed. "Girls need fathers who aren't afraid to talk to them about hard subjects. If you avoid them, she'll never fully trust you. Your mother handled the puberty talks with the girls, but I got into some other difficult subjects with them. And if you want Zoey's trust, you have to respect her opinions and trust her, too. That doesn't mean you have to agree with her or give in all the time, but when a teenage girl takes the time to say something beyond *whatever* or *nothing*, she's decided to let you into her head. She might yell, or cry, or mumble, and it's up to you to take a step back and think about *why* she's crying or yelling when she tells you whatever it is. Ask yourself if you've been not listening to her enough or if she is hurting because of some outside source. A friend, a boy, the loss of her grandmother. With Zoey, the stuff with her mother might come back for years when you least expect it. You need to always have that in your head. Like Aria with her nightmares. She doesn't have nightmares that I know of now, but she's still haunted, and it comes out in other ways. Watch for that so you can be there to catch her when she falls."

His father circled the pool table, looking for a shot as he spoke. "When we adopted Harlow, your mother told me what I think is the most important thing to remember with girls. How you treat her will determine how she's going to expect to be treated by every other man who comes into her life. If you keep that in mind with every conversation you have, every facial expression you make, you'll be in good shape."

"No pressure or anything," Kane said with an empathetic expression.

"I think I need something stronger than beer for this." Johnny scrubbed a hand down his face.

"You've got this," Kane said.

"I'd better, for Zoey's sake."

AFTER A FEW games of pool and sharing more than a few laughs, Johnny said, "I want to check on Zoey and bring in our things from the car. What do you think about having a bonfire tonight?"

"The wood is already in the pit," his father said as he and Kane played their last game of pool.

"Mind if I borrow this?" He motioned to the first full-size guitar his mother had ever given him, hanging on the wall by Kane's business degrees, Harlow's red-carpet pictures, and Aria's drawing awards. The guitar had been his mother's, and she'd given it to him when he turned twelve.

"Not at all. Did you forget your guitar?" his father asked.

"No. Zoey's learning to play." He took it off the wall and headed upstairs. He found his mother coming out of the kitchen with a plate of cookies. "Hey, Mom. Are you holding up okay?" He snagged a cookie and took a bite.

"I'm fine, sweetheart. Thanks for asking, but I'm really okay. I'll rest when I need to."

"Okay. Where's Zoey?"

"Harlow absconded with her and Aria. They're in the den, and, honey, we're so in love with her. Your girl has got grit. She told us about her mother, and she did not hold back about how she feels about her."

"Yeah. I'm glad I have Zoey, but I clearly wasn't thinking back then."

"You got famous so fast, and you had so much to deal with, we knew there would be some questionable decisions along the way. But look how wonderful you turned out, and now you have a beautiful daughter who thinks you're cool. Her word, not mine."

He grinned proudly. "She said that?"

"I think her exact words were, 'My dad and Jillian are so cool.' She's quite fond of Jillian."

"We both are."

"I gathered as much from what she shared with us. Will you be seeing her again?"

I sure as hell hope so. "At some point. She and Zoey want to make an outfit together."

"Zoey mentioned that, too, and Harlow was a little jealous, so Zoey called Jillian to ask if she could make Harlow an outfit. We all video chatted with her. She is lovely."

"You *what?*" Holy shit. He could only imagine the interrogation Harlow put her through.

"It was fine. Jillian was happy to talk with Zoey, and she and the girls hit it off. She seems like she's got a good head on her shoulders, and she clearly cares about Zoey. I'm glad Zoey has someone like her to look up to. They talked a little about your upcoming school visit, too, which Zoey is not happy about."

"I know, but we have a deal. It's a start."

"We heard all about your monthlong deal," his mother said.

"She must really feel comfortable with you guys to share all that."

"She seemed to be." She smiled. "She also said you're making music again."

"Yeah. I guess my life needed to implode in order for me to finally get some inspiration."

"It sounds like that time away with Jillian was good for both of you. I know your life is chaotic right now, and I'm sure it feels like you have too much in front of you to see an end to it, but we both know time is precious. You might want to let Zoey visit Jillian sooner rather than later."

If it were up to him, Jillian would be right there by his side. "I'll keep that in mind, Mom. I want to go check on Zoey. Would you mind if I gave this to her?" He held up the guitar. "She's learning to play. I'll make sure she takes good care of it."

"I think that would be wonderful."

He found Zoey sitting beside Harlow in the den, looking at something on Harlow's phone, while Aria drew on Zoey's sneakers. He pulled out his phone and took a picture. As he walked in, they looked up, and he snapped another.

"Wait," Harlow said, putting her arm around Zoey. "Aria, get up here so Johnny can take a picture."

Aria sat on Zoey's other side, leaning close to her, and Zoey beamed as he took the picture.

"Now a goofy one," Harlow urged.

They made silly faces, and he took another picture.

"Johnny, look!" Zoey popped to her feet and held out her arm, showing him where Aria had drawn the Bad Intentions logo.

"That's awesome. Maybe one day we'll have matching tattoos." That earned another bright smile.

"And look at my sneakers." She lifted one foot, showing him the designs Aria had drawn on that sneaker.

"I love it. Nice job, Aria."

"Thanks," Aria said softly.

"Would you mind if I borrowed Zoey for a second?"

"But we're not done," Zoey complained.

"I just want to talk to you for a minute. You can come right back," he promised.

"Okay." She turned to the girls. "I'll be right back." As they went into the hall, she said, "Did I do something wrong?"

"No, sunshine. I just wanted to see how you're doing and find out if you wanted to stay over or not before I bring our things in."

"I *do*. Harlow and Aria said we can watch a movie together, and your mom said we can have popcorn. We're going to sleep in Harlow's old bedroom. They said they'd make a sheet fort like they did when they were kids. Do you want to sleep in there with us?"

"That sounds like fun, but I think I'll stick to my own bed. We're having a bonfire after dinner. Are you still up for trying to play 'I Want to Hold Your Hand'?"

"You know I can't play the barre chords yet," she said quietly. Barre chords were hard for beginners because they required holding multiple strings at once.

"We'll do it just like we practiced, skipping all the B chords."

"You'll skip them, too?" she asked hopefully.

"Heck yeah. We're a team, remember?"

"Okay. I'll do it."

"Attagirl." He held up the guitar. "This was my first full-size guitar, and I want you to have it."

Her eyes widened with awe. "The one your mom gave you?"

"That's right."

"Are you *sure*?"

"There's no one else I'd rather have follow in my footsteps. Just promise you'll take care of it. It can't be replaced."

"I'd never let anything happen to it. You told me it was your most special thing."

"It was, but now I've got you." His heart screamed, *And Jillian,* but that was *if* she'd wait for him.

Zoey gave him a trembling-lipped smile and the tightest hug. "Thank you so much! Can I show Harlow and Aria?"

"It's yours. You can do whatever you'd like."

He handed her the guitar, and as she ran into the den, shouting, "Look what my dad gave me!" Kane and their father came down the hall.

"How does it feel?" his father asked.

Like someone important is missing a big moment.

Chapter Twenty-Two

"I'VE FLAGGED THE budgetary increases and highlighted the savings from the deals I've been able to negotiate." Liza put a folder on Jillian's desk. It was Friday afternoon, nearly three weeks since Jillian had left Colorado, and they were wrapping up their meeting about the launch.

The last two weeks had flown by in a chaotic state of launch preparations and keeping up with clients. Liza was working miracles to pull off an early-March launch for Wanderlust, and the *leak* had led to a flood of interest in the line. The fashion industry was buzzing with anticipation, and the general public was wild about the idea of letting go of societal expectations in fashion and a high-end fashion line at midline prices made for all body types. Moving forward with the launch had been a smart decision on all fronts. Burying herself in work had been exactly what she'd needed to refocus her energy during the day. Although her daily calls with Zoey, who was having trouble adjusting to school, and nightly calls with Johnny, who was doing everything he could to help Zoey while trying to fix relationships Dick had mishandled and pull his own life together and still managed to make Jillian feel special and wanted, left her feeling the same way his texts had in Colorado—satisfied *and* longing for much more.

"What's the bottom line?" Jillian asked.

"It's going to cost about twenty-three thousand more than our five percent wiggle room, even with the discounts."

"That's a lot less than I assumed it would be. You must have sold your soul to get deep discounts."

"I might have pulled a few strings. But the way your calendar is filling up with press requests, I think you made the right move going in a big, new direction. Interest in Wanderlust is still blowing up on social media, and not a single piece has been revealed."

"Let's just hope that when it is, people aren't disappointed."

"Not a chance. This is your best line yet. My daughters are itching to get their hands on it." Liza had three daughters, four granddaughters, and two grandsons.

"Order them whatever they want, on me."

"As generous as always. Thank you. How about I send it to them a month before the launch with a note that says sharing is caring, love Mom?"

"No wonder I like you so much. That sounds perfect." She'd already ordered one of everything for Liza, and she planned on giving it to her for Christmas, along with her other holiday gifts. Jillian pushed to her feet. "Thanks for the updates. I'll be in the studio if you need me."

She headed upstairs. The late-afternoon sun streamed through the windows, spilling over the sketches on her drawing table and bathing the rest of the studio where she spent so much time in light. Instead of going straight to work, as she'd tried to do these last few weeks, she took a moment to take stock in the plethora of mannequins dressed in outfits in various stages of completion, the many tables littered with fabric and other accoutrements, and the large pinboards with ideas and designs stuck to them, reminding herself of how far she'd come. Just as she'd done several times over the years when she'd felt lonely.

Loneliness had hit an all-time high last night when she'd gone to her parents' house for dinner with Jax and Jordan, Nick and Trixie, and Graham and Morgyn. Her family couldn't stop talking about how excited they were about her decision to launch Wanderlust, and her sisters-in-law and Jordan were excited to model for the show. Jillian hoped she came across with the same enthusiasm, but sitting at a table surrounded by couples in love had made her miss Johnny even more. She'd found herself fantasizing about him and Zoey being there with her. It had been easy to picture him joking with her brothers and Zoey talking through the trouble she was having at school with Jillian and her mother and the girls and getting all the love and support she deserved. Jillian knew she had that with Johnny's family. Zoey had told her that Harlow, Aria, and her Grandma Jan were keeping in touch with her, and she'd started talking with a therapist whom she seemed to like. But still. There was no such thing as having *too much* support.

She heard footsteps ascending the stairs and turned as Jax walked in, looking sharp as ever in his designer suit and tie. He wore his light brown hair short, and his dark eyes had seemed far more vibrant since he and Jordan had come together.

"Basking in the glory of your upcoming launch?" he asked as he sauntered toward her.

"Why, yes, yes I am." She sighed dramatically. "It's a rough life, but someone has to do it. What are you doing here?"

"Just checking up on you."

She scoffed and headed over to her drawing table. "You mean hoping some of my success wears off on you?" She was only teasing. Jax had hit the spotlight well before she had. He was a sought-after bridal gown designer and an excellent businessman, and he could practically read her mind. They often finished each other's sentences, and now that they were alone, that worried her a little.

"I should be so lucky," he said, glancing at the sketches. "Are these for the Rocker Girlz line?"

"Yeah. Do you like them?"

He looked over the sketches with a discerning eye. "I do. They're *saucy.*"

"Saucy?" She arched a brow. "Okay, old man."

"What's wrong with saucy?"

"Nothing, if you're a grandpa."

"I think *saucy* is a fine word. They're not cute, because young teens don't want to be called cute, and they're not sexy, for obvious reasons. They're edgy with a flair all their own. *Saucy.*"

"Okay, weirdo." She realized she'd picked up that word from Zoey, but she didn't stop to pick that apart. "I have work to do, so did you and your new vocabulary want something?"

"Just answers." He leaned his hip against the drawing table and crossed his arms.

"About…?"

"How you barely ate when we had dinner at Mom and Dad's and you were overly enthusiastic about Wanderlust."

"I didn't know there was a limit to enthusiasm. Don't you think I should be excited?" She stalked across the room.

"Yes. I think you should be elated, which was why your fake over-the-top excitement worried me. I know you, Jilly. I shared a womb with you. I can tell when something's off."

"Nothing is *off.*"

"You're really not going to tell me about this guy you're hung up on?"

"What guy?" She hadn't said a word to her brothers about Johnny outside of what he was dealing with. She spun around, meeting his gaze, trying to figure out if he was fishing, and *Oh God.* He knew. "I'm going to kill Jordan."

"Don't blame her. I tortured it out of her."

"You bastard. You made her break the girl code."

"What can I say? I'm good with my mouth."

"*Ew!* Now I have to bleach my ears." She strode across the room, heading nowhere, needing to escape his all-seeing eyes.

He laughed, but his amusement was short-lived. "Spill it, Jilly."

He walked around her so she had no choice but to look at him or childishly turn away again. She lifted her chin, holding his gaze, trying to figure out what to say. "What do you want me to say?"

"That you found someone who means a lot to you and you're hurting without him."

Why hearing that from Jax got her choked up, she had no idea, but she looked up at the ceiling to regain control before meeting his gaze.

"If anyone knows what that's like, it's me," he said empathetically. "I fell in love with Jordan the first time I met her, and she was engaged to someone else. I loved her from afar for eight months without knowing whether I'd ever see her again."

"I know, and you were a mess. Totally off your game that whole time. You've always been so in control, I never understood how that could happen. *Until now*," she said softly. "But I didn't fall for Johnny the first time I met him. I gave him hell. I don't even know *when* I fell for him. It snuck up on me, the way a design does. You know how when you start a sketch, every line you draw makes you feel something? And you like it, and then you aren't so sure, but the more you flesh it out and it comes to life, the more you start to *feel* it?"

"And then one line or a bit of texture or a pattern brings it all together, and suddenly it's the most perfect thing you've ever seen and you can't imagine it any other way."

"*Yes.* That's how it happened. I never saw it coming, and I can't imagine being close to anyone else."

"Sounds to me like you found your Diet Pepsi."

"Only you would call him that," she said with a laugh.

"That's the only thing you've ever been addicted to besides fashion."

"You're right, but the timing is all wrong for us, and you know what, Jax? It's fine. *I'm* fine. I love you for worrying about me and I know you mean well, but I'm focusing on work, and honestly, I'm so busy, I barely have time to *think* about Johnny and Zoey."

"Well, *that's* disappointing."

Johnny? Jillian spun around with her heart in her throat and lost her breath at the sight of him and Zoey. He was holding a huge bouquet of wildflowers, and they both looked stricken by her words. "What are you doing here?"

"Obviously *bothering* you," Zoey snapped, looking like she was going to cry.

"No, you're not." Jillian ran to her, pulling her into her arms. "I can't believe you're here. I only said that because I didn't want Jax to worry about me."

"You don't have to lie," she said, trying to push out of Jillian's arms.

Jillian was *not* losing this battle. She held tight. "I would *never* lie to you. Don't I make time for you every day?" She didn't wait for an answer. "*Yes*, I do, because you're important to me and because I love you. But missing someone you love is hard, and I thought I had tricked everyone into thinking I was fine, but Jax is my twin, and he saw through it and came here to check on me. I promise, Zoey, I *have* time for you, and when I don't, I'll make it."

The tension in Johnny's jaw eased.

As Jillian let go of Zoey, Zoey's untrusting gaze shifted to Jax.

"She's telling you the truth," Jax said. "My sister sucks at lying. Especially to me, but I didn't buy it for a second. I was about to tell her that when your dad spoke up."

Zoey pressed her lips together, and Jillian could tell she was embarrassed, so she pulled her back into her arms and said, "I need a hug so I don't cry, or my makeup will smear, and trust me, that's not pretty."

"I can vouch for that." Jax held out his hand. "You must be the infamous Johnny Butthead. I'm Jax."

"*Jax*," Jillian chided.

Johnny laughed and shook his hand. "It's nice to meet you." He touched Zoey's back. "And obviously this is my daughter, Zoey."

"Hi," she said a little bashfully. "Sorry about all that."

"All what? I didn't see anything." Jax winked.

Jillian ached to run to Johnny, but she didn't want to make things awkward with Zoey, so she said, "I still don't know what you're doing here."

"We had to come see the incredible pumpkin parade and festival you told us about." Johnny gathered her in his arms and gazed into her eyes. "That, and we missed you."

He pressed his lips to hers, and she pulled back, shocked. *"Johnny...?"*

"She knows," he said with a smile.

Jillian was sure she'd misheard him. "What?"

"I know you like each other and want to be boyfriend and girlfriend," Zoey explained. "And I know it might not work out, but I really hope it does, because I missed you as much as he did. But if it doesn't, Johnny said we can still be friends. I mean, if you want to."

Jillian was at a loss for words and a little afraid of shedding tears, she was so happy. Thankfully, Jax came to her rescue.

"Zoey, I hear you have an eye for fashion. Why don't we head over to the ice cream parlor and give your dad and Jillian time to talk? We can chat over sundaes."

"Can I go with him?" Zoey asked, wide-eyed.

"Sure. Let me give you some cash." Johnny reached for his wallet.

"I've got it," Jax said. "You just keep those tears at bay."

As they headed downstairs, Jillian said, "You *told* her?"

"I had to. These last few weeks have been hell. I hated hiding my feelings and pretending I'm not missing you every second of the day. I'm not good at it. Zoey could tell I wasn't happy. She asked me a few times if something was wrong, so I talked to Dare about it, and he said to be honest with her about everything."

Her heart was so full and beating so hard, she was surprised she could speak. "How did she take it?"

"She was pretty psyched. She said she had a feeling we liked each other. That when we were in Colorado, she saw the way I looked at you and noticed that I touched your hand a lot."

"Among *other* things. Why didn't you tell me you were going to tell her?"

"I wasn't sure I was going to, and then when she called you about school earlier in the week, I just couldn't pretend anymore. I didn't want to keep it from her, or anyone else."

"I can't believe you told her. I've missed you so much, and every time I talked to Zoey, I wanted to talk to you, too. I'm really glad you told her, but that was three days ago, and we talked every night. Why didn't you say anything?"

"And miss seeing the surprise on your face when we walked in? How about you stop asking questions and put that sexy mouth to better use before I lose my mind?"

He lowered his lips to hers, kissing her slowly and sweetly, as if he were savoring the feel and taste of her just as she was of him. "God, I've missed you," he said against her lips. "I feel like I can finally breathe."

She opened her mouth to say that made two of them, but his lips covered hers, and words no longer mattered.

JILLIAN WAS LIVING a dream she hadn't let herself fully imagine until now.

After Jax brought Zoey back, he pulled Jillian aside and said, *What a great kid. She's a tough little bird. She reminds me of you. She's got the same low filter and feistiness.* Jillian wasn't sure that was the best compliment, but she was glad he liked Zoey. She introduced Johnny and Zoey to Liza, who was instantly smitten with both of them, to Annabelle, who stumbled over her words every time Johnny was near her, and to the other girls who worked in her shop. Zoey went through every rack in the shop, commenting on her designs, and Jillian could do little more than smile, unable to believe she and Johnny were really there.

Johnny and Zoey had brought Winger and Rocker Boy with them, and Zoey set them up on the kitchen counter. Jillian was surprised by how much seeing the fish meant to her. They brought dinner in, and as they ate, Zoey reiterated that she felt out of place at school, and Jillian asked if there were any school clubs she could join where she might find kids who liked the same things she did, but Zoey said the kids were just too different from her. She was sticking it out, though, just as she'd promised, and Jillian was proud of her for that, even though she wished she could fix it for her.

After dinner, she showed them around the house, and Zoey asked a million questions in her studio. When they finally went back downstairs, Zoey claimed the first-floor guest room, and then they had a low-key evening, cuddling on the couch watching *Hocus Pocus 2* and sharing popcorn. Jillian had never been a cuddler, much less that comfortable with people in her home. But sitting with Johnny's arm around her and Zoey's head in her lap felt natural, like she'd found the place she was always meant to be.

As the movie came to an end, Zoey got up and said, "Can we go to Salem next year for Halloween?"

Johnny cocked a brow. "We'll see."

"Are you afraid?" Zoey teased.

"Of a few ghosts or witches? Nah. Nothing scares me, sunshine."

She looked at her hands. "How cool would it be if I had powers?"

"Okay, that might scare me," Johnny teased, earning an eye roll from Zoey.

"What kind of powers would you like?" Jillian asked.

Zoey shrugged. "The power to get rid of paparazzi and make everyone in the city slow down, or at least smile. Everyone walks around with mad faces."

Jillian was hoping she'd get used to the city by now and tried to make light of it. "They're just concentrating. A lot of people think things through when they walk from one place to the next. But if you get powers, you have to let me in your coven, because I want them, too. I'd like to be able to wiggle my nose or shake a stick and the dishes would magically get done." She wiggled her nose and looked at the empty popcorn bowls. "I guess that didn't work."

She carried the bowls into the kitchen and said hello to Winger and Rocker Boy, swimming in their little tank on the counter. She was glad Zoey had brought them. Seeing the little guys brought back memories of the carnival. She just finished washing the bowls when Johnny came in a few minutes later. He put his arms around her from behind, kissing her neck. He'd been openly affectionate all evening, holding her hand and giving her kisses here and there. He was careful not to do anything inappropriate, and it just built up the anticipation for what she hoped would come later. She hadn't brought up the subject of where he would sleep. She assumed he'd start out in her bed and end up in one of the other guest rooms.

He nipped at her earlobe, and she turned in his arms. "Where's Zoey?"

"Getting ready for bed, which is what I hope we're doing soon." He threaded his fingers into her hair and kissed her passionately.

"*Johnny*," she warned breathily. "She might catch us."

"I'm not doing anything dirty." He grabbed her butt and whispered, "*Yet.*"

She shivered with anticipation.

He reached for her hand. "Come on, let's go say good night." They went down the hall and found Zoey closing the curtains in the guest room. "Ready for bed, sunshine?"

"Almost. What time does the festival start tomorrow?"

"Around eleven, so feel free to sleep in," Jillian said. "It'll be a long day with the festival and Nick and Trixie's Halloween party. We need to figure out costumes for you guys for the party."

"Is there a costume store nearby?" Johnny asked.

Jillian scoffed. "Did you forget who you're talking to? I will whip you up a beautiful costume."

"You don't have to make one for me," Zoey said. "I know what I want to be, and Jax said he and Jordan would help me get ready. You just have to drop me off at their house before the party, and they'll bring me over."

"He did? That's fun. What are you thinking of dressing up as?" Jillian said.

"It's a secret. He told me all about your family, too. He said your parents are really nice, and that Graham and Zev are funny, and Nick is tough, but even though he looks mad, he's usually not."

"That about sums them up," Jillian said. "We'll probably run into some of them at the festival. Trixie's minis are in the parade."

"That's what Jax said. I can't wait to meet everyone. I'm really glad we're here. I just wish Beau and Char could've come."

"Me too."

"All right, kiddo. Try to get some sleep." Johnny pulled her into a hug and kissed the top of her head. "Love you."

"Love you, too." She hugged Jillian. "Good night. Love you."

Jillian didn't think her heart could get any fuller. "Love you, too, Zo."

Zoey climbed into bed, and they pulled the door most of the way closed behind them and went into the living room.

"Is all this domesticity freaking you out?" Johnny drew her into his arms.

Loving that he thought to ask, she said, "Not yet."

"I know we barged into your life today without warning." He brushed his lips over hers, his hands sliding down to her butt. "Do you need to catch up on work tonight?"

She realized she hadn't thought about work since they'd arrived, and she didn't care. "Now that you mention it." She pressed a kiss to the center of his chest. "I have some research to do for your tour wardrobe." She slid a hand between them, palming him through his jeans.

He made a low, guttural sound and covered her hand with his, squeezing as he lowered his mouth to hers. They kissed slowly, tenderly, but it quickly escalated into a passionate devouring. She moaned, and his hips pressed forward, his hand squeezing tighter as his cock hardened beneath her palm. He growled against her lips. "I need to be inside you."

"What about Zoey? Should we wait until she's asleep?"

"She'll be out soon. She was so excited to see you, she got up at five to pack before school." He kissed her again. "She also gave us permission to have a slumber party."

"Are you kidding?"

"Nope. On the drive here, she informed me that she knows adults have sex and that I don't have to pretend to sleep in a guest room for her benefit."

"Ohmygod." She grinned as they headed up the stairs. "What about you? Were you so excited to see me you got up at five, too?"

"What do you think?" As they stepped onto the landing, he looked down the hall toward her studio.

"We can't. It's above Zoey's room," she warned, guiding him toward her bedroom. "She'll hear us."

"Tomorrow, then, when she goes to Jax's."

A thrill darted through her as they walked into her room. She stood by the bed, watching his gaze sweep over the furniture, and she tried to see her private space through his eyes. It was substantial but elegant, with soft lines, decorated in gold, taupe, and cream, with splashes of color.

"Just as I pictured it," he said in a rough voice, tugging off his shirt and socks. "As beautiful as you are." He locked the door, eyes trained on her as he unbuckled his belt, stalking toward her like a lion on the prowl. He tangled his hand in her hair, tugging her head back. "It's been too damn long since I've had you to myself."

"Then kiss me," she challenged.

"I'm going to do a lot more than kiss you." He dragged his tongue along her lower lip. She tried to go up on her toes and capture his mouth, but he was holding her hair too tight. He moved behind her and unzipped her dress, pushing it to the floor. "So fucking gorgeous." He kissed her shoulder as he unhooked her bra, sending that to the floor, too. Goose bumps chased up her skin. His hand grazed her waist, and he circled her, and then his mouth was on hers, kissing her so thoroughly her knees buckled. He smiled against her lips and trapped her lower lip between his teeth, tugging hard enough to make her gasp. "I've been fantasizing about you for weeks."

"Then it's about time you got naked." She reached for the button on his jeans, need billowing inside her.

He hauled her against him, rubbing his scruff against her cheek. "On the bed, sweetheart." He smacked her ass as she crawled onto it, sending lust spiking through her body.

"I knew you wouldn't disappoint me," she said as she turned and lay on her back.

THE CHALLENGE IN Jillian's eyes was the sexiest thing Johnny had ever seen. "Baby, there are two things I'll never do to you in the bedroom. Share you or disappoint you." He straddled her and slid his belt out of the loops.

"Why, Mr. Bad," she said seductively. "What do you think you're going to do with *that*?"

"Punish you for making me wish I was a toy in your bathtub." He felt her shudder beneath him, her eyes blazing hotter.

"You loved it."

"Fucking right I did, and you're going to love this." He lifted her hand and kissed her palm. Then he took her other hand and dragged it down his chest, reveling in the feel of her fingers and the hunger in her eyes as he put her hands together and began winding his belt around them. He leaned forward and latched it around the decorative iron curls on the headboard, gazing down at her. "That doesn't hurt, does it?"

"Only the good kind of hurt," she said softly.

"God, I'm crazy about you." He took her in a deep but painfully slow kiss, wanting her needy and torturing them both. But he *loved* kissing her. Loved the way she was eager for more. He feasted his way down her soft, silky skin, slowing to enjoy her breasts. He teased her nipples, squeezing one while grazing his teeth over the other. She writhed and moaned, bowing off the mattress as he sucked it into his mouth.

"Johnny—"

The pleasure and need in her voice had him grinding against her center as he moved his mouth to her other breast, using his teeth more, earning sharp, sexy inhalations. "I fucking love your tits." He groped and licked, kissed and bit every inch of her as he moved lower, until she was panting, digging her heels into the mattress, a stream of whispered pleas falling from her lips. He slid his tongue around her belly button and clutched her waist. "I want to touch all of you at once." He licked and bit and sucked his way south and dragged his tongue over her panties, along her center. Her hips rose off the mattress, and he continued teasing until she was so wet, he tasted her through the thin material, and then he sank his teeth into the sensitive flesh between her sex and her inner thigh, sucking hard.

"Ah—"

"Just marking what's *mine*."

She panted and writhed as he stripped off the wet lace, her glistening pussy calling out to him. "Eyes on me, gorgeous." He held her gaze as he flicked her clit with the tip of his tongue while sliding his fingers through her wetness, lower with each swipe, until she was drenched from her pussy to her tightest hole. She rocked against his fingers, and he pushed two into her pussy, crooking them up, stroking that hidden spot that had her bowing off the mattress. "You like that, baby?"

"God, yesss."

"Then you're going to love this." He brought his other hand into play, getting his index finger wet, teasing that forbidden hole as he fucked her other with his fingers, and all at once, he took her clit between his teeth and pushed one finger into her ass.

"Ohmygod—"

She rode his fingers, moaning and whimpering, clenching her teeth. "That's it, baby. So fucking beautiful. Come for me." He lowered his mouth to her clit and quickened his efforts until she lost all control, bucking and moaning for all she was worth. Her inner muscles pulsed around his fingers, but it wasn't enough. He withdrew from her pussy, still fucking her ass, and devoured her sweetness.

"John—" She panted. "Johnny—"

He continued driving her wild until she shattered again, crying out and quickly clamping her mouth shut, mewling as she rode out her pleasure, until she lay spent, gasping for air, her body trembling. Only then did he withdraw from her sacred places and strip naked. What a beautiful sight she was, lying there watching as he sheathed his length and unbound her wrists. Her eyes were so full of *them* as he came down over her, he could feel her emotions wrapping around him, drawing him in like the most perfect lyrics.

She reached for him. "I need *you*."

"You've got me, baby." He cradled her beneath him as their bodies came together, and when he was buried to the hilt, he laced their fingers and gazed into her eyes. "I missed you so damn much."

"Show me." She craned to kiss him, and as their mouths came together, they began moving and quickly found their rhythm. She squeezed her inner muscles tightly around him. *"Faster."*

He thrust faster. She felt so good, so tight and eager and perfect, he felt himself getting lost in her and forced himself to slow down. *"Jesus,* baby. You feel too fucking good. I'm going to lose my mind."

Her eyes flamed. "I want you to lose your mind."

Their mouths crashed together, and they pumped and gyrated, groping and kissing. He pushed his hands beneath her ass, lifting and angling, taking her deeper, swallowing her needy sounds. All his emotions tangled together, pounding inside him, and she was right there with him. He felt the tension mounting in her body and tore his mouth away, sealing it over the curve of her neck as he teased that tight hole with his fingers.

She dug her fingernails into his flesh. *"Don't stop,"* she begged, holding on to him so tight, her entire body shook. He pushed his finger into her ass, and she cried, *"Yes—"* and bit down on his shoulder, hurling them both into oblivion. Violent waves of pleasure consumed him as they thrust and rocked, moaning and gritting out curses, their bodies ravaged with pleasure.

They finally collapsed, blissfully spent and unfathomably sated, in each other's arms. He rolled them onto their sides, kissing her softer, their hearts hammering to the same frantic beat.

He held her until he had no choice but to take care of the condom. She slipped into the bathroom afterward, and when she returned, she put on his T-shirt, and he reached for her as she climbed onto the bed, pulling her into his arms. She snuggled into him with her head on his shoulder. He kissed her forehead, holding her tighter, so fucking happy to have her in his arms. She ran her fingers over his cheek, her touch as soothing as it had been exciting.

Her sensual tigress's eyes fluttered open, and she purred like a kitten. "Do I really get to wake up with you in my bed? Or is this some kind of cruel joke or incredible dream?"

He held her tighter. She was everything he could ever want—a rock song and a ballad in one snarky, sensual, beautiful creature—and *this*, lying with her in his arms, with his daughter under the same roof, was everything he could ever need. "It's an incredible dream come true. One I hope we never have to wake up from."

Chapter Twenty-Three

MORNING TIPTOED IN, bringing the scents of rugged, sexy man and happiness. Jillian burrowed deeper into the confines of Johnny's warm, hard body, and for the first time ever, she wished they could stay in bed, making love and dozing off all day. It made no sense, since she was used to running on little sleep, but apparently running on little sleep and working used a lot less energy than staying up half the night devouring a man she adored.

"You're really here," she murmured against his chest.

"I am, baby, and there's no place else I'd rather be. But you're too far away." His hand slid down her back, and he pulled her closer.

He sounded so awake, she tilted her face up to look at him, and her heart skipped a beat at the emotions staring back at her. How can the mere sight of him do that? "You're sure this is okay and you shouldn't pretend you slept in the guest room?" She glanced at the dimly lit curtains. It couldn't be later than six o'clock. Surely Zoey was still sleeping.

"I spent the last three weeks wishing I could hold you. If you think I'm getting out of your bed, you're sorely mistaken." He brushed his lips over her cheek. "How can I have you in my arms and still miss you?"

"How could you not?" she teased on a yawn.

He laughed softly and nuzzled against her neck. He ran his hand up and down her back, whispering, "I want more of this."

"*Mm.* Me too."

"I'm serious, babe. I want to make this work. I don't want to go three weeks without seeing you again."

"I don't, either. I nearly lost my mind, I missed you guys so much."

"I know you're preparing for your launch, and November's going to be busy for us, too. We've got my family's fundraising gala honoring Lorelei to raise money for the Ronald McDonald house next Saturday. There's going to be select media coverage, and it would be the perfect time to let the world know we're together. Is there any chance you can come up and go with us?"

"I think so, but are you sure you're ready for that? Will it cause problems for Zoey?"

"We talked about it on the way here. I don't want to hide our relationship, and I don't want her to feel like she can't talk openly about us. She wants this as much as I do. The real question is, can *you* handle it?"

"With all the paparazzi hanging around Maryland?" she said sarcastically. "Of course I can. Does Zoey need a dress for the event?"

"She'll need an outfit. They do a theme every year, and this year it's disco."

"That sounds fun." She yawned. "I'm sure we can come up with great outfits."

"We can come back the weekend after that if you're free, but the third weekend in November is the American Music Awards in LA. Zoey's coming with me, and I was hoping I could convince you to come, too."

"I'll clear my schedule for the weekend you come back, and I wish I could go to LA, but I'll be in Virginia for my friend Amber's wedding. I think you met her and her fiancé, Dash, at the fundraiser last year."

"Dash Pennington? My cousin Dylan's wife, Tiffany, is a sports agent. She reps Dash and some of his buddies. I remember Amber. She was really sweet."

"I was kind of hoping you'd be my date, but I guess that's out."

"Sorry, babe, I wish I could go with you. What about Thanksgiving the following week? It'll be Zoey's first with my family. How would you feel about joining us, and then we can spend Thanksgiving weekend with your family?"

She cuddled closer. "That sounds perfect. Zoey and I can shop for a dress for her to wear to the awards ceremony when I come visit next weekend, and we can make her outfit from the Rocker Girlz line over her Thanksgiving break."

"I'm sure she'd love that."

"Listen to us, making future plans."

"It feels good." He kissed her forehead, and as she lay in the safety of his arms, the steady and sure beat of his heart lulling her to sleep, he whispered, "I'm falling for you, baby, and I'll do whatever it takes for us to have more of this."

His words took root inside her, just as he and Zoey had all those weeks ago.

JILLIAN AWOKE TO an empty bed and sunlight pouring in through the sliver of space between the curtains. She felt like she'd slept for a month and glanced at the clock, but it was only nine forty-five, which wasn't late for her. She padded into the bathroom, and after using the toilet and brushing her teeth, she headed downstairs.

She was greeted by the smell of something delicious and the sounds of Zoey and Johnny talking in the kitchen. What a glorious sound to wake up to. As she made her way to the kitchen, she saw a vase of gorgeous flowers on the table that hadn't been there last night, and the table was set with place mats and glasses Jillian hadn't seen since Emmaline had convinced her to buy them when she'd first moved in.

"I don't care what you say, I'm *not* telling you." Zoey sounded annoyed as she set a tray of muffins on top of the stove.

"I'm your father," Johnny said. "I should be the first to know."

"Oh good, you're up," Zoey said as Jillian walked in. She looked adorable in the gray hoodie with blue stars on it that they'd bought and jeans with butterfly-patterned patches on one thigh and studs on the pockets that she must have added herself.

"Sorry I slept so late. I don't know why I'm so tired."

Johnny turned from the cooktop where he was transferring eggs onto plates. His navy Henley looked absolutely breathtaking with that *knowing* gleam in his eyes and a panty-melting grin spreading across his lips. "Morning, beautiful. You're right on time for breakfast." He leaned down to kiss her.

"You know I don't eat breakfast."

"Yeah, yeah, I know." He smirked.

"Someone's got to take care of you so you don't starve," Zoey said, pulling a Diet Pepsi from the fridge and handing it to her.

"Thank you." Why did it make her feel so good that they cared about her nutrition of all things? "You might be able to entice me into one of those delicious-smelling muffins."

"They're chocolate chip. My favorite." Zoey handed her one.

Jillian took a bite. "*Mm.* Where did you get all this food and the flowers? They're beautiful."

"We went into town and picked a few things up," Johnny said.

"Your town is so *clean*," Zoey said. "And people smile when they see you. I understand why you love it here."

"The city is nice, too. You just have to get used to it," Jillian encouraged. "Did any fans bother you?"

"Girls stared at him," Zoey said.

"From a respectful distance," he added.

"I knew you'd be okay here."

"They're setting up for the festival already," Zoey said. "We saw signs for a pumpkin patch and a corn maze, and Johnny said we could go to them."

"I bet he gets lost in the maze," Jillian teased.

"Not a chance," he countered.

"We'll see about that," she said. "Are you going to try to go incognito to the festival, just in case?"

Johnny shook his head. "No way. I've done enough hiding for one lifetime. I want everyone to know I'm with my girls, and if I have to put my foot down and create a boundary, I'll do it. But I want Zoey to feel less like she's imprisoned."

"Thank God," Zoey said, exasperated.

Jillian sipped her soda, feeling a little giddy about that, and about *them*, as they talked about the day and made breakfast and she fed Winger and Rocker Boy. She looked around the kitchen she'd rarely spent time in, at the pretty table settings, the dirty mixing bowls in the sink, and the sprinkling of flour on the counters, and a new kind of happiness came over her. One she'd never anticipated. "You guys went all out this morning. I don't think I've ever even used my mixer, and the table looks beautiful. I had forgotten I had those place mats."

"Should we not have used them?" Zoey said.

"No. You can use anything," Jillian reassured her.

"I know you don't like people in your space, and I'm sorry we were arguing when you came in," Zoey said. "But he keeps pestering me to tell him what I'm going to dress up as at the party tonight."

Jillian couldn't help but smile. "I didn't think I liked people in my space, but I was wrong. I don't like many people in my space, but I like you guys being here, and to be honest, I have missed your squabbling."

Zoey smiled like she'd just been told she could ditch private school, and Johnny looked like he'd won Best Album of the Year.

As they put plates of food on the table and Zoey chattered about what they'd seen in town, the kitchen Jillian had built for resale value more than anything else suddenly felt like a gift in and of itself—and the people in it made her feel like she'd won something, too.

Something she had a feeling came only once in a lifetime.

JOHNNY THOUGHT HE'D known just how much he'd missed Jillian, but when she'd come into the kitchen, sleepy eyed and smiling, he'd been hit with it anew, and the euphoric feeling of finally being with her clung to him like a second skin as they headed into town later that morning. Pleasant Hill looked nothing like the sleepy town they'd driven through last night. A banner hung across the road announcing the pumpkin festival. Cornstalks were tied to every lamppost with enormous orange ribbons, fall flags waved from entranceways, and display windows were bursting with fall flowers, pumpkins, and other decorations. The sidewalks along Main Street were bustling with people going in and out of shops, and crowds milled around dozens of vendor tents in the park at the end of the street.

As they made their way through the crowds, Johnny held Jillian's hand, and he slung an arm around Zoey, trying to keep her close, but she ducked out from under it, giving him a look of disapproval. Apparently, it wasn't cool to have her father hanging on her, even if he was a rock star. He'd noticed a few people taking extended glances at them, but so far they'd kept their distance, which was refreshing.

"Jilly!" A pretty blonde waved from across the road as she and a tall, athletic-looking guy with longish brown hair jogged toward them.

"That's Zev and Carly," Jillian said, and ran to them.

"I've never seen anyone run in heels like she does," Zoey said.

He looked at Jillian as her brother twirled her around in the middle of the street. She was gorgeous in a pumpkin-colored sweater, skinny jeans with a tear in one knee, and knee-high brown leather boots, but it was her radiant smile that cut straight to Johnny's heart. "She's something else, isn't she?"

Jillian hugged Carly, who was all smiles, with a spray of freckles across her nose and bright blue eyes that matched her sweater. They talked a mile a minute as they approached.

"Johnny, Zoey, this is my brother Zev and his wife, Carly."

The pride in Jillian's voice made Johnny feel like a million bucks. "Jillian's told me a lot about you. You're the real-life Goonies, right?" He shook Zev's hand and nodded to Carly.

"You know it. We love your music, man," Zev said. He looked like a surfer, with his shaggy hair and wearing several leather bracelets and a Baja hoodie. "What are you doing in town? Is Jilly working on your wardrobe this weekend?"

"Um, not exactly," Jillian said. "We're kind of seeing each other."

"You slept in the same bed. That's more than *kind of*, isn't it?" Zoey asked.

"*Zoey.*" Johnny shook his head.

Zev barked out a laugh. "From the mouths of babes. I like your honesty, kid."

Jillian gazed adoringly at Johnny and said, "She's right. It's more than kind of."

"Much more." Johnny took her hand. "I'm crazy about your sister."

"So am I," Zoey said.

"As well you should be," Carly said. "She's an incredible person."

"Yes, she is." Johnny pulled Jillian against his side.

As he leaned down to kiss her, she said, "Sorry. I guess I should've warned my family."

Zev leaned around Carly and hollered toward the street as a mountain of a man wearing a cowboy hat and boots jogged by. "Lookin' good, cowboy!"

The guy stopped cold, and his eyes landed on Johnny and Jillian. His jaw clenched, and tree-trunk legs ate up the distance between them. He had to be some kind of bodybuilder, with biceps so large, his arms arced out from his sides. Johnny stood up taller.

"*Jilly,*" the guy said gruffly. "What's going on here?"

"Be nice, Nicky," Zev said with amusement. "Johnny is Jillian's new boyfriend, and this is Zoey, his daughter, who is now going to be careful about what she says."

Zev tossed Zoey a conspiratorial wink that Johnny hoped his daughter caught. He should probably be intimidated by Nick, but he didn't give a damn what the guy said or tried to do. He wasn't backing away from Jillian.

Johnny held out his hand. "Johnny Bad, nice to meet you."

Nick's eyes narrowed. "You're the dude she was with in Colorado?"

"Yes, and they really like each other," Zoey said. "My dad is not afraid of anyone, so you might want to back off."

"*Zoey*," Johnny chided her. "Let me handle this."

"But Jax told me that if Nick gets pissy just to give it right back to him," Zoey insisted.

"He did, did he?" Nick asked, eyes serious.

Zoey crossed her arms, meeting his stare. "Yup."

"Well, then, I guess he's got me all figured out." Nick slid a dark stare at Johnny. "It's nice to meet you, Bad. You hurt my sister, and you and I are going to have trouble."

"That's bullying, you know," Zoey said.

"No, little lady. That's *protecting*," Nick countered. "I'm sure your father will be doing the same for you when you're older."

"You got that right," Johnny said. "I get where you're coming from, Nick, but as I told Zev, I'm crazy about Jillian. She's in good hands."

"She better be," he warned.

"Okay, that's enough." Jillian planted a hand on her hip. "Nick, do I need to get your shock collar, or can you be nice?"

Nick cracked a grin. "I guess time will tell." He returned his attention to Zoey. "Beau told me you like horses. Is that right?"

"Yeah, I do," she said.

Nick addressed Johnny. "Trixie and I could use a hand walking the minis in the parade. I'd be happy to take your little lady with me."

"Really?" Zoey's eyes widened. "Wait, can you be nice?"

Jillian and Zev laughed.

"I can be nice, but if anyone bugs you, I won't be so nice to them," Nick said.

Zoey grinned and looked up at Johnny. "Can I go with him?"

Zoey hadn't gone anywhere without him yet, and the fair was so busy, he worried about her getting lost. But he had a feeling this was Nick's way of extending an olive branch.

As if Nick had read his mind, he said, "She'll be safe with me. It's a real special job, walking the horses, and we don't take it lightly. I'll be by her side the whole time."

"*Please?*" Zoey asked. "I promise to stay with him."

"Okay, sunshine. But you listen to him and Trixie, and don't go *anywhere* without Nick. Got it?"

"*Yes.* Thank you!" She hugged him.

"I'll text Jilly to meet up with you afterward," Nick promised, then returned his attention to Zoey. "Can those little legs of yours run?"

"What do *you* think?" Zoey said.

"I think if they're half as strong as your attitude, we'll make record time."

Nick reached for her hand, and as he and Zoey ran down the road, Zev clapped Johnny on the back and said, "That went better than I thought it would."

"How'd you think it would go?" Johnny asked.

"Let's just say I'm glad you're still standing." Zev reached for Carly. "We'd better find a spot to watch the parade."

Johnny put his arm around Jillian as they followed them through the crowd. "Any other Neanderthals I need to know about?"

"No." She lowered her voice seductively. "But I hear there's a sexy cavewoman dying to drag you into her lair."

THE PARADE WAS a festive procession of fall-themed floats, tractors pulling hay wagons full of people dressed in Halloween costumes, horses big and small, a high school marching band, Little League teams, people of all ages waving fall-colored flags, and a firetruck decorated to the hilt. And there amid the music and cheers was Zoey, waving to the crowd, wearing a cowgirl hat and smiling proudly as she held the reins of a miniature horse that was dressed up like a unicorn with wings and a spiral horn, wearing a pink vest that read RISING HOPE, MINIATURE THERAPY HORSE. Nick walked between Zoey and Trixie, his keen eyes keeping watch.

Johnny must've taken fifty pictures of what he had a feeling was one of the highlights of Zoey's life so far.

Zev and Carly took off after the parade to find Carly's parents. Two hours later, Zoey was still wearing the hat Nick and Trixie had given her and talking about how much she loved the miniature horses as they finished making their way through the festivities on Main Street. Or rather, *ate* their way through. It seemed like every shop offered pumpkin-flavored snacks. They ran into Jax and Jordan at Jillian's friend Emmaline's café and joined them for lunch. When Emmaline, a vivacious brunette, saw Johnny, she spilled the coffee she was making and exclaimed, *My latte worked!* Jillian told him about a *tribute* latte Emmaline was offering, and they all had a good laugh. He signed a few autographs, but everyone left them alone while they ate, and on their way out, Johnny made it clear to Emmaline that he was not entertaining any tribute offers.

Jax and Jordan headed down Main Street, and Johnny, Jillian, and Zoey made their way into the park, where kids were running around with ice cream cones and getting their faces painted, and crowds milled around tents offering arts, crafts, jewelry, clothes, baked goods, and a plethora of other things.

"Hey, Zo, want to get your face painted?" Johnny asked.

She rolled her eyes. "I'm not *five*."

He hooked his arm around her and hugged her to his side. "Give me a break. I'm still learning what's cool."

She grabbed her cowgirl hat and ducked out from beneath his arm.

"There's my parents." Jillian pointed to an attractive middle-aged couple standing by a tent. "Come on, let's say hi." She reached for Johnny's hand.

Her mother was slim, with straight blond hair cut just above her shoulders. Her mother's eyes lit up at the sight of them, while her father, a tall, broad-shouldered man with mostly gray hair, looked like he was trying to puzzle something out. Johnny wondered what she'd told her parents about them, if anything.

"*Jilly*. We were hoping we'd see you," her mother said. "Jax mentioned you had a couple of surprise visitors for the weekend, and I see you're holding hands with one of them."

"Real subtle, Mom." Jillian laughed, pressing herself closer to Johnny, and put a hand on Zoey's shoulder. "Mom, Dad, this is Johnny Bad and his daughter, Zoey, and yes, Johnny and I are seeing each other."

"Well, isn't that lovely," her mother said with a smile as bright and beautiful as her daughter's. "I'm Lily, and this is my husband, Clint. It's a pleasure to meet you both."

"It's nice to meet you as well," Johnny said, and shook Clint's hand.

"Hi," Zoey said.

"Hi, sweetheart," Lily said. "Jilly has told us so much about you."

"She *has*?" Zoey asked.

"Of course I did," Jillian said, earning a genuine smile from Zoey.

"We saw you in the parade," Clint said. "You looked darn good out there."

"Thank you. It was fun. Nick was a lot nicer once he figured out that he couldn't scare my dad away from Jillian," Zoey said.

Clint laughed. "I bet there's a story there."

"It's Nick," Jillian said. "There's always a story."

"He said I can ride one of his big horses while we're here," Zoey said.

"You must have made quite the impression on him. He doesn't let just anyone ride his babies," Lily said. "We were just heading over to Morgyn's booth. Why don't you tell us what it was like being in the parade on the way?"

Jillian and Zoey fell into line with Lily, and Clint and Johnny followed as Zoey recounted their initial meeting with Nick.

"I'd apologize for Nick's behavior, but it sounds like Zoey put him in his place," Clint said.

"I should probably talk with her about that so she doesn't get herself into trouble talking back to the wrong person."

"After all she's been through, it's not surprising that she's protective of you. How are you holding up with all the changes?" Clint asked. "The media really had a field day before you went on television. I was impressed by the stand you took."

"Thanks. I'm lucky. My older brother, Kane, is the best businessman I know, and he's taken charge of the legalities and getting things back on track, so I can focus on Zoey. And as far as Zoey and I go, we're figuring it out one day at a time."

"You must be doing a good job to have caught Jilly's eye."

"I have her to thank, actually. She doesn't pull any punches, does she?"

Clint chuckled. "She sure doesn't. She grew up with a brood of brothers. She had to be tough, or Nick and Beau would have determined where she went and what she did."

"Well, she's steered me in the right direction with Zoey many times, and she's still helping us communicate better and figure things out. I guess we have you and your wife to thank for that, too. She had to learn it somewhere."

"It was all her mother. I'm just along for the ride."

Johnny didn't believe that for a second.

They came to the only tie-dyed tent among a sea of white ones, with a LIFE REIMAGINED banner hanging across the front. About a dozen people were gathered around tables of jewelry, lamps, shoes, vases, and other items embellished in unique ways. There were displays of fall wreaths, antique furniture that had gorgeous hand-painted designs, and other eclectic items. Zoey made a beeline for a display of sweaters in the back of the tent that had patches and odd but interestingly placed buttons and other embellishments. There were two other young girls looking at the sweaters, and they said something to Zoey that made her smile. She touched the patches on her thigh and held out her arm, showing them the cuff of her hoodie, which she'd modified.

Johnny scrutinized the other girls. They had friendly faces. The brunette's hair was cut just above her shoulders, and she was wearing jeans, a T-shirt, and a denim jacket. The blonde's hair was longer, and she wore jeans and a sweatshirt. Johnny watched Zoey closely for any hints of discomfort, but she seemed to be okay.

"Those are Jilly's assistant Liza's granddaughters. Ginny and Cara," Clint said. "They're nice girls. Ginny is Zoey's age, and Cara is a year younger."

"I guess you can tell I'm not used to having Zoey out of reach."

"That happens with daughters. I'm still not used to it, and Jilly's an adult. But if you don't let them spread their wings, they'll rebel, and then you're really in trouble."

"I hear ya on that. My sister Harlow was a handful as a teenager."

Clint motioned to a pretty blonde wearing a floral dress and colorful cowgirl boots, helping customers. "That's our daughter-in-law, Morgyn, Graham's wife."

"Jillian told me about her. It looks like she's very talented."

"She is, and there's Graham." He nodded to a big guy coming around the side of the tent carrying a cardboard box. He was wearing an MIT baseball cap and a dark long-sleeved shirt. A handful of necklaces hung against his chest, some beaded, others with eclectic charms, and a number of leather and beaded bracelets adorned his wrists.

Graham spotted Jillian and broke into an adoring smile. "It's about time you made it over here." He set the box down and hugged her, then kissed his mother's cheek.

"Look at you. I *love* these." Jillian touched his necklaces.

"Gotta represent my girl," Graham said. "You're going to love Morgyn's new inventory."

"I can't wait to shop. But first I want you to meet Johnny." She turned around and reached for Johnny's hand, so different from her earlier comment about *kind of* seeing each other. "Johnny, this is my brother Graham."

"Well, I'll be damned," Graham said. "Johnny Bad in the flesh, and he's holding my sister's hand."

Johnny laughed.

"I've been a fan of your music since I was a kid," Graham said. "I don't want to go all fanboy on you, but, *man*, this is a big moment for me."

"Thanks. Jillian told me about the incredible work you're doing on the West Coast."

"Just trying to keep our world from going to hell in a handbasket," Graham said humbly. "I heard about your daughter. How's she doing? Is she here with you?"

"Zoey's great. She makes me a better man, as does your sister." He pointed to Zoey, chatting with the other girls, as Morgyn joined them. "She's right there, the one in the gray hoodie with the stars on it. She's probably asking Morgyn for all of her embellishment secrets."

"She's into clothes, huh?" Graham asked.

"She's got a sharp eye," Jillian said as Zoey, Morgyn, and the other two girls walked over.

"Dad, this is Ginny and Cara, and this is Morgyn. She made *everything* in here," Zoey gushed.

Her friends said, "Hi."

Johnny was momentarily stunned by Zoey's use of *Dad*, and by the look on Jillian's face, she'd caught it, too. He wondered if Zoey had even noticed her slip, but she was busy talking with her new friends. The fact that she had new friends felt like another milestone, so he didn't interrupt them and said, "Hi, Morgyn. I'm Johnny."

"I think the whole world knows who you are," Morgyn said. "It's nice to meet you. Zoey showed me what she did to her clothes. We're going to swap secrets at the party tonight."

"That's great."

"We're going to get our faces painted, and then we're going to watch the pie-eating contest," Ginny said to Zoey. "Want to go with us?"

Zoey looked hopefully up at him. "Can I?"

"You want to get your face painted?" he asked.

She nodded, and there was a silent message in her eyes that said, *Please don't call me out on what I said earlier.*

"I'm not really comfortable with you going without an adult," Johnny said. "How about if I go with you?"

"My grandma Liza is with us," Ginny said. "She's over there with my little sister. See her in the line for face painting?"

"I do, but I'd like to clear it with her first."

Zoey rolled her eyes.

"Sorry, sunshine, but if you want to go, then I've got to talk to Liza and make sure she has my number in case there's an emergency."

"Sunshine?" Morgyn asked. "That's what Graham calls me."

"Really?" Johnny asked.

"A beautiful endearment for beautiful girls." Graham nodded at Zoey. "How's it going, Zoey? I'm Jillian's brother Graham, and our dad used to do the same thing to us when we wanted to go places with friends. It's what parents do."

"I know," Zoey said exasperatedly, and then her eyes lit up. "Jax told me you guys live in a treehouse. Can I see it one day? Where do you go to the bathroom? Are there bugs and spiders in it?"

"A *real* treehouse?" Cara asked with disbelief.

As Graham and Morgyn told them all about their treehouse, Jillian whispered, "She's come a long way from *whatever.*"

"So have we," Johnny said, and kissed her.

Liza was happy to have Zoey join them, so Johnny and Jillian spent time with her parents. They walked through the park looking at crafts and getting to know each other. They were kind and insightful and not afraid to ask hard questions or dole out a little advice, just like their daughter. They teased each other and Jillian, the way families do, and it was easy to see why Jillian loved living so close to them.

After the pie-eating contest, Jillian's parents went home, and Johnny and Jillian caught up with Liza and the girls. Zoey and her friends still wanted to hang out, so they all headed over to the pumpkin patch together. They picked out pumpkins and carved them at a carving station. Jillian carved long eyelashes and plump lips into hers, and Johnny made his winking and smirking, while the girls carved triangular eyes and mouths with fangs, and Liza's pumpkin looked like it had seen a ghost, with a big O for a mouth.

Johnny got lost in the corn maze, and Zoey and Jillian had great fun teasing him about it.

They made it to the barn just in time to pile onto the last hayride of the day. As the trailer bumped and wobbled along the grass, with Jillian tucked beneath his arm and Zoey exchanging phone numbers with her friends, Johnny felt his world falling into place, and he couldn't imagine a more perfect way to end their afternoon.

Chapter Twenty-Four

JILLIAN TOOK ONE last glance in the mirror and flipped the visor up as Johnny opened her car door. Music floated up from Nick's barns as Johnny helped her out. They were late, and everyone else was already there. "They're going to know."

"What are you talking about?"

"You *know* what I'm talking about. My skin is flushed, and *look* at my eyes." She opened her eyes wider and pointed to them. "I look totally orgasmed out." As well she should, considering that after dropping Zoey off at Jax's house, she and Johnny had christened her studio, had gotten extra dirty in the shower, and then, as though they hadn't already had enough of each other, they got frisky on the way to the party and pulled over on the side road, where Johnny proceeded to drive her out of her freaking mind *again*. They'd stopped to use a restroom, and she'd hoped the freshly sated look in her eyes would be gone by now, but it was still there.

He laughed and drew her into his arms, looking at her like he didn't care if the whole world knew. "If you didn't look like the sexiest Egyptian goddess that ever walked this earth, maybe I could have kept my hands out from under your skirt."

She couldn't help but smile. She hadn't realized how sexy her costume was until he'd seen her in it and had practically drooled. The minidress was super short, with a sleeveless bustier and mesh side panels, a knit mesh drape from back to waist, and a gold faux leather belt with a hanging tie-shaped panel in the center. She wore metallic knit sleevelets and gold sandals that laced up her shins. The wide beaded collar and gold snakes around her upper arms were the perfect accessories.

"What are you worried about, baby?" he asked coaxingly. "That they'll know your man satisfies you? Because I'm pretty sure they know that already. You haven't stopped smiling once today. Even when Nick was being *Nick*, you beamed like a beacon."

"I did *not*." It was a blatant lie. She'd been on cloud nine since he and Zoey had arrived, and she was already wishing she could stop time so they'd never leave.

He cocked a brow. "You should've dressed as Pinocchio." He kissed her then, slow and sweet. "Stop worrying. I'm the dude wearing a skirt, and you know the guys are going to give me shit."

"You're a gladiator, and you've got better legs than all the men in that movie *300*. You look *hot*." She'd whipped up his costume in under an hour, with faux leather armor and skirt flaps that he wore over a black T-shirt and white skirt. She'd bound four black leather belts around his torso and secured a burgundy cape to one shoulder with a fancy black-and-gold shoulder guard. She'd added black leather bands around his biceps and wrists, and she'd even made leather shin guards that gave him a badass gladiator edge.

He cocked a brow and said, "Only for you, baby."

He kissed her again, and they followed a path lined by fake gravestones and skeletons crawling out of the ground toward the party. Bats hung from tree limbs, and cobwebs and ghosts were strewn over the pasture fences and riding rings. A bonfire was loaded with wood and ready to go near an enormous movie screen and a karaoke stage, and a circle of wooden witches wearing black robes and pointy hats held hands around a big black cauldron that had purple smoke coming out of it near long tables of food decorated with cobwebs, spiders, and crows. More skeletons, ghosts, and eerie figures were scattered around the ground in front of the massive off-white barns.

Nick's golden retrievers, Goldie and Rowdy, were running

around wearing lion manes. Graham, dressed up like Tarzan, and Jax, the perfect Phantom of the Opera, egged each other on as they threw beanbags into a giant wooden pumpkin with triangular holes for eyes and nose and a circle for a mouth. Nick, aka Batman, was with them, but he was busy staring at Trixie in her sexy Catwoman outfit in the distance. She and a few others were gathered beneath a tree, trying to eat something dangling from strings with their hands tied behind their backs, and Fred and Wilma Flintstone were cheering them on.

"Get your head in the game, Nick." Graham threw a beanbag at him.

"Oh shit," Johnny said as Nick lunged at Graham. Graham barely escaped, cracking up as Nick chased after him, his Batman cape flying from his shoulders. Jax headed for the food table where his Christine—Jordan dressed up in a long, fancy dress—was chatting with Morgyn, who was dressed as Tarzan's Jane in a leopard-print bikini and long cardigan. Morgyn was holding Pugsly, Nick's old pug. Pugsly wore devil horns on his head.

"We have a winner!" her mother shouted from the group by the trees, and cheers rang out.

"Where's Zoey?" Jillian called over to Jax.

He pointed to the cheering group and hollered, "Heads up! Jilly's here!"

Zoey came into focus, strutting toward them with the others in tow. She was wearing one of Jillian's colorful minidresses from her Multifarious line and high-heeled, knee-high boots. She stumbled and caught herself, grumbling, "Darn heels," as she approached. Her hair had been straightened, her makeup was perfect, and she carried a Diet Pepsi in one hand. She squared her shoulders and lifted her chin with the most serious face as she said, "Nice of you to show up, Mr. Bad Manners."

"Are you shittin' me?" Johnny laughed.

"Oh my gosh. Are you supposed to be *me*?" Jillian asked.

Zoey dramatically tossed her hair over her shoulder. "Does the name *Jillian Braden* mean anything to you? I don't care how much money you throw at me. I'm *never* leaving this party."

Laughter burst from Jillian's lips and from everyone else as she hugged Zoey. "You look awesome! Where did you get that dress?"

"Jax and Jordan took me to your shop, and then Jax cinched it so it would fit. Check out these boots Jordan loaned me." She lifted her leg, showing them the boots. "I can barely walk in them. Don't you love my hair? Jordan did it. Can I get a hair straightener?"

"Oh *man*. Is this what I have to look forward to?" Johnny asked, causing more laughter.

Jillian smacked him. "*Hey*, you're crazy about me, and I've hit a new level of fame. I've been elevated to Halloween-costume status."

"Your boyfriend is wearing a skirt. You might want to take it down a notch, Jilly," Nick said with a chuckle.

"Jealous that you don't have the legs for it?" Johnny countered.

"Tell 'em, baby," Jillian said as her father, who was dressed as Fred Flintstone, and Graham, in his leopard-skin loincloth, flanked Johnny and crossed their arms, staring Nick down.

"You got issues with men in skirts, son?" her father asked.

Nick put his hands up in surrender. "No, sir. I was joshin'."

"Put in your place by three guys in skirts," Zev said as he high-fived Graham, their father, and Johnny. Zev was dressed as Chunk from the *Goonies*, in a red satin jacket, plaid pants, and a Hawaiian shirt. He put his arm around Carly, who made the cutest Data ever in a short black wig, with a cardboard computer with fake buttons and wires hanging off it strapped to her chest over a gray sweater with a white collar. She wore a 007 belt buckle with eyes drawn in the zeroes and a long gray raincoat covered in patches.

"Hey, Bad," Nick said. "You any good at witch-hat ring toss? I'm putting my team together."

More laughter rang out.

Nick turned to Trixie. "I told you we should've done ax throwing."

With more chuckles, everyone followed Nick toward the witch hats, and Jillian sidled up to Jax and said, "Thank you for helping

Zoey figure out a costume."

"She knew what she wanted to be. She's completely enamored with you, Jilly."

She glanced at Zoey, walking with Johnny, Zev, and Carly. "That goes both ways."

"She told us about the outfit you guys are going to make together, and she asked if we thought it was weird that she felt like you were her best friend, only *old*." He laughed.

"Old? We're obviously going to need to have a talk about that, but I love that she trusts me so much."

"If she spends more time with Ginny and Cara, you may be kicked down a rung. She talked about them a lot, too."

"That would be a good thing. She needs to have friends her age, people she can complain to and figure things out with."

"Hurry up, you guys!" Zoey waved them over.

They joined the others, playing witch-hat ring toss, which turned into a drinking game for those who weren't driving. Zoey went into the barn and changed into jeans and sneakers as the couples raced to wrap their partners in toilet paper. The girls joked about how the guys only knew how to take things off, not put them on. Graham won, and then Zoey and Johnny kicked everyone's butts in a potato sack race, and when they raced around the hay bales the guys set up, Jax and Zev blew everyone else away. They took turns swatting at a giant pumpkin pinata, and Nick broke it open, sending gift cards and candy flying and giving him a reason to boast.

Jillian won a limbo contest, and she and the girls sang "It's Raining Men" into the karaoke microphone. In between the festivities, they ate too much delicious food. Nick and Trixie served pigs in blankets, only they used strips of dough to turn them into mummies, and they had spaghetti in the shape of brains, skeletons made out of vegetables, hamburgers with funny eyes on the buns, and stuffed orange peppers that were carved like jack-o'-lanterns. But the best part of Jillian's evening was sharing it with Johnny and Zoey.

Nick lit the bonfire, and as Zev and Carly belted out "Life Is a

Highway," Jillian filled a glass with bloodred punch, scooping around the gummy eyes floating in the punch bowl.

"What a party," her mother said as she sidled up to her in her white Wilma Flintstone dress and red wig.

"Nick and Trixie sure went all out. Everyone looks great, don't they?"

"They sure do. That Zoey is a hoot," her mother said. "When she first got here with Jax and Jordan, she was doing impressions of you. Jilly, I've never laughed so hard."

"Should I be offended?"

"My goodness, no. She did this whole morning routine with you not speaking before you got your Diet Pepsi, and then she strutted along the grass pretending to tell Johnny to keep up or get lost." Her mother smiled. "She's something else, and the way her daddy looks at you? Sweetheart, am I seeing what I think I'm seeing?"

Jillian looked across the yard at Johnny talking with her father and Graham, and her chest got all fluttery. "Probably," she admitted. "I've never felt like this before. I think about them all the time. I know Johnny can handle anything that comes their way, but I want to be with them, and I want to help with whatever I can, but at the same time, I have a line to launch, and I don't want my business to fall behind." She met her mother's caring eyes. "When they showed up yesterday, I felt like my whole world got brighter, and I didn't think twice about dropping everything so I could spend time with them."

"Love has a way of making everything fall into place."

Love. A shiver trickled down her spine.

"Is he as good to you as he appears to be?" her mother asked.

Jillian smiled. "Yes. He's wonderful to me. He's supportive of my work, and he never tries to change who I am. He does these little things that make me feel special, too, like giving me flowers and sending texts to say he's thinking of me." She left out the X-rated texts that made her pulse race, but in her heart they were just as important. "And he cooks for me, Mom, and doesn't make me feel like a loser because cooking isn't my thing, and he makes me breakfast."

Her mother's brows slanted. "But you don't eat breakfast."

"I know, and he still does it. What's really strange is that I find myself picking at *his* breakfast off *his* plate."

"Oh, baby girl, you've got it bad."

"That scares me a little. I've always known what I wanted and how to get there, and suddenly this guy and his daughter are dropped into my path, and I can't find my way around them."

"Maybe you're not supposed to. Things happen for a reason, honey."

"I know. I keep thinking about when we were in Colorado. I thought I was helping them, but all three of us were discovering new things and helping each other in ways probably none of us knew we needed. It's like I was transformed from Jillian, the busy high-powered fashion designer, to someone I didn't know I could be, and I liked that person. I liked slowing down enough to help them, and even though I don't normally like anything athletic, I looked forward to everything we did, and ever since they got here yesterday, I've felt that same shift. Last night we watched a movie, and even though I'd left work early, I wasn't thinking about how much work I had to do or new designs I wanted to make. I was just *happy*."

"And you're still launching Wanderlust and creating a new fashion line. I'd say maybe you've found a new kind of muse. One—or *two*—that are as good for your heart as they are for your creativity."

Cheers and applause rang out, drawing their attention as Johnny stepped up to the microphone carrying Nick's guitar.

"Looks like we're about to get a private show," her mother said.

Johnny's gaze landed on Jillian, and that secret smile meant only for her appeared. "This is a little something I've been working on since we got back from Colorado. It's called 'Star-Crossed.'"

Her heart skipped as he strummed a rockish beat and sang.

"It's twelve-oh-one and you're not here
But you're in my head, in my head

I see you so clear
See your smile, see your face
Hear those snarky things you say
Damn I hate when we're apart
I think you left your fingerprints on my heart

"You said we're star-crossed, destined to be apart
I see a different ending, and I'm not giving up your heart
Let's go back in time, back in time
Relive those weeks, those nights, those sweet in-betweens
Let's do it all, fall in love all over again
Let's hit repeat, baby, until it becomes our reality"

Jillian's heart lodged in her throat as her father came to her side and put a hand on her lower back.

"I'm going insane, addicted to your voice
My girl's not the same without you here
She's missing you, I'm missing you more
You're too damn far away"

A tear slipped down Jillian's cheek.

"You've opened a vein
I'm bleeding out
There's no way I'm going out like this
Need you near, need you here
You're in my head, in my head
I need you in my bed"

Nick glowered at him, and everyone laughed.

"We're texting all night
It's not enough, those words on the screen

I want you here where I can touch you, kiss you, love you
Wanna hop a flight, get you in my arms
And never let you go"

Johnny's eyes remained trained on hers as he sang it all again, and Jillian's heart felt like it was going to burst as he sang the last verse.

"You said we're star-crossed
But I see a different ending
Let's go back in time
Relive those weeks
Until they become
Our reality"

Cheers, applause, and whistles rang out. Johnny winked at Zoey, who was holding Pugsly and cheering along with everyone else, as he headed for Jillian.

"Now, that's a guy who's crazy about my girl." Her father kissed her cheek, nodded to Johnny, and as he walked away, Johnny gathered her in his arms.

"What are you doing to me, Johnny Bad? That song was…" She shook her head, at a loss for words, and rambled nervously. "It's not really a rock song, is it?"

"Yes, it is. That was the sweet version. I didn't think your family needed to hear the rock rendition that says, *In my head, you're on your knees.*"

She grinned. "I want to hear that one."

"Play your cards right, and we'll act it out." He sealed that tempting offer with a kiss. "You're my muse, baby. You've revived my love of music. The guys and I have been working on five new songs for an album."

"You're kidding? That's *wonderful.* Does that mean you're going on tour for the last album you put out? Because if that's the case, I need to work on your wardrobe."

"Then get on it, girl. We need to do the Brutally Bad tour. We can't let our fans down. We're thinking about doing it next summer, when Zoey's off school. That's assuming I can find the right school for her and she settles in before then. We have a lot to figure out, and I still have to convince my girlfriend to go on the road with us."

"On the road? Like live out of a tour bus? Do you have another girlfriend stashed away? Because I am not a tour-bus groupie."

"Groupies don't get on my bus." He brushed his lips over hers. "That spot is reserved for you."

"Johnny, I have a business to run. I can't just—"

Her words were silenced with a deep, delicious kiss.

"Get a room!" Zev said as he and Carly walked by.

"We'll watch Zoey for you," Carly offered.

Johnny grinned. "Is it awful that I'd let them?"

As he lowered his lips to hers, Nick hollered, "Hey, Bad, get your lips off my sister. It's movie time."

Johnny's jaw tensed. "Why do I have a feeling that's never going to change?"

"Because it probably won't."

"Guess he'll hate me, then." Johnny kissed her again as they made their way toward the others.

As everyone set out blankets around the bonfire, Nick said, "Who's up for an early trail ride tomorrow morning?"

"We are," their parents said.

"Count us in," Graham said.

"Us too," Zev and Jax said in unison.

"Can we go?" Zoey asked.

"Sorry, sunshine, but we're going home tomorrow morning," Johnny reminded her.

"Can't we go later?" she pleaded. "He said they're going early. *Please?*"

Johnny looked at Jillian. "Would you mind if we stuck around?"

"I don't know." She feigned an exasperated sigh. "I guess if I *have* to see more of you, I can deal with it."

"Can we?" Zoey asked again.

"Sure," Johnny said. "We'll stick around."

"*Yes!* Can I ask Ginny and Cara to go with us?" Zoey asked.

"That's up to Nick and Trixie," Johnny said.

Zoey ran over to Nick, clutching Pugsly in her arms. Whatever she said turned Nick's serious expression into a genuine smile as he answered. Nick looked across the grass at Jillian and winked as Zoey ran back, shouting, "He said I could!" She flopped onto the blanket and put Pugsly on her lap as she texted her friends.

Johnny sat on the blanket and pulled Jillian down between his legs, wrapping his arms around her. She looked over her shoulder and whispered, "Sure you don't want to build a studio in Maryland?"

"Sure you don't want to open a shop in New York?"

As tempting as it was, she couldn't imagine moving away from Maryland any more than she could imagine him moving away from New York. That reality came with a side of longing, but she shoved it down deep, because even if a long-distance relationship was the only way to make it work, she'd take it. Family aside, being with Johnny and Zoey part time brought her more happiness than having anyone else in her life full time ever had.

Chapter Twenty-Five

THE TRAIL RIDE brought memories of their time in Colorado, although the terrain and the company were totally different. Johnny loved seeing Jillian with her family, hearing her volleying banter with her brothers, and what a joy it was to see Zoey and her friends giggling and making plans for the next time they'd be together. Johnny should be flying high after the morning he and Jillian had shared. It wasn't just making love to her that had made it so memorable. It was the way she'd looked at him and touched him, like she never wanted to let him go. Hell, he was right there with her.

Leaving was going to suck. The weekend had gone by too fast, and he knew what tomorrow would bring. He'd wake to an empty bed, wishing Jillian were there beside him. Zoey would complain about going to school, and when she got home in the afternoon, she'd share a litany of reasons she hated it. He and Jillian would text throughout the day, and after Zoey was asleep, they'd talk for hours. They'd only just agreed to do this long-distance thing for real, and he was already sick of it.

But as they put their horses in the barn, he slung an arm around Jillian, vowing not to let that ruin the little time they had left.

"Coming through!" Zoey said as she, Ginny, and Cara ran past, giggling, with the dogs on their heels.

"Zoey needs a dog," Carly said as she and Zev caught up to them. *And friends closer to home.* "Maybe one day," Johnny said.

"No time like the present," Zev said.

"At the moment I'm trying to figure out if I can kidnap your sister without getting thrown in jail."

"Like I said, no time like the present," Zev said.

"*Hello?*" Jillian said. "I'm right here, and I have a business to run. I think people might notice if I disappeared."

"Mom would notice she had more leftovers," Zev teased.

"Shut up." Jillian swatted him. "I'll have you know that I can make spaghetti and meatballs now."

Zev arched a brow. "Chef Boyardee doesn't count."

And so the morning passed with laughter and light conversation until it was time for Johnny and Zoey to leave. Zoey hugged Jillian for what felt like forever, raving about how much fun she'd had and eliciting promises of more to come.

As Zoey climbed into the car, Johnny pulled Jillian into his arms, gazing into the eyes that bewitched him even from hundreds of miles away. "Thanks for letting us crash your weekend."

"I loved every second of it. Thank you for not being able to stay away."

He laughed and kissed her, telling himself that this wasn't the end of a great weekend but the beginning of many wonderful things to come.

Chapter Twenty-Six

JILLIAN HAD NEVER been so thankful for an overloaded schedule as she was this week. She'd even managed to squeeze in dinner and shopping for Amber's wedding gifts with Trixie and Jordan, and since Morgyn was still in town, she joined them, too. They'd had a great time, but seeing Johnny and Zoey last weekend and talking with the girls about them had only made Jillian miss them more. But as it turned out, Johnny was a very attentive boyfriend who never let her miss him for long.

She woke every morning to a different text from him. Sometimes they were steamy, other times sweet, but they were consistent and loving, and aside from waking in his arms, they were the best greeting she could wish for. They were both busy during the day and texted when they could, and her pulse quickened like a teen with a crush every time his name appeared on her phone. Video calls had become their go-to form of nightly communication, and not just for sexy times. His handsome face was the last thing she saw every night. But after their calls, she'd lie awake overthinking, and usually got up and worked until two or three in the morning.

She was more tired than usual, but Trixie reminded her that she was working at full speed for the launch, trying to stock her shop for the holidays, *and* she'd never expended that much emotional energy missing someone before. Jillian knew she was right, and it wasn't just Johnny she missed. Zoey had been texting with Ginny and Cara all week, and her texts to Jillian had come about every other day. She was glad Zoey had found friends, but even though the hoopla over her and Johnny had dissipated, Zoey still wasn't making friends at school or loving city life. Johnny was doing everything he could to make sure she had as typical a childhood as possible. He was trying to get her out more and establishing boundaries when they were in public to try to ease her discomfort. Even though Jillian knew he was doing the right thing, she worried about both of them. Being on guard all the time was taking a toll on Johnny, and she knew it was just as hard for Zoey. By Friday night, she was itching to get her arms around them.

She parked in the garage of Johnny's building and texted him. *Just got here. See you in a few minutes.* They had a big surprise for Zoey, and Jillian couldn't wait to see her face.

As she pocketed her phone, she looked over the seat at Ginny and Cara. She and Johnny hoped that by bringing her friends to the city, she might start to see how fun city life could be, which also might encourage her to make more friends at school.

"Ready for the big surprise?" Ginny and Cara were great travelers. They'd chatted almost the whole way about music, school, clothes, boys, and how excited they were to see Zoey and to go to the fundraising gala with them. Johnny had spoken to their parents about the press and what the girls could expect, and Jillian had bought fantastic outfits for all five of them and had them shipped to Johnny's.

"*Yes*," they said excitedly.

They got their luggage from the trunk and made their way up to the penthouse. When the elevator doors opened, Johnny was there, gorgeous as could be in a black Henley and jeans. His hair looked finger combed, and his eyes were so full of emotions, Jillian nearly ran to him. But she managed to stay put and follow their plan as he put his finger to his lips, keeping the girls quiet, and whispered, "She's in her room, right down that hall."

As the girls hurried down the hall, Johnny drew Jillian into his arms. "Five days was too long." He lowered his lips to hers as squeals and giggles rang out in the other room, and they both smiled. "How can that sound make me as happy as having you in my arms?"

Zoey and her friends ran down the hall, and Zoey launched herself at Jillian. "Thank you! I can't believe you brought them! I'm so glad you're here. I've missed you."

"I've missed you, too. I'm impressed that Ginny and Cara were able to keep their visit a secret."

"Grandma made us promise," Ginny said.

"I'll have to thank her for that," Johnny said.

Zoey threw her arms around him. "Thank you *so* much. I can't believe they're really here for the whole weekend. Can they go shopping with us for my dress tomorrow?"

"That's the plan," Johnny said. "Are you girls hungry? I've got reservations at one of Zoey's favorite restaurants."

"*Yes*," they all said at once.

"Zoey, why don't you put some shoes on and we'll head out."

He reached for Jillian's hand. "How about you, beautiful? Is your stomach feeling better?"

She'd been so excited to see them, she hadn't been able to eat all day. "Much. It's amazing what seeing you does to me. I'm starved." She went up on her toes and kissed him. "For dinner and *dessert*."

"*Mm.* I see you brought my dirty girl." He kissed her again, and just as he took it deeper, the girls came running into the room. He whispered, "Is it bedtime yet?" and put on a winning smile for his very excited daughter and her friends. "Okay, ladies, let's hit the town."

THEY WENT TO an Italian restaurant that wasn't too fancy and was perfect for giddy girls. Several people took second and third looks at them, and Jillian noticed that Johnny gave off an air of confidence that was a little standoffish to strangers, which she assumed was purposeful to establish boundaries. The girls seemed blissfully unaware of the eyes on them as they chatted happily, giggling and eating everything in sight. *Bravo, Daddy Bad.* It was amazing how far they'd come, and Jillian was glad she'd been there at the start, or she'd never know how hard he'd fought to get them there.

After dinner, they went to Times Square to show the girls the lights of the city. Johnny held Jillian's hand, his watchful eyes scanning their surroundings. Ginny and Cara *ooh*ed and *aah*ed, pointing to the lights and stores with awestruck exuberance. Zoey wasn't as unguarded as she'd been in the restaurant and not nearly as free spirited as she'd been at the pumpkin festival. She stuck close to Johnny and Jillian.

"I can't believe you don't like it here," Ginny said. "It's exciting."

"I love the lights," Cara said. "Is it like this every day?"

"Yup," Zoey said.

"You were right about it being crowded," Cara said. "And it *is* loud. Why are people honking their horns? It's not like the cars in front of them can go anywhere."

"That's part of what makes it fun," Ginny said. "Everyone has someplace to be."

"But *where* are they going?" Cara asked. "There aren't any houses or neighborhoods."

"I don't know. To hotels and parties, I guess," Ginny said.

"Maybe they're going to see famous people," Cara said.

"My dad's famous, and no one comes to see him but work people and Jillian." Zoey looked up at Johnny. "Right, Dad?"

Johnny squeezed Jillian's hand. She knew how much Zoey calling him Dad meant to him. He'd told her that she'd called him that only a few times since the festival.

"The guys in my band are my friends."

"They don't count, because they work with you," Zoey said.

"They count to me," Johnny said. "If they left the band, we'd still be friends." He motioned to an ice cream shop up ahead. "Who wants ice cream?"

The girls cheered.

Johnny treated them to sundaes and surprised them all with a carriage ride through Central Park. The carriage was black with purple seats and neon purple lights underneath. The horse's harness was purple, with a tall plume of matching feathers on top of its bridle. The driver gave them blankets because it was a chilly night, and then they were off, riding through the moonlit park.

Johnny put his arm around Jillian, keeping her close. "I'm glad you're here, baby. I don't care what we're doing. I just want you by my side."

Didn't he know she wished she always was?

"This is awesome," Zoey said, taking pictures with her phone.

"They do this at Christmas in Pleasant Hill. You can ride right through town," Ginny said. "Our Grandma took us one year."

"You can?" Zoey asked excitedly. "Can we do that? Can we go to Jilly's at Christmastime?"

"I think we can make that happen," he said, sharing a smile with Jillian.

Jillian silently cheered at the promise of seeing them at Christmas.

"Yes!" Zoey said. "Jilly, if we get the outfit done over Thanksgiving break, can we make another over Christmas break?"

"We can try. We'll just have to pick out the one you want to make so I can be sure to have the materials on hand."

"Can we help?" Ginny asked.

"Grandma taught us to sew," Cara added.

"So did my grandma," Zoey said. "Can they, Jillian?"

"I don't see why not. We'll do it in my office studio and make a girls' weekend out of it."

The girls all spoke at once, and their excitement was contagious. Johnny played with the ends of Jillian's hair and whispered, for her ears only, "Not mom material, huh?"

She gave him a deadpan look.

"I didn't think I was father material, either," he whispered. "And look at me. I'm nailing it."

She laughed softly. "And it makes you even hotter, which is a problem. Now I can't *stop* looking at you."

He waggled his brows.

As they rolled by the carousel, the pond, the lake, and Bow Bridge, the girls asked a million questions and took loads of pictures. With every landmark, Johnny whispered in Jillian's ear. "I want to kiss you on that bridge…I want to touch you on that carousel…I want to make love to you by that pond…"

"I'm sensing a theme here," Jillian said.

He pulled her closer, kissing her cheek and whispering, "About time you caught on. We will leave no spot unchristened."

Oh, how she loved that idea.

He continued whispering sweet things to her. Even with three chatty girls, riding through the park cozied up to Johnny was magical. It might have been even more magical because they got to share it with Zoey. As she and her friends raved about the sights and asked if they could come back tomorrow to see the park in the daylight, Jillian thought back to Johnny's comment last weekend about her opening a shop in New York.

She tried to picture herself living there. What would it be like if she left the home she'd always known to be with them? Could she be happy that far away from her family? Living in the noisy, busy city? Could she continue working with Liza remotely? Would her being there help Zoey like the city more or find a school she enjoyed? Or was Zoey simply not a city girl, like Jillian?

It was too much to think about, and it didn't matter anyway. She and Johnny weren't there yet, even if it felt like they could be. She gazed up at the starry sky, seeking the brightest star to wish upon. But she didn't know what to wish for. Their love was real, even if they hadn't said those three special words. She felt it every time he looked at her, felt her love for him and Zoey growing deeper by the day, so she wished for the thing that mattered most, for Zoey to be happy.

She rested her head on Johnny's shoulder, grateful for the time they made for each other and looking forward to Thanksgiving and Christmas.

Chapter Twenty-Seven

IT WAS AMAZING how much life three teenage girls could bring into a room. The morning was a cacophony of commotion as they took over the kitchen, cooked breakfast for everyone, cleaned up after themselves, and then disappeared into Zoey's room until it was time to go shopping.

What Johnny thought would be a quick trip to find Zoey a dress for the awards ceremony turned into an all-day affair. Running around the city with three teenage girls had nearly done Johnny in, but he'd been the perfect dad, carrying packages, telling Zoey how beautiful she looked in everything she tried on, and keeping them safe. While she and her friends were in the dressing room, he'd pulled Jillian in for long-awaited smooches. She was incredible with the girls and endlessly patient. She knew just how to guide them away from clothes that were too revealing or not quite right, and she could spot an outfit from across the store and know it would be the perfect style for them.

The girls loved shopping with her, and from the light in Jillian's eyes, Johnny knew she was enjoying it, too. They'd gotten quite a haul and had bought Zoey several cute outfits, a gorgeous dress for the awards ceremony, a pair of wedged heels and low-heeled boots, and all sorts of accessories. He also bought a couple of cute things for each of her friends, which delighted them, and he picked out a few sexy outfits for Jillian. His favorite was a pair of pajamas that was even tinier than the ones she'd worn in Colorado.

When they got home, the girls disappeared into Zoey's room again, and Jillian went to put her clothes away in his bedroom. Johnny sat on the couch, glad for a moment of peace.

Twenty minutes later he went to check on Jillian and found her fast asleep on his bed. She looked so peaceful, lying on her side on top of the blankets with one arm tucked beneath the pillow. His Energizer Bunny had finally run out of steam, and it was probably his fault. She'd been working like a fiend, had driven hours to see them, and then he'd kept her up late last night. They'd waited until they were sure the girls were asleep before coming together, and they'd moved painfully slowly, trying to be quiet. It had made their lovemaking insanely intense. He'd held her so tight as she'd come, and his own release had mounted, they'd both tried to keep from making a sound. He'd felt every clench, every gasp and sigh, and had seen the need in her eyes as he'd thrust slowly, driving in so deep, they'd truly felt like one being. His body pulsed hot with memories of taking her right up to the edge a second time and holding her there, their bodies trembling with need as he gyrated his hips, his muscles aching with restraint.

Damn, he was getting turned on just thinking about it. She affected him like no one ever had. He wanted to take care of her, to lie behind her and hold her so she felt safe and slept soundly, as much as he wanted to be buried deep inside her and do all the dirty things they enjoyed.

He brushed a kiss to her forehead and quietly left the room. He heard voices and giggles coming from behind Zoey's door and knocked. When she opened it, Ginny and Cara were sitting on the bed, surrounded by the clothes the three of them had gotten.

"Hey, Zo. Jilly's taking a nap, and I'll be in the studio if you need me."

"Okay," she said.

He headed downstairs, feeling complete in a way he never had, and he knew it was because Zoey was happy, and Jillian was there, and the penthouse that had gone from feeling like his sanctuary to a place that was too silent finally felt like *home*.

TWO HOURS LATER, when he headed back upstairs, the girls were still giggling. He knocked again, and Zoey said, "Come in." As he pushed the door open, she said, "We're in here."

He headed into her sewing room.

"Look what we did," Zoey said excitedly.

Ginny and Cara held up the·yellow and pink cropped hoodies he'd bought them. They'd replaced the front pocket of Ginny's hoodie with a pocket made from fabric with hearts all over it, and Cara's had been replaced with skull-pattern fabric.

"Those look great."

"Look at the back of mine." Ginny turned her hoodie around, showing him a jagged line of tiny skulls sewn just above the hem.

"And look!" Cara held out the sleeve of her hoodie, showing a trail of hearts from shoulder to wrist.

The things Zoey did to her clothes often blew him away, and these were no exception. The little touches she added really set them apart. He was starting to think this might not be a passing phase, and she might have found her calling. "Those look incredible. You girls have a knack for this."

"Thanks!" they all said.

"It's time to get ready for the fundraiser."

The three of them gasped and squealed.

He left them alone to get ready and headed into his bedroom, closing the door behind him. Jillian was still sleeping. He sat beside her and ran his hand down her back, kissing her cheek. "Hey, Sleeping Beauty."

Her eyes fluttered open. "Sorry. I must've dozed off. What time is it?"

"Time to get ready for the fundraising gala."

She sat up. "*What?* How long did I sleep?"

"A couple of hours."

"Ohmygod. I'm so sorry. The girls—"

She pushed to her feet, but he stood and drew her into his arms. "They're getting ready."

"Okay, I'll be quick in the shower."

"So will I." He kissed her deeply, crushing her body to his. "The question is, can you be *quiet*?"

"There's only one way to guarantee that." Her eyes turned seductive. "A full mouth can't speak." She flashed the wickedest grin and sauntered toward the bathroom. "Let's go, Mr. Bad. Time's a wastin'."

They were naked and in the shower in record time. He captured her mouth in a demanding kiss and pushed two fingers inside her, using his thumb where she needed it most. "I fucking love your body," he growled against her lips.

"And I love your dirty mouth. Now shut up and kiss me."

She pulled his mouth to hers beneath the warm shower spray, and, *man*, he loved that. He knew her body by heart, knew just how to make it sing, and he was determined to see her lose control. It didn't take long before she was riding his hand, whimpering into their kisses. He put pressure on her clit, and she cried out into his mouth, her hips bucking wildly, until she went slack in his arms and her head tipped back. "How do you do that to me so fast?"

"Motivation." He dipped his head, grazing his teeth over her nipple, and she slammed her mouth shut, reaching for his cock. "I want to fuck that pretty mouth of yours."

With a wicked grin, she pushed him against the tile wall and bent over, taking him in her mouth, sucking and stroking to perfection as the water streamed down her gorgeous body. He cupped her jaw with one hand, running his thumb over the edge of her lips, feeling his cock moving in and out of them, and fondled her breast with the other. She moaned around his dick, and the vibration made his entire body throb.

"Touch yourself."

Her eyes flicked up to his, full of desire as she reached between her legs.

"That's my dirty girl."

She worked him faster. What a beautiful sight she was. He gritted his teeth against the need to come, wanting to bring *her* even more pleasure. He had a dire need to make love to her, but there was no time. "We're going down to my studio tonight, and I'm going to fuck you so good, there's no way you'll be silent."

Her eyes widened.

"It's soundproof."

She smiled around his cock, and he stroked her jaw. "We've got to hurry, baby. Do you want me to come in your mouth or on your stomach while I make you come again?"

She slipped his dick out of her mouth, blinking wide eyes up at him. "What do you think?"

Her lips were pink and swollen, so fucking sexy he could barely stand it. The need to pleasure her was stronger than the need to live out this fantasy. He hauled her up to her feet and sank to his knees, stroking himself with one hand as he buried his face between her legs. He licked and sucked and ate his fill. Just as she started to come, heat seared down his spine. He swapped his mouth for his hand and rose, kissing her roughly as she rode out her pleasure, and he gave in to his own.

JOHNNY PUT ON the black bell-bottoms, black-and-mesh glittery shirt, and silver platform shoes Jillian had gotten him and headed into the bathroom. Jillian was leaning over the vanity in a black bra and panties, putting on eye makeup.

He wrapped his arms around her from behind and kissed her shoulder. "Do you have any idea how crazy I am about you?"

"Texts at three a.m. crazy?" She turned in his arms. "Dried flowers in my books crazy?" She unbuttoned his shirt nearly all the way down to his waist and kissed his chest. "Multiple orgasm crazy?"

"Yes to all of the above, and tonight the whole world will know it." He kissed her softly. He was looking forward to introducing her to his family, even though his mother and sisters had already video chatted with her, and he was excited to introduce her to the guys in his band.

"It's going to be a big night for all of us." She grinned. "You take care of Zoey around those photographers, and I'll take care of Ginny and Cara. We've got this."

"We sure do. I'll go check on the girls. Think you'll be ready soon?"

"I just need to finish my makeup and slip into my jumpsuit." She'd color-coordinated their outfits right down to her silver heels. Her sexy one-piece jumpsuit had thin stripes of black glittery material and mesh, a plunging neckline, and a thick black belt.

"I can't wait to slip you *out* of that jumpsuit."

"That's what I'm counting on." She went up on her toes and kissed him. "Now get out of here. You're slowing me down."

He swatted her ass and walked out.

The girls were looking out the living room windows, and they were cute as could be. Jillian had sent go-go boots with all three outfits. Zoey wore a glittery, off-the-shoulder, silver-blue-and-purple one-piece jumpsuit with a silver belt, the perfect outfit for a girl who didn't love wearing skirts or dresses. Cara wore a psychedelic minidress with bell sleeves and a matching scarf in her hair, and Ginny wore magenta bell-bottoms with an orange-pink-and-yellow bell-sleeved blouse that tied above her belly button.

Zoey turned around, and her jaw dropped. "Wow, Dad, you look great."

Every time she called him Dad, which seemed to be haphazard, it hit him like an arrow to his heart. *Dad* felt like the highest honor a guy could achieve, and he wondered if he'd ever get used to it.

Her friends spun around, chiming in with agreement about his clothes.

"Thanks, girls. So do you. I wanted to talk with you again about what to expect at the gala." He reiterated what he'd told them over breakfast, about photographers being there when they got out of the limousine, and what they should do. His cousins had ample security at the hotel, and they had hand-selected the media that was allowed inside the ballroom. "The press will stay behind a velvet rope and take pictures as we walk in. Just stay close to me and Jillian, and everything will be fine. Okay?"

They all nodded.

"Do you have any questions?"

They shook their heads.

He put a hand on Zoey's shoulder. "Sunshine, can I talk to you in private for a minute?"

She went with him into the hallway.

"I know you don't like cameras any more than I do. Are you still okay with going?"

She nodded. "Yes."

"If you feel funny or get nervous, just take my hand."

"I won't need to. I'll be fine," she said confidently.

"Okay, and once we're inside, there won't be any cameras, and they have security at every entrance to the ballroom, so you can relax and have fun."

"I know. You told me."

"Right." He hugged her. "You look beautiful. We're going to have a good time tonight."

Half an hour later, the girls were bouncing off the seats in the limousine as they pulled up to the hotel. Johnny squeezed Jillian's hand. "Are you ready for our coming-out party, beautiful?"

"One hundred percent *yes*."

He looked at the girls. "Ready to make your grand entrance, ladies?"

"Yes," Ginny and Cara said loudly, while Zoey's response was a little less sure.

The driver opened their door, and Johnny climbed out. He took Jillian's hand, helping her out, and then he did the same for Zoey and her friends. As he put his hand on Jillian's and Zoey's backs, Zoey reached for his hand instead. He gave her a reassuring squeeze and a wink.

Jillian put her arm around the other two girls. Zoey had a death grip on Johnny's hand as they smiled for the cameras and made their way into the hotel. Their coats were efficiently taken to a coatroom, and they followed a red carpet into a ballroom bustling with people dressed in colorful outfits from the seventies. Once the doors closed behind them, Zoey's grip finally eased. Jillian didn't miss a beat, making sure the girls were okay as Johnny spoke privately to Zoey.

"Are you okay, sunshine?"

"Yeah. There were so many cameras."

"I know, and you did great. I'm proud of you."

She peered around him. "Wow, look at all the lights."

Massive disco balls hung from the ceiling, showering dancers and mingling crowds in shimmering light. A band decked out in seventies attire played on a stage at the far end of the room. Pictures of Lorelei Bad and children who had stayed at the Ronald McDonald house decorated the walls, and enormous lava lamps and clear tubes with gold and silver balls rose from the center of enormous round tables draped in gold tablecloths.

"Wasn't that cool?" Ginny said.

"Yeah," Zoey said. "And a little freaky with all those flashes."

"I'm still seeing spots," Cara said.

"Hey, you guys! Zoey!"

Zoey's eyes lit up as Harlow hurried over in a colorful minidress with a cutout around her belly button and a silver ring between her breasts.

"Oh my gosh, it's *Harlow Bad*," Ginny said excitedly.

"Hey, gorgeous." Johnny hugged Harlow.

"Look at you, Mr. Disco," Harlow teased. "And you brought a *bunch* of gorgeous ladies. Zoey, you look amazing."

"Thank you. So do you." Zoey hugged her.

"And I finally get to meet Jillian in person." Harlow looked her up and down. "Girl, that outfit is *hot*."

"So is yours." Jillian hugged her. "Harlow, these are Zoey's friends, Ginny and Cara."

"Hi," Harlow said. "You two look fantastic."

"I've seen all your movies," Ginny said. "Well, the ones my mom will let me watch."

"Me too," Cara said.

Harlow grinned. "I like you girls already."

"Is Aria here?" Zoey asked.

"No. This is a little too much for her," Harlow said. "She usually donates tattoo work for the auction instead of coming." A glimmer of excitement shone in her eyes. "How would you girls like to learn all the cool disco dances?"

Three sets of excited, hopeful eyes landed on Johnny. "Okay, but I was hoping to introduce Zoey to Mick and everyone."

"I'll make sure she meets them," Harlow promised.

"Come on, Dad. Please?" Zoey urged.

His heartstrings might as well be wrapped around her little finger. "Okay, but stay with Harlow."

"We will!" She hugged him, and the girls all talked at once as they followed Harlow with stars in their eyes.

"You just made three girls very happy," Jillian said.

Johnny drew her into his arms. "And now I've got you alone, which makes me very happy."

"Alone with about two hundred other people."

"Good enough for me." He pressed his lips to hers as Dion and Adrian sidled up to them.

Dion was six three, with short dreads, several of which were dyed blond. He wore leather pants and a sparkling black shirt with see-through sleeves. His skin was as dark as Adrian's was pale. Adrian looked just like Kurt Cobain, with blond hair that fell in front of his eyes. He was a few inches shorter than Dion, and he always wore dark eyeliner. At the moment he had a trim goatee and was dressed in a white polyester suit and bright blue shirt.

"So, this is the *fine* lady who stole our man's heart." Dion looked Jillian up and down and whistled.

"Get your eyes off my girl, asshole," Johnny teased. "Jillian, this is Dion and Adrian."

"It's nice to meet you. I've heard a lot about you."

"All lies, I'm sure," Adrian said. "We hear you're not afraid to give our boy hell."

She slid her arm around Johnny. "Someone's got to keep him in line."

"If you get tired of reeling him in, hit me up, beautiful. I'll treat you right," Dion said.

"Sorry, but I think Johnny has ruined me for all other men."

My girl can definitely hold her own.

Dion flashed a cocky grin. "You say that, but you've never had a taste of this." He gestured to his body.

Johnny shook his head, laughing softly.

"Where's Mini Bad?" Adrian asked.

"Harlow took off with her and her friends." Johnny glanced at the dance floor and saw Zoey and her friends dancing with his sister.

"By the way, Johnny, I'm taking Harlow home tonight." Dion smirked.

"Good luck with that," he said.

"Look at you going from one girl to the next," Jillian teased.

"Don't worry, sweetheart." Dion grinned. "There's always room for a third."

Jillian raised her brows. "I can see designing your wardrobe is going to be entertaining."

"Taking our clothes off could be even better," Dion retorted.

"Okay, Romeo, let's get you out of here before Johnny kicks you out of the band." Adrian shoved Dion away from them.

"You know I love you, man," Dion said over his shoulder.

"They're really nice. Is Chad here, too?"

"No. He's spending the weekend with his ex and his kids. I think they might be reconciling."

"Really? Is that a good thing?"

"I think so. He's never stopped loving her." He pulled her into a kiss. "Ready to meet my parents in person?"

"If you're sure you're ready for that."

Baby, I'm ready for everything. "Who are you kidding? I want to show you off to everyone."

As they made their way around the room, Johnny introduced Jillian to his cousins, and as they walked away, he drew her into his arms and gazed into her gorgeous eyes. "Have I told you how glad I am that you're here with us?" He pressed his lips to hers.

"Maybe once or twice."

"Jilly!" Victory hurried over, looking like a go-go dancer straight out of an Austin Powers movie.

"Vic! You look gorgeous." Jillian hugged her. "I didn't know you'd be here."

"And I didn't know you and Johnny were together." She eyed Johnny. "Why is your agent the last to know? I think I should collect a matchmaking fee."

"I'd be happy to pay you." He drew Jillian to his side. "Jilly's the best thing that ever happened to me and Zoey."

"I love that. If anyone knows how the right person can make a difference in someone's life, it's me." Victory lost her husband, Ivan Bauer, who had founded Blank Space Entertainment, a few years ago and had taken over the business. "I saw your teenybopper shaking her booty on the dance floor. Does she have your musical talents?"

"Listen to you, always on the prowl for new business," Jillian teased.

"Hey, someone's got to represent our young people and turn

them into stars," Victory said.

"And you're the right person to do it," Johnny confirmed. "Zoey's good on the guitar and she has a hell of a voice, but I think her passion lies in fashion."

"She's got a great eye." Jillian told her about Zoey's input on the Rocker Girlz line she was developing.

"*Nice*," Victory said. "Then she's already got the best in the business on her side."

They talked for a few more minutes, and as they made their way around the room looking for his parents, he introduced Jillian to half the people there. She was warm, friendly, funny, and so comfortable with everyone, they were drawn to her, just like he was. By the time they found his parents, he was sure his love for her was radiating from his very being.

His mother looked gorgeous in a red disco dress, gold hoop earrings, and a brunette wig, and his father pulled off a Travolta wig, a white polyester suit, and a black shirt to perfection.

"Mom, you remember Jillian."

"Yes, of course. Hi, sweetie. I'm so happy to finally meet you in person." She hugged Jillian, and then she hugged Johnny. "You both look wonderful."

"Thank you," Jillian said. "So do you. *Saturday Night Fever*, right? Tony and Stephanie?"

"That's right," his father said. "I'm Bruce. I've heard such nice things about you from my family, I feel like I know you already." He embraced her. "Thank you for everything you've done to help Johnny and Zoey through a really tough transition."

"Oh, I didn't do much," she said.

"I see you are as humble as you are beautiful," his father said.

"Thank you, but honestly, all I did was make a few suggestions. Your son worked hard to be the father Zoey needed, and Zoey's come a long way down a difficult road. They deserve all the credit."

"They already know otherwise," Johnny said, kissing her cheek.

"Harlow introduced Zoey and her friends to everyone," his

mother said. "They told us all about the carriage ride through the park and shopping this afternoon. Zoey and her friends seem like they're thick as thieves. It's hard to believe they just met."

Johnny looked at Jillian and said, "Some people are meant to be in each other's lives."

"Even if they start out at each other's throats," she added playfully.

"We know a little something about that," his father said.

"We met in college, and Bruce thought I was a stuck-up brat," his mother explained.

"I never used those words," his father said, drawing his mother against his side. "I believe I said you were out of my league."

"You said I was the type of girl who expected to be wined and dined." She looked at Jillian. "Which I *wasn't*. We were in college. I expected to be beer'd and pizza'd, and he wasn't used to that. Bruce was quite the ladies' man in his day. He thought he could just call me pretty and get me in the back seat of his car."

Johnny laughed. "Dad, you scoundrel."

"Now I know where you got it from," Jillian said.

"What are you talking about? You made the first move on *me*."

"I did *not*. You came downstairs shirtless and tried to get me to share my Twix bar."

"He didn't get that from me," his father said. "My game is a lot stronger than candy bars."

They laughed, and the song "Ring My Bell" came on. "Bruce, it's our song. You kids want to join us on the dance floor?" his mother asked.

"What do you say, baby? Want to show my folks how it's done?"

"My friends don't call me the dancing queen for nothing," Jillian said. "Oh wait, they don't call me that."

They danced and laughed with his parents. His parents went to sit down after the first dance, but he and Jillian stayed on the dance floor. She knew all the moves to the Hustle, the Disco Finger, and the Bump. Johnny noticed more than a few guys checking her out. *Eat your hearts out. She's all mine.* Harlow, Zoey, and her friends joined them, and they danced until the band announced that dinner was going to be served.

They sat with his family, and dinner was delicious. Jillian and Kane fell into playful banter, which his parents got a kick out of. Harlow pumped Jillian for details about their relationship, and Zoey and her friends raved about the fun they were having and made plans for a sleepover next weekend when he and Zoey would be in Maryland. Jillian informed them that she had new designs for the Rocker Girlz line she'd like to run by them, which the girls were thrilled about, and that led to a conversation about the upcoming launch of her Wanderlust line. She told them all about how the line had come to be and about the models she was going to use.

As the night wore on, the auction was held, and his cousins gave a speech about their late sister and how much they appreciated everyone's support for the Ronald McDonald house. Johnny and Jillian mingled until Harlow and the girls dragged Jillian to the dance floor again, and Johnny and Kane caught up with their cousins Mick, Carson, and Dylan.

Dylan clapped Johnny on the shoulder. "You're the only guy I know who could have his entire life blow up and still come out on top."

"With a beautiful woman on your arm, too," Mick added.

"Another bachelor bites the dust," Kane said.

"Is Big Daddy Kane jealous?" Carson teased, and everyone chuckled, except Kane.

Kane scoffed. "There's not a woman on earth who could keep up with me. Could you see me slowing down to do that?" He motioned to Brett dancing with his toddler, Brenna, and his pregnant wife, Sophie.

"You got something against family?" Dylan asked. He and his wife, Tiffany, had a ten-month-old son.

"Careful how you answer," Mick warned. His wife, Amanda, and Carson's wife, Tawny, were pregnant, and Carson and Tawny had also adopted a daughter.

"You *know* I'm all about family," Kane said. "But come on, guys. How did it happen? I mean, I knew Dylan would fall in love. He was always a little soft."

Dylan smirked. "Considering my wife says I outlast the moon, you might want to rephrase that."

"I meant softhearted," Kane clarified. "And, Carson, I had a feeling there was someone from your past that you'd never gotten over. Tawny is definitely your match, and I love Amanda and Sophie, but, Mick, you and Brett were the ultimate bachelors, and you fell like dominoes."

Mick nodded. "And I'm still falling in love with my wife every minute of the day. When you find that, there's no turning back. Just ask your brother."

"You got that right," Johnny said as he gazed out at the dance floor, mesmerized by Jillian holding Dylan's little boy as she danced with Tiffany, Harlow, Zoey, and their friends. Jillian tickled the baby's foot and turned so Zoey could see him.

"John, I don't recall you ever bringing a woman to this event," Carson said. "Must be serious."

"You see how he's looking at her," Dylan said. "Cupid shot him in the ass with about a dozen arrows."

"Are you going to put a ring on her finger?" Mick asked.

Hell yes, he'd put a ring on her finger if he thought she'd accept. But he doubted any woman would be chomping at the bit for a long-distance husband. Especially a woman who deserved to be given the world—and thought she could build it on her own.

JILLIAN COULDN'T REMEMBER the last time she'd had so much fun at an event. Johnny was beyond attentive, holding her hand, whispering sweet *and* naughty things, dancing with her, and introducing her to everyone. His family was as warm and wonderful in person as she'd known they'd be. Kane had his own brand of warmth, but she liked his arrogance and clever wit, and she loved him for the many ways he was helping Johnny. She'd missed meeting Aria in person, but she'd see her in a few weeks at Thanksgiving, and she was excited to see everyone else then, too.

They didn't get home until after midnight, and although the girls had talked the whole ride home, once they were in bed, they went out like lights. Jillian sat on Johnny's bed to take off her heels, her gaze moving to the picture on his nightstand of the two of them on the Ferris wheel. Her heart filled up, and on the heels of that happiness was the reality that she was leaving again tomorrow. She swallowed against the sadness rising inside her, and she toyed once again with the idea of moving to the city and what it would be like waking up in Johnny's arms and seeing Zoey every morning. She imagined working on her designs while Johnny was recording music. She even imagined working *in* the studio while he recorded. She loved listening to loud music while she worked, and what could be better than being serenaded by the man who had stealthily stolen her heart?

She was reaching for her heels to put them in the closet when that special man walked in.

"There's my beautiful girl." He took her hand, lifting her to her feet, and kissed her. "Are you exhausted?"

"Never too tired for you."

"Thank you, babe. I want to show you something."

As he led her out of the bedroom, what he'd said in the shower came back to her. "Is this *something* in your studio?"

He didn't respond, and he was acting a little coy as they headed downstairs. He'd shown her his studio one night while they were video chatting, but as they entered, she realized it was much larger than she'd thought. Leather couches and chairs and a wood-and-steel table created a conversation nook atop a handsome area rug to their left. It was easy to picture him sitting there with his bandmates, hashing out songs. To their right was a small stage with drums, microphones, a keyboard, amplifiers, and about a dozen guitars hanging on the walls. Speakers and other musical accoutrements were scattered on the floor. She could see him there, too, playing with his band, speakers blaring.

Directly across from where they stood was a soundboard, an enormous desk with electronics where the producer sat when recording music, facing the glass window of the recording studio. The walls housed complicated speakers.

"So this is where the magic happens."

"I always thought so." He gazed down at her, those dark eyes reeling her in. "But then it happened in Colorado." He pressed his lips to hers. "And in Maryland." He kissed her again. "And here in New York."

Her pulse quickened. "We *are* talking about music, aren't we?"

He raised his brows. "I thought we were talking about magic." He walked over to the soundboard. "We recorded this for our album, and I wanted you to be the first to hear it."

He flicked a few switches, and the song he'd sung at Nick's party came on, but it was the dirty rock version with his band. The pulsing beat and his husky singing voice gave her chills. "Ohmygod, *Johnny*. This is amazing. It's gritty and seductive and *explosive*."

"Just like us, baby." He gathered her in his arms. "I've got several more in the works that are just as powerful, and that's all because of you, my beautiful muse. The last few years, I thought I was falling out of love with music and the grind that goes along with it, and then my mother got sick, and I found out about Zoey, and everything Dick did, and on the heels of *that* wake-up call, you blew into my life, breathing fire and ready to tear me apart, and I thought that was *it*. The universe was telling me that the musical part of my life was over. But that wake-up call was nothing compared to the kaleidoscope of emotions and determination you brought out in me. I misread the signs, baby, and I misread myself. I wasn't falling out of love with music, and the universe wasn't telling me the musical part of my life was over. It was bringing me the missing pieces of my life that I needed to dig deeper and rediscover, not just my love of music but *myself*, and become the man I was always meant to be. You snuck up on me, baby, with your tough love, feisty attitude, and your beautiful spirit, which could probably find a ray of light in a dungeon. My world, *our* world, is better with you in it, and I hope yours is better with us in it, because I know who I'm supposed to be now. Music is a part of me, just like you and Zoey are, and I have fallen madly, *passionately* in love with you."

Tears sprang to her eyes. "You have?"

"Yes, babe, and I wish I could figure out how we could be together all the time, but short of convincing you to move in with us while we figure out everything with Zoey, I don't have an answer. But one day I will, and then we'll be together every night."

Her heart felt like it was going to beat right out of her body. "I hope so, because you snuck up on me, too, Rocker Boy, with your barn candles, dirty talk, and dried flowers. I never saw you and Zoey coming, and once I started falling, I didn't want to stop."

A tease rose in his eyes. "Tell me something I don't know."

"Hey," she said with a laugh. "Don't pretend like I'm a sure thing."

He brushed his lips over hers. "Baby, you've been a sure thing since the first time we kissed."

"You think you know me?"

"I know you pretty damn well."

"Is that so?" She went up on her toes and whispered, "Bet you didn't know I'm not wearing any panties," and sauntered away.

His arm swept around her from behind. She squealed as he hauled her back against his chest. "Where do you think you're going?" He kissed her neck, his scruff tickling her skin as he unbuckled her belt.

"Wherever I want," she challenged.

He grabbed both sides of her plunging neckline and tore her jumpsuit right down the middle. Holy moly that was hot! Laughter tumbled out as he tightened his hold on her with one hand, his other sliding between her legs, turning her laughter into a hungry moan.

"*Where* does my sexy girl want to go?" His deep, gravelly voice was pure seduction.

She reached up, guiding his mouth back to her neck as she said, "Nowhere. My plan worked. I'm *exactly* where I wanted to be."

Chapter Twenty-Eight

JILLIAN PUT THE last bow on Amber's wedding gifts and wrinkled her nose at the smell of burnt pancakes turning her stomach. She eyed the blackened circles like they were the enemy. She didn't even know why she'd made them. She wasn't particularly hungry. She'd just missed Johnny and Zoey, and it had made her feel like they weren't so far away. She had woken up to a text that he'd sent at the crack of dawn. *Waking up without you sucks. Wish you were coming with us.* It had been two weeks since the gala, and he and Zoey were leaving this morning for LA with his bandmates.

"Good morning, guys." She sprinkled fish food into Winger and Rocker Boy's tank. Johnny and Zoey had left them there when they visited last weekend. Jillian was surprised to find that she liked the company. "Liza's going to feed you while I'm away for Amber's wedding, so be good for her." Rocker Boy came to the surface, nibbled on a flake, then swam away. "I don't blame you. I don't like the smell of burnt pancakes either."

Her phone rang with a video call from Johnny. Excitement skated through her as she answered it. "Hi. I didn't expect to hear from you until after you landed in LA."

"Did you really think I'd leave without hearing your voice? We're going to be boarding soon. How're you feeling this morning? Any better?"

She'd been a little rundown lately, and her stomach had been off a couple of days the last two weeks. She was pretty sure it was stress, but she'd worried she might have to miss the wedding if she was coming down with something. She'd gone to bed early last night, and thankfully, she was feeling better today. "Much better. I'm good. But the pancakes I tried to make weren't so lucky." She picked up the plate and dumped the circular bricks in the trash.

"Aw, babe. That's why you need to be with us."

"I have a zillion reasons I want to be with you, but I'm perfectly capable of feeding myself, thank you very much." She obviously wasn't great in the cooking department, but she didn't need to admit that. "I just got distracted while I was making them. I went upstairs to get Amber's gifts, and then I changed my outfit and answered a few texts. If the smoke alarms hadn't gone off, I probably wouldn't have even come back to the kitchen. I swear my brain has been all over the place lately."

"Of course it has. You're running on even less sleep than when I met you. Can we talk about you sneaking out of bed last weekend?"

When they were there last weekend, they'd gone to Nick's to ride horses Saturday morning and to Jillian's parents' house for dinner Saturday night, and then Ginny and Cara had slept over with Zoey. Jillian wouldn't trade that time with them for anything, but the work she used to do at night during the week—much of which was now often spent catching up with Johnny—and on the weekends still needed to get done. She was barely keeping up. "I told you that I just couldn't sleep."

"Which is my fault. I'm wearing you out."

"I love the way you wear me out."

"*Jilly*," he said thoughtfully. "I'm worried about you. You were a midnight owl when we first got together, and I'm well aware of all the work time you give up for me and Zoey. The last thing I want is to screw up your career. If you need more time to work, just say the word. Maybe we should cut back on seeing each other every weekend."

"Don't you *dare*. I'll have withdrawals."

"Thank God, because I would, too. But we have to do something. Promise me you'll get some rest this weekend."

"That might be tough with the wedding." She was driving to the wedding venue today, which was an hour outside of Oak Falls, Virginia, and was staying there overnight. She wouldn't be home until tomorrow around noon, and she had a list of changes to make to designs that were due last week and commissions she'd agreed to do before booking the launch. "But I'm fine, really. I'll rest next week."

"Over Thanksgiving?"

"Is it Thanksgiving already? I'll rest after the holidays." She carried Amber's presents into the foyer and set the boxes down by the door.

"Right before your launch? You know that's not happening." His voice was thick with concern. "Do I have to kidnap you and force you to take some time off? Because if that's what it takes to get you to take care of yourself, I'll do it."

"That's a fantastic idea. After my launch, I'll need a month or so to handle any issues that arise, and *then* we can disappear to a tropical island and fan each other with palm fronds as we drink margaritas and lie in the sun."

"Now, that sounds good. Are we wearing clothes in this fantasy?"

"Only when Zoey's around."

He chuckled. "I'd do that in a heartbeat, but I got a text from the guys this morning, and everyone's on board for a summer tour. We're meeting up after the awards tonight to finalize dates so we can get the ball rolling."

"That's exciting, and now I've got to get your wardrobe done. Can you see if the guys can meet with me the next time I'm in New York? I think that's the first weekend in December."

"Sure. Have you thought any more about going on the road with us? You can rest during the tour and hang with me and Zoey."

She wanted to be with them more than anything, but she had to be realistic. "*Rest* and *tour* seem contradictory."

"It's not that bad."

"I've seen tour documentaries, and it's every bit that bad."

"Damn documentaries. Seriously, though. I wish you were with us all the time. I'll make sure you have a hotel suite in every city we tour, fully equipped with whatever design tools you need."

God, this man's love knew no limits. She had no doubt he'd do that and much more for her. "I'll think about it."

"Don't mess with me, baby."

"I'm not. Hotel rooms aren't as enticing as palm fronds and margaritas, but you and Zoey beat those out any day of the week. How long will you be touring?"

"Six or seven weeks over the summer for the US tour, so I can take Zoey with me, and then we'll do a European tour in November when she has fall break. I'll hire a tutor for the road."

"Does that mean Zoey's feeling better about school and she'll go to the same one next fall?"

"No. She still hates it, and I didn't like the principal of the last school I checked out. We're still figuring out where she'll go next fall, but every school has fall break, so she'll only miss about three weeks."

"But that would be really hard for her to start at a new school and then be gone two months later."

"I know, but I'm not going to hire a stranger to stay with her, and I don't want to put that pressure on my parents."

"What if there was another option?" Her heart raced at what she was about to suggest. "I've been thinking about our situation and about what you said about convincing me to move to New York. It's not realistic to think you'd move to Maryland. You have your band and your studio and Zoey's been through enough of an upheaval. But I can work from anywhere, so maybe Zoey wouldn't have to miss school."

"Are you saying what I think you're saying?"

"I'm saying that I've been toying with the idea of moving there if you still want me to."

"Are you kidding?" he practically yelled. "Baby, I'll send a moving truck today."

She laughed. "Let's not get ahead of ourselves. I haven't figured it all out with my work and Liza, but it *would* mean Zoey wouldn't have to miss school in November."

"Jilly, baby. *God*, I'm so fucking happy. What about your family? And I thought you said you didn't like the city enough to live there."

She wasn't sure how she felt about moving away from her family and to the city, but she was sure of her love for him and Zoey. "I hate being away from you and Zoey more than I think I'd dislike living in the city, and if I'm not near my family, they won't have to make so much food for dinner."

He laughed. "God, baby. I wish you were here right now so I could show you how happy I am that you're even considering this. Hold on a sec." He pulled the phone away from his ear, talking with someone. When he came back on the line, he said, "I have to go. Kane's pilot is ready. I love you, baby, and I won't say anything to Zoey until you're sure."

"I love you, too. Hug her for me, and send me a picture of the two of you when you're all dolled up. I'm sorry I'm not there with you. Good luck."

"I don't need luck. I've got my girls. Everything else is icing on the cake."

AMBER AND DASH'S wedding took place at Chaverly Hall, an estate that looked like it came straight out of *Pride and Prejudice*, which was beautifully perfect for Amber's love of literature. The luxurious and massive three-story stone mansion stood sentinel over meticulously manicured lawns and gardens. The ceremony was touching and beautiful, and Jillian doubted it left anyone dry eyed. Amber and Dash said their vows beneath the stars in a gorgeous gazebo decorated with white and pink lilies and sparkling lights, in front of an ivy-covered stone wall with heart-shaped archways on either side of the gazebo. Amber was the picture of graceful elegance in the hand-beaded gown Jax had made for her, and Dash was every bit the dashing groom in a black tuxedo, and what his sisters called his *toddler smile*—the kind of smile that was so big it looked fake but was genuine for Dash—never left his lips.

Over the last few years, Jillian had watched her friends and brothers say their vows with envy, wondering when it would be her turn. But as she took it all in—Amber and Dash gazing into each other's eyes as they were pronounced man and wife, while Reno, Amber's epilepsy seizure-alert dog, sat dutifully beside her in his black bow tie, and her five sisters and maid of honor, beautiful in their fall-colored dresses, and Dash's handsome best man and groomsmen in dark tuxedos, stood in support—she tried to picture herself and Johnny standing before the people they loved, exchanging their vows with Zoey by their sides. As much as she wanted that, there were things she wanted even more, like just being *with* them. The dress, the ceremony, reciting vows of forever for all to see were no longer as high on her list of hopes.

Being with the man who loved and respected her, and his wonderful daughter, would be enough, and if she had to move to New York for that to come true, it was a small price to pay for happiness. She checked her messages, hoping to see one from Johnny. She'd texted him a picture of her in her dress before leaving her room in the mansion. He hadn't responded yet, but she knew his day was going to be busy. She imagined him and Zoey checking into the hotel and Zoey being excited to check everything out before getting ready for their big evening.

After the kiss of the century, Amber and Dash were swept away for pictures by his brother Hawk, a renowned photographer, then they joined everyone else for the reception, which was now in full swing in a grand ballroom with opulent vases overflowing with colorful bouquets. Tables draped in white boasted gorgeous glass centerpieces filled with acorns and twinkling lights, and an elegant array of chandeliers surrounded by an assortment of greenery and lilies illuminated a gold-and-white dance floor.

Amber's brother, Axsel, and his band played "Rewrite the Stars" for Amber and Dash's first dance, and they'd been playing upbeat music ever since. Jillian danced with Trixie and several of Amber's sisters, and Amber's bestie, Lindsay Roberts, a professional wedding planner who had planned their magical night. After a few songs, Jillian felt a little light-headed and went to get a glass of ice water. Trixie and Brindle followed her over to the bar, where they found Pepper, Amber's older sister. Pepper was a scientist, and when she was in graduate school, she'd developed a seizure-alert necklace, which was now sold all over the world. Pepper was also Sable's twin, and her polar opposite. While Sable was brunette, brash, and ornery, Pepper's hair was a mix of browns and blondes, and she was sweet and gracious.

Brindle and Trixie ordered mixed drinks. Jillian got ice water and put the cool glass to her cheek. "Is it hot in here?"

"Not really, but you were dancing," Pepper said. "Your body temperature is probably elevated."

"You're probably thinking of your hot rock star," Brindle added. "It's a shame Johnny couldn't come. I couldn't believe it when I saw the pictures of you attending the fundraiser with him. I was like, *No way. Jillian and Johnny Butthead?*"

"Brindle, that's not nice," Pepper said.

"Oh, don't worry, Jillian is very fond of his butt and *both* of his heads." Trixie waggled her brows.

"*Yes*, I am. Onstage is not the only place my man is talented," Jillian said.

Jillian's cousin Clay sauntered over, looking handsome in his tuxedo, his dark hair brushed away from his face. As the starting quarterback for the New York Giants, the team Dash had played for before retiring, he was one of Dash's closest friends. His eyes were trained on Pepper, who was blushing a red streak.

"Ladies," Clay said, as he went farther down the bar to join his teammates, Troy and Tyrell.

"I swear the Braden men are blessed with good genes," Pepper said.

"Now's your chance," Brindle said. "Make your move. Go flirt with him."

Pepper looked away. "I'm not into football players. I just think he's handsome."

"Are you kidding? Dash is amazing," Trixie said.

"Yes, but he's not your typical jock," Pepper said. "He doesn't even play football anymore. He's an author now."

Brindle let out an exasperated sigh. "You're such an overthinker. You don't need to be into him to get him *into* you, if you know what I mean."

Pepper's lips pursed. "We have nothing in common. Nothing to talk about."

"How do you know?" Jillian asked. "There's more going on in Clay's head than football plays. He's my cousin, and he's a great guy."

"Besides, you don't need to *talk*, Pep," Brindle pushed. "You can keep his mouth busy in other ways."

"*Brindle*," Pepper snapped.

Brindle rolled her eyes. "I just want you to be happy. You're an incredible person, and you're never going to meet anyone if you spend all your time in your lab doing research."

"Don't say that," Trixie chided. "She'll meet someone when the time is right. Although my vote is for a night of debauchery with Clay."

Pepper glowered at her.

"If I've learned one thing lately, it's that love comes when you're not looking for it," Jillian said encouragingly. "Just look at me and Johnny."

"Char swears the magic of the inn brought you two together," Pepper said. "But there's no evidence proving that places can help people fall in love."

"Maybe not, but I believe in it," Jillian said. "And I'm glad we started there, because that kind of magic never ends."

"That's what happened with me and Nick," Trixie said.

"You fell in love at the inn?" Pepper asked.

"No, but we were touched by the magic of the inn," Trixie said. "It was a little more than two years ago, after the Mad Prix wilderness race I competed in."

"I remember that. You got wasted," Jillian said.

"I got a little *tipsy*," Trixie corrected her. "Nick walked me to my room and sat there all night in case I got sick. I didn't even know he'd stayed, and he swears after that night he couldn't get me out of his head."

"That's the magic of the inn." Jillian sipped her water.

"Well, Trace and I didn't need an inn," Brindle said. "I have loved that man since I was thirteen years old." Brindle was married to one of Trixie's older brothers.

"You've had my brother tied up in knots for just as long," Trixie said.

"I wish I'd known Johnny that long, but with his stardom and my focus on fashion, we never would have made it."

"You don't know that," Brindle said.

"Yes, I do. I've been laser focused on fashion since I was yay high." Jillian held her hand by her hip.

"Until Johnny," Trixie pointed out.

"Exactly. I think we came together at just the right time," Jillian said. "I'm actually thinking about moving to the city to be with them."

"Are you *kidding*?" Brindle asked.

"What?" The shock in Trixie's voice was inescapable.

"You must be really sure about him to move your business and move away from your family," Pepper said.

"I am, and I know he and Zoey can't move to Maryland. I still have a lot to figure out, but I want to be with them."

Trixie fake cried and hugged her. "I want to be selfish and tell you to stay, but I moved for Nick, and these last few weeks, you've been happier than I ever remember seeing you. I love you."

"I love you, too, and thank you for not trying to guilt me into staying."

"I'd totally guilt you if I lived there," Brindle teased. "But the truth is, I'd move anywhere for Trace."

Jillian smiled. "Where is your handsome cowboy? He's usually all over you."

"He went to change Emma Lou, but that was a while ago." Emma Lou was Brindle and Trace's little girl. Brindle looked around and smiled as she pointed across the room to Trace talking with her and Pepper's older sister, Grace, and her husband, Reed. Grace was holding Emma Lou. "There they are. I hope Gracie gets pregnant soon. I hate that they're having trouble."

"I'm sure Char and Beau's pregnancy announcement didn't help," Jillian said. Charlotte and Beau had shared their news with their family and friends right before the wedding. Everyone was thrilled for them, and Jillian's parents were elated about having their first grandchild on the way.

"She didn't seem upset by it," Brindle said.

"You know how Grace is," Pepper said. "She's happy for them, and she and Reed are seeing a fertility doctor. They're hopeful they'll get pregnant soon."

"We should send all our positive pregnancy mojo their way," Trixie suggested.

"They can have it *all*," Jillian said, as the band started playing one of Trixie's favorite songs.

"Let's go dance!" Trixie exclaimed, and tried to drag them all to the dance floor, but Pepper waved her hands, backing away.

Jillian's light-headedness was settling, but now her stomach felt funky. "I think I'll sit this one out."

They mingled until they were seated for dinner. Jillian sat with her family, except for Graham, who was at the head table with Morgyn and the rest of the wedding party. The champagne toasts were heartwarming, and Amber and Dash looked so in love, it made

Jillian miss Johnny even more.

She listened to the conversations going on around her, nervously contemplating the best way to tell her family that she was thinking about moving. Beau and Char were making plans for a nursery, and Zev and Carly were heading straight from Virginia to Colorado for the winter. Jax and Jordan were making plans to see Sully again, and Nick and Trixie were talking about a horse they were thinking about getting. Jillian ate a few bites as she waited for a lull in the conversations, but the smell of the food made her nauseous.

Damn nerves. She pushed her plate away and sat back.

"You don't like it, honey?" her mother asked. She was wearing a cinnamon dress that matched her father's tie.

"I do. I'm just not that hungry."

"Are you feeling okay?" her mother asked.

"Yeah." She sipped her water, but even that had trouble staying down.

"You weren't feeling well the last two times you had dinner with us," her father said. "And you look a little green around the gills. Are you sure you're okay?"

"I'm fine." *Liar, liar.* She hated lying. "Actually, I'm not fine, Dad."

"I had a feeling," he said. "Are your long hours catching up to you?"

"My bet is on her missing Johnny and Zoey," Jax said from her other side.

Of course he'd know. He always knew.

"Is that it, honey?" her mother asked.

"Yes, and only seeing them on weekends is hard." She drew in a deep breath. "I think I want to move to New York."

That brought the conversations around the table to a screeching halt. Nick's brows slanted, but thankfully everyone else was smiling, with the exception of her father, whose expression was one of nonjudgmental concern.

"When did this come up?" Nick asked.

"It didn't *come up*," Jillian said. "I've been thinking about it for a few weeks, and don't tell me you wouldn't have moved to Virginia to be with Trixie, because I know you would've done whatever it took to be with her."

Trixie put her arm around Nick. "She's right, and you know it."

"I didn't say I was against her moving," he said gruffly. "I just want to know where her head is."

"This has nothing to do with her head," their father said. "And everything to do with her heart. Jilly, you know we'll support whatever you decide. But what about your business?"

"I have to talk with Liza and Annabelle, but if Liza agrees to continue working with me remotely, and she works in the office, she'd be there to handle anything Annabelle needs help with. There's a lot to figure out, but I'd like to move in that direction."

"Don't take this wrong, but are you sure you're ready to be a stepmom?" Nick asked.

"Zoey's a teenager, not a baby," Jillian said sharply. "She doesn't need me to survive. She needs love and emotional support, and I'm good at that."

Nick nodded. "You're very good at it, and I'm glad you see that. But you don't love the city any more than she does, so where does that leave the two of you?"

"*Nick*," her father warned.

"What? I'm happy for her. I support whatever she wants to do," Nick insisted. "Johnny's a stand-up guy, and he and Zoey obviously love her. But she's talking about moving the business she worked her ass off to create, and I don't care how in love anyone is, it won't change the things she doesn't like about the city. It's still going to be chaotic and impersonal."

"It's okay, Dad," Jillian said, touched by Nick's outburst of concern. "You're right, Nick, but I feel like I could live in a freaking gutter with Johnny and Zoey and be happy."

Nick arched a brow.

"Okay, not a gutter. A tent," Jillian said. "With a bathroom, and heat and air-conditioning. You *know* what I mean. It's not the place that matters. It's the people, and I *love* them."

"That's all that matters. I won't like you being so far away," Nick said with such honesty, Jillian struggled against tears. "But if it's what you want, I'll help you move."

"Thank you." She tried to blink her eyes dry.

"I think it's great, Jilly," Beau said. "I've never seen you as happy as you were with them in Colorado."

"I second that," Char said.

"I'm happy for you, too," Zev said. "You've never really traveled beyond business trips. A change of scenery might be good for your creativity."

"Does Johnny cook?" Carly asked, and everyone laughed.

"Yes," Jillian said. "And so does Zoey." She looked at Jax. "No words of wisdom from my twinnie?"

"I'm just trying to imagine my life without you right around the corner."

"It's going to be weird," she said.

"Or wonderful," Jax teased.

"Hey."

"You know I love you." He pulled her into a hug. "I couldn't be happier for you. I knew the day he showed up in your office that you two wouldn't be able to stay away from each other for long."

"I think I did, too."

Her father lifted his glass in a toast. "To all our children's happiness."

"Hear, hear," the guys said, and everyone clinked glasses.

Jillian took a sip just as the waiter walked by with a tray of something that had everyone saying, *"Mm,"* and her stomach lurching. She pushed to her feet. "Excuse me for a second. I'm just going to run to the ladies' room."

She tried to walk normally, despite the wave of nausea rolling through her, and once she was out of the ballroom, she hightailed it into the closest restroom and made a beeline for a stall. She made it just in time for the little she'd eaten throughout the day to come back up. She wiped her mouth with toilet paper, flushed it down, and leaned against the stall door, trying to catch her breath before going to wash her hands.

When she opened the stall door, Sable was standing there, gorgeous in a cinnamon off-the-shoulder gown with a twist-knot bodice and slit along her right leg. Her makeup looked professionally done, and her long brown hair was gathered over one shoulder and secured with a ribbon. A far cry from the jeans-clad, cowgirl-boot-and-hat-wearing mechanic Jillian was used to.

Sable was several inches taller than Jillian, and her face was so serious, Jillian felt like a kid caught skipping school. "*Great*. An audience."

"You look like hell," Sable said. "How much did you drink?"

"Just a little champagne with the toasts." Jillian brushed past her, washed her hands, and rinsed out her mouth. A quick glance in the mirror confirmed Sable's observation. She turned away from the mirror and grabbed paper towels, using them to pat beads of sweat from her forehead.

"Do you have a fever?"

Jillian shook her head. "I'm just worn out. I'm not sick."

"Being worn out doesn't make you barf." Sable crossed her arms.

"Well, I guess it does to me. Plus, I've been nervous all evening. That didn't help." She threw out the paper towel and leaned against the sink, putting her hand over her gurgling stomach.

"You sure you're not sick?" Sable reached over and touched her forehead. Her brows knitted. "Have you thrown up a lot lately?"

"Once or twice the last couple of weeks."

"Is that normal for you? You're not bulimic, are you?"

"Seriously?" Jillian shook her head.

"Just checking. Any chance you're pregnant?"

"Jesus, you go right for the…" *Oh shit. When was my last period?*

"Now, *that'll* make you puke."

"I'm not pregnant. I can't be. We're always careful." She remembered the night in the shed, and in the shower, and panic set in. "*Oh no. Nonono.* We were careful *most* of the time, but he…he pulled out."

"*Christ.* Now you sound like a sixteen-year-old who didn't want to stop in the back seat of a car. FYI, just the tip counts, too."

Jillian glowered at her.

"When was your last period?"

"I don't *know.*" She paced, wringing her hands together, trying to remember. "It's not regular. I get it every four or six weeks, and just go with the flow."

"Well, you're obviously not doing that *this* month."

"You're *not* helping. I can't be pregnant. What would that do to Zoey? And I have a launch coming up and the band's wardrobe to make, and Johnny has his tour. *Ohmygod,* Sable. I totally forgot to tell you you're opening for his tour."

Sable scowled. "I'm *what?*"

"It's all in writing. You can thank me later." She continued pacing, her heart and mind racing.

"Thanking you is *not* what I'm thinking, but we can table that discussion for another time. You need a pregnancy test. Want me to go to the store?"

"*No.* You need to stay at the reception, and I'm telling you, I'm not pregnant. The universe would not put a baby inside *me.* I'm not mother material."

"What the fuck is mother material?" Sable snapped.

"I don't know. It's what I'm *not.*" Tears welled in Jillian's eyes. "It's someone who puts a baby first and remembers to feed it and change it and make sure it gets its shots. Someone who can slow down enough to rock it and nurture it. I *burn* pancakes, for Pete's sake!"

"Who cares about pancakes?"

"The baby will when it's eating bricks or starving. I *can't* have a baby. Johnny *just* got Zoey, and this could be bad for their relationship. Ohmygod, Sable, what am I going to do?"

Sable took her by the shoulders, her face a mask of seriousness.

"Breathe, Jillian. Just fucking breathe."

Jillian took a deep breath and blew it out raggedly as tears slid down her cheeks.

"Now, stop crying. *Why* do girls cry all the time? Tears never helped a damn thing."

"I *don't* cry all the time."

Sable gave her a *yeah right* look. "There's a drugstore around the corner. You go up to your room and get cleaned up, and I'll get a test, and bring it to you."

"No. I appreciate your help, but this is your sister's wedding."

"My sister is so gaga over Dash, she wouldn't notice if the whole room cleared out."

"Still. I'm not letting you leave because of me. I can handle this." She grabbed a paper towel and dabbed at her tears, hoping she was right. "I'm getting all worked up for nothing. I'm sure it's just stress." *It has to be.* "Thank you for letting me freak out."

Sable sighed. "As if I had a choice?"

"Well, you didn't slap me, and I might have done that to you if you'd gone off on a tangent." Jillian hugged her, and with another deep breath, she drew her shoulders back, lifted her chin, and headed out of the bathroom.

After congratulations and goodbyes, she told Amber, Dash, and her family that she was exhausted and going to bed early and went up to her room. She brushed her teeth, washed her face, and changed out of her dress. Feeling like a teenager sneaking out of her parents' house, she headed out to buy a pregnancy test and hoped nobody saw her when she came back in.

Chapter Twenty-Nine

JILLIAN STARED AT the tiny plus sign, unable to stop a rush of tears as a knock on her door sounded. Who the hell was looking for her, and why didn't they just text? She set the test stick on the counter and went to look out the peephole, seeing a very serious-faced Sable.

As she opened the door, Sable strode in. "Did you do it yet?" She spun around and saw Jillian's tears. "Oh shit." As if she heard the worry in her own voice, she said, "It's okay. It's going to be okay."

"No, it's *not*. Nothing will be okay ever again." Jillian paced. "You should go back to the party before they miss you."

Sable planted a hand on her hip. "I'm not letting you go through this alone."

There was another knock on the door. "Who is *that*?" Jillian whispered.

"How should I know?"

Jillian looked out the peephole, and her chest constricted at the sight of her bestie. "It's Trixie." She breathed deeply, swiping at her tears, and tried to hold it together as she opened the door, but Trixie took one look at her and said, "What's wrong?" causing the dam to burst.

"Everything." Jillian grabbed her wrist and pulled her into the room, closing the door behind her. "I got sick earlier, and Sable asked if I could be pregnant, and—"

Trixie's eyes widened. "Ohmygod, Jilly, you're *pregnant*?"

She could do little more than nod and cry.

"I'm guessing these aren't happy tears." Trixie pulled her into her arms. "It's okay. We'll figure this out."

She pushed out of Trixie's arms and paced. "How could I be so careless? I'm not ready. He's not ready. I'm supposed to be moving to New York. What am I going to do?" Her phone rang from the counter in the bathroom, and she headed in to get it. Her gaze landed on the pregnancy test just long enough to send a pang through her chest. *A baby. Our baby.* Love and worry intertwined in a confusing mix of emotions. She grabbed her phone and saw Johnny's name on the screen. Panic spread like wildfire through her chest, causing more tears as she went back into the bedroom. "It's him. I can't tell him before the awards ceremony."

"Yes, you can. This is his problem, too," Sable said.

Jillian shook her head. "Not tonight."

"Bullshit. *That's* why I don't like celebrities. Fucking egomaniacs. A stupid award should *not* come before this."

"*Sable*," Trixie chided. "Jilly, do what feels right to you. If you don't want to tell him now, then wait until tomorrow. Do you want us to stay while you talk to him?"

"No. It'll be harder if you're here. Thank you, though." She hugged them, promising to let them know how it went, and answered the call as they left the room. "Hey," she managed.

"I just saw your text. You look gorgeous, babe. I'm sorry I didn't get back to you sooner. We were out, and then we had to get ready. I just texted you some pictures of everyone. Zoey looks beautiful, and she's having fun with the guys. Chad brought his ex. They're going to give it another try. How's the wedding? I wish I were there with you."

His happiness brought more tears. They were just getting started, and this baby could change everything. "It's wonderful." Her voice cracked, and she squeezed her eyes shut.

"Jilly, what's wrong?"

"Nothing. I'm fine. Just emotional from the ceremony."

"That had to be at least an hour ago. Talk to me, baby."

She shook her head even though he couldn't see her. "I'm fine. We can talk tomorrow." There was no masking the heartache in her voice. "Go have fun, and give Zoey a hug for me."

"Babe, I'm not going anywhere until you tell me what's wrong."

"Johnny, I can't," she pleaded.

"You *can*, baby. You can tell me anything. You know you can."

Not like this.

"Jillian, you're scaring me. What's going on?"

"Nothing." She tried to stop her tears, but they fell like rivers.

"I'm not hanging up until you tell me."

A video call from him rang through, and she closed her eyes, gathering the courage to accept it. She wiped her eyes and touched the green icon. His handsome face and those loving dark eyes appeared, bringing an onslaught of more tears.

"Aw, baby. What could be that bad? Did someone hurt you? Is your family okay?"

She shook her head. She heard a knock from his end, and he looked to his right, forcing out, "I'll be right there." Then he looked at her again, his eyes imploring her. "I love you, Jilly. Whatever it is, we'll get through it."

"I don't want to tell you like this."

"Tell me *what*? Come on, babe. Everyone's waiting on me, and I'm *not* ending this call until I know what's going on. I will stand right here all night if I have to."

"I'm…" She couldn't do it and sank down to the edge of the bed.

"Damn it, Jillian, I'm not fucking around. You've got me worried. Tell me what's wrong."

"I'm *pregnant*." Sobs fell from her lips, and through the blur of tears she saw his jaw slacken and disbelief rise in his eyes. The next few seconds passed in slow motion, and she felt every change in him as if it were taking place in her. A storm of confusion and worry pushed that disbelief aside, and his jaw tightened.

She heard Zoey holler, "*Dad!* The photographer is waiting. Kane said we have to go *now*."

Hearing Zoey's voice and her use of *Dad* brought a tidal wave of tears. "*Go.* I'm sorry. I love you. We'll talk tomorrow." She ended the call and lay back on the bed. Her phone vibrated and a text message popped up. She opened it with a shaky finger, and the group of pictures he'd sent before their call appeared, with the picture of Johnny and Zoey dressed for the event on top. Johnny had his arm around Zoey, and they were both beaming. The caption read *Wish you were here. We love you.* She looked through the other pictures of them with his bandmates and Chad's ex. Everyone looked so happy, and now she'd ruined his night.

She knew Sable and Trixie would be at her door if she didn't text them, so she sent a quick message to each telling them she and Johnny would talk tomorrow, and she was going to bed. Closing her eyes against hot tears, she curled onto her side as the phone vibrated in rapid succession. She forced herself to look at it. Trixie sent a heart emoji, and *I'm here if you need me*, and Sable, the queen of tough love, texted, *You're stronger than you think. Whatever you decide has to be right for YOU, and if Bad pisses you off, I'll take care of him.*

Another message popped up, and her chest constricted at the sight of Johnny's name. She opened the message, reading the three simple words that made her feel better and hurt worse—*I love you.*

JOHNNY'S HEART THUNDERED as he knocked on the door. Hell, it hadn't stopped thundering since those two life-altering words—*I'm pregnant*—had hit his ears. Too anxious to wait, he knocked again, louder. He heard a muffled voice and footsteps.

The door opened, and Jillian blinked sleepily up at him. "It's four in the morning. What are you doing here?" Her hair was a mess, her eyes puffy and red, and she was wearing his favorite sleeping shorts and tank. The ones she'd worn the first morning he'd seen her in

Colorado.

He stepped inside and gathered her in his arms, holding her tight. "I would've climbed through the phone if I could have."

"Where's Zoey? How did you get here so fast? I thought the awards went until eleven."

"I got a suite here. She's there with Kane. We didn't go to the awards. The guys accepted it."

"You *won*." She stepped out of his arms. "This is exactly what I didn't want to happen. This was a big night for you, and I ruined it."

"You haven't ruined anything." He took her face between his hands, holding her stare. "I've accepted enough awards to last a lifetime, but there's only one of you, and if you think I could step onstage and pretend everything is great when you're across the country, hurting, then you don't know me at all."

"*Johnny.* What about Zoey? She was so excited to go. What did you tell her about why you were missing the awards?"

"I told her that you were having a hard time with something and I'd feel better if I were here with you. Kane offered to take her to the event, but she said if you were having a hard time, she'd rather be here for you, too."

Her shoulders sank, tears falling down her cheeks. "She's the best, isn't she? I'm sorry this is such a mess. I shouldn't have told you before the event."

"You *absolutely* should have. There's nothing we can't handle, and there's no place I'd rather be than right here." He took her hand and led her to the bed, sitting down beside her. "I love you, Jilly, and before we talk about everything, you need to know that I'll support whatever you decide."

"Even if I'm not ready to have a baby? I'm not saying I've decided anything, but I have concerns, starting with Zoey. Would it be fair to bring another child into her life right now?"

"I don't know of any kid who has a choice when their family grows, and most seem to do okay with it. It might be tough on her, or maybe it'll make her happy to have a sibling to love. We have no way of knowing because this isn't her decision, and she isn't going to know about it unless we decide to move forward with the pregnancy. If we do, we'll just work twice as hard to make sure she knows our love for her isn't based on her being an only child."

"You're right. I just worry about her."

"I do, too. But right now I'm more concerned about you. Do you want to talk about what you're thinking?"

"I don't even know what I'm thinking. I have things I want to accomplish, and I can't imagine doing them with a baby. I know that sounds selfish, but I'm not done being *me* yet."

"And you feel like you'd lose a part of yourself if we had a baby?"

"I don't know what to think. I'm scared, and confused, and you've already had one child thrust upon you."

"That was totally different, and as I told you, you and Zoey are the best things that have ever happened to me, regardless of how we came to be. If we decide to do this, we'll do it together, and we'll figure it out just like we are with Zoey. I'd be by your side the whole time for feedings and diaper changes and stroller rides and toddler tantrums. But a bigger concern is whether you feel like your relationship with me and Zoey has cost you anything."

"Only work time, but I think living together will help with that because right now we only have weekends together, and we're starved for that time. But if we have a baby, I won't want to move away from my family. I'll *need* their support, and my mom can help me learn all the things I need to know."

"Then we'll live in Maryland. I don't care where we live, as long as we're together, and Zoey hates the city anyway. Her friends live near you, and she cries when we leave."

"She *does?*"

"Yes. She cried after you left New York, too, but it was worse this time. She made me swear not to tell you, so don't let her know I spilled the beans."

"I won't. I had no idea going back and forth was so hard on her. But you can't *move*. What about your band, and Kane, and being near your parents?"

"As far as the band goes, we're going to make adjustments anyway. Chad told us he's moving to Virginia to be with his family. And Kane and my parents are only a few hours from Maryland. Baby, if you want to do this, we'll figure it out in a way that works for all of us. I know how important your business is. It's not like we can't afford to hire help with a baby if we need it, and if we're in Maryland, I'd imagine your parents will be first in line to pitch in."

"They'd probably never give it back," she said with a smile, but it faded, and worry rose in her eyes again. "I'm scared, Johnny. What if I'm not good at being a mom?"

"I know that worries you, but I don't think you can help *but* be a good mother. It doesn't matter if you cook or clean or do any of that crap. You won't forget to feed or change a baby. They cry and let you know when they need something. Give yourself a little credit, Jilly. You remember to feed Winger and Rocker Boy, and they're *fish*. They can't tell you when they're hungry, and they need to be fed two or three times a day. Besides, from my limited experience, I think eighty percent of raising a child is loving it enough to be there and try your best. You fell in love with Zoey, and she's not even your blood."

"I love her like she is."

"That's what I'm saying. Imagine holding a baby you and I created."

Her eyes teared up.

"That kind of love breeds the rest."

"It didn't for Zoey's mom."

"We both know there's something very wrong with that woman. But there's nothing wrong with you. You love with your whole heart. I understand why you're scared, but you saw me the day we met. I wasn't ready to be a dad, and here I am, doing my best. Even on the most frustrating days, when I think everything I do is wrong, I don't regret being Zoey's dad. I love her enough to try to figure out how to do it right, and you've always helped me with that, which tells me you'll be a wonderful mom. But if you're not ready, that decision won't change how I feel about you."

He lifted her chin and brushed his thumb over her lower lip. "I love *you*, Jillian. I'll love our kids whether we have them now or a few years from now, and I'll love you even if we never have children."

Her eyes dampened. "I love you, too." She swallowed hard and put her hand on his leg. "Do *you* want a baby right now?"

"I didn't think I did. I couldn't fathom bringing a baby into our lives when we're anything but settled, and I have no idea if or when things will fall into place. But on the flight here, I thought about us and Zoey and how far we've all come. I know you don't think you're mother material, but from the very first time we met, you've proven otherwise. You set aside all your hard feelings toward me when you didn't know me from a hole in the wall, and you dropped everything to help a girl you'd known for all of five minutes. I ask myself all the time how we got so lucky that you walked into our lives when you did."

"I'm not sure that's lucky. You said I was breathing fire, remember?"

"How could I ever forget? I have singe marks on my ribs."

She smiled, and he leaned in and kissed her. He took her hand in his and rubbed his thumb over the back of it. "None of us had any idea what would happen when we got on that plane, but we all took that risk."

"I wasn't sure you'd make it off alive if I didn't go."

"Neither was I. But that's when I got lucky. You didn't care that I erected walls around myself on that plane. You kicked your way through them, plunked down beside me, and forced me to talk to you. Nobody ever forces me to do anything. To most of the world, I'm Johnny Bad, the untouchable, unapproachable rock star, but you never saw me as that guy, did you?"

"Only when I thought of you as Johnny Butthead."

"Ah yes, good old Johnny Butthead. The asshole who blew you off too many times. But you saw past that before you even knew my reasons, and you took me for the man I am, faults and all. The man who needed to step up to be Zoey's dad. You were pushy and snarky and so fucking adorable, you unearthed parts of me and capabilities in me that I didn't even know existed."

"I didn't do anything special. I was just there." Her heart was racing.

"Everything about you is special, and Zoey and I are lucky to have you in our lives. Baby, you saw in me what I didn't see in myself, and I see in you what you don't see in yourself. I see past your fears and insecurities to the incredible woman who can't help but love and try to help others. You don't fake who you are or hide behind a damn thing, and you don't let anyone else hide their true feelings, either. That is beautiful and special and so fucking real, and *that's* what being a parent is about. Loving and caring so fiercely, you get to the heart of matters even when no one else wants to, and you find ways to work them out. All those things are what will make you a great mother."

"Do you really believe that?" A tear slipped down her cheek, and he wiped it away.

"How could I not? I've seen it with my own eyes. I've felt your love for me and Zoey in everything you've done. But there's no pressure. I'm just letting you know that you don't have to live up to anyone else's standards. You're perfect just the way you are."

More tears fell. "But this timing is awful. You're going on tour, and I'm launching a new line."

"The timing for us wasn't great, either, but we made it work. I'll move the tour up to April, right after your launch, and you and Zoey can come with me, or if it's too hard while you're pregnant, then we'll video chat while I'm on the road. I assume the baby would be due in July sometime, and that would give us a few months to get settled before we do the European tour."

"This doesn't scare you?"

"Sure, as much as having a baby would scare anyone, but you and I are phenomenal together. I honestly don't think there's anything we can't handle." He took her hand between both of his, brushing her tears away with the pads of his thumbs. "On the flight to LA this morning, I told Zoey, Kane, and the guys that after this tour I'm done touring for a few years. I'll keep making music, but I want to be there for Zoey, for the years she has left before she's off to college or whatever she decides to pursue, and I want to build a life with *you*, Jillian, whether or not we have more kids. I want to have bonfires and go to pumpkin festivals, with or without a BabyBjörn strapped to my chest."

She laughed softly.

"I want to do right by both of you. I want to see Zoey loving school and having fun with her friends and making outfits that you design together, and I want to cheer you on while you launch Wanderlust and Rocker Girlz and whatever else you dream up. When Zoey goes out in the world to blaze her own path, I want to know that I did everything I could to help her heal the wounds her mother left behind. And if we have kids, I want to be there for all the things I missed with Zoey. I want to see them take their first steps and put on their first fashion show at some ridiculously young age. I want to teach them to play their first instrument, and I want to be the tooth fairy and Santa Claus. I want to be part of it all. I've been on this hamster wheel for twenty years, baby. Now it's *our* turn."

She exhaled a long breath. "I was so worried that you'd be upset."

"I was shocked, and I'll admit my first thoughts included a lot of cursing, but even before you told me, when I looked into my future, I saw you and Zoey, and room for more." He leaned in and kissed her. "It's late, and we don't have to make any decisions tonight. Why don't we get some sleep and talk in the morning?"

"Okay."

They stood, and she stepped toward the door. He caught her hand, bringing her back into his arms. "I'm staying with you tonight."

"What about Zoey?"

"She's with Kane. She's fine, and she knows we'll see her later. Come on, let's get you back in bed. I want to take a quick shower."

Jillian was asleep when he crawled into bed behind her and drew her into his arms. She snuggled against him and whispered, "Thank you for coming. I'm sorry you missed the event."

"I'm sorry I put you in this position."

"You didn't. *We* did, and even though this happened, I wouldn't change a thing about the way we came together. I love us."

His heart turned over in his chest. "I love us, too, baby."

Chapter Thirty

JILLIAN AWOKE BEFORE Johnny, and she lay still with her head on his arm and her hand on his chest, trying not to wake him. She couldn't believe he'd blown off the event and had come all that way to be with her. But then again, she could believe it, because Johnny had always made her a priority even when he was wrestling with the worst of things with Zoey.

She thought about Zoey, and it broke her heart to think she'd cried when they left. Would she want to live in Maryland? How would she feel about a baby? Would she want to share Johnny in that way? Or would it upend her world again? Could Jillian give her and a baby enough attention? Could she give Johnny enough attention?

Jillian loved other people's babies. She didn't know *why* she was so afraid of not being able to care for her own. She hadn't thought she'd ever give up design time for anyone, yet here she was, putting Johnny and Zoey first every weekend and taking Zoey's calls at all hours of the day and evening. She didn't want to give up that time with them, and she'd have even less time for work with a baby. A surprising thought tiptoed in. She *could* take on less work, launch fashion lines less often, like Johnny was doing with touring. Would she be happy doing that, or would she always be one of those people who put their career ahead of their family?

She rolled onto her back and put her hand on her belly, trying to imagine her life with a baby in it. She saw chaotic mornings that came too early and included dirty diapers and baby burps that led to milk stains on her shoulders. She could hire a nanny to watch the baby while she was at work, but could she leave her tiny baby? No way. She knew she couldn't. She'd have to bring the baby to the office. She could have a babysitter there, couldn't she? Would she trust someone she didn't know? How did people do that? Zoey was fourteen and Johnny wouldn't leave her with anyone but family.

She closed her eyes, imagining a little boy with Johnny's dark eyes and thick dark hair. Picturing that tiny baby in Johnny's arms tugged at all her heartstrings. Maybe they'd have a little girl, and she'd hate fashion. Wouldn't that be something? Maybe she'd like sports and Jillian would have to learn all about them if she wanted to keep up with her. She laughed softly and felt Johnny's warm hand cover hers, his fingertips grazing her stomach as his lips touched hers. She opened her eyes and found him smiling down at her.

"What was that laugh for?"

"I was just thinking about if we had a little girl who liked sports and hated fashion."

He laughed. "Or a boy who hated music?"

"I don't care what our kids love or hate as long as they're happy and good to others."

"Me too, babe."

"I don't *think* I'd put work ahead of a baby, because I don't do that with you and Zoey, but do you think I would?"

"Sometimes you might have to, if you're near a launch or on a tight deadline, but that's okay," he said supportively. "I'll be there to pick up the slack."

And just like that her love for him bloomed impossibly bigger. Her father's words came back to her. *When the right people come into your life, the ones who are meant to stay there forever, that kind of connection is bigger than we are. We can't escape it, and most of the time we don't understand it, but that's what makes it so special. That kind of love is everlasting.*

With that in her heart, she said, "What if we decide to have this baby and Zoey doesn't want to move?"

"I don't have a good answer for that. I guess we'll cross that bridge when we come to it. Are you worried about missing your family?"

"A little, but I'm more worried about not having help to learn how to do things right."

"Does my *winger* want to be a planner?"

"Johnny, I'm being serious."

"I know, and I didn't think it was possible to love you more than I already do, but I love you even more for that. I'm pretty sure we'll figure things out together no matter where we live, but we could always hire a baby nurse to show us whatever we need to know. If we end up in New York, we have a big penthouse, and your parents could come stay for a few weeks at a time, and if that's not enough, or they can't, then we'll ask my parents for help or get a live-in nanny."

She loved that he had such faith in the two of them and that he was willing to do whatever it took.

"There's no pressure, babe."

"I know, but I just turned thirty, and I know we didn't plan this pregnancy, but I didn't plan on falling in love with you and Zoey, either, and I love you so much that sometimes I physically ache with it, wishing I could feel your arms around me or hug Zoey when she's upset."

"I feel that way about you, too."

"I was really freaked out last night when I took that pregnancy test. But this morning, I don't feel so frantic. I'm scared, but I know you'll be there, and I'm worried about Zoey, but like you said, we'll just love her more."

His brows knitted. "Are you saying you want to have this baby with me?"

She nodded, her eyes tearing up. "I want to have this baby with you."

They both laughed as he kissed her. "Baby, we're gonna have a *baby*."

"It might breathe fire," she teased.

He scooted lower, speaking to her belly. "Hey, little one, this is your daddy. Just so you know, I'm investing in fireproof suits, so breathe fire all you want, because nothing will stop us from loving you."

Jillian laughed and cried as he kissed her stomach and continued kissing his way up her body until he was gazing lovingly into her eyes.

"Should we wait to tell Zoey? Give you some time to be sure?"

"I won't change my mind. We made this baby, and we might not have been in love at the time, but we are now. Our baby was touched by the magic of the inn, too, and I'm pretty sure it already owns a piece of my heart, just like you and Zoey do. But I think we should wait to tell Zoey, or anyone else, until I've seen a doctor and we make sure everything is okay. Maybe until I'm through the first trimester, just in case?"

"Okay." He kissed her again. "I love you, Jillian." He laced their hands together. "One day I'm going to put a ring on that finger."

She couldn't resist teasing him. "Don't act like I'm a sure thing, Mr. Bad."

"You can be anything you want, as long as you're *mine*."

As their bodies came together, he lowered his lips to hers, breathing air into her tired lungs and love into her overflowing heart.

Chapter Thirty-One

THE NEXT FOUR weeks were a whirlwind of morning sickness that was more like guess-when-it'll-hit sickness, because it came and went with no rhyme or reason. Jillian had worked like crazy, traveled to and from New York, had visits from Johnny and Zoey in Maryland, had gone holiday shopping with Trixie and Jordan, enjoyed two wonderful Thanksgiving celebrations, and through it all, she struggled to keep her pregnancy, and nausea, a secret, though she and Johnny were bursting at the seams to tell everyone their big news.

Thanksgiving was nothing short of wonderful with Johnny's family, and they'd enjoyed a second celebration with Jillian's family that weekend. They had a lot to be thankful for. Jillian had seen her doctor two weeks ago, and she'd gone for a sonogram earlier this week. Today was Saturday, and she was officially eleven and a half weeks pregnant with twins. They'd been stunned by the news, and then they'd laughed, because while they'd started making plans for a baby, they now had to make plans for two. They were telling Zoey today, and if all went well, they'd tell their families next weekend when they saw them for the holidays.

Jillian took one last look in the mirror. Her oversize sweater covered her little baby bump. She looked more like she'd eaten a good meal than like she was pregnant. "Good morning, babies." She and Johnny talked to their babies often, and like with the fish, she enjoyed their company even though they couldn't talk back. "We're telling your sister about you today, so let's try not to upset Mommy's stomach, okay?"

She was nervous about talking with Zoey, despite having rehearsed with Johnny every possible scenario and outcome more times than she cared to admit. She'd been reading everything she could about pregnancy, telling siblings about pregnancy, and caring for babies. They'd decided to be direct and honest with Zoey. Jillian found herself skipping pages often in the baby book. It turned out that she already knew much of what the books contained. Then again, as with fashion, she wanted to do this right, so she eventually went back to read those pages *just in case.*

She made her way downstairs and heard Johnny and Zoey in the kitchen, remembering the first time she'd woken up and found them together in a kitchen. It was the second day they were in Colorado. Johnny had tried so hard to get through to Zoey then, and now they were joking around with each other. Or so she thought. Maybe they were arguing. It was hard to tell with them sometimes.

"We'll let Jilly settle it," Zoey said from where she leaned against the counter peeling a clementine. She looked cute in a striped miniskirt and gray cropped sweater, with thick gray tights and black flat-bottomed boots. "Jilly, Dad says we can't get a dog because it would be too hard to travel back and forth, but dogs travel with families all the time."

Zoey called him Dad most of the time now, and she'd started asking for a dog a couple of weeks ago. They'd already decided to surprise her with one for Christmas. Johnny arched a brow, his secret smile saying, *I love you. She called me Dad,* which he still couldn't get enough of, and *This is it, baby, our big day.* "I brewed you a cup of tea." He handed it to her and leaned in for a kiss.

"Thank you." She'd swapped her beloved Diet Pepsi for peppermint tea and seltzer water. She wasn't thrilled with either, but she'd read about peppermint calming nausea, and it was helping a lot.

"Some people would call that bribery." Zoey popped a section of clementine into her mouth.

"I'd give you the same answer even without the tea. I'm afraid I have to defer to your dad about getting a dog, since he's the one who would be driving with it."

Zoey rolled her eyes.

"Aria and Kane texted about the New Year's party. They can both make it," Johnny said. They'd decided to host a New Year's party at Jillian's house so their families could meet.

"Does Aria mind driving that far?" Jillian asked.

"Her friend Zeke Wicked will drive with her. He never leaves her hanging, and Kane's going to Oak Falls after the New Year to hear Sable play," Johnny said. "He said not to tell her because it's better if she doesn't know she's being assessed."

"Good idea. He'll love her band." Jillian would forever be grateful to Sable and Trixie for being there for her the night she'd found out she was pregnant and for keeping their secret. Although Sable wasn't keen on the idea of opening for the tour, she'd agreed to think about it. Apparently, hitting it big wasn't high on her list of priorities. But Jillian thought Sable was just worried she might not be good enough, which she *was*. She and her band were too good not to be discovered, and Jillian hoped Kane would love them and convince Sable to take the gig.

Zoey ate another piece of her clementine. "Ginny asked if I could go shopping with her and Cara and Cara's mom for Christmas presents for you guys."

"You don't have to get us anything," Johnny said.

"I know, but I want to. I've been saving my allowance."

"That's sweet of you," Jillian said. "Did you ask the girls if they're able to come over to start work on your outfits later?"

"Yeah. They can after we go shopping. Can they spend the night?"

Johnny looked at Jillian, silently seeking approval. She nodded, and he said, "Sure, sunshine, but Jilly and I have something we'd like to talk with you about first."

"What?" Zoey asked, popping another piece into her mouth.

"Maybe we should sit down," Johnny suggested.

"Is something wrong?" Zoey asked as they all sat at the table, her eyes filling with worry.

"No, but it's important. You know how much we love you, and that will never change, no matter what."

"You're making me nervous," Zoey said. "Are you sure it's not bad? Is Jilly sick? Is that why you're drinking tea instead of soda lately?"

"Not a bad sick," Jillian said, and glanced at Johnny. He nodded almost imperceptibly, and she hoped for the best. "I'm pregnant."

The air rushed from Zoey's lungs. "Oh, thank God." She sank back in the chair with her hand over her chest. "I thought you were going to say you were dying."

"No, sunshine," Johnny said at the same time Jillian said, "No, honey."

"Does that mean you're going to get married?" Zoey asked excitedly.

"One day," Johnny said. "Are you okay with our family growing?"

Zoey shrugged. "I like babies. Why wouldn't I be?"

"I don't know," he said, looking adorably confused. "Do you want to talk about it? Do you have questions?"

"I know how babies are made," she said, full of attitude.

"Zoey, we're having twins," Jillian blurted out, unable to hold it back.

"*Twins?*" she exclaimed. "Can I help name them? Can we name one after my grandma?"

"We have some time before we have to worry about names," Johnny said. "They're not due until July."

"We're not sure what we're having yet, but we can think about that," Jillian said.

"Thanks." Zoey's brow furrowed. "Wait. Will they live *here*, with Jilly?"

"That was another thing we wanted to talk with you about,"

Johnny said. "We thought it would be better if we moved here so we could all live together, and you could go to school with Ginny."

"*Really?* Oh my God! *Yes!*" She sprang to her feet and hugged him. "Thank you! Manifesting really works!" Then she ran to Jillian and hugged her, too. "When can we move?"

Johnny laughed. "Soon. *Manifesting?*"

"Yeah. I learned about it when we were at the inn. I heard Char telling Jillian that she was going to manifest a relationship between her characters, and I've been hoping you guys would get married since you told me you were boyfriend and girlfriend." She was talking so fast, they couldn't get a word in edgewise. "I know you're not getting married yet, but living together is the same thing. Can I go call Ginny and Cara?"

"Sure, sunshine." As she ran out of the kitchen, Johnny took Jillian's hand and drew her into his arms. "My daughter manifested us."

"Be glad that's all she got from that conversation. Char and I were talking in code about some pretty spicy things."

"You were? Things we should explore?" His hand slid down to her butt.

"Things we *already* explored, but I'm totally into repeated pleasure."

Chapter Thirty-Two

WINTER BLEW ACROSS the East Coast with whipping winds and blankets of snow. But Jillian and Johnny must have had angels on their shoulders, because they were able to make it to Boston to share their news and celebrate with Johnny's family over the holidays and back to Maryland to do the same with Jillian's. Everyone was happy for them, although Nick had told Johnny he should've put a ring on Jillian's finger before announcing the pregnancy and the move. Her old-fashioned brother would probably still be protecting her when she was sixty, but Johnny didn't mind. Nick had been protecting her long before Johnny had come on the scene, and he'd taken Zoey under his wing, which meant she had one more person watching out for her.

Zoey had been so excited about moving, they'd already moved most of their things into Jillian's—*their*—home. Zoey was starting public school right after the break, but Johnny wasn't letting go of the reins just because they were in a safe small town. He'd arranged for private security to watch over her from a distance, allowing Zoey to finally settle in and just be a kid again. She'd already made arrangements to help Nick with his horses a couple of days a week after school.

It was crazy how much could change in a few months.

It was New Year's Eve, and their party was in full swing. Both of their families and Zoey's friends and their families had joined them. Twinkling lights glittered on the Christmas tree. Their stockings still hung from the mantel, on which were pictures of the three of them, their families, and Winger and Rocker Boy's decorative new fish tank, which Jillian insisted on buying because *Our fish need a little luxury, too.*

The living room was buzzing with excitement as the clock neared midnight. Johnny gazed across the room at his beautiful sweetheart talking with their mothers. She was in her element, surrounded by the people she loved and carrying the babies they'd made in her burgeoning belly.

"Looks to me like you made the right move coming to Maryland," Clint said as he sidled up to Johnny. "Any regrets?"

Johnny followed his gaze to Zoey, sitting on the floor with her friends by the patio doors. The girls were wearing their new outfits they'd made with Jillian and giggling as Zoey rubbed noses with her new puppy, Manny, short for manifest. Johnny wondered how she'd use her manifestation powers in years to come.

"It's hard to have regrets when I go to bed every night with the woman I love in my arms and my daughter happier than I've ever seen her." He was drawn to Jillian again, and as if she felt the heat of his stare, she glanced over, and that gorgeous smile turned seductive. He had a feeling twenty years from now she'd still be able to seduce him with little more than that smile. "But I do have one."

"What's that?" Clint asked.

"A lifetime with Jillian doesn't seem long enough. I wish I'd met her years ago."

"Based on the look on my daughter's face, I'd say she feels the same. Jilly told me you were making one of the extra bedrooms into a sewing room for Zoey instead of having her share Jilly's studio."

"That's right. That studio has been Jilly's sanctuary since she bought the place. She's going to have enough of her space encroached upon once the babies get here. I would hate for her to lose that, too. We're also talking about building a recording studio out back."

"So you have an escape?"

"Partially, but it would also allow me to have the guys come here to record instead of heading back to the city."

Clint grinned. "You're a smart man, Johnny. It's funny how priorities change, isn't it?"

"You can say that again."

"It's almost midnight!" Harlow announced. "If you're planning on kissing someone when that ball drops, you'd better make sure you're next to the right person."

Johnny made his way toward Jillian amid a flurry of commotion.

JILLIAN'S HEART RACED as Johnny closed the distance between them, looking beyond handsome in a black dress shirt and slacks. His gaze slid down the length of her, leaving a trail of goose bumps in its wake. How was it possible that he still took her breath away?

He reached for her, and she eyed his outstretched hand, arching a brow. "Would you like something, Mr. Bad?"

He hauled her into his arms. "I'd like that dress on the floor and your naked body beneath me."

Yes, please. "I think our guests might take issue with that."

He kissed her cheek and whispered, "We could sneak upstairs."

Oh, how she loved his passion. "The ball is going to drop in a minute."

"*Clock*blocked on New Year's Eve."

She laughed.

"Sixty seconds!" Trixie called out.

Johnny kept her close. "Are you happy?"

"I couldn't be happier."

"Any regrets?"

"The slice of cheesecake I ate isn't playing nicely with the twins, but that's about it."

He chuckled as the countdown started, and everyone turned to watch the ball make the final descent, chanting, "Ten. Nine. Eight...Four. Three. Two. *One!* Happy New Year!" Jillian turned to kiss Johnny, and her jaw dropped at the sight of him down on one knee, holding the most breathtaking ring she'd ever seen.

"Hi, baby. I was going to do this after the awards ceremony, but then we found out you were pregnant, and I didn't want you to think I was doing it just because of that."

Nervous laughter bubbled out as tears filled her eyes.

"Everything about us has been unconventional from the start. From the way we met to the places we made love and the fact that I wear the apron in the family. But I wouldn't change a thing about us, because, baby, I love your fire-breathing passion and your fierce love for me and Zoey. I love your brilliant mind, your creative spirit, your beautiful body, and the way you believe with all your heart that having your parents cook for you is still considered feeding yourself."

Chuckles rose around them as he pushed to his feet, gazing into her eyes.

"I want to raise Zoey and our babies and look back fifty years from now and remember all the silly things they did and the ridiculous arguments we had. I want a lifetime of loving you and helping you make your dreams come true. I want to hear you tell me you're not a sure thing even when you've been my wife for sixty years."

She laughed, tears streaming down her cheeks.

"I don't care if we get married before or after the babies are born, as long as one day I get to see you walk down the aisle and know we'll become husband and wife and share the same last name. With or without a hyphen."

"Me too!" Zoey interjected.

Jillian's heart stumbled, drawing more tears as he choked out, "Really?"

Zoey nodded. "I want to be a real family. I want the same last name as you guys."

"I'd love that," Jillian said. Trixie handed her tissues for the flood of tears raining down her cheeks.

Johnny winked at Zoey, and then he took Jillian's left hand in his and gazed deeply into her eyes. "Jillian Marielle Braden, will you do me the honor of marrying me and letting me love you, spoil you, and cook for you for the rest of our lives?"

"*Yes!* A million times yes!"

He slid the ring on her finger, and she launched herself into his arms, kissing him with everything she had as cheers and congratulations rang out. They were passed from one set of loving arms to the next, and when Jillian finally landed back in Johnny's strong embrace, elated and passionately in love, she thanked her lucky stars that she hadn't walked out of his penthouse all those weeks ago.

Ready for more Bradens & Montgomerys?

Fall in love with Kane Bad and Sable Montgomery

in FALLING FOR MR. BAD

A Braden + Bad Boys After Dark Crossover Novel

She's a badass musician and mechanic given the opportunity of a lifetime, but she has no patience for glitz, glamour, or overinflated egos. He's a billionaire tasked with wrangling her into submission, and he has no time for drama. Going head-to-head has never been so much fun. Especially since neither one is afraid to play dirty.

Love loyal cowboys and hot bikers?
The Whiskeys: Dark Knights at Redemption Ranch.

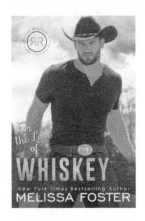

When Sullivan Tate escaped from a cult, leaving behind the only life she'd ever known, she thought she'd already endured the most difficult things she'd ever have to deal with. She knew she needed to figure out who she was, but she hadn't expected to fall for overprotective and sexy-as-hell Callahan "Cowboy" Whiskey along the way. How can she give her heart to a man who has always known exactly who he is when she's only just begun figuring that out about herself?

Have you met the Wickeds?

What happens when you're not looking for love, but it walks in the door?

Madigan Wicked's heart is not up for grabs. She's been there, done that, and she's not going back for seconds. She pours her heart and soul into her family, her puppetry and storytelling performances, and her greeting card line. But she's not opposed to having a night of fun, and the gruff, sinfully hot, definitely-not-looking-for-love mysterious stranger she runs into at a bar might be just the right man to enjoy it with.

Ex-con Tobias Riggs has lost enough for one lifetime. The only family member in his corner doesn't remember him, and the people he thought would always be in his life walked away. He's just trying to make it through each day, and the last thing he's looking for is any sort of connection. When chemistry ignites with the snarky, sexy storyteller whose lips he can't stop thinking about, he gives in to a night of passion.

Though neither is open to love, it's been known to bully its way into even the most resisting hearts. But can it survive the wicked truth of Tobias's dark past?

An abundance of heat, humor, and heart?

Start the Seaside Summers series FREE in digital format

Fall in love at Seaside, featuring a group of fun, sexy friends who gather each summer at their Cape Cod cottages. They're funny, flawed, and will have you begging to enter their circle of friends.

Bella Abbascia has returned to Seaside Cottages in Wellfleet, Massachusetts, as she does every summer. Only this year, Bella has more on her mind than sunbathing and skinny-dipping with her girlfriends. She's quit her job, put her house on the market, and sworn off relationships while she builds a new life in her favorite place on earth. That is, until good-time Bella's prank takes a bad turn and a sinfully sexy police officer appears on the scene.

Single father and police officer Caden Grant left Boston with his fourteen-year-old son, Evan, after his partner was killed in the line of duty. He hopes to find a safer life in the small resort town of Wellfleet, and when he meets Bella during a night patrol shift, he realizes he's found the one thing he'd never allowed himself to hope for—or even realized he was missing.

After fourteen years of focusing solely on his son, Caden cannot resist the intense attraction he feels toward beautiful Bella, and Bella's powerless to fight the heat of their budding romance. But starting over proves more difficult than either of them imagined, and when Evan gets mixed up with the wrong kids, Caden's loyalty is put to the test. Will he give up everything to protect his son—even Bella?

New to the Love in Bloom series?

If this is your first Love in Bloom book, there are many more love stories featuring loyal, sassy, and sexy heroes and heroines waiting for you. The Bradens & Montgomerys is just one of the series in the Love in Bloom big-family romance collection. Each Love in Bloom book is written to be enjoyed as a stand-alone novel or as part of the larger series. There are no cliffhangers and no unresolved issues. Characters from each series make appearances in future books, so you never miss an engagement, wedding, or birth. You might enjoy my other series within the Love in Bloom big-family romance collection, starting with the very first book in the entire Love in Bloom series, SISTERS IN LOVE.

See the Entire Love in Bloom Collection
www.MelissaFoster.com/love-bloom-series

Download Free First-in-Series eBooks
www.MelissaFoster.com/free-ebooks

Download Series Checklists, Family Trees, and Publication Schedules
www.MelissaFoster.com/reader-goodies

More Books By Melissa Foster

LOVE IN BLOOM SERIES

SNOW SISTERS
Sisters in Love
Sisters in Bloom
Sisters in White

THE BRADENS at Weston
Lovers at Heart, Reimagined
Destined for Love
Friendship on Fire
Sea of Love
Bursting with Love
Hearts at Play

THE BRADENS at Trusty
Taken by Love
Fated for Love
Romancing My Love
Flirting with Love
Dreaming of Love
Crashing into Love

THE BRADENS at Peaceful Harbor
Healed by Love
Surrender My Love
River of Love
Crushing on Love
Whisper of Love
Thrill of Love

THE BRADENS & MONTGOMERYS at Pleasant Hill – Oak Falls
Embracing Her Heart
Anything for Love

Trails of Love
Wild Crazy Hearts
Making You Mine
Searching for Love
Hot for Love
Sweet Sexy Heart
Then Came Love
Rocked by Love
Falling For Mr. Bad (Previously *Our Wicked Hearts*)
Claiming Her Heart

THE BRADEN NOVELLAS

Promise My Love
Our New Love
Daring Her Love
Story of Love
Love at Last
A Very Braden Christmas

THE REMINGTONS

Game of Love
Stroke of Love
Flames of Love
Slope of Love
Read, Write, Love
Touched by Love

SEASIDE SUMMERS

Seaside Dreams
Seaside Hearts
Seaside Sunsets
Seaside Secrets
Seaside Nights
Seaside Embrace
Seaside Lovers
Seaside Whispers
Seaside Serenade

The Real Thing
Only for You
Love Like Ours
Finding My Girl

HARMONY POINTE
Call Her Mine
This is Love
She Loves Me

THE WICKEDS: DARK KNIGHTS AT BAYSIDE
A Little Bit Wicked
The Wicked Aftermath
Crazy, Wicked Love
The Wicked Truth
His Wicked Ways

SILVER HARBOR
Maybe We Will
Maybe We Should
Maybe We Won't

WILD BOYS AFTER DARK
Logan
Heath
Jackson
Cooper

BAD BOYS AFTER DARK
Mick
Dylan
Carson
Brett

HARBORSIDE NIGHTS SERIES
Includes characters from the Love in Bloom series
Catching Cassidy

Discovering Delilah
Tempting Tristan

More Books by Melissa
Chasing Amanda (mystery/suspense)
Come Back to Me (mystery/suspense)
Have No Shame (historical fiction/romance)
Love, Lies & Mystery (3-book bundle)
Megan's Way (literary fiction)
Traces of Kara (psychological thriller)
Where Petals Fall (suspense)

Acknowledgments

There were so many threads that needed to be wound through this story, it was probably one of the hardest I've ever written. Many thanks to my good friend and assistant Lisa Filipe for catching me when I fell off the ledge and kicking my butt right back up to the top. It was worth the late nights and weekends. I fell desperately in love with Jillian, Johnny, and Zoey, and I hope you did as well. I loved getting to know Johnny's family and visiting with Mick and his brothers. I look forward to writing each of Johnny's siblings' books, starting with FALLING FOR MR. BAD, Kane Bad and Sable Montgomery's love story.

I am inspired on a daily basis by my fans and friends, many of whom are in my fan club on Facebook. If you haven't yet joined my fan club, please do. We have a great time chatting about the Love in Bloom hunky heroes and sassy heroines. You never know when you'll inspire a story or a character and end up in one of my books, as several fan club members have already discovered.
www.Facebook.com/groups/MelissaFosterFans

To stay abreast of what's going on in our fictional boyfriends' worlds and sales, like and follow my Facebook fan page.
www.Facebook.com/MelissaFosterAuthor

Sign up for my newsletter to keep up to date with new releases and special promotions and events and to receive an exclusive short story featuring Jack Remington and Savannah Braden.
www.MelissaFoster.com/Newsletter

And don't forget to download your free Reader Goodies! For free ebooks, family trees, publication schedules, series checklists, and more, please visit the special Reader Goodies page that I've set up for you!

www.MelissaFoster.com/Reader-Goodies

As always, loads of gratitude to my incredible team of editors and proofreaders: Kristen Weber, Penina Lopez, Elaini Caruso, Juliette Hill, Lynn Mullan, and Justinn Harrison, and my *last set of eagle eyes*, Lee Fisher.

I am forever grateful to my family, assistants, and friends who have become family for their endless support and friendship. Thank you for always having my back, even when I'm deep in the deadline zone and probably unbearably annoying.

Meet Melissa

www.MelissaFoster.com

Melissa Foster is a *New York Times, Wall Street Journal,* and *USA Today* bestselling and award-winning author. Her books have been recommended by *USA Today*'s book blog, *Hagerstown* magazine, *The Patriot,* and several other print venues. Melissa has painted and donated several murals to the Hospital for Sick Children in Washington, DC.

Visit Melissa on her website or chat with her on social media. Melissa enjoys discussing her books with book clubs and reader groups and welcomes an invitation to your event. Melissa's books are available through most online retailers in paperback, digital, and audio formats.